A TIME TO MOVE ON
When one door closes . . .

A Novel

LINDA ELLEN LYNCH

Copyright © 2021 Linda Ellen Lynch. All rights reserved. No part of this book may be used or reproduced in any form without express written permission from the author and/or publisher except for brief quotes, approved excerpts, articles, and reviews. For information, quotes from the author, or interview requests, contact the publisher. Printed in the United States of America

Other books by Linda Ellen Lynch, available on Amazon.com, Kindle, barnesandnoble.com, and by request/stocked in select retail locations.

Secrets on Sand Beach
Blood
Emerald Valley
What the Heart Wants

ISBN 978-1-970037-80-7
Library of Congress Control Number: 2021922403

Cover artwork by Gary G. McGrath

Disclaimer – This is a novel. Any resemblance to persons living or deceased is coincidental. No portion of this book may be used or reproduced by methods available now or in the future. All rights retained by the author without a legal agreement.

Crippled Beagle Publishing
Knoxville, Tennessee
crippledbeaglepublishing.com

Printed in the UNITED STATES OF AMERICA

ACKNOWLEDMENTS

A heartfelt thank you to Paula Zigant, my friend, for your able assistance in the original editing of this book, and Gilberto Mendoza, my gardener, for allowing me to observe his Mexican language patterns in a quest for typical use of this language when living in America. Kudos to my friend and neighbor, Gary G. McGrath, for his book cover illustration.

For Brenda and Randy, my children.
Without you, my life would be meaningless.

CHAPTER 1

Striking, strawberry blonde, tall, blue-eyed, strong-willed Joyce Christine (Scott) Morgan, known as JC to friends and family, would be turning thirty in two months. For the past three years she has made it clear there should be no celebration, just as there had been no celebrations involving her attendance at private or public events since she had become a widow. Her husband of three years, Rex Morgan, died after being thrown by the wild stallion he was attempting to break. In her mind the door to happiness slammed shut on the fateful day Rex took his last breath lying face down in the corral, his neck at an odd angle, his throat crushed by repeated blows by the wild stallion's sharp hooves.

The Scott Ranch foreman Andy Mendoza was beside himself with anguish as unrestrained tears rolled down his weathered face. He repeatedly, viciously kicked at the dusty ground with the toe of his well-worn boot on the day Rex Morgan was killed. "I try tell Mr. Rex stallion one mean ornery cuss that shoulda been sold or put down, but he no listen! I try stop him. Sorry I no shoot black devil! I sorry JC!"

Instead of being comforted, JC consoled the normally unflappable foreman and, later, the whole contingent of mostly Mexican ranch hands who worked on the Scott Ranch, many of them for years. "I know you tried to stop him Andy, but we both know Rex was hardheaded. When he made up his mind to tackle a job, he meant to see it through no matter what it would take. I don't place blame on you or anyone else working here on the ranch for what happened, myself included. My pleas, along with yours, to keep him from trying to break that horse fell on deaf ears. It is my hope you and the rest of the cowhands will stay on and help me manage the ranch. My brother, Sam, has made it clear he will not be available to help. I can't do it alone."

Andy lowered his head and kicked at the ground less vigorously with the toe of his boot, something he was prone to do when he believed he had little or no control over a situation. "You not worry about cowhands. They stay on, but I stay only for little while on one condition. Make two conditions," he replied. When she heard him say he planned to stay on for only a little while, her stomach fell. She feared what was might say.

"Name them," replied JC, warily.

"That brother of yours, he keep distance from me, even if he own half of ranch since your momma, daddy, and Mr. Rex die, God rest their souls." Andy crossed himself before continuing. "Me 'n Sam no see eye to eye, ma'am. Never have 'n never will!"

"You don't need to worry about Sam," replied CJ. "I already bought out his half of the ranch two weeks after Mom died. Sorry, I should have told you. He's leaving at the end of the week to finish the last semester of college in San Antonio. He plans to set up a law practice there after he passes the bar exam. We all know he isn't cut out for ranching. You and the other hands are part of my family, and I do not want to lose any of you. Stop and think, Andy. You're the one who taught me to ride when I was three years old. You dried my tears when I got bucked off and made me get up and get right back on the horse. You were there when I was a bratty eleven-year-old who knocked a hornet's nest out of a tree after being warned to stay away. When I got stung, you were there to toss me in the watering trough to avoid more stings. You ended up taking more than a few stings yourself. You were there to lend your support when both my parents passed away. Those are only a few of the many times you have been there for me. Although good parents, my mother and father were often too busy to deal with my adolescent problems. You have been my friend and confidant, offering wise advice, along with correcting me, by saying the right words when I needed to hear them the most. That means you and I go back a lot of years. I would do almost anything to keep you working here at the Scott Ranch."

Andy was a twenty-year-old, half-starved ragtag cowboy from across the border. He was born south of Juárez, Mexico. One day, looking for a job, he knocked on the back kitchen door of the Scott Ranch house. That was thirty-one years ago. As luck would have it, Jeb Scott, JC's father, was short a hand and hired him on the spot. That turned out to be a wise decision. Andy knew how to keep the other ranch hands in check without animosity. Plus, he tended to the needs of running a large cattle ranch without being told daily what to do. It didn't take long before Andy more than proved himself worthy of being named ranch foreman when the then seventy-year-old foreman retired.

Andy nodded and smiled, remembering the time a horse ran away with then four-year-old JC. Instead of showing panic, she squealed with delight and spurred the hapless creature on. It had taken him the better part of fifteen minutes to catch up to the runaway and pull JC to safety. As for the hornet episode, it was one he would rather forget. To him, JC was a little sister. As she matured, he began to think of her as the daughter he did not have, having never married. "If memory serves right, you have birthday soon. You need celebrate. Mr. Rex would not want you give up living. You still young." Andy stopped short of saying she needed to find a new husband and produce an heir to keep the ranch in the family. He doubted, with good reason, that Sam would not produce an heir.

JC answered with a sad smile. "I'm not ready to go back to any sort of social life, Andy. I miss Rex and the life we shared. And now that I am responsible for overseeing ranch operations, I don't have time for a social life. Now tell me, what is the second condition to keep you working here?"

Andy blushed, not knowing how to start. "You know Andy getting older and it more hard fix fences, do branding, and drive cattle to market. I stay on 'til you name new foreman, but don't take too long. I find senorita want make wife before we both too old to make babies." Saying something this personal made him blush even more and kick at the ground again.

Despite the shock of hearing the news he was planning to leave and wanted to get married, JC clapped her hands gleefully. "That's wonderful news! You have found a nice lady you want to settle down with soon. You don't have to leave. When you marry you and your wife can live in the apartment upstairs in the barn, the one the vet uses while waiting for horses or cows to give birth if they have a problem. I will have it enlarged enough to take care of you, your wife and many babies. I will even have it immediately redecorated to your liking."

"Thank you, but my lady want go back Mexico be near family. I do what she asks. That not easy for me, but need make her happy." That said he gave her a shy grin. "One more condition be you need take good look at Emilio Vasquez to be new foreman. He honest cowboy, real smart and know ranching. He work on Scott ranch five years just like me before I foreman. He no give you trouble. Other cowhands like him." While JC felt a huge tug on her heartstrings at the news Andy was planning to leave, she knew the day would come sooner or later when he would retire. She wasn't expecting it so soon. He was only fifty-one years old. She didn't want to spoil his happiness by voicing her dismay.

"I can't honestly say I know Emilio personally, although I'm sure I've seen him around the ranch. But if Dad hired him and you kept him on, he must be a good person and excellent ranch hand. I will take your recommendation under serious consideration. I hate to see you go, but I understand you need to have a life and family of your own. I wish you and your bride-to-be the very best, and I had better get an invitation to the wedding or there will be hell to pay!" She smiled when she made the last statement to let Andy know she was only kidding about receiving a wedding invitation. She knew there was no doubt she would receive one.

"Our families, they come from Mexico. There are many brothers, sisters, aunts, uncles, cousins and parents. They come early. Help with cleaning and decorations. Okay they pitch tents in pasture, and we use big horse barn for fiesta after wedding ceremony?" inquired Andy.

"Of course they can pitch tents and use the barn," replied JC. "I will order coolers, a freshwater tanker, and a large outdoor grill for cooking to be brought in, even outdoor toilets. Just give me a date and an approximate number of guests to get things ordered and delivered in time. When do you plan to have the wedding?"

"You no need bring in toilets, water, or grill. They used to living off land."

"Nonsense!" exclaimed JC. "I will not have your families living off the land on the Scott Ranch! Think of it as my wedding present." Andy shook his head, smiled, gave her a quick fatherly type hug and told her she was a generous lady.

"You didn't give me a wedding date," JC reminded him.

"Three weeks from this day. That give Emilio time make plan that work for him. Fall roundup, it not start for month. Buyer for cattle all set, so he no worry about that part. How you say I haggle, and buyer he give good price. I know his price better than auction price. He pay extra two-dollar for pound above cows for steers. He know Scott Ranch cows and steers always good buy. No need go through auction and pay auction man. Buyer, he give check after head count. You need make plan with banker man and give name who will deposit check like always. That man should be Emilio Vasquez."

"Thank you, Andy. It looks like you have everything under control, but then you always do. I sure hope this Emilio fellow can do the same IF I decide to promote him to foreman. I will let you know before I leave for Houston. I will be chaperoning the kids from Winchester School. Remember? That's the school where I help teach English. We leave on Thursday." The two-day delay before leaving would give her time to casually ask questions concerning how other the cowboys felt about Emilio being named as the new foreman.

"Emilio, he twenty-five year younger than me. Already teach him how you want things be done. He do lot better than me. You make big mistake if you no make him foreman," insisted Andy.

"I can't imagine anyone doing a better job than you have, my dear friend," replied JC.

Embarrassed by the compliment, Andy shrugged his shoulders. Instead of kicking the ground he allowed his thoughts to wander while JC continued to sing his praises. *I hope she listen to me not brother when choose new foreman. Sam know nothing about ranching and no want to learn! He only want what ranch bring in - money. Cowboys no like him. I no like him! He no like us! Sam one strange hombre! Wish he go away and no come back, but no can say this to JC. He her brother and she love him. She no understand he no care about her or ranch.*

CHAPTER 2

Sam Judson Scott, JC's only sibling, could hardly wait to cash the initial check made out for four hundred fifty thousand dollars, cut by the attorney when their mother died of a broken heart two months after their ailing father passed away. This sad event was followed a week later by Rex Morgan's untimely and fatal accident. Sam had the audacity to approach JC immediately following the reading of their mother's will as they were walking to his car from the attorney's office. To say JC was surprised by what he had to say is an understatement. It sent a chill through her that was followed by sheer anger when she learned he wanted to speak to her about buying out his half of the ranch.

"Can't you at least wait until we get in the car to talk about this?" she sharply questioned. "Mom has been gone for only two weeks and Rex a week. Your request has to hold some sort of a record for being insensitive!" Not one prone to crying, JC found herself near tears. "I would think the check for four hundred fifty thousand dollars the attorney just gave you would tide you over for a while. What in the world are you thinking? Our parents, grand and great grandparents put their hearts and souls into Scott Ranch! I can hardly believe you are willing to sell your half!"

Sam scowled. "That four hundred fifty grand is just a mere drop in the bucket! Mom could have been more generous with us instead of tying up the bulk of the estate in a trust where we are forced to jump through hoops to get a few measly dollars every year! I hate this ranch! I hate the one-horse town of Midline, even if it is the county seat. The founding fathers should have named it Nowhere, Texas. If you got out more often you would realize there is nothing to offer in this pitiful god forsaken place for someone like me."

"I didn't realize you felt so strongly."

"Well, I do!" exclaimed Sam. "Nobody around here has ever given two hoots if I lived or died, and I'm tired of always being left out. I was always the last one chosen for sports all through grade and high school. I was the one shunned and made fun of by the popular crowd, even in college. Dad made it clear I was a disappointment, and he couldn't stand being around me for more than few minutes at a time."

"I care about you. Mom cared about you," offered JC. She could not offer any positive words concerning the way their father had treated him. Sam was right. Their father had made it abundantly clear he wasn't interested in the welfare of his only son beyond that of handing him money whenever he asked for it, if it sent Sam off in a direction where he didn't have interact with him.

"You two are the only exceptions," he conceded. "And Mom is dead."

"Let me take a closer look at the books then talk to the bank trust rep as soon as we get back to the ranch to see if there's a way and enough ready cash to buy you out. I wouldn't want to stand in the way of your needs, even if that means sacrificing some of the needs of the ranch. You are aware things have been tight in the cash flow department, especially with the downturn in the economy and beef prices the lowest in years, aren't you?"

"We both know there should be more than enough ready cash in the trust. It's only a matter of you sweet-talking the bank's trust fund manager into parting with some of that cash," snapped Sam. "So, you have to put off buying a few more head of cattle for a couple of years if buying me out makes you a little short. Either you buy me out within the next two weeks, or I'll find someone who will!" That said, he got in the car, slammed the door, turned on the ignition, and spun the wheels of his new BMW with a screech as he backed out of the attorney's parking lot. Neither of them spoke during his high-speed, forty-mile drive to the Scott Ranch.

JC's heart lurched and she paled at his threat. The ranch was the only life she had ever known or wanted. The property consisted of sixteen thousand acres, fourteen thousand in grasslands and hay and the rest in foothills with a mountain range off to the west. A huge log construction bunkhouse able to house twenty full-time cowboys, including a separate room for the ranch foreman, helped keep a steady compliment of reliable employees. The eat-in kitchen and a shower room were benefits that rivaled those of an exclusive gym. The ranch boasted two horse barns, with fifteen stalls in one and twenty-five in the main barn (which featured an apartment on the second level). Also, two large, open-sided pole barns held hay under tarpaulins, equipment, repair supplies, and planting, harvesting tools. These made up the outbuildings on the valley floor.

Originally, the living quarters for ranch hands had been a small, crude, tin-roofed log structure able to house two cowboys sleeping on cots, a wobbly handmade table, two chairs, and a ceramic bowl and pitcher as means to wash up. A stone, wood-burning fireplace kept the tenants warm when the weather turned cold. Clothing was washed in the river that flowed at the foot of the mountains. Meals were taken in the kitchen of the ranch house or cooked outside over an open fire pit in a black, cast iron kettle. Meals were typically stew, bacon and beans, or steaks cooked on a makeshift grill. Coffee was made available outside in the fire pit using a large, blue and white granite pot with matching cups. The pit, covered by a sand-colored tarpaulin, served to protect the fire and men from the summer sun, winter snow, or spring rain. Periodically, high winds accompanying thunderstorms sent everyone inside the ranch or bunkhouse.

The original ranch house started out with one bedroom situated behind a large kitchen, both spaces heated by a potbellied stove, which was also used for cooking during stormy weather. The original 'bathroom' consisted of a pitcher and bowl in the bedroom, just like that found in the bunkhouse, both of which sat on a handmade table. A path leading out back to a one-hole privy, complete with the traditional half-moon carved in the door to provide minimum ventilation.

The current ranch house had been enlarged in stages. The first addition was comprised of six guest rooms, each of which included a full bath with hot and cold running water and walk-in closets after a gasoline powered generator two oil producing wells were installed. These rooms were added to accommodate guests, visiting family members, or those stranded in the area due to severe weather. The next phase consisted of a huge living room featuring a floor-to-ceiling fieldstone fireplace across one wall and large picture window overlooking the porch, corral, grassland, and mountains. This came about when Grandfather Jeb wanted to impress the lady he intended to marry. Phase three was a library, also utilized as a den. All phases were completed over a ten-year period once electricity became a reality in the form of a propane-powered generator. The generator remained in working order as a backup when modern powerlines fell prey to vicious storms.

The large wooden bunkhouse and smaller of the two horse barns were also due to the efforts of JC's grandfather. He used the accommodations to lure more cowhands to work on the ranch as it became more and more successful. He jokingly liked to tell everyone the additions were what made JC's grandmother accept his proposal of marriage, which, if the facts were known, was probably true. The target of his affection was a city girl used to the finer things of life. She oversaw the ranch's modernization and secured Jeb's promise of continued updating of the kitchen before agreeing to the marriage. JC's mother kept that tradition going, as would JC.

Sam is not aware, or to be more accurate, does not care if the economic downturn and apparently low beef prices have made things a little tight in the cash flow department the past couple of years since the death of their parents. He has been away, living the life of a playboy in San Antonio, while attending three and a half years of undergraduate school with minimal passing grades. As far as JC can tell, Sam always had everything he needed—in fact, far more than he needed. She regretted she did not let him know that she had been forced to dip into her personal savings and pawn her nicer jewelry to keep the sixteen-thousand-acre ranch afloat until the next cattle sale. And that wouldn't be for another four months after the fall roundup. He was also unaware she had set aside every penny earned as a part-time teacher's aide at The

Winchester School, along with the initial inherited money from their mother's bequest, to provide funds for an addition to the school where she helps migrant workers and their children learn to speak English.

The school had been developed four years ago to serve the growing needs of Mexican migrant workers and their children, not that Sam would have cared had he known. It was common knowledge among the ranch cowhands that Sam looked down his nose at the Mexican cowboys. He was arrogant and vocal about his dislike in their presence, unless members of the Scott family or their close friends were within earshot. Then butter would melt on his forked tongue. This, along with other unspoken issues, was why Andy and the other ranch hands wanted nothing to do with Sam.

CHAPTER 3

In Sam's defense, if it could be called that, JC had not seen much of him during his college years beyond a couple of awkward visits while he was living in San Antonio in an upscale home purchased with the help of their father. This took place while Sam was in undergraduate school. Her father had never mentioned his help with the home. She learned this bit of information while going over the financial ledgers after both parents died. On her first visit she was dumbfounded by the luxurious trappings of the house in a neighborhood of equally expensive homes. Sam offered no reason for this choice, where he had obtained the money to buy it, or why he never wanted her to spend more than a few hours there at any one time. There were always a multitude of excuses involving unspecified 'things' he needed to do when she did make time for the three-hour drive each way to visit him. On her third visit she teased him about the choice of such an expensive home. His quick response was delivered with hostility. She never mentioned the home again, nor did she visit while he attended law school.

The last time she saw Sam was at the party she sponsored in his honor at the Cattleman's Country Club in Midline following his passing the bar exam a year ago. She figured he bothered to attend the party to collect the gifts he knew would be forthcoming. She was right. He stayed an hour and left without saying thank you or goodbye to anyone. This was the reason she was now taken by surprise when he arrived at the ranch unannounced and all smiles, acting like the long-lost brother who should be welcomed home with open arms. He had made no effort to contact her in over a year, nor had he returned any of her phone calls.

"Hello stranger," said JC, a definite touch of coolness to her voice when he showed up without calling ahead to find out if it was convenient. "What brings you to this neck of the woods? I haven't heard a word from you since your graduation from law school and the party I gave for you. Let me guess. You need money. Am I right?" She folded her arms across her chest and gave him a challenging look.

Sam gave her a lopsided grin. "Nice to see you, too, Sis. As a matter of fact, I could use a few dollars. Life is expensive when you are paying tuition, maintaining a home and a social life, taking the bar exam, and setting up a new law office. That damned banker, Clarence Mooney, the stuffed shirt in charge of the trust fund, said I'm tapped out of my share of the fund for the year and it's only early September!" (The will specified he and JC could have access to twenty thousand dollars each year from the trust, no strings attached.) "But the main reason I'm here is to see you and make a proposal regarding a way for me to earn some much-needed cash, and at the same time, help you—if you agree to what I have in mind."

JC was not buying that his main purposes there were to see her and offer help. He had had a lot of chances to help over the years and didn't. "Don't tell me you blew through the six and a half million paid to you for your half of the ranch by my half of the trust. That inheritance money direct from Mom's personal account plus the generous gifts I and others gave you after you passed the bar should have kept you going for a long time.," declared JC. "I must say I find it more than a little irresponsible. In fact, it's absolutely outrageous!"

"What can I say or do?" he offered with a shrug. "It costs money, a hell of a lot of money, to live in San Antonio and set up a new law office in a lucrative location on the riverfront," replied Sam. The devil-may-care look on his face did not help his cause.

"Well, for starters you could sell that huge mansion you call home and find somewhere less expensive to live," remarked JC. "I assume the new BMW I see parked out there in the driveway is yours?" She continued without waiting for an answer. "It must be yours since I drive a nine-year-old Ford 150, bare bones pickup truck with over two hundred fifty thousand miles on it. And none of the ranch hands own or drive a BMW."

"Don't judge me!" growled Sam. "You of all people should be aware you have to spend money to make money if you want to get ahead in this world. Especially when it comes to making really big money. And I do plan to make really big money. Why else would I have gone to the trouble of becoming an attorney? Did you think I was going to stick around here, mucking out horse stalls, rounding up cattle, or mending fences? I am not stupid enough to live here on this damned ranch for the rest of my life like you are doing!"

JC ignored his remark, although it stung. "I am aware of what you want, but there are ways to spend money in a prudent manner that will produce the needed return. For starters, you could have avoided buying that expensive house and banked what you took from our father to buy it. I am sure the utilities, insurance, and maintenance costs must be astronomical on that huge place. Buying it was not one of the ways to conserve resources. You could have lived in one of the dorms just like everybody else while attending undergraduate school, then shared an apartment with a couple of other law school students. You could have signed up for the college meal plan at both locations. You apparently chose to eat out in fancy restaurants every meal. The few times I visited your house there was no evidence of a stocked pantry, stocked refrigerator, or any kitchen appliances or cooking utensils in use. Except for the refrigerator full of fancy beers, expensive wine, and junk food in the pantry, the kitchen didn't look used beyond an empty pizza box left on the kitchen counter. You could drive a less expensive car, resulting in cheaper insurance and repairs." JC noticed the deepening scowl on Sam's face, but kept on talking. "You could have passed on buying designer clothing and all those trips abroad whenever there was a school break. There is nothing wrong with buying clothes at discount stores like I do. As for those trips abroad, couldn't you have waited until you established your law office and it was producing an adequate income?"

Sam glared at her with the sullen look of a grounded, angry teenager on his boyish yet handsome thirty-three-year-old face. Nobody had ever questioned his choices before now, and he didn't like it one bit.

"I could have done a lot of things, but it was my money, and that was how I wanted to spend it!" JC is aware what he considered 'his money' was the generous allowance provided by their parents, handouts whenever he asked, and now the proceeds from their bequests and his selling his share of the ranch and gifts. "Look, Sis, I didn't come here to fight with you. I came here to offer you a proposition that will allow me to earn a few dollars while I develop a larger client base for my law practice. I will be helping you at the same time, so it won't be a handout," insisted Sam defensively.

"I'm all ears, but you need to keep in mind I will listen with extreme caution. It was easy for you to con our parents into giving you money whenever you asked when they were alive, but I warn you, I am not the local bank like they were. I have a ranch to maintain, and that includes a large payroll to meet every month, supply costs, and stock to buy in order to keep this place going. You need to understand that my job is not easy," replied his indignant sister.

"I'll grant you it must be one hell of a huge responsibility. That must be why you look so frazzled and worn out," said Sam. "That's why I'm going to propose that you allow me to take over the bookkeeping and make sure the bills are paid. You've always said you aren't good with numbers and I am. That is the least I can do. If you will make arrangements with Mr. Mooney at the bank, I can run payroll and pay bills through my law office equipment. Bills can be sent to me directly for approval and payment along with your invoices, names, and hours for payroll checks to be dispersed from monies taken from the trust fund set aside for that purpose. All Mr. Mooney has to do is put his stamp of approval on expenditures when I provide copies of various merchant statements. Then he can release the funds to me, and I will send payroll checks for the cowhands to you via overnight mail. That way you won't have to worry about a thing except making an estimated yearly budget, buying livestock, overseeing the ordering of supplies, and telling the hired hands what needs to be done around here on the ranch. I would be willing to take on that responsibility, for let's say, a mere fifty thousand dollars a year."

JC looked at him like he was a Martian who just landed from outer space. “You have got to be kidding! You, who squandered your inheritance from Mom, including half the value of the ranch? And you want me to let you take on the responsibility for managing the financial end of this operation? Do you think I’m a total idiot? The answer is NO!”

Not one to be denied, Sam turned on the charm. He knew his sister loved him despite his being an irresponsible jerk. He was more than willing to play that card to the hilt. He took on a hangdog look. “I’m not that stupid college kid anymore. I’ve learned my lesson in handling money. If it will make you feel better, I’m willing to put my house up for sale and find less expensive housing. Please don’t ask me to give up the BMW or nice clothes, though. I need to drive a suitable car and look the part of a successful attorney when dealing with upscale clients. It won’t be me paying the bills. It will be my accountant and the bank trust fund, but only after I check everything for accuracy and authorize payment. Come on, Sis! Don’t you trust me? I’m family. This would free up more time for you to continue helping those migrant workers and their kids over at the Winchester School.” He was well aware helping those kids and their parents was a weak spot for his sister. He believed mentioning it would more than likely be his ace in the hole. If she had she known what Sam was really thinking, JC would have told him to get lost. While it was true that he was a lot more adept at figures than she was, not to mention she was tired of burning the midnight oil working on balancing the books, she doubted the best interests of the ranch or helping her were Sam's primary reasons for making the offer.

At the same time, she had to admit that she did want to spend more time teaching English and United States customs to parents and children of Mexican workers. She enjoyed enabling them to live better lives. Still, she had reservations. "Let me sleep on it and get back to you with a phone call tomorrow."

"In that case, I'll call my secretary and instruct her to clear my calendar for tomorrow. I will stay on the ranch tonight to be here for your answer in the morning," replied Sam, knowing full well he had nothing of importance to tend to tomorrow. "I'm really sorry I haven't been here for you these past few years. You can trust me. I've grown up, and I love you JC. I promise I will be a better brother in the future. I know it has to have been rough for you with Mom, Dad, and Rex all passing so close together. I should have been more helpful." There were crocodile tears his in eyes when he walked over to where JC stood with her arms crossed. He put both arms around her shoulders and gave her a bear hug. "You're my only family," he whispered. "Please, won't you give me a chance to lighten your load and be a better brother?" When JC began to well up Sam knew he had won his case despite the fact he knew she would be spending a sleepless night mulling over what would become his self-serving proposition. He was right. The next morning, the dark circles under her eyes made it evident JC had not slept.

Over breakfast prepared and served by the unusually quiet, long-term housekeeper/cook Rosa Sanchez, JC presented her response to Sam's proposition. Normally a woman with a lighthearted, outgoing, ready smile and tendency to chatter, Rosa remained distant and quiet as she overheard JC make her counter proposal to Sam. Already distressed at having overheard his proposition and observing him hug his sister yesterday with what she regarded as fake tears, she became even more upset when she heard JC agree for him to take over paying bills and writing payroll checks for the fee of thirty thousand dollars a year (instead of the fifty thousand he asked for yesterday). Even with the lesser amount, Rosa knew this figure had to be against JC's better judgment. *God help her,* she silently lamented as she went about cleaning the kitchen and loading the dishwasher when the meal was finished.

He is family. He needs money, I need help and I can spend more time with the kids and their parents at the Winchester School, JC silently reasoned during her overnight deliberations. *Those are the only reasons for me to give in to his offer. I sure hope I'm not making a big mistake, although I'm not willing to lay out fifty grand when finances are already tight. I don't want to dip into the trust fund principle after having been forced to do so in order to buy out Sam's half of the ranch. He will have to settle for thirty grand a year divided into four equal payments per year over the next two years or no deal. He can take it or leave it.*

While not happy with the thirty-thousand-dollar figure or extended payment, Sam agreed to it when it became clear this was the deal she was willing to offer or there would be no agreement. Her counteroffer of thirty thousand, payable in four quarterly payments over the next two years, made him think his sister might be a little smarter than he gave her credit for, so he decided to take it and be thankful. He knew this money would buy time to secure more paying clients and continue to maintain his current lifestyle, at least for a while longer.

After serving breakfast, Rosa left the dining room instead of joining JC and Sam for breakfast as she usually did when she and JC dined alone. She returned to the kitchen where she crossed herself reverently and said a prayer. "Please God you no let my baby how you say be snookered by Sam." This was said before she whispered to her helper, nineteen-year-old Miguel Lopez, as he cleaned the black and silver electric range. "Rosa know Sam not good brother. He always get what he want using silver tongue and good looks." Miguel nodded his head in agreement but remained silent, allowing her to continue. "He no give care about ranch or sister! If he did, he here to help when his Daddy, Momma, then Mr. Rex die! He not even show face at church services, only graveside services! Only come to ranch back then when he know there be celebration of life after burials, so he eat, drink 'n run mouth, so everybody know he almost attorney!" She paused to roll her eyes in a show of disgust. "He not even wait, insist JC buy him out after their momma's will read at lawyer man's office! I invited there for share of money, so I hear him tell JC she pay now, or he find somebody buy his half of ranch when they still in parking lot. What kind 'o brother do that to sister?"

"You right Rosa. Sam not good for many reasons," said a red-faced Miguel as he started walking toward the kitchen's back door.

"What reasons?" Rosa called after him. Miguel hurried on, allowing the screen door to slam shut behind him. Rosa sighed and punched down the bread dough she was kneading a lot harder than necessary. She had a rather good idea what the other reasons were that Miguel was referring to, but she wanted him to verify out loud what she had strongly suspected for a long time. "Rosa know Sam strange, but not know how he strange. I will find way for Miguel to tell Rosa why he not like Sam, even if other cowhands not tell Rosa."

CHAPTER 4

On their wedding day, Andy and his new bride made a lovely couple. She was dressed in a colorful, long, full-skirted floral print dress edged with yards of white, handmade lace on the hem, bodice and puffed, elbow-length sleeves. Her coal black hair and dark eyes shined like polished onyx. Andy was wearing an equally colorful guayabera shirt accented with a string tie featuring a silver religious medal, black dress pants, a spotless white Stetson hat and brand spanking new snakeskin boots. Silk flowers and ribbons of every conceivable color had been placed throughout the larger of the two Scott Ranch horse barns where the reception was held. Everyone arrived after Andy and his bride exchanged vows at St. Michael's church during a late afternoon ceremony. Starched white linens covered tables made from sawhorses and plywood. The tables were laden with every imaginable kind of homemade food, including pit-cooked cabrito supplied by relatives and friends. Three Scott Ranch cowhands doubling as bartenders stood by with a good supply of sangria, beer, tequila, and California red and white wines ready to quench the thirst of anyone in need of being quenched. A variety of soft drinks kept the children and teetotalers happy, all soft drinks compliments of JC. She wanted to provide all of the drinks, but her tight budget would not allow for the expensive alcoholic beverages.

Providing portable toilets, a water tanker, cast iron grill and cash wedding gifts were already a strain. She would have to rely on oilwell revenues and the calving of existing cows to cover the costs to supply additions to the herds.

"We glad you come to wedding JC," said a beaming but unusually shy Andy. "This my wife Maria." The way he looked at Maria and nodded toward JC, gave Maria the nod that she could be less formal with JC than a mere handshake. JC couldn't help thinking Andy had done very well for himself in choosing such a lovely woman for his wife. She was a beauty with the aura of a woman who knew what she wanted. It was obvious she wanted Andy and he wanted her, evident by the way they looked at each other.

"You make a lovely bride," offered JC. "May I give you a hug? Andy must have forgotten to tell you that you are now a part of my family. And wild horses could not have kept me away from the wedding!"

"Maria no speak or understand much English, so I tell her what you say," said Andy. He leaned in to whisper something in Maria's ear. She smiled again and opened her arms to receive and return the offered hug.

"We like sisters?" she questioned in broken English.

"Si. Sisters, Maria," replied JC. She made an effort to inconspicuously hand her an envelope containing five hundred United States dollars while using a soft tone of voice. "You do not need to tell Andy. This is for you to buy whatever you want when you get to Mexico." Although

Maria did not understand much of what was said, she did understand green associated with money when she peeked inside the envelope. Her eyes grew wide, and her mouth formed a perfect O; and so did Andy's as he excused himself from the person speaking to him and stepped forward to peer over her shoulder. Maria prepared to hand the envelope over to him. He started to reach for it when JC interceded with a playful slap to his hand. "There is an envelope for you, too. That one is strictly for Maria," she pretended to scold him. He could not help noticing his envelope was fatter than Maria's when JC pulled it from her purse and handed it to him. It contained five thousand American dollars, worth double that amount in Mexican pesos. His eyes widened and his jaw dropped when he looked inside. He opened his mouth to speak, but no words were forthcoming. JC held up her hand in a gesture meant to convey he did not need to speak and added, "Don't say a word. This is just a small token of appreciation to help you get started in your new life."

It took several seconds, but Andy was able to speak. "But . . . but you, Mr. Rex and parents . . . all pay and treat Andy good many years. You no need give this much," he sputtered.

"If I could, I would double the amount; but the recession, poor beef prices and the payout to Sam have made things a little tight," replied JC. Before Andy could say anything in response to JC's comment on beef prices,

Mariachi band struck up the Mexican Hat Dance. Maria playfully grabbed one of JC's hands, and Andy grabbed the other, making it impossible for her not to become part of the circle of happy dancers. The dancers surrounded a large, black velvet sombrero highlighted with a woven silver hatband and tassels spaced around its brim. In all the excitement, Andy's plan to refute JC's use of the word *poor* regarding beef prices was soon forgotten. The pace picked up. One of the dancers to the left of Maria turned out to be none other than Emilio Vasquez, the cowboy Andy had recommended to take his place as ranch foreman.

Emilio Vasquez was no exception to any other man when it came to noticing JC's charms and beauty. He had fallen in love with her the first day he laid eyes on her at the Scott Ranch when applying for a job five years ago. At the time he was made aware by another ranch hand, who had observed his smitten look, that she was married to Rex Morgan, and if he hoped to land and keep a job, it was hands off. It was common knowledge among the cowboys that you didn't mess around with the boss man's wife—not that Emilio would have even considered making advances toward a married woman. This is when Emilio decided to keep his distance to eliminate any possibility Rex Morgan would think he was hitting on JC.

Emilio was acutely aware there were plenty of unmarried, and even married women, who let it be known they were available at the Lonesome Dove Cantina the first time he went there. But he was shy and pretended he didn't know what they were talking about when they made suggestive moves toward him. He chose not to take advantage of their come hither glances or outright propositions on the rare occasions he would later drop in at The Dove, as it was locally known, on a Saturday night for a beer after a week of hard work on the ranch. He also made it a point to steer clear of the main ranch house, only sneaking occasional peeks at JC from afar, something he continued to do for the almost three years since Rex's death. He hoped that would change after being named the new foreman, when it would become necessary to have personal contact with her to conduct ranch business, even though he felt she would not be interested in a lowly cowboy.

At the wedding reception it took a lot of courage for him to ask JC to dance. The band began to play a Texas twostep. Even though Rex was now out of the picture, and it had been made clear she could dance with the cowboys on this special occasion, as she indicated during her welcoming toast to the bride and groom, he felt uncomfortable asking. JC agreed to dance with him. She had seen him from a distance around the ranch after Andy had pointed him out on several occasions. She knew it would be considered rude to turn him down since he was one of her employees, and especially since Andy had recommended him as the new foreman. She finally agreed this was the best course of action. Andy convinced her that Emilio understood how things were to be done on the ranch and that she would not have to waste time instructing him. Plus, she had discretely asked several ranch hands about Emilio, all of whom gave him the nod. The bank trust manager informed JC that Emilio had a clean record. Most of all, she trusted Andy's judgment.

"Forgive me, I know I've seen you from a distance around the ranch, but your name escapes me at the moment," JC said when they joined the others for a dance in the open space cleared for that purpose in the main barn. His name had not escaped her, but she felt the need to use that as an excuse. She wasn't certain why this was necessary beyond the fact he was extremely handsome, so handsome that she had to say *something* or make a total fool of herself by openly staring at him.

"There is no need for you to ask for forgiveness ma'am. I know there are a number of cowboys working full time here at the ranch, along with extras Andy hires during roundup, branding, and the drive to market. You can't be expected to know everyone by name. My name is Emilio Vazquez. Andy and I have become good friends in the five years I have been working here."

JC's face turned red. She felt herself begin to perspire, first on her forehead, followed by her upper lip and then between her generously endowed breasts. *So, this is Emilio up close*, she thought. *Andy neglected to remind me he is tall, good looking, speaks perfect English, and dances like a dream; and that beautiful head of thick black hair, perfect white teeth, sexy smile and those dark smoldering eyes . . . Snap out of it!* she told herself. *He's a ranch hand, make that the ranch foreman, but even then, he is still your employee, so pull yourself together pronto!*

"Mr. Vasquez I am doubly embarrassed. Andy recommended you should take his place as foreman. I took his suggestion to heart and told him to promote you to foreman. I . . . I should have told you myself, but I . . . I found myself roped into being a chaperone for a three-day field trip for The Winchester School. We visited an art gallery and attended a play in Houston. During the time I was gone you needed to know as soon as possible that you were offered the job in order to prepare for the upcoming fall roundup and trail drive, should you accept the offer. Obviously, you took the offer, so welcome to becoming what I hope will be a permanent member of the Scott Ranch family. At least I hope it's permanent." She knew she was rambling and hoped he didn't realize it.

"I understand and thank you for the promotion. It is an honor I do not take lightly. I will do my best to make you proud for many years to come. I am aware you devote a lot of time and resources to the migrant workers and their children at The Winchester School. Thank you from the bottom of my heart. If it weren't for people like you helping to teach them English and U.S. ways, a lot of them would not make it beyond a life of hard work as cowpunchers or planting and harvesting fruits and vegetables. And that would be such a waste of talent."

JC felt herself blush even deeper. "I agree with you. There appears to be a lot of talent among both the children and their parents, but I get lots of help. The financial support from many folks makes sure the families have food, clothing, school supplies, and decent places to live. Oh my, I think the song ended and we're still dancing."

Emilio wanted to gaze into the eyes of the lovely creature he was holding in his arms, but he only glanced. The look, although brief, made JC feel a tingly sensation throughout her entire body.

"Yes, the song has ended, but another will begin. We can keep dancing if you would like to continue," he offered.

Oh, those smoldering eyes . . . JC would have liked nothing more than to continue dancing with him all evening, but she knew she should keep it casual since he was an employee. She didn't want the other cowhands or guests to think he was getting special treatment. "I promised Juan the next dance," she offered lamely, knowing the white lie was better than offending Emilio by refusing to continue dancing with him.

"Then you must keep your promise, but you need to know I saw him leave with a lady friend a while ago. He must have forgotten or if he mentioned it, she didn't want you dancing with him. After all you are a threat to her, you being a pretty lady. I would hate to see a pretty lady like you standing in a corner all alone, so we could dance the next one before I call it a night, but only if you are willing. I wish I could linger to enjoy the festivities, but tomorrow will be a long day with the fall roundup, and the branding of yearlings already in progress before herding seven thousand head cattle off on the two-day drive to the railhead in two weeks before this coming Thursday morning." Emilio didn't know why he was explaining all this to JC when she was in charge of running the ranch, but like her he found the need to continue talking. "Normally I would be staying at the line shack or out in a field makeshift camp, but I felt it would be rude not to attend Andy's wedding." He too was aware he was rambling while thinking, I would love to continue dancing with you all night, but I would be too tempted to kiss you, and I know that would not be acceptable in front of all these people, not to mention doing such a thing could get me fired.

JC smiled and said she understood his need to call it an early night, while thinking she was grateful, he was being a gentleman in making allowances for her lie regarding Juan. "Never let it be said I was left standing alone to face sympathetic stares in a corner. I would be delighted to continue dancing with you for the next dance. Then I, too, must call it a night, but not until after a proper sendoff for Maria and Andy following the cutting of the wedding cake."

"We can continue to dance if you call me Emilio and I may call you JC," he responded in a lighted hearted teasing manner in an attempt to put her and himself at ease. "Mr. Vasquez is my father," he added with another heartwarming playful smile that sent more goosebumps racing up her arms and the back of her neck. "And I want you to know I understand I cannot call you JC when I'm working, but that isn't until tomorrow when you become Ms. Morgan, the boss lady again." He held her a little closer than he probably should have, but JC pulled only slightly away while maintaining her poise and a smile. His head was reeling with the smell of her delicate perfume in addition to consuming a glass of red wine. *God help me! I'm in love with her,* he reacted to his immediate desire, *but I'm not sure she returns my feelings.*

"Deal," said JC a little too brightly. She was pleased to have an excuse to continue dancing with him on an informal first name basis. "For the next dance before you leave, you are Emilio and I'm JC." *If you only knew how my heart is beating like a trip hammer while you are holding me in your arms* was the thought invading her mind. But she held that thought for only a few moments. Just as quickly as it came, she put it out of her mind by reminding herself that even though he was now the ranch foreman, it still meant he was her employee; and she never fraternized beyond dancing with employees on special occasions like weddings, holidays, or fiestas. This had been true even before she married the local bank owner's son, Rex Morgan. This was an ultimatum at the insistence of her mother who felt it unbecoming for a lady to show interest in the lives of the ranch hands beyond being social when attending special events; a standard JC continues to maintain with the exception of Andy, even though her mother frowned upon their connection.

Later that night while lying alone in her bed, JC allowed herself to relive the unexpected feelings experienced while dancing with Emilio. Those thoughts sent goosebumps all over her body, not just up her arms and the back of her neck. If she concentrated, she could still almost still smell his spicy aftershave and masculine odor. She didn't want to linger on these feelings knowing they could be a two-edged sword. She liked dancing with him, while at the same time there was the feeling, she was being unfaithful to Rex's memory. This led to her tossing and turning for the better part of two hours before she got up, put on her robe and slippers to exit her bedroom and start walking down the shadow filled hallway, past the den, across the living room and into the kitchen for a glass of milk. The grandmother clock on the mantle chimed three a.m. She didn't realize Rosa was sitting quietly at the kitchen table in the darkness. She, too, was unable to sleep, but not for the same reason JC could not sleep. Rosa continued to feel concern about Sam taking over the financial management of the ranch, but felt it was none of her business to mention it.

JC had the sensation someone was watching her as soon as she took a step into the kitchen. She hesitated and quickly glanced around in the pitch-dark room, but did not see Rosa, wearing a dark blue nightgown, sitting at the far side of the kitchen table until the refrigerator light came on when she opened the door. "Oh, it's you, Rosa! You scared the living daylights out of me!"

"Rosa, sorry about that, but couldn't sleep." She and steady boyfriend Roberto were spending the night in one of the guest rooms. They had not wanted to make the drive to his house late that night after imbibing in more than a few drinks at the wedding reception. She explained her presence in the kitchen was due to all the excitement surrounding activities associated with the wedding and reception. "You tell Rosa why you no can sleep?" She asked the question knowing the reason, but she wanted JC to acknowledge it concerned one ranch foreman by the name of Emilio Vasquez.

"Probably for the same reason you can't sleep, all of the excitement surrounding the wedding," was all JC offered in reply. Rosa wagged her index finger at her after snapping on the light fixture comprised of deer antlers and fifteen forty-watt bulbs centered above the huge round oak table. "Rosa does not think so. Rosa is sure it because of Emilio Vasquez. I see way he look at you tonight. I see way you look at him all dreamy eyed when you dance, and this good thing yes? You should dream about him, not awake to drink milk in wee hours of morning."

"Don't be silly! We were just dancing. I was only being sociable and so was he."

Rosa sniffed and shook her head. "Ha! If Rosa believe that, she be crowned Midline Queen for Taco Festival! And that not happen. I fat winkled old woman. They want pretty young thing. He in love with you and you afraid return his love. Rosa know these things." This was followed by an exaggerated sigh on her part.

"Sorry Rosa, but you don't know anything about how I feel when it comes to Emilio," declared JC just before she fled back to her bedroom without drinking the milk she had poured, leaving Rosa feeling even more deeply troubled. Deep sleep continued to elude JC for the remainder of the night. Every time she drifted off, she awakened with a start, her heart pounding wildly while dreaming of being held by Emilio. Rosa's words, "he in love with you and Rosa know these things," kept repeating in her head. JC didn't want to think about returning his love and what that could entail. In her mind her heart still belonged to Rex. To think about loving another man, even one as intelligent, good looking and sexy as Emilio just wasn't in the cards. She convinced herself the time wasn't right for her to move on and find a new love, even one as handsome and smart as Emilio Vasquez.

Several hours later found Rosa with a forced a smile when JC entered the kitchen. She did not comment about their earlier conversation regarding Emilio, although she very much wanted to. "You look like what cat drag in," was all she said with a scowl before preparing their breakfast of crisp bacon, fluffy buttermilk pancakes, maple syrup, scrambled eggs, and coffee.

"You sure know how to start my day with that kind of a comment," answered JC dryly before filling her mouth with scrambled egg. She did this in an effort to avoid any more conversation, for at least the next minute or two, that could include any reference to Emilio Vasquez.

Rosa then decided she was not to be deterred and pressed on while grinning mischievously. "I bet Emilio know better way start your day. But you need give him chance." JC continued to eat without responding to Rosa's comment. When she finished the eggs and the last swallow of coffee, she sat the cup down on the table, got up and announced she was going riding up to the north pasture to check on the heard as though there had been no conversation between them regarding Emilio.

"See you at lunchtime," was her only comment before hurriedly leaving to go saddle up and ride her favorite horse to check on the upland herd. By her doing this it would free up one of the cowboys to mend fences and she would not have to listen to Rosa in her quest to link her with Emilio.

"You sidestep Rosa for now JC, but Rosa not finished. Rosa know Emilio good match for you," she said aloud into the now quiet kitchen. "Rosa just need find way to make you see and Rosa will find way!"

CHAPTER 5

Several weeks after Andy and Maria's wedding, Sam approached their aging Aunt Pearl when he was making one of his rare appearances at the ranch in an attempt to foster the relationship with his sister and possibly get more money. Pearl happened to be visiting, even though JC was working in the larger of the two barns mucking out horse stalls. Pearl had made herself comfortable in the living room, intending to wait until JC finished, knowing they planned to have lunch together. The arrival of Sam was not expected, but Pearl made an effort to be civil toward him. While she didn't openly show hostility, she always felt uneasy when he was around, especially when she knew he usually only came around when he wanted money.

Aunt Pearl, the widow of Ira Scott, JC's uncle, had moved in at the ranch immediately following Rex's death to provide much needed solace and support to JC. She ended up staying much longer than either one of them anticipated. JC loved her widowed aunt and appreciated her being there, so said nothing about her returning to her home in the suburbs in the small town of Midline, Texas located forty miles north of the ranch. When Rosa asked how long Pearl was going to stay after several months had passed, JC had responded by saying, for as long as she wants. Rosa had smiled and nodded approval. But she couldn't help thinking it would make any future plans she had in mind a little more difficult to carry out with an extra very observant person occupying the bedroom suite across the hall from where JC's bedroom suite was located. Rosa expressed sadness when Pearl announced she would be leaving a year later to go to her home, Rosa felt relieved. She was fully aware Pearl Scott was an extremely wealthy widow, a force to be reconned with, who was not shy when it came to expressing opinions or taking actions she deemed appropriate.

"What are we going to do about celebrating JC's thirtieth birthday?" asked Sam in an effort to break the ice when Pearl made no further effort to engage in conversation beyond that of a hello and nod of her head in his direction. "That's a milestone we can't allow to go by without some sort of a celebration, even if she doesn't want a party. Almost three years is more than enough time for her to mourn Rex's death and get on with a life beyond devoting it to this ranch while she's still young enough to find a new husband and provide an heir to this god forsaken place," said Sam while Pearl continued to flip through a magazine.

"Why should you give a diddly squat if she finds a new husband and has kids," retorted feisty and outspoken sixty-eight-year-old Pearl Scott. "She isn't the only one that's getting a bit long in the tooth! If I am not mistaken, you're three years older than her. It isn't like you don't have the equipment to produce an heir if you weren't so danged hung up on finding the perfect woman like you been tellin' all of us for the past ten years. 'N when it comes to having a party for JC, what do you expect me to do? Hogtie and drag her kickin' and screamin' to a party just because you want her to celebrate so you have the chance shoot off your mouth 'n play bigtime attorney with the guests? And furthermore, she will mourn Rex's death for as long as it takes, be it three, five years or more!"

"Don't get all riled up, Aunt Pearl," said Sam. "It's just that I hate to see her spend the rest of her life dedicated to managing this ranch without a husband and kids. She's young, and don't you dare tell her I said so, but she's still a good looker when she decides to get dressed up, use a little lipstick, and curl her hair. But what will she look like in another five or ten years the way she works outside doing the work of three men in all kinds of weather? She should be out there kicking up her heels at the Country Club or in bars having fun. I'm sure there's more than one suitable man around this area who would like nothing more than to become her husband and what all that entails."

Pearl gave him a sour look. "I assume you mean kick up her heels and raisin' hell just like you did all through high school, then college and still continue to do? If she should do such a thing as you suggest, just who in the name of all that is holy do you think will run this ranch? You can bet your sorry ass it sure won't be you, Mr. Playboy!"

Sam's face turned bright red, and he slinked down a little farther in his chair. There were times he liked to think he cared about his aunt, but her blunt outspoken ways often threw him for a loop, and he didn't know how to respond. He was aware she did not know he batted for the other team, something he became aware of at an early age, but managed to keep under wraps until after he left home for college. He knew he felt different when it came to girls, but it didn't fully dawn on him he was gay until he became a junior in college and met Ross Vandenberg. It had been Ross who helped him accept that fact when the two of them became roommates then lovers after Ross began partying regularly in the house Sam purchased. At the same time, Sam still managed to keep his sexual preference under wraps back home with the exception of coming on to Rosa's helper, Miguel, who had rebuffed him. It had not taken Ross long to figure out Sam was gay and the wealthy sugar daddy he had been looking for ever since his last lover left him high and dry with no visible means of support beyond that of part-time bartender, and now mooched in grand style off Sam.

Gathering his wits, Sam turned the conversation with Aunt Pearl back to the celebration of JC's birthday. "I think we should have a surprise party at that poor excuse for a club in Midline," he offered.

"I hope you are not referrin' to that disgraceful place known as The Lonesome Dove Cantina," replied Pearl sarcastically. "It's just a front for a whorehouse! You and most people around these parts know it! Decent folks just don't talk about it out in the open."

"Of course I'm not referring to The Dove!" exclaimed Sam. "Please give me a little more credit for better taste than that! I was referring to the Cattleman's Country Club and Golf Course. And The Dove is not a whorehouse! It's a cantina where many of the Mexican cowhands gather when they have some free time and a dollar or two to spare burning a hole in their pocket for a shot of tequila, or a beer and a little music. So, what if they tend to fraternize with the willing women who happen to be there?"

"Whatever," Pearl replied sharply. "I still think it's nothin' but a whorehouse. But the Cattleman's, now you are talkin' Sammy boy! That's a mighty good suggestion. We could set things up with the head honcho, and JC would never suspect a thing since she doesn't go there anymore. We could invite some 'o her former high school 'n community college classmates along with the couples she and Rex used to have out here to the ranch for dinner or their parties. Why I'd bet more than half the town would come. Then there's the new ranch foreman, what's his name? He's now management since Andy got himself hitched and took off for Mexico with that new wife of his, so he needs to be invited, too."

"You must mean Emilio Vasquez," replied Sam with an obvious sneer. "That's all we need is some Mexican greaser trying to gain entrance to the Country Club to create a scene when told he can't enter!"

"I will not sit here listenin' to you referrin' to the ranch foreman as some greaser!" declared Aunt Pearl. "He's incredibly good at what he does, or Andy would not have recommended him for the job, and your sister would not have approved him. As the leader of the ranch hands now, he needs to be invited to join the party! Why Sam Scott! I'm ashamed of you! Your momma didn't teach you to look down your nose at Mexicans and I won't stand for it, neither!"

Sam knew if he didn't express remorse for what he said immediately, all bets would be off for Aunt Pearl helping pull off the party. He was well aware it would have to be her to come up with a way to lure JC to the Cattleman's since she would refuse if he asked her to join him. That, and he knew the club manager had taken a dislike to him. He hated to admit it was true; he was the one who wanted a party to flaunt his success at becoming an attorney and possibly gain new clients. It left him with a sour taste in his mouth at having to apologize, but he answered by saying, "I didn't mean it when I called Emilio a greaser. It was a poor choice of words on my part, and I'm very sorry."

"You damn well better be sorry, and to prove it, you will personally invite him to the party!" decreed Pearl. "If you refuse, I will make sure everyone at the Cattleman's knows you are nothin' but a racist who should not be trusted with any 'o their legal business!"

"You wouldn't dare!" exclaimed Sam. Aunt Pearl leaned forward in her chair, her face only a few inches from his face. Her eyes narrowed. "You wanna try me? Just think about what happened to that good for nothin' loudmouth Cyrus Parker when he made me angry tellin' lies about my deceased husband's ethics while he was in the oil business when he didn't have a lick 'o evidence! In fact, he didn't even know Ira all that well to know he was as honest as the day is long! That was more than ten years ago 'n Cyrus is still an outcast 'round these parts and I don't see that changin' any time soon if I have anythin' to say about it!"

Sam scowled. "I remember Cyrus. You singlehandedly almost succeeded in running him out of Texas, and for all essential purposes, you have succeeded by making him a social outcast around here. He doesn't even venture into town anymore for fear of running into you. I will be happy to invite Emilio to the party." He so much wanted to add, 'you vindictive old bat!' But he refrained. He needed Aunt Pearl's influence to secure the party room at the Club, find a way to lure JC there and possibly pick up a majority of the tab for expenses. He knew he didn't have enough funds in his checking account or a sufficient unencumbered credit card balance to make the required deposit to secure one of the party rooms. Those hopes for her paying for everything were soon dashed when Pearl informed him it would be him paying the majority of costs for the party.

"Now that you are a big fancy attorney in San Antonio, I think it's only fair that you pick up the tab at the Cattleman's for food, drinks and a band. That's what any good brother would do for his sister. I'll pay for and send out invitations, make the necessary arrangements at the Club and supply a few 'o the decorations." She frowned and glared at him. "Just because I'm doin' that doesn't mean you don't have to personally invite Emilio Vasquez to the party or pay the tab," she cautioned. "Do we have a deal?"

Challenged, Sam swallowed hard, but he agreed. "Just don't go overboard when you order food, booze and a band. Speaking of booze, I think it should be a no host bar. It's only been a year since I graduated from law school, passed the bar exam and set up shop, and I'm still in the process of securing more major clients." Pearl had no idea he was cash strapped due to his irresponsible party boy lifestyle financed exclusively for himself and his lover.

"Don't you go playin' poor mouth with me Sammy Boy! I know you forced JC to ante up a whole bunch 'o cash to buy out your half of the ranch right after your momma died; and in case you forgot, I was at the readin' of her will when all of us, includin' you Sammy Boy, were handed a check for four hundred and fifty thousand big ones. In your case, that was in addition to the buyout money, not to mention the generous cash gifts you got at the party your sister paid for and the twenty grand each year, no strings attached, you get to withdraw from the trust fund." Sam hated it when she referred to him as Sammy Boy, but he had sense enough to keep it to himself rather than incur her disfavor any more than he already done after voicing his feelings with regard to Emilio Vasquez.

"Aunt Pearl, I said I would pay for the party! I just ask that you not go overboard," replied Sam while desperately trying to conceal his anger. He could not remember a time when he hated anyone more than he hated Aunt Pearl at this moment. He thought she was bossy, vindictive, and overbearing, even though she was usually right on target with her outspoken opinions and decisive actions.

Realizing she was getting under his skin, Pearl decided to have a little fun with her nephew. "Gee whiz Sammy Boy, and here I was under the distinct impression you meant I would have carte blanche when it came to hirin' a band, orderin' the food 'n booze since it was you who asked for the party and want me to make all the arrangements. Anything less and I'm not goin' to be a party to a cheap party! I have a reputation to uphold of bein' the hostess with the mostess around here, and I'll be a horn-swoggled lizard afore I give up that reputation just to save you a buck or two!"

God forbid you should have to give up that reputation, thought Sam. At the same time, he knew she had him backed into a corner if he didn't comply with her wishes. It could cost him money if JC gave him the boot on Pearl's say so for his self-serving plan of handling the ranch finances. He had every reason to believe Aunt Pearl would snoop around until she discovered a reason to blackball him with his sister, something he could not afford to have happen or his world would come tumbling down like that proverbial house of cards. "Do what you need to do, but I'm holding out for the no host bar," he said. "And please, I'm begging you, don't go overboard when you order food and negotiate a fair price for use of the party room and when hiring a band. I have had, and will continue to have, a lot of expenses until I get a reputation built up by winning some noteworthy cases."

Aunt Pearl settled back comfortably in her chair and propped up her feet on the matching brown leather ottoman. She took a leisurely sip of her iced tea, then gave Sam a wink and sly smirk that said, sure I will. Pearl would never know how close she came to becoming a statistic if he only had the guts to carry out what he was thinking and wanted to do.

"One of these days I'm going to snap totally and murder that bitch!" he muttered darkly under his breath on his way out the front door to his new dark blue BMW. "It will be a cold day in hell before I invite Emilio Vasquez to the birthday party! I'm sure the old bitch will forget what she said." He had been planning to join JC and Aunt Pearl for lunch, but in his current state of mind he had the rare, good sense to leave before he said or did anything he might regret.

When JC came in for lunch after mucking out the horse stalls, she asked Aunt Pearl what happened to Sam. "I saw his car pull up earlier, but it's gone. I thought he would be joining us for lunch."

"I have no idea. He didn't say where he was goin'," replied Aunt Pearl with a sweet innocent smile. "I guess he thought he had to see a man about a horse."

CHAPTER 6

As soon as she and JC finished lunch, Pearl set off on a jaunt to the only variety and dry goods store in Midline. She was grateful that she had managed to avoid answering JC when she asked why Sam had not remained to join them for lunch. Pearl's mind was now on purchasing blank birthday party invitations instead of having to make a trip to San Antonio or Austin to have them specially printed. She did not think the long drive to either location was an option. Time was running short, and they needed to be available to mail out two weeks in advance of the party. That gave her less than three weeks to track down names and addresses of those to be invited. "I hate sendin' out this type of an invitation, but I don't really have any alternative other than to call everybody," she continued to mumble under her breath. "I don't have that kinda free time to make calls 'cause I'll have to listen to everybody give me their life history from day one," she continued to mutter even though she knew it was expected and considered good manners to listen if she did end up having to make phone calls. JC knew better than to ask Aunt Pearl to speak up when it was time for her to leave the ranch, so she thanked her for coming and bid her goodbye.

While walking into the variety store, Pearl thought maybe she could get Mary Jane Withers, the owner's former wife, to help her find what she needed so she wouldn't have to waste time and deal with her ex-husband Bob, plus Mary Jane knew most of JC's friends and their addresses. "I hope she doesn't want to bend my ear about the details involvin' her divorce from Bob and how she managed to get half ownership in the store, full ownership of their ranch, that fancy sports car, along with half of their joint bank account in addition to alimony."

Not being able to locate Mary Jane, she retreated to the aisle displaying cards of all descriptions when she heard a familiar voice. It was Bob Withers, the former husband of his fourth wife, Mary Jane, who often made it a point to be seen wandering about in the store just to annoy her former husband. But today was not one of those days, so her absence left Pearl to deal with Bob.

Bob fancied himself to be God's gift to women and a legend in his own mind. His glory days of playing high school football had faded from the minds of just about everyone else but him. While there was no doubt he had been a ruggedly handsome guy when he played football in high school, he was now fifty-four years old, more than seventy pounds overweight, sporting a beer gut, receding salt and pepper hair and rotten teeth.

His latest conquest had been Lucy Parker, a woman known for loose morals, but choosy about the men with whom she unleased her passion, unless they had money. And at the time, she believed Bob had money. He put the moves on her in of all places, the church basement storage room! This was done in response to a challenge made by his drinking buddies at The Roadrunner Saloon that he would not be able to bed Lucy within twenty-four hours – a challenge he took on late that afternoon after consuming six beers, three Jell-O shots and four shots of whiskey over a three-hour period while playing their usual Wednesday afternoon poker game. And as bad luck would have it, with the help of the little blue pill, Bob won the bet on that same Wednesday night during a prayer meeting going on upstairs in the church sanctuary, on an old pew stored in the basement near the kitchen of the First Baptist Church. Of course, Mary Jane took offense and filed for divorce when members of the Ladies Aide Society confronted her with this information the following the prayer meeting.

Bob's indiscretion was alleged to have been seen by one of the members who kept a pulse on the morals of everyone in town. She had come forward to say she had been horrified to witness what had taken place between Bob and Lucy while she was making coffee in the nearby kitchen. And she felt a moral obligation to pass along the word in detail to what she had seen, and that she would be willing to testify to that fact in a court of law should Mary Jane decide to file for divorce. Playing the part of the wronged wife, nobody knew Mary Jane had been looking for a reason to divorce Bob. She had become suspicious his indiscretions involved several women other than just Lucy, although she couldn't prove it in court until there was an eyewitness willing to testify on her behalf to his flagrant indiscretion.

In order to speed the divorce along, Mary Jane offered Bob fifty thousand dollars in cash if he would waive court proceedings and sign the divorce paperwork. Being the greedy bastard that he was, Bob eagerly signed the papers before it dawned on him fifty thousand dollars was a pittance when compared to half the value of the variety store, their joint bank account, the sports car and the ranch after he took the time to read what he had signed. He had appearances to keep up, including an expensive membership at The Cattleman's Country Club and Golf Course, he would need to continue buying nice clothing, plus he would need a place to live in the style to which he had become accustomed, along with purchasing a car. The location he could now afford to call home did not begin to live up to those standards. It didn't even come close. Mary Jane's sharp attorney had seen to it she got the ranch outright and Bob got the mortgage and only half of the money in their joint account, plus alimony payments of three grand a month to Mary Jane until she should remarry. The fifty-grand came from her half of the shared bank account since she made the offer. She liked to say her momma "didn't raise no fool," which, if she had given any serious thought, was debatable. She paid Bob the fifty thousand from what the judge had declared was her half of the money in awarding her the three hundred thousand dollars. Duh!

Bob felt he needed to be at least a tiny bit grateful since Mary Jane paid for him to remain on their health insurance plan for six months as part of the divorce settlement. At least he wouldn't have to pay out of pocket for Viagra. But that meant he needed to find another wealthy wife within that six-month window or go without sex after he was sure to become short on funds with those additional alimony payments, car payments, the condo mortgage, the order to provide money to pay half of the utilities and insurance premiums on the business and keep the store stocked and open during normal business hours. Due to snowstorms, the variety store was lucky to bring in the three grand a month to cover the alimony. Affordable health care insurance at his age, being overweight with high blood pressure was out of the question. He didn't want to think about the problems with his sex life associated with not having health insurance when he could no longer afford to pay for Viagra out of pocket. He still liked to think of himself as a stud, even though he was dependent on the expensive little blue pills to perform.

"Why hello there Miss Pearl" exclaimed Bob. "My, don't you look lovely today," he purred in what he perceived to be a sexy voice. It was a voice that grated on Pearl's nerves. "What brings you to my humble establishment? I never expected to see a lady of means like you shop here." Pearl smiled sweetly while thinking, what a worn-out line of B.S., since he knew she shopped there routinely. Not wanting to give Bob the real reason she was there, she told him she needed a sympathy card for Allie Masters, who had lost her husband recently. I should not have let him know Allie is now a widow, thought Pearl as soon as she said it. That slimy bastard will be after her like flies on fresh cow shit! It didn't dawn on Pearl that she might be Bob's next target as a means for his financial salvation.

"Miss Pearl, I would be honored to show you the latest new card selections. In fact, I insist," said Bob. Pearl took a step back away from him. His breath reminded her of the smell associated with a dry feed lot holding a large herd of cattle in the hot summer sun before they were sent off in rail cars to market the next day. It was all she could do to keep her composure and not gag. "That won't be necessary, Mr. Withers. "I am perfectly capable of makin' a card selection without any help. I'm sure you have more important matters to attend to besides wastin' your time showin' me greetin' cards." She paused and cocked her head as if to listen. "Why I think I hear someone up front at the cash register wantin' to pay. Shouldn't you go check?" Bob excused himself and went to go see who was there since he couldn't afford to miss a single sale, even if it were only for a pack of chewing gum.

Not only did Pearl intensely dislike Bob, but she did also not want him to know she wanted to purchase birthday party invitations. A known gossip, she knew before nightfall he would let it be known all over the county that she was hosting such a party. This would start rumors and hurt feelings if someone who thought they should receive one did not. This was something the hostess with the mostest could not allow to happen. She quickly grabbed all dozen packages, each containing twelve invitations. She hurried to the soda fountain to pay Abigale Spivey, the soda jerk, instead of going to the front counter cash register before Bob had a chance to see what was happening. She did not intend to include him on the list of invitees. Luck was on her side. He was engaged in an animated conversation with a woman who had her back to her. Pearl did not stick around to find out who the woman might be and continued on her way out of the store. It was with a sigh of relief she escaped through the side door unnoticed while Bob was focused on making flirty small talk with the female customer. "He'll be madder 'n old a wet hen once he learns he's not been invited to the party, but he'll just have to get over it. It isn't like we are close friends or even friends for that matter," Pearl muttered under her breath. What Pearl didn't realize was Bob did not miss the fact she had made a purchase and left. He just didn't know what the purchase was and could not, as a busybody, stand the thought not knowing.

After he finished talking with the other customer, he was nosey enough to wander back to the soda counter and ask Abigale to tell him what Pearl had purchased. Abigale stammered and shrugged her shoulders, but Bob kept persisting. “Come on, Abbie,” he pleaded. “It’s not like it’s a national security matter or you are sworn to secrecy. I will find out sooner or later when I do a stock check to see what I need to be order in the card section. Come on, you can tell me.”

“Well, if you must know, she bought all dozen packages of those fill in the name, place, time and date invitation cards for a birthday party.”

“Did you find out the name of the person the party is being given for and where it is to take place?”

Abigale gave him a disgusted look and kept wiping imaginary spills from the pink and grey streaked marble topped soda fountain counter. The early lunch crowd had left an hour ago with her leaving it spotless, as she usually did, within half an hour of the last customer leaving. “No, I didn’t. I figured it weren’t none ‘o my business, unlike some folks I know.” Bob acted as though he didn’t hear the put down in regard to him being nosey.

“Dang it woman, you should have asked! I was hoping to get closer to Miss Pearl, her being a widow and me being single again. If I at least knew where the party was going to be held, I might just happen to be in the neighborhood and make a casual call with a box of our best chocolates.”

"Miss Pearl is way out of your league, Bob. We both know you'll soon be needin' more money than this place brings in durin' the comin' winter months. Best set yer sights on the widder, Allie Masters. She's more your style 'n she now owns the Lazy Bar M ranch since her husband, Will, died a couple weeks ago."

She may be more my style, since I like my women a little on the trashy side, but I have inside information, me being on the Board of Directors at the bank. That is how I know that ranch of hers is mortgaged to the hilt, something Bob did not disclose to Abigale. "I prefer a woman a little more refined than Allie," he answered instead of saying what he was thinking. Thoroughly disgusted that Abigale had not inquired further about the party, he left the soda fountain totally unaware she was grateful he was leaving the area. She had studied his face while deep in thought during the time she was being questioned. *I hope that old buzzard ain't seriously thinkin' about chasin' after Miss Pearl or, God forbid, Miss JC, them both bein' wealthy widows. Naw, he wouldn't git to first base with neither one 'o them. Miss Pearl is a dried up mouthy old biddy who ain't lookin' to find a man, but Miss JC... now there's a nice-lookin' filly who is gettin' awful lonesome since Mr. Rex died nigh onto three years ago. I'm sure ole Bob don't stand a chance with her. But then again, I done witnessed some stranger bed fellers in my day.*

CHAPTER 7

Abigale's suspicions regarding Bob possibly giving thought to going after Pearl was almost right on the money in respect to him going after either Pearl or JC. After giving it some thought, he devised a plan to seduce JC into marrying him, and he knew just how he was going to do it. Perhaps seduce isn't quite the right word; duress might turn out to be a more appropriate word to get what he wanted.

In his haste to get to the bank, Bob hurried right on past Allie Masters without speaking or even a nod of his head considering she was the woman he had spoken to less than ten minutes ago in the variety store. Allie had stood there listening, totally captivated by Bob's line of B.S., almost swooning when he asked her to join him for coffee the following morning over at the Bluebonnet Café. His invitation was made when it became apparent she was planning to make a large purchase when initiating the conversation by asking about ordering a dozen pairs of expensive tennis shoes in assorted colors she had seen on a TV infomercial – shoes he knew he could order at a discount allowing for a good markup in price.

She was less than pleased when Bob walked past her and her lady friend and did not speak. "Well, I never!" she exclaimed to the female shopping companion who had just joined her. "Did you see that? Bob didn't even bother to nod or speak; and he just asked me not ten minutes ago to join him for coffee at the Bluebonnet Café in the morning! He was so charming when we were talking in the store it made my heart flutter."

Her companion, Millie Mayberry, sniffed. "I didn't know you were that hard up for male companionship already with Will dying only three weeks ago. I will admit Bob was very handsome and fit when we were back in high school, but Allie, that was thirty-four years ago! Take another good look. Not only does he have a beer gut, his hair is non-existent on top and his teeth haven't seen the inside of a dentist's office in years. On top of that he usually has B.O. and breath bad enough to gag a maggot. Have you already forgotten Mary Jane dumped him for fornicating with that little tramp, Lucy Parker, in the church basement of all places! Gwendolyn Moore caught them in the act when she went down to the kitchen to make coffee for everyone after the Wednesday night prayer meeting. Why it wouldn't surprise me one bit if he has one of them social diseases after messing around with the likes of Lucy! And Wayne Purcell's cousin, twice removed, told me Lucy wasn't the first woman Bob messed around with after he up and married Mary Jane! Wayne's great niece on his mother's side, Myrtle Conroy, confirmed that story, so it must be the gospel truth!"

Allie tossed her ridiculous dyed red Shirley Temple curls over her shoulders. "That's enough, Millie! You made your point. Now let's you and me mosey on back over to the variety store since Bob probably won't be there for a while. We might hear us some juicy gossip while we sit at the counter having an ice cream soda. A lot of people don't remember how their voices carry when they think nobody is close by to hear them talk while they shop." Actually, she was hoping Bob would reappear and apologize for not speaking, and that could lead to him asking her out to dinner. The remote chance to have a dinner date with her dream man far outweighed his faults as far as she was concerned. She figured she could whip him into shape with her womanly charms if given half the chance.

Millie didn't fully realize her rants against Bob were being ignored. Allie still carried the torch for Bob, just as she had done all through high school when he was repeatedly voted captain of the football team by his teammates. During those years, Allie often fanaticized he would ask her out. It didn't happen back then or in the year after graduation before she married her now deceased husband. But she had never given up hope. She could hardly believe he had just asked her to join him for coffee now that she was a widow and him a bachelor again. In her mind, her dreams were about to come true, even if it took thirty-three years of marriage, the death of a husband and birth of four now grown kids before he asked her out. He must have had a lot on his mind, or he would have at least nodded was what she chose to believe. When he had asked her to join him for coffee Allie had no idea Bob was simply looking for a warm body with a few extra dollars to spend while filling in the gap between now and his plan to marry JC Morgan.

"I wonder what made Bob in such a big hurry when he was headed toward the bank," said Millie. She sucked on the straw of her soda hard enough to make a loud slurping noise that made her giggle.

"Oh, he probably just wants to count his money. I heard on the grapevine Mary Jane gave him a hundred thousand dollars to sign the divorce papers quick like with no fuss."

"That's funny. I heard it was seventy-five thousand dollars. If Jack and I had that kind of extra money, I'd be in the bank counting it every day."

Allie laughed. "The way you spend money, Millie, in no time there wouldn't be much left to count!"

In a strange sort of way, both women were right in thinking Bob was going to the bank to count his money. He needed to make sure there was at least twenty-five thousand dollars left in his personal account after making the down payment on his condo and buying a used car, if what he had in mind was going to work. During their two-year marriage Mary Jane took care of financial matters for Bob after he told her he didn't have the time or inclination to deal with them. After checking his account, he calculated he had three thousand nine hundred fifty-two dollars and sixty-three cents to spare above the twenty-five thousand he would need to buy up Sam Scott's illegal loan from the trust fund. This was not a whole lot after paying for business related expenses in addition to the down payment on the condo, minimal used furniture and a used car. That would leave just enough to cover next month's mortgage payments on his condo, the ranch, pay utility and phone bills at the condo and half the utilities and liability insurance at the store for the month per the divorce decree. This would leave just enough to purchase more store brand cornflakes, dried milk, beans, TV dinners and coffee for the coming month. Adding fresh stock to the store would just have to wait unless he could talk suppliers into extending credit. That would mean Mary Jane would also have to wait on next month's alimony check until he was all set financially after marrying JC and riding on the Scott Ranch gravy train. The thought of forcing Mary Jane to wait for her money brought a big smile to his face.

CHAPTER 8

Weekends, especially Saturday nights, were always hardest for JC. This had been her and Rex's date night, even before they were married. That pattern had continued for three years after they were married. Without fail, they would get dressed up and go to the Cattleman's Country Club for dinner, then drinks and dancing in the lounge while socializing with other couples. After returning to the ranch following their marriage, they often took long walks in the moonlight with their faithful collie, Jess, followed by love making.

But that all ended the day Rex was thrown from the wild stallion he was determined to break or die trying. A broken neck and crushed windpipe fulfilled the dying part before one of the cowhands chased down and shot the stallion. JC was still reeling from the death of her father and mother at the time Rex was killed. Even with the tender care of Aunt Pearl, Rosa and the sympathies expressed by then foreman Andy Mendoza and the ranch hands, she thought her life was over. She blamed herself for not insisting more firmly that the wild stallion be sold or put down before Rex had the opportunity to try and break him. More than three years have now passed, and she continues to cope with her losses by refusing all social encounters and throwing herself into whatever needs to be done to keep the ranch running smoothly.

On this particular Friday night, she shoved the sirloin steak Rosa had prepared to the middle of the table untouched. The melted butter usually making it succulent had begun to congeal. She sat back in her chair and stared at the far dining room wall while muttering. "I'll be thirty years old in less than a month. That means I've got another fifty or more years to live on my own and maintain this ranch. I have to get out of here for a while or I'll go crazy! I never dreamed being responsible for managing this spread could be so hard!" Only this morning, Rosa had let her know their credit at the local grocery store had been cancelled for lack of payment over the past three months. This had been verified by a letter from the store owner later that afternoon when the mail was delivered, along with statements from the vet's office and the feed store showing charges two months in arrears. Sam was not taking her calls to find out why this was happening since he was the one being paid to be responsible for keeping the bills current and meeting payroll.

After her third call to his office, Sam's secretary, June Maddox, became less than cordial. "Mrs. Morgan, I keep telling you Sam has taken the weekend off, and he didn't say where he was going. I'm sure he will call you first thing Monday morning." The tone of irritation in her voice let JC know June was tired of the interruptions.

The miles between them did not allow JC to know Sam was sitting in his office with the door closed refusing to take any calls. Not only had he been getting calls from the owner of the Midline Grocery store for lack of payment, he had been made aware by the bank trust manager there was that bank note for twenty-five thousand dollars due and payable in three weeks or the best thousand acres of ranch grazing land would be put up for auction to satisfy the loan. When JC pressed for an explanation regarding the loan, the trust manager had abruptly hung up after saying he had a pressing business problem and would have to get back to her as soon as possible, which to date has not happened.

Sam couldn't believe he had illegally agreed to put up that part of the ranch as collateral for such a pittance since he had sold his interest to JC but felt justified because his back was against the wall and that was the only amount the less than honest manager of the bank trust fund would allow. His office rent was due, along with the mortgage on the house he promised JC he would sell but had yet to list with a broker. His lover, Ross Vandenberg's, expensive drug habit and tastes had kept eroding what little money he had accumulated from the few clients he managed to represent, many of them slow in paying. And there was the upcoming birthday party for JC. "I can't believe I thought the bank trust officer, Clayton Mooney was my friend and lover on the side. We both knew he was granting the loan to me for sexual favor's rendered; something he had no right to do under the terms of the trust along with me no longer owning any part of the ranch!" He put his head in his hands and cried. "My God! How am I going to repay the loan and meet the other bills on a long-time basis? I can't even keep up with the day-to-day bills at the ranch, my house or my office! How am I going to pay for a birthday party and still keep Ross happy? He expects the best of everything, and if I can no longer provide it, then he will leave me for someone who can! If Aunt Pearl finds out, she will never let me live this down! If JC finds out, she will end our financial arrangement and disown me! I can't believe I allowed that weasel, Ross, to play me for the past five long years! I will be ruined and could end up in prison!" Sam continued to sit with his head in his hands, tears streaming down his face while remembering it wasn't that long ago when he and Ross had sat sharing a romantic dinner at their favorite restaurant to celebrate their five-year anniversary together as lovers. After what had transpired between he and Ross that night, he had given a brief thought to committing suicide, but knew he was too much of a coward to take his own life.

"Here's to five happy years," Sam recalled having said on that Friday evening a month ago. "As a present for you, I've arranged for us to take a weekend road trip to exciting New Orleans with dinner on Friday evening at Commanders Palace. Saturday morning, there is a three-hour brunch river cruise aboard a paddle wheeler. Then we can enjoy a late lunch at the Oyster Bar and take in a show at the nightclub featuring The Dueling Pianos on Saturday night after an early dinner at Two Jacques restaurant." He had not booked a meal at world famous Brennan's due to what he considered the high cost.

Ross had smiled, his eyes taking on the sexy, mysterious look that had always captivated Sam. "That is so sweet of you, my love, but I was hoping we would go back to Paris, the land of love and city of lights. Paris is sooo divine this time of year." Ross had not given any thought about providing a present for Sam.

"I would love to be able to do that, my sweet," Sam recalled saying. "But right now, I'm a little strapped for cash. Clients have been slow in paying. But if you insist, we could go to Paris for a week if you loan me around thirty thousand dollars. Of course, I would pay you back."

The sexy, mysterious look quickly vanished from Ross's face. "You can't be serious, Sam! Me lend you thirty thousand bucks? I'm lucky to have ten-thousand in my checking account at any one time." The mysterious, pouty, sexy look had turned into an unflattering scowl in a matter of a few seconds.

Sam continued to sit there in his office chair with the door closed remembering he had swallowed hard before asking, "Could you lend me the ten thousand? I have ranch payroll, office rent and mortgage on the house to meet. I'm tapped out of my share of the trust fund for the year. If I ask for more money JC will become suspicious, and Clarence Mooney at the bank tells me he can be of no further help." He didn't mention the grocery store demanding payment or the illegal bank loan he and Clarence cooked up was coming due among other unpaid bills. He couldn't even bring himself to think about the power and phone companies, each a month in arrears at not only the ranch, but at his home and office as well. He could stall JC a little while longer telling her it was just a bank oversight and the grocery, vet and cattle feed bill would be paid by the time she could figure it out and ask what was going on, but those bills would be paid only if Ross came up with the ten-grand. But the utility companies, payroll for the ranch hands, his secretary's salary and mortgage on his home were each quite another matter unless he could think of a way to come up with more cash. And at the present time, he didn't have an answer how to come up with such a large sum of money in a short amount time.

Continuing to reflect on the night of the five-year celebration served to bring back the memory of Ross batting his eyes, losing the scowl and licking his pouty lips provocatively. "I will lend you the ten thousand dollars if you promise me one thing."

Right now, I would promise you the moon and stars, Sam had thought to himself. Sitting there, he shuddered, remembered running his hand along Ross's inner thigh up to his crotch under the table causing Ross to squirm and giggle in such a way that he became aroused. "And what would that be?" Sam had inquired with a wicked come-hither grin, along with a promise of more intimate things to come when they got home.

"When you take me to the most fashionable clothing salon in Paris, you will buy me a dozen pairs of silk underwear. I simply adore the feel of silk against my skin," gushed Ross. "And of course, we will stay at the same five-star hotel near downtown where we stayed last time, won't we?"

It had been Sam's turn to fake a smile and nod. "You have a deal. Can you transfer the cash into my account early tomorrow morning?" *Never mind any trip to Paris. That will be a long, long time in the future, if ever. The way things are presently going, unless I can talk Clarence Mooney into giving me more cash from the trust to add to your pitiful ten-grand we will be history* had become the focus among his thoughts.

"Not quite so fast, my dear," Ross had responded. "I will need a signed note stating you will pay me back, including the signature of a notary public." Sam still remembered staring at him in total disbelief with tears and uttering, "After me devoting five years to paying for everything and you are asking me to sign a note? I am so hurt!"

Ross had sighed and rolled his eyes. "Save the theatrics, darling. Business is business. You should be grateful I'm not charging you interest and allowing you up to six months for repayment. By the way, I still expect my regular weekly thousand-dollar allowance. Sign the note as requested or no goodies. I can go to Paris any time I want to buy silk underwear with or without you." The threat struck home with Sam that Ross could leave him, and at the time, it was not a pleasant thought on top of all of his other overwhelming troubles.

"All right, I'll sign the note," Sam agreed. "Have it on my office desk no later than ten o'clock tomorrow morning."

"If you would be so kind, dear one, I would like another bottle of that lovely French champagne," Ross had requested with another pouty smile. Sam had managed to suppress a scowl, remembering he had given Ross what could be interpreted as a loving look while thinking, people in hell would like ice water, and they have about as much chance of that happening as you do getting another bottle of that expensive champagne. Instead, he had signaled the waiter for another bottle, hoping his credit card would not be denied when presented to pay the bill. He had done this thinking he could not afford to anger Ross.

As he sat there in his office remembering that evening, suddenly an evil plan crossed Sam's mind. He would make sure Ross would not have any idea he would be dead in the not-too-distant future, but not before a nice, big insurance policy on his life was taken out with himself as the beneficiary, even if Ross did transfer the ten-grand to his account.

Sam had found it necessary to contact three different insurance companies before he could persuade one agent to write the insurance policy on Ross's life. "It pays to be persistent," he reasoned without any thought of what the consequences could be when murder was involved.

CHAPTER 9

The melted butter on JC's perfectly cooked charbroiled sirloin steak had definitely congealed without her taking a single bite. Rosa had left for the night at JC's insistence more than twenty minutes ago to visit local family members of her boyfriend. This left the dining room in relative silence. She picked up the platter, got up, walked to and opened the front door, tossing the steak off across the porch onto the lawn for the dogs to enjoy. She returned to the kitchen, rinsed then deposited the dirty plate and silverware in the dishwasher. Walking into the living room the late afternoon sounds associated with log construction creaking after a warm mid-September fall day frayed her nerves more than they were already frayed.

"I have to get out of here! I need a place away from here to think. I know, I'll pack a few things, saddle up and ride up to the mountain line shack. There won't be anyone using it since the remaining herds up there have been driven to the low land corrals in preparation for branding and the drive to the railhead next Thursday morning. Nobody will be using it again until more herds are driven down to the lowland pasture for the winter, and that won't be for another two weeks." She checked the clock on the mantle. It was ten minutes passed five p.m. "If I hurry, I'll be there before it gets too dark. At least up there I'll have howling coyotes for companions since we haven't had any really cold nights or snowfall yet to send them scurrying off into their winter dens."

The line shack was not your typical barren one room uninsulated wood shack containing a set of bunk beds, small table, two chairs and a potbellied wood fired stove with an outhouse out back like the one existing there eighty years ago. Rex had that one demolished and built a special one for their little getaways in addition to accommodating the foreman during the yearly spring and fall roundups. It contained two rooms, including a full bathroom with hot and cold running water, a bedroom with a queen size bed, two night tables, two generator powered lamps and two kerosene lanterns for use should the generator fail, a mirrored dresser and small, but compact closet for storing linens and a few items of clothing. The other room, a matching twenty feet long by sixteen feet wide, served as the living room complete with a floor to ceiling fieldstone fireplace across one end, dining area, pantry and L-shaped kitchen that included a propane fired kitchen stove and refrigerator in the other end. At this altitude, air conditioning was not necessary. The wood burning fireplace and wool blankets supplied heat on cold nights. A well was drilled with a hand pump added should the propane fired pump engine fail. A huge picture window with side vents that opened and closed allowed access to a view across the expanse of a ten-foot wide by twelve-foot-long covered front porch and the meandering river half a mile below. Beautiful ruggedly framed pictures of the ranch, some taken by aircraft, hung over the mantle. The same type of curtainless window could be found in the bedroom. Only there, the unobstructed view was toward the elevated mountain peaks off in the distance, often snow covered up beyond the tree line.

JC hoped the shack's pantry had been restocked with canned goods and coffee. Just in case that hadn't been done, she tossed a couple of cans of soup, evaporated milk, a box of crackers, a small jar of peanut butter, a plastic bag filled with sugar and one filled with ground coffee in one of her saddle bags along with two changes of clothing in the other. "Everything else I need should be there, linens, bedding, toothbrush, toothpaste and bath soap. If the propane tank hasn't been filled, I can always gather up or chop mesquite for the fireplace and pump water by hand," she mused. "If necessary, I can build a campfire and cook outdoors. And who will be there if my deodorant fails should the water be too cold to take a shower?" She took one last look around the ranch house, locked the doors and declared she and her horse were ready to ride. She did not leave a note to her whereabouts, thinking she would be back before Rosa returned late on Sunday night.

And ride they did! Her favorite horse, a cinnamon-colored gelding by the name of JoJo standing sixteen hands high at the chest, knew the way. JC gave him his head, allowing him to gallop full speed across the flat pastureland. He was just as anxious to make tracks across the pasture leading up to the mountain shack as his mistress. He barely slowed to a trot when they approached the arroyo and broad meandering river at the foot of the mountains. Luckily, the riverbed was shallow enough at this point there was no need for him to swim. He did slow to a walk and become more careful where he stepped on the journey up the narrow steep rock-strewn mountain trail leading to the shack. Any misstep would send both horse and rider plunging down the rugged drop off hundreds of feet to land among the rocks and scrub pines below. They would not be found for days, whether or not they survived with what would undoubtedly be serious disabling injuries if not immediate death.

The closer they got to the shack, the more spectacular the sunset became, giving way to streaks of bright reds, oranges, purples, and gold while the red ball descended below the mountain peaks. As the sun passed out of sight, the colors became muted into softer shades melding into varying shades of pink, violets and multiple shades of blue and gray. The temperature also began a steady decline the farther up the trail they went. JC was happy she made the decision to add a light jacket and tossed it across the saddle horn as an afterthought. She would need it for the last mile before making it to the shack. Night was settling in faster than she anticipated. This would mean the only source of light would be from the full moon and stars. She did not like riding up here in the dark. It could prove to be downright dangerous. This is when creatures of the night, such as rattle snakes, mountain lions, poisonous lizards and two legged creatures on the prowl came out from under their respective rocks or hiding places seeking prey. “I should have left a half an hour sooner,” she lamented to JoJo. The horse shook his head and softly nickered as though he understood what she said.

Rounding the last bend in the trail before reaching the gentle plateau where the shack stood, JC was surprised to see pale yellow light shining through the front window a quarter of a mile in off in the distance. She had not been informed any of the cowhands would be there. It would not be the first time someone had broken into the shack. Those types, usually rustlers, were not known to be all that friendly. She unsheathed the shotgun fastened to the side of her saddle, knowing she knew how to use it if necessary. “Well here goes nothing, ready or not,” she whispered to JoJo. Arriving at the shack, she did not try to quietly toss JoJo’s reins across the hitching post in order to give any unwelcome guest the opportunity to exit through the back door. Stomping her boots on the walk across the front porch floor, flinging open the door, shotgun poised waist high ready for action was probably not the smartest move on her part, having given the intruder or intruders a heads up to expect company had they decided not to exit.

"What the hell are you doing in my house!" she announced loudly before she realized who was making an effort to get up off the sofa in front of the fireplace.

"Mrs. Morgan, please don't shoot! It's me, Emilio! His hands were raised high above his head in the air. The book he had been reading landed with a thud on the floor at his feet.

"Emilio? What are you doing here?" demanded JC.

"I could ask you the same question. In fact, I'm asking that question. You have not been up here to the shack. . ." He stopped before adding, since Rex died. "Had I known you were headed up here, I would never have come."

"I could say the same about you being here. Don't you usually go to the Lonesome Dove Cantina on your off time?"

"No, ma'am. I usually stay in my room at the bunkhouse, listen to music, watch TV, jawbone with the boys, or go riding. Sometimes I come up here to clear my head." Then he quickly added, "I always restock anything I use from out of my pay, and I don't usually start the generator or turn on the lights, but tonight I wanted to read. I hope that's okay." He lowered his hands and stooped just enough to be able to slowly bend, retrieve the fallen book and lay it on the sofa before returning his hands fully into the air.

JC lowered the shotgun to her side. "Do you mind if I come on inside? It's been a long ride up here and I'm saddle weary and hungry." As an afterthought she added, "You can relax and put your hands down now. I have no intention of shooting you." She walked on inside and leaned the shotgun in a nearby corner.

"You don't have to ask if you can come inside. It's your shack," said Emilio. "There's canned chili simmering on the stove . . . that's if you like chili. If not, there is some canned hash and several different kinds of canned soup. I'm sorry, but there aren't any potatoes, salad vegetables or fresh meat, except for some hotdogs I brought with me. Would you care to join me for some canned chili? I did add extra chili and onion powder. And I will be glad to sleep outside. I have a bedroll stashed under the roof overhang next to my saddlebags and saddle. I'm used to sleeping out under the stars. Speaking of saddles, please allow me to get your horse settled for the night. I don't think either one of us want to make the ride back down the mountain at night on that narrow trail."

"You don't need to take care of my horse, nor do you need to sleep outside on the ground. I can take care of JoJo. And no, I don't want to make that ride back down the mountain, and since you arrived first you get the bedroom. I'll sleep on the sofa."

"Oh no, ma'am, you get the bedroom! I insist. I also insist that I take care of JoJo if you will be so kind as to put the biscuits in the oven while I feed and hobble him. They're sourdough rising over there on the kitchen counter under the red and white stripped dish towel. I'm sure the oven should be at the proper temperature by now."

"You made biscuits?"

"Yes, ma'am. I always keep sourdough starter going in the pantry during roundup time, and there was some left for when we round up the remaining herds in a few days. My mother insisted I learn how to make biscuits." Actually, it was their cook, but he didn't want her to know they had a cook when he lived at home. "She said there would be times they might save my life. Of course, I don't know if these biscuits will be fit to eat or best used to build walls or walkways."

JC had to laugh at his last comment. "All right, you've got a deal. You take care of JoJo, and I'll bake your biscuits and dish up the chili. I happen to love chili."

"Taking care of horses is man's work," continued Emilio. "Woman's work is in the kitchen."

JC bristled at those comments and voiced her displeasure. "There is no such thing as man or woman's work! It is whoever is handy and able to get the job done!" Emilio didn't know how to respond to her terse statement so he answered by saying, "Sorry, there isn't any butter to go with the biscuits, ma'am, but there may be strawberry preserves in the pantry. I thought I saw a jar in there when I stayed here a couple of weeks ago during the first roundup."

“I’ll manage without butter, and please stop calling me ma’am!” she commented sharply. I don’t know how well I’ll manage with you sleeping in the room next to me with only a door and wall between us was what she could not help thinking. “And since we are spending the night here in the shack together, you can call me JC. Oops, that didn’t sound right. What I mean is . . .”

Emilio smiled without looking in her direction on his way across the room while striding toward the front door. He stopped suddenly to interrupt before she could finish what she was saying. “You don’t have to explain. I know what you meant.” His next thought was, *Shame on me. I sure hope you don’t know what I was thinking, or I could be in deep trouble!* He decided it would be best not to think about only a wall and door between them or things could get complicated.

While Emilio was taking care of JoJo, this gave JC time to get her emotions under control. She had placed the biscuits in the oven five minutes ago when there was a loud knock at the front door. She started to walk toward the shotgun leaning in the corner and picked it up in case it was someone unfriendly since there was no reason for Emilio to knock. “Come in,” she called. It took a couple of seconds after she realized by looking through the peep hole it was Emilio doing the knocking. “You don’t have to knock, just come on in,” she shouted, recovering from the fleeting fear of not knowing who could be out there. “Biscuits will be ready in about ten more minutes. That will give you plenty of time to go wash up in the bathroom." She hoped he didn't notice her placing the shotgun back in the closest corner. If he did, he didn't mention it or why he had knocked on the door.

"I can use the kitchen sink to wash up and not make a mess in the bathroom," offered Emilio.

"You could, but wouldn't it be better if you used the bathroom sink? I don't want horsehair in my chili. And I did check the pantry and found some of my homemade wild strawberry jam."

"Strawberry jam will be just fine. It's one of my favorites," he said on the way to the bathroom.

"That's good, because jam on the biscuits will have to double as dessert since I didn't see anything else that could qualify, unless you can whip up a cake or you like dried prunes," she called to him across the room. "I did bring crackers and a jar of peanut butter, but those wouldn't make very good dessert."

"Sorry, biscuits and coffee are my only culinary accomplishments. That is unless you count fatback and beans cooked over an open fire out on the trail if the cook gets a burr under his saddle when the hands object to the same fare every day and he takes off," he said with a barely audible chuckle.

Conversation during the meal proved to be a challenge for both of them. JC found herself chattering on about the fact she thought there would be a long, hard cold winter. Emilio rambled on about the roundup, branding, fence mending and upcoming cattle drive to the railhead in Midline.

"I sure hope the fall cattle sale is more profitable than the spring sale," said JC, worry unmistakable in her demeanor and voice.

Emilio looked perplexed. "Why do you say that? Andy told me based on the number of head that included twenty thousand head of cows and nine hundred head of steers, it was one of the best sales in years."

"Are you sure it was that good?" she questioned.

"I'm sure. I was there when the buyer handed Andy the check after the head count. It was hard not to see the amount. In fact, Andy waved the check in my face he was so happy. I also went with him when he deposited it in the Midline bank before we went for an early lunch that Saturday morning. I remember a lady cashier sending us to a Mr. Mooney to make the deposit. She said trust manager informed the tellers he would make any deposits. When Andy asked for a receipt this Mr. Mooney said that would not be necessary. The amount would be posted on the following month's bank statement. I thought that was strange, but I didn't think it was my place to say anything. Anyway, this Mr. Mooney didn't give Andy the opportunity to question not getting a receipt, saying he had a meeting with an important customer and he was late. And off he went, leaving us standing there with our mouths hanging open. We had no choice but to leave or tackle and force him produce a receipt. We didn't think that would be appropriate in front of other customers."

"I'm curious. Do you happen to remember the amount of the check?"

"Seven hundred thousand eight hundred dollars," he replied. "That figure was based on three hundred and fifty dollars each for cows and the extra five dollars each for what the buyer considered prime steers."

"Are you sure the check wasn't for seventy thousand eight hundred dollars?"

"No, ma'am. I am one hundred percent sure it was not for that amount," insisted Emilio.

JC's heart sank. When she had made a quick check of the deposit statement in early April, it had been recorded at the lesser figure. Unable to continue eating, she laid the half-eaten biscuit on the table instead of her plate. She closed her eyes and took a deep breath letting it out slowly. She could not help wondering if she had been shorted on other cattle sale checks over the two years since Sam had been paid to take over the responsibility of the finances.

"Is something wrong, JC?" asked Emilio.

"I hope not, Emilio. I certainly hope not!" In her heart of hearts, JC knew something was very wrong. She had been experiencing the uneasy feeling something had not been right after Sam had taken over the financials, but she had failed to act on the feeling. There was something fishy with Sam dealing exclusively with the bank manager of the ranch trust fund when any one of the senior cashiers could have handled the approved invoices, payouts and any deposits. When she confronted Sam earlier about this arrangement, he insisted it was best that he deal exclusively with the ranch trust fund manager, Clarence Mooney, and she didn't have to worry her pretty little head about finances. It was only this afternoon when she fully suspected it was her mistake to have trusted Sam after she received those troubling notices in the mail involving not only the grocery bills having not been paid for the past three months just as Rosa had mentioned earlier, but the grain and vet bills had not been paid for two months. The grocer's bill also stated that no more credit would be extended until the balance was paid in full. "I should never have let Sam take over the financial end of running the ranch," she said barely above a whisper, while covering her face with her napkin in order to stem the sudden flow of tears.

Emilio got up from his chair, walked over behind her and placed a hand on her shoulder. "Who and what are you talking about?" he asked softly.

"My brother, Sam . . . I foolishly agreed to paying him to take over all of the ranch accounting, including paying all of the bills and payroll. He is better with figures than I am. He asked me to set it up with Mr. Mooney, the bank overseer of the trust fund our mother put in place before she died. Invoices and checks were to be run through Sam's office equipment and paid from the trust account after Sam and Mr. Mooney approved them. It seemed like a good idea at the time. Sam wanted to do something to help me when he realized he had not been the brother he should have been. This afternoon I received notices in the mail of bills not having been paid for several months. Please tell me you and the other cowhands have been getting your monthly checks."

"As a matter of fact, none of us got paid this month, but we thought it was just a bank oversight and you would take care of it. I was planning to mention it to you on Monday. I was not aware Sam was responsible for paying our salaries or the bills." JC began to cry in earnest. Not knowing what to do with a crying woman, Emilio continued to stand behind her chair nervously patting her on the shoulder. He had never seen his mother, sister or aunts cry, not that they had anything to cry about. His beautiful Spanish mother led a fairytale life. His father treated his mother like a China doll that would break should her every wish not be granted, nor had his sister, brother or aunts gone without. "I'm sure it is just a misunderstanding. Mr. Mooney will be able to explain and take care of it on Monday," he finally offered. "I know the bank cut back the Saturday hours to half a day so there won't be time for you to get there from here until Monday. Have you tried calling your brother?"

“Yes, three times. His secretary kept telling me he’s out of town and she doesn’t know where he is or how he can be contacted. And you are right about the banking hours only being until noon on Saturday.” She wiped her eyes and then blew her nose on the plain white paper napkin.

The information concerning the lack of knowledge of Sam’s whereabouts caused Emilio to be at an even greater loss for words, but only for a moment. He cleared his throat and gave her shoulder a couple of more intense pats. “Why don’t you finish your meal and I’ll go outside, scare up some wood and build a campfire? It’s not too cold for a campfire yet. Yes, sir, ah, I mean ma’am, ah, JC, there is nothing like sitting on a blanket around a nice warm blazing campfire under the stars and a full moon to clear the mind and put things in their proper perspective.” JC, not knowing what else to say, just nodded in agreement.

When he had gone outside, she took the opportunity to scrape the remainder of her uneaten food into the plastic lined trash can and cover it with paper towels. “I can’t believe Sam is doing this to me! All I’ve ever done is go out of my way to help him. I just don’t understand why he would do this to me! And as for Mr. Mooney, we have always enjoyed a good business relationship ever since he took over Rex’s job as the trust manager after Rex married me, and that has continued after Rex died. But I have a feeling he is somehow mixed up in this gosh awful mess!”

Emilio could not help hearing muttering and the slamming of dishes, pot and pans coming from the open panels of the kitchen window as he gathered up mesquite to start the campfire. Tossing on a couple of ponderosa pine logs taken from under the shack overhang after the initial flame took hold, he spread out a saddle blanket close by the fire. Then he stepped back to sit on his haunches and stare up at the night sky in order to give him time to think about how best to handle the situation before JC finished up in the kitchen to join him. The fire was toasty warm, but a chill crept up the back of his neck, and he shuddered. "Dad, I wish you could be here to tell me what to do next because I don't have a clue," he muttered under his breath.

CHAPTER 10

JC could have blamed what happened next on Emilio's response to her being upset, but that was only part of it. There was no denying he was easy to talk to or that he was handsome and sexually appealing. The fire and view of the countryside below with a few twinkling lights from distant ranch houses was so relaxing. The stars and full orange moon lent a romantic air to intensify Emilio's appealing attributes. It seemed so natural for him to be sitting there beside her on the blanket while she poured her heart out over Rex's death and the fact her brother, and possibly the bank trust officer, were stealing from her. Before either one of them realized what was happening, Emilio reached out to wrap his arm around her shoulder, the motion sending them off balance resulting in both of them ending up lying beside each other on the blanket instead of sitting side by side. Without thinking of the consequences, Emilio pulled her close to his chest and kissed her. At first, she responded before pulling away. "We can't be doing this," she moaned. At the same time, she wanted to do this and a whole lot more. It had been quite a while since she felt a man's touch or kiss, and it felt right to her under the circumstances.

Emilio knew she was right. He should not be holding or kissing her. She was his employer. He was just a hired hand, even if he was now the foreman on the ranch she owned.

He wanted to believe it was possible for a relationship between them to work, yet she knew nothing of his background. He thought nobody on the ranch or in the ranching community knew his family was extremely wealthy ranch owners in Mexico, but at that moment it didn't matter. All he could think about was holding her close and kissing her; reason be damned to where that might lead if she were willing to take the next step.

Not wanting to live his life as a spoiled rich kid, Emilio had left home with his father's blessing at the age of sixteen to come to the United States and seek his fortune after completing and excelling in a private school. The first ten years, he worked as a cowboy on several different ranches to earn money, finally making his way to the Scott Ranch where he had now worked for the past almost five years. He lived frugally, waiting for the perfect opportunity to buy land. He knew someday he would be expected to return to the family ranch, marry a local girl and raise a family, but that would not happen until he made his dream of becoming a U.S. citizen a reality. He had just recently fulfilled the U.S. citizenship dream. But his attraction for JC had thrown a monkey wrench into the timing of his plans to buy his own ranch, build it up and sell it, then to return home to marry a local Mexican girl and eventually take over the family ranch for his father. He groaned softly. There was no denying he had loved JC from the first moment he laid eyes on her. He prided himself on the fact that he was able to keep his distance from her while Rex was still alive. He knew he felt enough time had passed since Rex died that was no longer a roadblock to him and JC having a romantic relationship. He pulled her back to his chest and kissed her more passionately. This time she did not pull away and kissed him in return.

Passion and physical need took away any misgivings for both of them. He began nuzzling her neck with kisses while whispering endearments in Spanish words she understood. And when she didn't make any further effort to pull away his hand slid toward the snaps on her shirt. Her bare shoulders looked like cream in the moonlight to the point it took his breath away. He did not have to fumble with her bra. She unfastened, removed, and tossed it aside along with the shirt as he helped her slip out of her jeans and panties. In a matter of minutes, they breathlessly lay practically naked on the blanket, gasping for air after their lips met, their tongues exploring, their hands caressing. She begged him to enter her. He willingly did so, knowing he should take more time to explore every part of her body, and she his body. But those thoughts were lost in their heightened state of arousal. Neither of them gave a thought about using protection. After climaxing they lay back on the blanket, sweat glistening on their bodies, both breathing hard. "I think you made the coyotes stop howling to listen," whispered Emilio, his lips pressed against her cheek, his hand caressing her bare stomach sending shivers up her arms that had nothing to do with the temperature outside. He pulled the saddle blanket up around her, but with both of them lying on it, it didn't cover much, but it didn't seem to matter to either one of them.

"Are you saying I was noisy?" she questioned as she ran her hand through his hair and nibbled on his ear.

"I can't honestly say I remember. I need to listen more carefully when you cry out again," he responded before kissing her left breast.

When they made love this time JC would swear she heard the angels sing. "You are not sleeping outside!" she declared breathlessly. She still had no thought about using protection since she and Rex had tried unsuccessfully to become pregnant for more than two years prior to his death. Thorough testing revealed a very high probability of her being unable to conceive due to a backward tilted uterus in conjunction with Rex's low sperm count. They had even started to consider adoption. "We need to go inside to the bed to continue in comfort. I'm cold, and this ground is getting harder by the minute."

"Harder than me?" Emilio joked with a mischievous grin that made her blush visibly, even in the dimming firelight.

"I will decide and give you an answer to that question after we go inside to bed," she replied with a come-hither smile. He did not hesitate to kick out the dying embers, scoop her up and carry her naked body across the lawn, up onto the porch, kicking the shack door open then shutting it behind them with his foot before heading straight for the bedroom. The coyotes remained silent, even with uninhibited sounds associated with lovemaking being emitted through four walls and closed windows surrounding the pair. He found it unnecessary to press her for an answer to his question. From the satisfied look on her face, it was obvious what it would have been. Being a devout Catholic, the use of protection never entered his mind.

The next morning, Emilio was up, dressed and had already made coffee without awakening JC. When she walked into the kitchen area fully dressed forty-five minutes later, he knew what she was going to say before she said it. "About last night, Emilio . . . It was a lovely dream, but we can't let it happen again."

"Can you make that statement while you look me in the eyes? And if you do that makes you a liar!" he passionately responded.

"Are you calling me a liar? You know perfectly well we both fell under the spell of the campfire, a full moon and the stars. We were both lonely and simply needed someone to offer comfort. You and I live in different worlds. A serious relationship would never work out!" JC was on the verge of tears but willed herself not to let them fall. She was able to do that because she was angry with herself for allowing her emotions and physical need to overrule her head last night.

Emilio refused to look away from her, his dark eyes blazing. "Are you telling me I'm not good enough to live in your world? It's because you think I'm Mexican isn't it? Well, Miss High and Mighty, I'm more Spanish than greaser! In fact, I'm a U.S. citizen, and that means I have citizenship in both countries, and I will also have you know the majority of my ancestors are of Spanish Hidalgo heritage! That makes me more Spanish than Mexican!" There was no doubt he was indignant.

JC felt awful. "It's not like that!" she declared.

"Then you need to tell me what it is like! We both know it wasn't just the stars, moon and campfire! It was about two people who need each other more than a one-night stand. I love you, JC. I have loved you since the first time I saw you, but you were married at the time. You should know by now I do not date married women! In fact, I have not dated anyone in the five years since I first saw you. Now you are no longer married, and I'm sorry about what happened to Rex, but I still love you, and I have a strong suspicion after what took place between us last night you love me too. But for reasons known only to you, you are afraid to admit it. I am telling you my love for you will not ever change, and you need to at least think about moving on in a relationship with me!"

JC started to cry, turned and ran from the shack. She rushed to where her horse, JoJo, was calmly grazing, a hobble on his front feet. She removed and tossed it aside then jumped on his back, to urge him across the yard and onto the trail, while hanging onto his mane for dear life. She had not stopped to put a bit in his mouth, saddle up or grab her saddle bags. Without control of reins, JoJo was left strictly on his own when it came to slowing down when they reached the narrow mountain trail, then the river and arroyo. She cried as though her heart would break during the three-mile ride across the open pasture back to the ranch house. Arriving late morning, she stumbled through the ranch house door after handing JoJo off to one of the startled cowboys who had stepped outside the bunkhouse for a smoke after having eaten an early lunch before heading out to mend more fences. She didn't stop to say hello or ask Rosa why she returned early from her family visit as she would have done any other time.

Rosa took one look at JC when she rushed past her into the ranch house without saying where she had been or a simple hello. "It got to be a man. Only man make woman cry like that," Rosa muttered. She was just about to ask who the man could be when JC made tracks for her bedroom and slammed the door. Rosa knew she would not get any answers from her today. But it would not be for lack of trying. She had taken care of JC from the day her parents brought her home from the hospital, and she wasn't about to let some unknown man make her cry without a darn good reason. Although she knocked on the bedroom door multiple times, JC told her go away in a voice made raspy from crying.

"JC, you come to door! You tell Rosa who make you cry. I make person sorry!" she pleaded not once, but several times. Her pleas were met by silence interrupted by the sound of dry sobs. Rosa tried the doorknob. The door was locked. She could not remember a time when she had been locked out of JC's room, even during the tumultuous teenage years. With a heavy heart and a deep sigh, she returned to the solace of the kitchen and a cup of hot coffee. "I find out who do this to you. I make them sorry!" she vowed.

CHAPTER 11

The owner of the town florist, Billy Joe McClain, arrived to knock on the ranch house front door early the following Monday morning an hour before the store would normally open. Rosa answered the door, a look of surprise on her face.

"I've got two dozen long stemmed red roses for Miss JC," he announced. "Somebody sure wanted to make a statement, roses being seventy-five dollars a dozen these days, and that's not counting the delivery fee."

Rosa took the vase, set it on a nearby table, thanked Billy Joe and sent him on his way after a quick cup of coffee then called for JC to come into the living room.

"Lord have mercy!" she called in an overly loud voice. "JC you come quick! Somebody send you roses, lots 'o red roses!" It must be man who made her cry, thought Rosa. A haggard looking JC appeared, her face splotched, her eyes red and swollen, the result of crying well into the night and morning. She was still wearing a housecoat and nightgown even though it was now past the time she would usually have eaten breakfast and headed out to feed the horses.

"Who in the heck would be sending me roses?" she questioned irritably.

"Rosa not look for card."

"Would you please check and see if you can find one?"

Rosa ran her hand through the flowers. "I no see card."

Assuming the roses were from Emilio, JC gave them to Rosa. "You no want beautiful flowers? You tell Rosa why you no want. Somebody spend big money to make you happy."

"It's a long story, and I don't want to talk about it," JC answered. "Just take the roses and get them out of my sight!" Rosa frowned, but did as she was asked, all the while muttering under her breath on the walk to the back porch located off the kitchen. JC returned to her room and shut the door where she remained the rest of the day. Rosa knew better than to knock or try to enter by the way JC had hurried back to her bedroom and slammed the door once again. Both lunch and dinner were left untouched on trays placed on the hallway table where Rosa had left them outside JC's room.

There was no card included with the second bouquet of roses delivered the following morning. This time, JC stormed out to the bunkhouse to pound on the door, demanding to speak with Emilio. As fate would have it, he had just arrived back at the ranch from the line shack only moments before. By the angry look on her face and the way she was standing on the porch with her hands on her hips and a look of fury in her eyes, he knew something was up, and it could not be anything good.

"I was just on my way to return your saddle, reins and saddlebags," he said, a touch of coldness in his voice. "I stayed at the shack the last two last nights and put everything back in order."

She was so angry it didn't register in her mind that he had stayed at the line shack. "You need to stop sending me roses!" she demanded. "Flowers are not going to mend the rift between us. In fact, I'm giving serious thought to firing you and hiring a new foreman!"

Emilio frowned. "How could I have sent you flowers? I just told you I spent last two nights up at the shack. There is no cell phone service up there for me to have called the florist, and I sure as heck didn't ride into town to place an order in the middle of the night or early this morning! As for you firing me and hiring a new foreman, please don't bother to waste any time. Just keep in mind doing so will mean you need to find someone qualified in a big hurry to finish the branding and be trail boss for the cattle drive by four a.m. on Thursday morning. Then you need to make arrangements with the buyer and the bank for that new person to make the check deposit. And with such short notice, that alone will present a problem when the buyer and bank manager will demand a background check of that person, like what was done with me, and that could take more than a week."

"I . . . I said I was only thinking about firing you," stammered JC. "Are you sure you didn't send me those roses?"

"I. Did. Not. Send. You. Roses!" he repeated, enunciating each word clearly before he slammed the bunkhouse door in her face.

JC stood there with her mouth hanging open for several seconds. Nobody had ever slammed a door in her face until now. She turned and stormed back to the ranch house, sorry she had not fired Emilio on the spot. At least that is what she told herself until the reality of his words hit home. "If I didn't need him for the cattle drive and sale he would be history!" When she made that statement, she knew there were at least five other cowboys working on the ranch who could easily handle the forty-mile drive to the railhead without a trail boss if necessary. But none of them were well known to the buyer or authorized to accept payment and make bank deposits since they could not read English or speak the language fluently. While they were good cowboys, she did not fully trust the Anglos when large amounts of money were involved.

Rosa happened to look out JC's bedroom window as she was cleaning. She had a clear view aimed toward the bunkhouse, and from the angry look on the faces of Emilio and JC she knew. "Ah," she smiled. "Now Rosa know what man make JC cry. Emilio he is good man. Rosa need make sure JC know he good man, but not before Rosa learn what he say to make her cry. Then give him big piece Rosa's mind!"

CHAPTER 12

Over the past week, JC knew something was up with her students at The Winchester School, especially little girls who gathered in a group to giggle and whisper with one another with glances in JC's direction. Each time she approached they would stop talking and scatter as soon as a boy tossed a warning stone near them. Then it dawned on her. They were hatching up the usual 'surprise' for her birthday. Every year for the past four years, a homemade chocolate cake, vanilla ice cream and handmade cards appeared around an hour before dismissal time on her birthday, or on Friday if it happened to fall on the weekend when school was not in session. This allowed her to dismiss any thought that serious mischief was afoot. At the same time, it reminded her she would be another year older without Rex by her side. She did her best to act surprised as the children and their parents all joined in sharing refreshments after singing their rendition of "Happy Birthday" and presenting her with a beautiful clay hand crafted flowerpot filled with bluebonnets. JC had no idea her dedication and kindness would be repaid many times over in the future.

JC had spoken earlier on the phone with Mr. Mooney at the bank regarding the nonpayment notices. He repeatedly kept reassuring her the lack of payments was only a computer glitch, and he would personally see to it everyone was paid. All she had to do was provide him with the figures of what was owed and to whom, and checks would be sent according to the invoices she had received in the mail. He didn't tell her he would be taking the payments from the trust fund without Sam's authorization, along with a sizable chunk of cash for himself like he had been doing for the years after her parents and Rex died. While she wanted to believe it was a computer glitch, that little voice in her gut kept asking, why did Mr. Mooney seem so nervous and keep repeating himself? At the same time, she felt obligated to believe what he was saying. After all, he was the person in charge of the trust fund that paid expenses to keep the ranch in good standing with the merchants. That, and her former father-in-law was the principal owner of the bank. But the question remained: were Mr. Mooney and Sam in cahoots? When she questioned him again, he did not fully explain the discrepancy in the check deposit from the spring cattle sale, saying only that he would check into the matter and get back to her. She would have called her father-in-law, Harold Morgan, to ask questions, but he and his wife were on a yearlong around the world tour somewhere in Asia according to the schedule he had sent to her shortly before their departure last month.

While the elder Morgans had been civil toward her since Rex's death, JC had the feeling they blamed her for not being more forceful in insisting the stallion causing their son's death be sold or put down. She had also always believed they thought Rex could have chosen a more appropriate wife, one with more social standing other than being the daughter of a ranch owner, even a very well to do ranch owner. It did not help that she had not attended a prestigious four-year college, instead choosing the local community college offering a two-year course in ranch management at which she had excelled. They had visited the ranch only twice in the three years since their son's death, and she had not received invitations to their family events or holiday parties. Their two visits to the ranch had left JC feeling like she was walking on eggshells that would be crushed if she said the wrong thing. The Morgans left on their trip, leaving her with the impression she was not to call and check on them during their travels, nor would they call to check on her.

Early on Saturday morning, a week before JC's birthday, Aunt Pearl called. She had returned to her suburban home in Midline the previous year. "Hello, JC. It's Aunt Pearl. I need your help. My Sunday school class is sponsoring a big fundraiser over at the Cattleman's Country Club this coming Saturday night. The proceeds are going to help Shirley Summers. Her mother died in Austin, and she can't afford to make the trip, pay for the funeral or buy a headstone. One of the ladies who said she would help in my booth called off sick with the flu. I'm desperate! Would you come and help me?" It would be later when JC wondered why Pearl hadn't offered to pay for her friend's trip and funeral expenses as she was prone to do when a friend needed a helping hand.

JC hesitated. "Aunt Pearl, you know I have trouble getting away. I have a ranch to run, and the cattle drive to the railhead is planned to start early tomorrow morning. I'll be tuckered out making sure the cowhands have the supplies they need for the two-day trip that could end up being longer if there is a hitch such as a stampede or severe weather. Besides, I don't have anything fancy to wear. None of my nice dresses fit since I've lost so much weight since Rex died. I ended up giving away all of my nice clothes to charity. Are you sure you can't find someone else to give you a hand?"

Not one to accept excuses or take no for an answer, Pearl insisted she and JC go shopping. "Meet me at the Bluebonnet Café at twelve noon sharp for lunch tomorrow, and don't be late. Then we'll trot ourselves over to the She Shoppe for some new duds 'n shoes. It will be my treat as a birthday present. I'm tellin' you there is nobody else available to help me. Lord knows I've tried to find somebody!" She crossed her fingers knowing that was a necessary lie.

"But Aunt Pearl, I forgot to mention in addition to the cattle drive, there's a purebred horse about to drop her foal. Most of the cowhands will be tied up on the cattle drive. I need to be here to make sure nothing goes wrong."

"Honey, horses have been droppin' foals all alone since the beginnin' 'o time. That mare is going to give birth whether you are there or not. If it's such a worry, surely you can get one of the cowboys or the vet to babysit if you are all that concerned. Don't make excuses! Not every cowhand workin' on the ranch will be out on the trail for the cattle drive. Thursday twelve noon sharp at the Bluebonnet Café! Be there!" The phone line went dead.

"First, I have a door slammed in my face, and now, I have Aunt Pearl hang up on me! These are a couple of firsts I could do without!" muttered JC. "I can't just not show up for lunch, or I'll never hear the end of it, but at the same time, I can't stand the thought of all those people at the restaurant or Country Club whispering and staring at me with pity . . . Oh, what the hell! I suppose its past time for me to move on and start trying to live a somewhat normal life again."

The next morning after looking in her closet, JC determined she wasn't fibbing when she said she had nothing nice to wear. Three long sleeved well-worn shirts with pearl snap buttons hung next to three other shirts, the sleeves cut off to accommodate hot days, along with four pairs of Levis. That left one pink and white striped shirt with sleeves in relatively good condition. The sight sent chills up her arms as it reminded her once again, she had donated her nice clothes to charity shortly after Rex died. At the time, she decided there would be no need for them in the future since her social life was over. It was easy to see dress shoes were non-existent, unless she counted the one pair of Dingo boots she had polished months ago and never got around to wearing because she always selected the other same old well-worn pair on a daily basis.

Thursday morning arrived. JC waved goodbye to the herd and cowhands driving them to the trailhead at four in the morning. After eating breakfast and feeding the horses, it was fast becoming time to shower and select something to wear for lunch and go shopping with Aunt Pearl. She ended up choosing the pink and white striped shirt with sleeves to go with the least worn looking pair of Levis and the polished Dingo's. "Well, at least everything is clean," she muttered. "Guess I need to remind Rosa I won't be here for lunch." She went about getting a quick shower and dressing before heading for the kitchen.

"That good news," said Rosa with a grin when informed JC would not be there for lunch. "You meet nice gentleman for lunch?"

"No, Rosa. It's just Aunt Pearl."

Rosa frowned. "That too bad, I don't mean Miss Pearl bad. Rosa think it better you go have lunch with handsome cowboy we both know, but you need give hint 'n let him take you."

"If you are referring to Emilio Vasquez, that's entirely enough, Rosa! You know I never socialize with employees unless it's a wedding, fiesta or a funeral, and none of those things are happening today, so back off!"

Rosa looked hurt at hearing the harsh words. However, the unexpected outburst did not silence her. "If Rosa thirty years younger I not think twice for Emilio take me to lunch or dinner, but breakfast even better." She paused to give an impish grin. "Breakfast mean we spend night together, but back then when I young I be happy cook any meal he want!" JC found she was uncomfortable at the reference Rosa just made about spending the night with Emilio. She immediately regretted she had spoken harshly, but felt she needed to put a stop to what she considered foolishness on Rosa's part.

"I'm sorry, Rosa. I didn't mean to snap at you. You know I think of you as a part of my family, but please, no more talk about Emilio."

Her request was ignored. "Rosa wish you give Emilio chance. He one good hombre. You know why he not go to Lonesome Dove Café? He not say why to you, so I tell you why. He save pay to buy more cattle for his ranch."

The look of surprise on JC's face was unmistakable. "Emilio owns a ranch? Where?" she asked.

"Maybe Rosa say too much." She held a hand up to her mouth before adding, "He no want anybody know he own ranch."

"It's all right. You and I are dear friends. You can tell me. Who am I going to tell? I seldom leave the ranch except to help teach English at The Winchester School three afternoons a week, and a lot of those people are kids or their parents who barely speak English. When I rarely do go into town, I spend time with Aunt Pearl."

It was easy to see Rosa was torn whether to reveal what she knew or not. "Okay I tell you, but you swear you no tell nobody else."

"I swear on my mother's grave."

"He buy John Winters' ranch when he and wife decide sell move to Dallas three years ago."

"That's interesting. I didn't know the ranch was even up for sale, or I might have made arrangements to buy it. Part of that land abuts the south side of this ranch over by the river. I'm surprised John didn't give me first dibs."

"Mr. Winters, he no mention sale to you then, but he tell Andy who tell Emilio. Mr. Rex just die and you real upset." Rosa was frantically searching her mind for a way to change the subject. "What time you meet Miss Pearl? Clock on wall say quarter past eleven. It almost hour drive to Midline on good day and you not put on lipstick or comb hair yet. Miss Pearl she get all upset if you late."

"Guess I do need to get a move on it. I'm due to meet her at noon. I have to admit she is a stickler for promptness, and that means I will have to exceed the speed limit. Where in the dickens is my tube of lipstick?" Then she remembered it was still in one of her saddlebags Emilio had returned to the barn, not to the ranch house following that fateful night three weeks ago. Instead, he stowed both of them, along with her saddle, in the horse barn for her to pick up whenever she got around to it rather than have contact with her beyond that involving necessary ranch business. It would take at least five or six minutes each way to make the walk out to the barn and back, making her extremely late. "Looks like I will have to do without lipstick. If I run my fingers through my hair and tie it back in a ponytail, that should look all right," said JC with a shrug.

"Here, use Rosa's comb and lipstick." She pulled a tube of bright red lipstick from her apron pocket, a color JC would never have worn in private, let alone in public, along with a black plastic comb with several missing teeth. JC didn't think twice about using either item any more than she would have refused to use her mother's lipstick or comb. Without any more thought she went to the hall bathroom located off the kitchen and dabbed a little lipstick on her chapped lips. When she looked in the mirror, she had to admit the color didn't look too bad after she blotted it with a piece of toilet paper. In fact, she had to admit it gave a much-needed touch of color to her weather worn, tired looking face. She deftly combed her hair into the usual ponytail and secured it with the rubber band she had placed on her wrist while dressing. When she returned to the kitchen, she planted a kiss on Rosa's cheek, leaving a faint imprint before dropping the comb and tube of lipstick in her apron pocket while teasing. "What will your boyfriend, Roberto, think when he sees you with lipstick on your face?"

Rosa shrugged her shoulders. "Maybe make him jealous? You go now Missy before you make more trouble for Rosa." She gave JC a swat on the butt with a dish towel as she turned to make her exit.

"I don't know what I would do without you, Rosa," she laughingly called over her shoulder.

"You think of something. Maybe you think about cowboy who tall with dark eyes and curly black hair," answered Rosa.

Rather than respond, JC pretended she didn't hear what Rosa said and kept on walking toward the door.

CHAPTER 13

Aunt Pearl was already seated at a table in the Bluebonnet Café when JC arrived. Margaret Blosser, the current manager, met her as soon as she entered the cafe. "Well, hello there, stranger! Pearl's over there at the table right beside the fake oak tree." Pearl waved her hand. JC gave Margaret a hasty hello and swiftly threaded her way through the tables to the table where Pearl was seated, Margaret trailing close behind with a menu in her hand. She didn't want to linger up front to become the attention of everyone where Margaret would have insisted on asking her where she had been for so long, expecting the full version, which she undoubtedly already knew.

As soon as JC approached the table, Aunt Pearl pointed to her wristwatch and tapped on the crystal. "I said twelve noon sharp! You're nine minutes late!"

"Sorry. I couldn't find a parking place," she offered, ignoring the frown on her aunt's face.

Margaret handed the menu to JC. "I will leave you two ladies to decide on what you would like for lunch. LuAnn will be your waitress. She can fill you in on the specials of the day." She paused a moment before telling JC it was good to see her again and she shouldn't wait so long to come back.

"I'll bet that was hard for her to say," remarked JC. "I would think she would be happy when she did not have to see me, seeing as how she always made no bones about the fact she had the hots for Rex, even though she was older than him and he ignored her."

"My, but we are being catty today," remarked Pearl. "But let's not waste time talking about Margaret. From the looks of that getup you're wearin' we need to spend some serious time shoppin'! I'm orderin' the chicken salad plate, how about you?"

"The chicken salad plate will be just fine."

"Good. Now gettin' back to about helpin' out with my booth at the Cattleman's on Saturday night. Be there promptly at seven p.m. Not a minute before or a minute after! Use the valet so you don't ruin your shoes by parkin' in that godforsaken potholed lot and walkin' to the clubhouse."

"Would you like for me to donate something for the sale?"

"Thank you, but that won't be necessary. I have more donations than I have room to display them." Pearl crossed her fingers on the hand hidden from view in her lap.

"Do you need help setting up your booth? If they don't have anything scheduled at the country club, I could come by to help around five o'clock on Friday evening. If they do, I could come early on Saturday morning," offered JC.

Pearl had to think fast. She wasn't one to routinely lie, but she had to come up with something plausible in a big hurry. "Joe Tucker and his boys are comin' to set up the sale tables around ten on Saturday mornin' so that won't be necessary."

Pearl sighed with relief when LuAnn approached the table to take their order. She stopped her in mid-sentence when Luann started rattling off the specials letting her know they both wanted the chicken salad plate. Aunt Pearl deftly changed the subject after they ordered. "How are things goin' at the ranch? I miss bein' there, but I felt it was high time I pulled up stakes and headed for my own barn. Have you thought about hirin' a couple more people to help you out? Rosa is gettin' up there in years. It must be hard for her to do the cookin', laundry and the cleanin'. That house is one big place with all those bath and bedrooms, even if they aren't used much anymore. It's not like you don't have the money to hire more help for her and yourself."

"Aunt Pearl, I have a lot of competent people working at the ranch. I don't need any more help. As for Rosa, I have made an effort to not let her realize I am taking some of the burden off her shoulders without offending her by cleaning up after myself and doing some light cooking and laundry instead of waiting for her to do it." JC did not want Aunt Pearl to know there were financial troubles that might include Sam and the bank trust manager, and she could not afford to hire more help at the present time.

"If you don't need extra help tell me why in tarnation you look so bone tired and haggard?" Pearl shot back.

Before JC could answer, she continued, "I wasn't necessarily talkin' about cookin' 'n cleanin' at the ranch house. I'm talkin' about the fact you stay out there all alone with no companionship beyond the hired help. You never go out to join friends anymore. Rex wouldn't want you wastin' away like you're doin'. You and I both know if it had been you to go first, he would have mourned a proper amount 'o time then found himself a new wife."

JC wanted to sink through the floor and disappear. "Please, Aunt Pearl. People around us can hear you! It's only been two years since Rex died, and I'm still mourning. Can't you see that?" She started to push back her chair in preparation to get up and leave.

Aunt Pearl reached out to firmly grasp her arm. "I'm sorry. Please don't go. It's just that I really hate seein' you doin' the work that should be done by hired hands. Besides, it's goin' onto three years, not two since Rex died. It's not just me who feels this way. A lot of people love you and hate to see you workin' hard and not takin' the time to take care 'o yourself or be happy with some sort 'o male companionship. You need to take a good look at me. I coulda had a new husband years ago after your Uncle Ira died. I sent potential suitors packin' instead 'o marryin' again, something I now regret." She shook her head with a look of sadness on her face. "It was foolish of me wastin' years mournin' for a man who wasn't comin' back when I coulda had a new love and life. You need to face the fact

Rex isn't gonna come back and you need to get on with your life while you are still young. It's that or you'll end up just like me, old, livin' alone with only regrets to keep me company." JC pulled her chair back toward the table, giving Pearl the opportunity to let go of her arm.

"But I thought you were happy living alone."

"Nothin' could be farther from the truth! I make sure I don't ever let anybody see me cry. I do my cryin' at night when I'm alone. When I was married, I didn't have the sharp tongue I'm famous for now. Thank the good Lord above most folks pass it off as me bein' a lonely old widow woman or I wouldn't have any friends!"

LuAnn approached their table with the salad plates. "Will there be anything else I can get for you ladies?"

"I'll take more iced tea, and this time LuAnn, make it unsweet tea like I ordered the first time!" barked Pearl, pointing to the untouched glass of sweet tea. "Too bad you can't read your own writin' or know which tea is which!" LuAnn's face turned scarlet. She apologized, then turned around to head for the kitchen again, saying she would make it right. "See what I mean?" said Pearl. "I coulda been a lot nicer, but bein' lonely makes a body grouchy. Let's eat and get outta here. We got places to go 'n people to see, and that isn't gettin' done by us sittin' here flappin' our gums yammerin'!" They ate in silence. JC was relieved when they finished their meals. Aunt Pearl paid the check in spite of her offer to do so, and they were able to be on their way. But that didn't happen until after JC felt she was the target of whispers and nods in her direction, all of which made her feel extremely uncomfortable. She had no way of knowing if the whispers were of sympathy or about the way she was dressed. The women involved in observing her were obviously more stylishly dressed.

"To hell with all of you," she muttered. She was tempted to go over to one of the tables to ask if they wanted to take pictures, since pictures lasted longer than their small minds could possibly remember seeing with their eyes. Aunt Pearl, sensing JC's mounting discomfort, hurried her out the door before she could say or do anything she might later regret.

CHAPTER 14

The She Shoppe had always been intimidating to JC. It had been even when she and her mother shopped there when she was knee high to a grasshopper. As she evolved into her teenage years, she felt even more intimidated by the clerks with their perfect hair, perfect makeup, perfect clothing and almost snotty attitude. As an adult, that had not changed even though she was now a willowy five feet nine inches tall with a figure to die for, skin that looked like fresh peach ice cream (before taking over the ranch) and the money to buy out the entire store should she choose to do so before the economic downturn and possible theft from the trust fund.

Jane Trumbull, the owner dressed to the nines, greeted them as soon as they entered the store. "Well, if it isn't Miss Pearl and . . . who is this? JC Morgan?" She said JC's name as though she could not believe she was seeing the same woman she had known in the past. Jane recovered quickly. "How may I be of service to you ladies today? We just received a new fall collection of dresses. I'm sure we can find something to your liking if you let me know the occasion. You might like to know we now offer custom fitting since hiring a full-time seamstress two months ago." JC didn't miss the look of distaste on Jane's face as she surveyed the clothing she was wearing. It didn't help knowing Jane had dated Rex a few times in high school, with her confiding in friends she was sure they would marry after graduating from college. JC did not like her then, and that feeling had not changed, especially when she had continued to shamelessly flirt with Rex in front of her and their friends at the Cattlemen's Country Club, even after JC and Rex were married. Rex ignored her, but it still made JC uncomfortable. Jane had known and relished in that knowledge.

"Please accept my heartfelt condolences regarding Rex's passing, Mrs. Morgan," offered Jane, looking straight at JC with an almost imperceptible smirk on what JC thought was an overly made-up face. "That must be why we haven't seen you in town or at the Country Club in what? Three years? My goodness sakes, how time does fly! It doesn't seem that long ago since we were all in high school. Such a shame Rex was thrown from a horse and died leaving you all alone way out there to manage that big ranch with your brother off attending college then law school. Forgive me. I am assuming you are still alone, and if so, I'm so sorry about that as well."

Sure, you're sorry, thought JC. You are about as sorry as the cat that ate the canary. "I need a nice dress and some shoes," she announced curtly.

"I'll get right on it, but I need to know the occasion so we don't waste time on dresses that would not be appropriate."

"I would rather take a look around by myself if you don't mind." This was JC's thinly veiled way of saying, 'Lady, I don't need or want your help!' Jane knew she was being dismissed. "Please feel free to look around, Mrs. Morgan. Just let one of us know if you find something to your liking. Should I happen to be busy with other customers, there are several ladies working in the store who would be delighted to help you." Just to make a point, and have the last word before walking away, Jane added in a cool voice while focusing intently on what JC was wearing, "I'm sure any one of them will be more than happy to assist you in finding more suitable clothing, Mrs. Morgan."

"I can't stand that woman!" announced JC through clinched teeth as soon as Jane was out of hearing range. "She, like almost everyone else in the county, knows I'm still living alone! There was no reason she had to mention that fact other than pure meanness! And did you see the way she looked at my clothes? It was like they were something that should be used for mop rags!"

Aunt Pearl smiled. "See what I told you earlier? You are beginnin' to sound just like me."

"But that bitch kept referring to me as Mrs. Morgan when she is fully aware Rex died, and I have not dated or remarried. She has to know everyone calls me JC. She also knows calling me Mrs. Morgan is like twisting a knife in my heart."

"Stop and think dear. It has always been store policy to refer to customers by their title, unless instructed to call them by their first name. I don't remember as an adult you tellin' Jane she could call you JC," admonished Aunt Pearl. In an effort to comfort her niece, she continued, "Come on. Forget about her. You 'n me need to take a look at the new 'collection', as Jane calls them." Pearl began sorting through the rack of dresses. "My, my! These dresses all seem to show a lot of bosom! But you got what it takes to fill any one 'o them out right nice." She pulled one off the rack and held it up for JC to take a closer look. "Hmmm . . . What do you think about this little turquoise number?"

"Aunt Pearl it is lovely, but what will people think? I can't go around showing 'the girls' in public!"

"I say if you've got it, flaunt it! And Honey, you got it!" JC had to laugh when her aunt wiggled her thick brown eyebrows like Groucho Marks would have done.

"But that dress would mean having to buy a new strapless bra."

"What's stoppin' you from doin' that? I'm payin' so you can't use money for an excuse not to buy one. Get with the program, girl! I'll go find one 'o the other sales ladies to take your measurements since you can't stand bein' around Jane." Off Pearl went on her mission, leaving JC standing in the middle of the store holding the turquoise dress. To avoid further embarrassment, she wandered over to a free standing antique full-length mirror and held the dress up in front of herself. “I guess Aunt Pearl does have an eye for color. But that neckline is something that needs to be addressed in the privacy of the changing room,” she murmured. In the mirror’s reflection, she could see Aunt Pearl watching and mouth the words, “Don’t give the sales ladies a hard time.”

“When have I ever given anyone a hard time?” JC mouthed back.

“You don’t want me to answer that, dear,” was her aunt’s audible reply.

Louise, the sales lady waylaid by Pearl, smiled as she approached. “Miss JC, why don’t you follow me to one of the dressing rooms where I can take your measurements in a more private setting?” Pearl had given her the authority to call her JC, mentioning that fact to her niece quietly. “We cannot do a proper dress fitting until we have a proper undergarment. Is this the dress you are considering?” continued Louise.

JC felt the color mounting on her cheeks. “It is the dress Aunt Pearl is considering me wearing.”

“Well, then, I must say she has excellent taste. The color and style are perfect for you. It’s one of the newest creations by Bonnie Bluebelle, the New York designer, via Dallas where her career actually began. She is the one everyone is raving about.” Oh no, thought JC. The translation means a huge price tag!

Right about then, Pearl opened and stuck her head through the dressing room door. "I know my niece is going to balk at the price of the dress, Louise. Don't you pay her no never mind. If the dress fits, she will need suitable shoes and an evenin' bag. Put everything on my tab. I'm going to do a little shoppin' of my own. Come find me when she's dressed in that little turquoise number."

"Yes, Miss Pearl."

Standing there in her plain white cotton underwear, JC felt like a fool when Louise closed the dressing room door behind her after taking her measurements. "I don't know what I'm doing here," she muttered. Her embarrassment only increased when Louise returned a short time later with a set of flesh colored lace panties and matching regular bra in addition to the strapless bra required by the dress.

"Miss Pearl wants you to have these," announced Louise. JC nearly fainted when she saw the price tags – a whopping one hundred and fifty dollars for the two pieces of underwear, not including the strapless bra and fifteen hundred for the dress! "I can't possibly accept these! They are much too expensive! I have never paid more than eight dollars for a pair of panties or thirty dollars for a bra," gasped JC.

"You will have to be the one to tell your Aunt you can't accept them. I don't want to deal with her. In case you are not aware, she often buys such lovely things for herself, and she wants you to have them, too. I may be speaking out of turn, but just learn to enjoy what she is willing to give you and know that in doing so it will make her happy."

I can't imagine Aunt Pearl wearing expensive lace underwear, thought JC. Not at her age and certainly not when there is not a man in her life anymore. Not when she barrels around town wearing those two-piece sweat suits and tennis shoes, but that just goes to show you can't judge a woman by what you see on the surface.

Louise didn't miss the mark when it came to guessing what Pearl's reaction would be upon seeing JC in the turquoise dress. Pearl literally doubled over and clapped her hands. "Oh my God, JC, you look like one 'o those New York models pictured in a slick magazine ad! You have to say yes to the dress! And those classy silver heels! The men at the Cattleman's will have their tongues draggin' clean down on the floor and hopefully open their wallets big and wide to purchase items at the fundraiser."

"But Aunt Pearl, the underwear, the dress, bag and shoes come to almost two thousand dollars with tax, and I don't have the jewelry to set off the dress. And take a good look at my skin, nails and hair! They are a total disaster! This outfit is like putting a silk dress on a sow's ear, or some such saying like that."

"You do need somethin' sparkly to set off that dress," declared Aunt Pearl without acknowledging JC's protest. "I know your momma and daddy gave you some real nice stuff, so we need to look through it and find just the right pair of earrings, then again, maybe not, since styles in jewelry change." She was unaware JC had been forced to pawn the nicer jewelry given to her as gifts by her parents when she made a trip to San Antonio to visit Sam. This had been done to keep the ranch afloat during the economic downturn just prior to her parent's death released the necessary funds into the trust. She did this without their knowledge in an effort to keep them and Rex from worrying.

"I was just thinkin' your mother's jewelry would be old and not up to the current way of thinkin'," conceded Pearl. "Honey, you are worth every penny I've spent and more," declared Aunt Pearl. "I never had a daughter to dress up and spoil. Please don't deprive me of this chance to spoil you, especially with your birthday right around the corner. You can bet there would have come a time when Rex would have spoiled you with whatever your heart desired. The ranch was just startin' to make really big bucks again just before he . . ." She got choked up and could not finish the sentence. It didn't take her long before she straightened her shoulders, stood erect, cleared her throat and announced it was time to do more shopping. "Have these purchases delivered to the Scott Ranch yet today," she instructed Louise in a no-nonsense voice before they headed for the She Shoppe's delicately etched glass and oak door.

"I will see to it personally, Miss Pearl. Thank you for shopping with us, and I hope to see both of you again soon," replied Louise. That is not likely to happen any time soon on my part, thought JC. You don't sell work shirts or jeans meant to be worn while shoveling horse manure, pitching hay or mending fences.

"Thank you, Aunt Pearl. Where are we off to now? Do you need to rest a while? Would you like to take a break for some tea? Will we need to drive? If so, would you like to use my truck?" questioned JC.

"Don't ask so many questions, young lady! Just follow me and keep your pretty little trap shut! You will know where we're goin' when we get there!"

CHAPTER 15

JC could not believe it when, after a three-block walk, Aunt Pearl opened the sturdy glass door of the local jewelry store and turned to JC, who held back instead of going inside. "Well, what are you waitin' for? I'm not gonna stand here holdin' the door open for you all day!" exclaimed Pearl.

"But Aunt Pearl, unless you plan to look for something for yourself, I'll go wait in the truck."

"Do I look like I need any more jewelry? Get your fanny inside the store right now! You need sparkly earrings to set off that dress, that's unless you have somethin' stashed away at the ranch house. And don't tell me you can use somethin' that was your mothers or the gifts your parents gave you. While it was all real nice stuff, it's all outdated since she had most of hers before she married your dad and it's been at least ten years since they gave you anything."

"But Aunt Pearl, you have already spent a bundle on me at the She Shoppe. I can't allow you to spend anything more!"

Pearl allowed the jewelry store door close and put her hands on her hips as they stood face to face on the sidewalk outside. "Since when do you start tellin' me what I can or cannot do, young lady? I am tellin' you that you need somethin' sparkly to set off that dress so the women will be jealous, and the men will open their wallets! There is nothin' like a little jealousy to spur women on to outspend their competition, especially when their menfolk are payin', and the men don't want to be outdone neither!"

JC shook her head in wonder. "You are one shrewd woman, Aunt Pearl. How can I argue with that line of thinking?"

"You can't, so get movin' on inside and head over to the earring counter and pick out somethin' pretty."

"May I help you?" asked the prissy young man standing behind the glass enclosed counter dressed in a Brooks Brothers dark blue suit, starched white shirt and subdued tricolor tie. His nails were manicured and polished with clear lacquer. His nose and clean-shaven face had taken on the appearance of smelling something unpleasant as he focused on JC and what she was wearing.

Aunt Pearl spoke up boldly. "You certainly can be of help, young man. My niece needs some diamond earrings, and not those small cheap lookin' ones like you just set out on the counter!"

After giving JC the once over as soon as they entered the store heading for the earring counter, the salesman had arbitrarily made the decision they would not be looking at anything located in the expensive display tray. The look on his face had been one, just like the one Jane had, of dismissing JC due to the type of clothing she was wearing and her need for hairstyling and a manicure. He had arbitrarily selected a tray featuring diamond chips set in silver plating in the price range between seventy-nine and two hundred dollars in an effort to place the tray on the counter for their inspection as soon as possible.

"Not that tray. We want the one on the end," declared Pearl as she pointed to the tray filled with more expensive goods. He didn't waste any time returning the inexpensive tray and produced the tray demanded by Pearl. "Now that's more like it!" she declared. "You must be new here, or you'd know I don't buy cheap jewelry!" she declared.

The young man could not have bowed and scraped any more that what he did when he rang up a three thousand, five-hundred-dollar, six-carat diamond and platinum pair of dangly earrings, a choice reluctantly agreed upon by JC and encouraged by Aunt Pearl as she slapped her platinum credit card on the counter.

"Do you think he would follow me out to the ranch house and wash the windows?" remarked JC after they made their exit onto the sidewalk and the store's door had closed behind them.

"My dear girl, not only would he wash the windows, he would wash your truck and you if you would let him!" she said with a brittle laugh. "You need to stop seein' yourself as a poor miserable widow. You are a beautiful and desirable woman. I will admit you need a haircut, facial, nail trim and probably a pedicure, but that can be taken care of at the spa at nearby Willow Dale Resort. That can be one more of my birthday presents to you. I'll make an appointment for both of us for ten a.m. on Saturday mornin'. Then we'll have a late lunch in their fancy dinin' room before we retire for a nap at our respective abodes to be in shape for stunnin' the britches off those who think only they are the cream of society at the Cattleman's on Saturday evenin'." Aunt Pearl lifted her right pinkie finger bearing a ring encrusted with emeralds in the shape of a horseshoe and pushed her sterling silver framed bifocals down on her nose in a failed attempt to look snobbish. JC knew it would be impossible to argue since she was laughing so hard she thought she would wet her pants. So, she thanked her aunt for the earrings while deciding how to best to respond to the assessment of other people who would attend what she believed to be a fundraiser, thought better of it and decided it wasn't worth commenting on that issue in light of what Aunt Pearl had just done for her, instead saying, "You never cease to amaze me, Aunt Pearl. To hear and see the way you just acted and spoke, anyone who doesn't know you would think you are high society. Let me amend that statement to almost close to high society."

"Whatever do you mean, almost close, my dear? We both have considerably more money than a majority of those pretenders who like to show off at the Country Club. I know I do, and so do you."

JC took a deep breath. "That isn't exactly the case for me when it comes to having a lot of money."

Aunt Pearl gave her a sharp look. "What are you sayin'? I attended the spring cattle sale. I know the number of head you had in the sale, and I keep abreast of beef prices, so I know you did right good by the look on your foreman's face. The way he looked 'n danced around wavin' the buyer's check in the face of his sidekick, I'd say you did fantastic! With the interest from the trust fund and your mom's check from her personal account bequeathed at the readin' 'o the will, along with the no strings twenty grand yearly you can take from the trust, not to mention revenue from the oil wells, you should be rakin' in the dough hand over fist!"

JC took another deep breath before deciding it was time to inform Aunt Pearl about her suspicions of theft involving Sam and Mr. Mooney at the bank, in addition to the notices of nonpayment. She knew it was probably past the time she needed to seek the advice of someone who cared deeply about her and the survival of the Scott Ranch. "We need to talk, but let's do it in the truck," said JC. Pearl listened without comment, her face growing flushed, eyes narrowing to slits, lips puckering with increasing anger by the minute. She allowed JC to continue uninterrupted until she finished talking before she added her two cents.

"You leave your brother to me! And as for that scum bag Mooney, if he thinks I'll pull my money outa the bank, I can make him squirm and sing like a canary. Yes, ma'am. You leave it to me to handle this situation!" JC had no doubt her Aunt would do exactly what needed to be done whether she wanted her to or not. "You run along on home, 'n don't you worry about it. I got things to do and people to call," said Aunt Pearl. "I'll make the Saturday spa appointment for ten 'n pick you up at nine. Now don't forget, nine a.m. sharp on Saturday with lunch afterward." The two women embraced and said their goodbyes, each heading off in a different direction, Pearl to her truck at a rapid pace for a woman of her age.

Little did Sam suspect he would be walking into a hornet's nest Saturday night at JC's birthday bash. As soon as she arrived home, Pearl was on the phone speaking with no less than six power broker type individuals before the last call asking to speak with the manager at the Cattleman's Country Club. The receptionist was polite in asking who was calling and with whom did she wish to speak. "You can put me through to the manager, Bradley Miller, pronto! Tell him it's Pearl Scott. I'll wait, but not long!" Less than a minute later, Bradley answered. Pearl timed him as she was accustomed to doing no matter how important the person on the other end of line believed themselves to be. She would not hesitate to voice her displeasure if the person took longer than she thought they should.

"Hello, Miss Pearl. What can I do for you today?"

"Nice of you to be so prompt, Bradley. I hope it doesn't cause you a problem, but I would like to upgrade a few items regardin' the food, beverages and band I called about earlier in regard to JC's birthday party scheduled for this Saturday evenin'. I know the changes don't give you much time, but I'm sure you can pull them off."

"For you, Miss Pearl, it won't be a problem. Just fill me in."

"Do you have a pen and paper handy?"

"Yes, ma'am. I sure do."

"For starters, you can cancel the Swedish meatballs over buttered noodles and green beans almondine. Replace them with a sixteen ounce per person charbroiled filet mignon instead. I'm thinkin' Idaho baked potatoes with the works on the side and mushroom caps in that wonderful red wine sauce to go with the steaks. I'm cancelling the no host bar in favor of top shelf booze and French champagne, as much as our guests want to drink during the servin' of appetizers on silver platters by waiters wonderin' amongst the crowd, you know things like oysters on the half shell, clams casino, spicy veal meatballs, crab dip, several cheeses baked in pastry, 'n make sure that's French champagne. Then have waiters keep the champagne 'n booze comin' throughout the evenin'." It came as no surprise when Bradley said he thought that would be great. "To start dinner let's go with jumbo shrimp cocktails, fresh fruit for anyone allergic to seafood, followed by a mixed greens salad and a choice of dressin': ranch, blue cheese, Italian, honey mustard, Asian. And while you're at it, add artichoke hearts and bacon bits, not that imitation kind, to the salads. For dessert how about havin' your chef whip up some baked Alaska? I want it served traditional flaming style on silver platters by ten waiters dressed in white formal shirts and black slacks, along with the usual French music accompaniment. A little lemon sorbet would be nice after the entrees. This is to be billed to Sam Scott, JC's brother, since he is now a hotshot attorney over in San Antonio. He wants to do somethin' special for his sister. Lord knows she's done a lot for him! I almost forgot. He wants a twelve-piece orchestra instead of the four-piece band. He let me know I needed to take care of the changes since he's so busy . . . Sure, I can give you an address where to send the bill, or better yet, he can pay up the night of the party. Your choice . . . I agree. He should pay the night of the party. The deposit needs to be made in advance so you can bill that to my credit card on file. He and I can settle up later for that, but now that you mention it, you are right. It would be best to collect from him for the rest 'o the charges next week since it will take time to tally up all those drinks. Don't hesitate to contact me, not Sam, if any problems should arise between now and then. I'm sure you have my phone number on file . . . You do? That's good. I know Sam has some big cases comin' up, so you probably can't reach him 'n that's why he asked me to take care of makin' the original arrangements and now the changes. I thank you kindly for takin' care of everythin' on such short notice."

Pearl knew there was not a snowball's chance in hell she would get the nonrefundable deposit back from Sam, but she didn't care. It would be worth it to be able to stick him with the rest of what would be monumental charges incurred by at least a hundred and forty guests.

"None of the changes will be a problem, Miss Pearl. By calling today it gives me plenty of time to contact my suppliers, the chef and line up an orchestra. I know who I'll call for the music. The leader of the band I have in mind is a friend of mine, and he owes me a favor. They have played here before for a couple of weddings, and everyone loved them. Feel free to call me anytime should you want to make any other changes. You have a real good day."

Pearl leaned back from her custom-made mahogany desk in her brown leather swivel desk chair. The look on her face was one of satisfaction. "That will teach you to mess around with family finances, Sammy Boy! I would love to see the look on your face when you get that bill! Now it's time to pay a little visit to that little piss ant, Clarence Mooney! I'm sure he will dirty his drawers by the time I'm finished with him if he's had a hand in stealin' from JC and possibly even me! Never did like him. He reminds me of a big, fat, bug eyed rat caught dead to rights in the corncrib when the light gets snapped on at night. You can bet your bottom dollar there will be a bank crash if I take my money outta that bank, 'n you can print that on the front page 'o that weekly rag of a newspaper!"

Pearl did not waste any time arriving at the bank on Friday night barely minutes before closing time, demanding to see Clarence Mooney. She did not wait for his secretary to escort her into his office after the woman strongly suggested Pearl come back tomorrow morning. Pearl let her know in no uncertain terms, including several four-letter words, that would not be convenient and then proceeded to march past the dismayed secretary into Clayton's office with the unhappy woman trailing not far behind. "I'm sorry, Mr. Mooney. I tried to tell Miss Pearl she should come back in the morning since we are just about to close." Before she could say anything more, Pearl began to speak.

"Clarence, you 'n me need to have a little chat so you can send this little lady on her way 'n have her shut the door behind her on the way out. This might take a little time, and I'm sure you won't be wantin' anyone listenin' in on what we have to discuss!"

The look on Clarence's face was one of concern mixed with fear, but he did not ask Pearl to leave. Her extreme wealth and excellent standing in the community when it came to supporting charitable causes were much too important to the bank's reputation and survival to send her on her way. Even more important was the fact he had not yet stolen all of the money from her trust account he would need to move on to a new life. He had always resented answering to the bank's owner, Harold Morgan. Harold and Pearl were old friends, so that alone was an incentive that he could not afford to offend her. This made him feel he had no choice but to hear what she wanted to discuss with him. And from where he sat, the intense expression he could see on Pearl's face, was one causing sweat to break out on his forehead and upper lip, along with what was sure to cause a bout of indigestion.

CHAPTER 16

After a long day mending downed fences following a severe thunderstorm resulting in a stampede by one large herd, weary Scott Ranch cowboys gathered around on the bunkhouse lawn sitting on bales of straw. Some were nursing a cup of coffee, some shooting the breeze outside after eating supper. Emilio did not join them as he normally would have done.

"Wonder what's eatin' boss man," said Pedro. "He been actin' like sick calf for couple weeks 'n barely has anythin' to say, 'cept bark orders. Ya don't think he got burr under saddle or been shot down by female at The Dove?"

"Maybe he sad 'cause he didn't get invite to Miss JC's surprise birthday party," offered Raul. "He don't go much to Dove."

"How you know Miss JC have surprise birthday party Raul?" asked Poncho.

"My friend, he clean manager's office at Cattleman's. He hear him talk to Miss Pearl on phone about it."

"Oh, Emilio get invitation all right. I see when I pick up everybody's mail. I know Miss Rosa see, too, and she make sure he get it," interjected Jose. "Even if he not get invite, no reason he act like he got corncob stuck up his ass!" This comment brought snorts and chuckles from several of the men.

"I wonder where he sneaked off to today? Seems like every time I turn around, he's gone off somewhere!" remarked Tex, one of the five Anglos working on the ranch.

"It not your business where he go!" came Jose's quick reply. "All you need know is your job for day and when he not here I tell you." This comment yielded a handful of dried horse manure thrown at him. It was not the first time the two men clashed, nor would it be the last. It was evident Tex did not like the fact Jose was second in command when he felt it should be him. As a result, he took every opportunity to question Jose's orders or make disparaging remarks directed toward him when Emilio was absent.

"Easy man or I kick you in ass!" declared Jose, brushing the manure off his shirt and face.

"You and who's posse, you poor excuse for cowboy! I can use you to mop the bunkhouse floor with one hand tied behind my back!" declared Tex. "Just keep sending those threatening remarks my way, and you will find out what I can do!"

"I scared," remarked Jose. "You run mouth, but you no take action."

All the men began elbowing each other and sniggering. They delighted in watching and listening to the two men verbally spar. None of them were aware JC had quietly approached from behind until she spoke. "Who is going to mop up who with one hand tied behind their back? You know I do not allow any fighting!" The men immediately stopped laughing. Some coughed nervously and sat up straighter on their straw bale as she continued to approach. Tex slowly backed away from Jose. "We only joke around," offered Jose. Tex did not offer any comment as he continued to glower in Jose's direction after positioning himself with legs apart and arms crossed over his chest a few feet away.

The look on JC's face hovered between a frown and smile as she scrutinized the faces of the two men. "It's a good thing you two are just joking, or both of you could find yourselves without a job!"

"What brings you out to bunkhouse?" asked Raul in an effort to distract her.

"I am looking for Emilio. I just got a call from Bill Fletcher over at the adjoining ranch to the southwest. He tells me there is a fence in need of repair between their pastureland and mine where the river meets the rocks down below the line shack. He says it looks like it's been deliberately cut, so be on the lookout for rustlers. I know from past experience Bill can get hostile if he thinks our cattle have wandered onto their pastureland."

"Sorry JC, we didn't get that far make repair there today, but not be problem. We do tomorrow. Emilio own that ranch. Fletcher only foreman so work for Emilio and he make sure he no give you trouble."

JC had dismissed the thought Rosa let her know Emilio now owned that ranch, something she had promised not to reveal to anyone. Even though the cowhands apparently knew about the purchase, she was determined to keep that promise and act as if she was unaware by continuing to give a reason why she needed to speak with Emilio. “Okay, but I still want you to let Emilio know I’m looking for him. We need to go over the budget for feed, buying more cattle, vet care and general maintenance for the coming year.” Jose nodded to let her know he understood what she said.

“Oh, JC, Emilio tell me remind you saddlebags in horse barn,” said Jose. She was glad twilight had given way to a deeper dusk and they had not turned on the bunkhouse porch lights or lighted a campfire to see the look on her face. She didn’t want anyone to see the look of guilt and shame over what had taken place between her and Emilio up at the line shack when she had left without those articles in such a hurry.

“I know where they are. I just haven’t had time to bring the saddlebags up to the ranch house.” That wasn’t exactly the truth. She didn’t want to pick them up and be reminded of the time they spent together at the line shack.

“Jose happy bring saddlebags to house for you.”

“That will not be necessary,” retorted JC more sharply than she intended. Fearing her voice would betray her if she said anything additional, she turned away and started to walk slowly up the well-worn river rock covered path leading to the main house. Thinking she was out of earshot and spoiling for a fight, Tex continued in his effort to anger Jose by making the comment Jose must not be one of JC's favorite people, or she would have allowed him to bring the saddlebags to the house.

Tex was the type of cowboy who usually stays in one place just long enough to earn enough money to move on to the next ranch. But for some unknown reason, at least unknown to the other cowhands and JC, he was finishing his third year working on the Scott ranch. He kept Elida, a lovely young French woman with scarlet hair and green eyes a secret to keep from being teased unmercifully when he went out of his way to present a macho image. Elida is a shapely well-liked dancer at The Lonesome Dove Cantina. She only had eyes for Tex in such a way the other cowboys did not know they had an ongoing relationship, or so they both thought.

"Shut the hell up, or I tell rest 'o the cowhands about woman!" Jose threatened in a whisper just loud enough for Tex to hear, but the others did not hear due to resuming their playful, loud horsing around. "You think I stupid? I know about Elida, and I tell everyone!"

"You open your piehole about her, and you're a dead man," was the stage whisper response near Jose's left ear. Jose blanched. Tex now stood only inches from him. He knew the powerfully built man could take him out in a heartbeat when fully angered. His stance and clenched fists left no doubt Tex was very angry.

"Stay cool, man," offered Jose as he stepped back. Tex continued to close the distance between them, a scowl on his face that could only be interpreted as a dire warning of what he intended to do. While Tex didn't say anything more, hoping to fool JC into thinking hostilities had passed, Jose could see him clutch and un-clutch those unusually large meaty fists. Tex had glanced up to notice JC had not made it far enough away and had overheard what transpired between the two of them, so he backed away from Jose slightly, thinking it was a sufficient move to make her think there was no longer a problem. She was not fooled.

"Remember Tex, no fighting," she called, sensing the hostilities had escalated. This caused him to back farther away from Jose and take a seat on an empty bale of straw. That didn't stop JC from retracing several steps to take a closer look at both men before resuming her exit while thinking about what she had overheard. *So, that's the problem and what is keeping you here, Tex. I should have known it was a woman. All I can say is more power to her. Although he is a little rough around the edges, Tex is a darned good cowhand, and I would hate to lose him if he decides to fight, making me forced to fire him. I need to have a talk with Jose first thing tomorrow morning to insist he keep this information concerning Elida to himself.*

"I think we all need mosey off to bed before we canned," proposed Jose in an effort to defuse the hostile situation between himself and Tex. "Tomorrow is long day." The rest of the men, stifling yawns, agreed with him with the exception of Tex. He headed for his truck, got in and sped off in a cloud of dust. It would be much later when he returned to the bunkhouse. More than a few drinks while observing Elida dance hoping she would help him be successful in his effort to control his anger failed, and he left. He knew he had to control his temper or lose his job and be forced to move on. And for once in his life, he felt deep love for Elida and did not want to lose her. At the same time, he felt a gnawing anger for revenge toward Jose.

It wasn't five minutes before the lights went out in the main bunkhouse after the cowhands entered. Emilio's separate quarters remained dark throughout the evening and into the night. A matter of minutes after boots hit the floor and clothing was removed down to underwear, a chorus of loud snores could be heard all the way to the next ranch located miles across the low land pasture.

In the Scott Ranch house, JC's bedroom light remained on well into the night. The reason she was awake had nothing to do with the loud snores. "What am I going to do about Emilio?" she wondered aloud. She tossed aside the steamy novel she had been reading. The angst for the heroine in the novel was fictional. Angst regarding feelings she found herself developing for Emilio were real, and she did not know what to do about them.

CHAPTER 17

The second hand seven-hundred-watt microwave signaled Bob Wilkins' TV dinner was ready. Eating alone was one of the things he hated most since Mary Jane terminated their rocky marriage. He poured himself another glass of cheap red wine, his third so far. It was a good bet more glasses would follow until the box was empty. Then he would stretch out on the sagging sofa after eating the gooey mass of macaroni and cheese while standing in front of the worn grey Formica topped kitchen counter located in his one bedroom, one bath, second floor condo.

"Damn that woman all to hell! That bitch Mary Jane didn't know when she had it good! It's not like she didn't know I was not a virgin who had a high sex drive when I married her! So, I have to take Viagra now and that bothered her. So what! Be glad you won't be living like this for much longer," he mumbled angrily between bites. "JC should be getting all warmed up and ready to be romanced after those roses I had sent to her. And if that doesn't do the trick, I've got a nice little piece of legal paperwork to back 'em up with plan B in the persuasion department." He couldn't help congratulating himself at what he thought was a fool proof plan to force JC into marrying him in order to retain those thousand acres of her precious ranch "And if that doesn't work, I always have plan C." Moments later, he went into an alcohol induced sleep on the sofa, thinking he had two more days before plan A, the roses, would be all it would take to put him on easy street for the rest of his life.

The next morning, he awakened with the nasty, dry mouth hangover associated with drinking large amounts of cheap red wine. With a great deal of effort, he managed to sit up on the edge of the sofa to hold his aching head in his hands. “I’ve got to get it together. I have to wash and iron my tux shirt,” he told himself. “Sure hope that shirt still fits because I don’t have ready cash to go buy another one, me having to pay that bitch Mary Jane alimony, along with the mortgage on this fleabag of a condo and springing for those roses I had sent to JC. But first, I need a cup of coffee and a couple of aspirin.” He wrinkled his nose in disgust when arriving at the kitchen counter. The sight of leftover coffee from the night before still sitting in the glass pot was not appetizing. Since the coffee can was empty of fresh grounds, he had to make do by warming up mud-colored dregs poured into a cracked cup; the cup having been salvaged from the storage area of the dry goods/variety store where unsalable goods ended up until he could make a dump run. He again cursed Mary Jane because she had kept all the China along with the furnishings, forcing him to buy cheap secondhand furniture or forage for household items, like the coffee cup, in the variety store bone pile.

Once he learned where the party was being held, it didn’t matter he had not received an invitation to JC’s birthday party. He had brazenly asked around and learned where it would be held and the name of the birthday person. In his devious mind, the lack of an invitation was simply the result of an oversight by Pearl. "The worst thing they can do is throw me out of the Cattleman's, but when Miss JC sees me all dressed up, and I let her know it was me what sent her all those roses, she will be all over me like flies on honey. I can already hear wedding bells, especially when I turn on the charm."

A few minutes later, a sense of darkness swept over him as he took a sip of the lukewarm bitter coffee in order to swallow the aspirin. "Of course, if the roses don't work, I will be forced to embarrass her in front of all those people and use Plan B. I have a strong feeling I will not be required to resort to Plan C, since there isn't a doubt in my mind I will get what I want without resulting to the use of violence. At least I hope so. I can't imagine being locked up in prison or having to take off for parts unknown." It was with an air of regained confidence he sat down in the broken-down lounge chair and soon drifted off to dream about owning the Scott Ranch and making love to JC. He was totally unaware his heavy breathing and snores caused fluttering of the yellowing plastic vertical blind strips covering the dirty living room window.

Bob had not meant to cut Allie short the day he was headed to the bank. He always liked to keep his options open, but it had been urgent timewise that he find out if

Sam's loan had not been repaid. After unloading a line of B.S. to a lonely female cashier that Friday while using his charming act, and the fact he was a member of the bank board, she did not have the time to research the records thoroughly before closing time approached. He was aware Sam's loan was due tomorrow before the bank closed at noon. He distracted her more by having her check his bank account numbers again to reassure himself that he had enough cash to buy the loan. He debated whether to withdraw the cash immediately or wait until morning. If I take it now, I'll lose some interest, and there is no way Sam can pay off the loan, so I don't have a thing to worry about, he decided. At promptly nine a.m. when the bank opened on Saturday morning, Bob withdrew the cash in the form of a cashier's check, then walked into Clarence Mooney's office like he owned the bank and demanded he be allowed to buy Sam Scott's loan, which would allow him, as the loan's owner, to collect from JC one way or another.

By the intense scary glint in Bob's eyes, Clarence knew it would be in his best interest to let him pay off the loan and provide fake copies of the loan agreement, even though the loan had already been paid off by another interested party just moments before closing time last night. Clarence was smart enough to know it wouldn't look good, and he could lose his job if the banks' owner and president of the Board, Harold Morgan, were to find out he had allowed the illegal loan against the Scott Ranch to take place, especially since JC was still his daughter-in-law. There was no doubt in his mind there would be hell to pay if Harold were to find out. Even if he did not appear to have a close relationship with JC, she was still a Morgan. Clarence's next thought was to save his ass. That thought was that money could be sneaked back into the trust fund, erase any computer or paper trail and nobody would be the wiser. "Hell no to that happening! I can erase the computer information and get rid of the paper trail, and that twenty-five thousand can be added to what I have already been able to set aside, and when the timing is right for me to make some changes, I will be ready to move on from this god forsaken place, and I'll have another easy twenty-five thousand," he mumbled in a quiet voice so as not to be overheard by his secretary.

But that decision had been made before Pearl Scott came waltzing into the bank in all of her glory to make a personal call one minute before closing time yesterday. That visit had made him very much aware he now needed to produce three hundred thousand dollars to cover his pilfering of JC's trust fund in addition to the twenty-five grand, not figuring in interest due, and hope Pearl didn't know he had been stealing from her account for the past ten years to the tune of almost nine million dollars. The twenty-five thousand, while paltry, would be in addition to his half of the take from the scam he and Sam Scott cooked up by stealing from the Scott trusts to keep them both living on easy street and still have enough for him to set aside to cover his intentions. And he knew those figures did not include what he had stolen from other trust funds ever since he became the trust officer.

Clayton felt he was forced to meet Pearl's demands or spend a very long time in federal prison for embezzlement, not to mention what his wife was capable of doing if she found out he was gay and a thief.

"Looks like I will have to take action faster than I've planned and steal more funds a lot sooner than anticipated before we leave town," he had muttered soon after Pearl left. "I should have taken action long ago to make sure Bob Wilkins was voted off the bank board. Had I done so, he wouldn't have known about the loan, and I would be home free, but that idiot got greedy for a mere twenty-five thousand dollars! I let that slimy bastard have way too much control over the other board members. By the time JC or that busybody Pearl Scott would have figured out their trusts were practically bankrupt, I would have been a multi-billionaire, leaving Sam to take the hit. He will still take a hit. Oh well, I can't be worried about Sam Scott, that unfaithful faggot! I just hope he doesn't spill the beans that we've been lovers for the past three years when he gets dragged in for questioning by the Feds. There is no doubt my wife would not understand if she heard about our affair or the thefts. When I think about that Ross guy and Sam spending time together, I'd like to scratch both their eyes out! Surely Sam knew I knew about Ross, but that's all in the past and doesn't matter now. I will be on my way, along with my wife, Penny, to my coffee plantation in Brazil before anyone knows we are gone. The hell with selling my mansion!

"The state of Texas can have it as far as I'm concerned. All I care about is getting away from here as fast as possible before Pearl and the others can prove I've been systematically stealing from them. Penny will be delighted to move. She has always wanted to live in Brazil ever since we visited there, and once we're there I'll make sure she won't find out I'm gay or about the stolen money. I'll just have to figure out a way to keep her quiet about the quick move before she blabs to her friends. I am so glad I made sure ownership of the Brazil coffee plantation cannot be traced back to me. Ah, I can smell the coffee brewing already!"

A lot of local folks thought it strange when Clayton and Penny Mooney seemed to disappear off the face of the earth, leaving their mansion deserted with the servants locked out less than a week later. It wasn't until after Pearl Scott happened to mention his involvement with theft of money from her and JC's trusts they understood why this had taken place. Many of them ended up kissing sizable portions of their fortunes goodbye and having to settle for the government FDIC requirement mandating they recoup only two hundred fifty thousand dollars of their hard-earned money when the bank was forced into receivership.

Luckily for Pearl and JC, they withdrew the money they had left before that happened as soon as they figured out their trust funds had been scammed. There was the possibility for JC to recoup some of her losses from the sale of Sam's luxurious house, its furnishings and the BMW, but that would only happen after a judgment was reached following his conviction for theft and fraud. That could take years, and she couldn't afford to take a chance the sale might come up short. Such a loss could signal the end or forced sale of the Scott Ranch if Aunt Pearl hadn't stepped in to help.

Pearl had so much money she didn't care if she ever recouped her losses from this trust fund. It was only one of many accounts and investments set up in multiple banks throughout the country and abroad by her late husband, Ira Scott. She was smart enough to invest in rental properties, both residential and commercial, in various locations throughout the tri-state area in addition to revenue producing oil wells, stocks and high interest-bearing bonds with earned interest, making her a billionaire.

JC was relieved to learn Mr. Mooney, before leaving town, had paid back her three hundred thousand dollars, but without interest, only hours before the bank was sent into receivership just hours before he and his wife left town. Pearl wasn't that lucky for whatever reason. She could only guess it was because Clayton felt she had more money than God with more coming in on a regular basis, along with the fact he was angry that she had called him out and forced his hand. Although she would be required to find a new bank for her money and the FDIC payment rather than keep that money under the mattress, Pearl didn't dwell on it for now. "There will be plenty of time for me to deal with Clarence Mooney when I'm ready," she told those who offered opinions she should file a lawsuit against him immediately, if not sooner. "Let ole Clarence think he got away with stealing," she voiced repeatedly. "I will be ready to spring a big surprise on him when I'm ready."

CHAPTER 18

Bob Wilkins was not the only one having erotic thoughts on the Friday night before the Saturday surprise birthday party for JC. Ross Vandenberg was moaning with pleasure as Sam went through the motions of making love to him. Sam's mind was definitely not focused on giving pleasure. His goal was to get Ross into a drunken stupor to carry out his plan, but Ross resisted, sensing something was not right with Sam. "Are you still angry that I made you sign the loan note for the ten grand?" he asked. Preoccupied, Sam didn't answer. "Earth to Sam! Earth to Sam! I said, are you still angry with me because of me insisting that you sign the loan note?"

"What? No, I'm not angry. Here, let me pour you another glass of wine. I just have a lot of things on my mind." Things like killing you, how long it will take for you to die, the bank note due tomorrow before noon and all the other bills, not to mention the money Clarence Mooney and I have been stealing from the ranch trust, thought Sam. At this time, Sam had no idea Clayton had also been stealing from his Aunt Pearl's trust as well as other people's to finance his and Sam's high living while he was planning to secretly take off with his wife to live in a foreign country, leaving him to deal with the fallout.

"I have the perfect solution to help you relax," purred Ross. "I took the liberty of turning on the hot tub heater earlier this morning. It should be at a perfect temperature by now."

You must have read my mind, only I wasn't planning to heat the water, thought Sam. "That sounds like a very good idea. I'll race you. Last one in is a monkey!"

Sam deliberately tripped, allowing Ross to be the first one in the hot tub, knowing he would be the last one out. Sam had made up his mind weeks ago Ross would be the last one out, but not until Monday when the cleaning lady would find his bloated body to be retrieved by the coroner. Ross wasn't aware his death, made to look like an accident, would end up netting Sam two hundred and fifty thousand dollars. He would not know until he rifled through Sam's desk looking for money after surfacing, getting out of the hot tub, drying off and dressing. The torn in half insurance information sheet in the middle drawer stated it would have been five hundred thousand if Ross had held steady a job and Sam was not in arrears paying bills. What appeared to be a legitimate contract written only two weeks ago, according to the posted date, had been written in the amount of two hundred and fifty thousand dollars with Sam listed as the sole beneficiary.

It had not been for lack of trying on Sam's part to get the five hundred-thousand-dollar figure. He had diligently tried to convince two of the three insurance agents he contacted that Ross worked as a full-time bartender, when in fact, his job was only part time relieving the full-time bartender on a sporadic basis at a low-class biker bar hangout, also a source for him to buy illegal drugs.

The two hundred fifty-thousand-dollar policy was issued only after Sam lied and said he held half ownership in the well-known Scott Ranch, and he would be totally responsible for paying the premiums a year in advance following the fall sale of a large herd of cattle in a matter of days. Luck was with Sam when the agent bought his lie and didn't bother to check his ranch ownership claim or credit score because he thought he could spot a good risk and was anxious to go on a three-week cruise with a hot blonde the following day.

There was just one major problem for Sam. Ross did not die. As a former surfer and one-time Olympic swimming champion, his talent for holding his breath under water for prolonged periods of time paid off more than he could ever have anticipated. Now he was very much alive, extremely angry, and determined to get revenge. "That bastard left for Midline to attend a party for his sister after he thought he killed me! Guess what, Sam? You low down son-of-a bitch! I know exactly what I'm going to do to let you know you can't go around killing somebody and walk away to attend a party and expect to get paid for it! You can be damned sure you will curse the day we met before I'm through with you!" With those angry words, he set out to start the process of getting even by logging on to their shared computer and renting a car and driver on the black web; a less than legitimate service asking no questions beyond what the client needed and did they have the ability to pay. Advance payment was made by an untraceable computer link with funds taken from Ross's checking account. "Lucky for me, and too bad for you, I didn't get around to transferring the ten-grand to your checking account, Sam," he muttered once the illicit deal had been verified.

CHAPTER 19

Dusk was settling in when Emilio arrived at the Scott Ranch line shack. He had not been back since the weekend two weeks ago when he and JC ended up making love. He thought revisiting the scene might help him come to grips with the realization she was not interested in him romantically. It was troubling to think that night had only been the result of the campfire, stars and moon, along with both of them needing someone to offer comfort, just as she had told him the following morning before she left in a hurry without bothering to saddle her horse, pick up her clothing or saddlebags.

He hobbled his horse then gathered up the supplies he bought in order to take them into the shack. He knew he needed to cut some mesquite for a campfire, so after arriving, he placed the items on the kitchen table before going outside to retrieve the hatchet kept under the porch for use in emergencies. While it wasn't an emergency, he did want a campfire since he planned cook dinner and sleep out under the stars and half-moon. He couldn't stand the thought of sleeping in the bed he and JC had shared. He needed to be outside where he could contemplate whether he should continue working at the Scott ranch or move on. He didn't bother to prepare supper, instead he went back inside the shack to get a couple of hot dogs from the package he brought with him. He speared two on a stick, roasting them over the fire until almost burned, then he ate them without a bun. By that time, the coffee was ready in the old blue and white speckled granite coffee pot. The waning moon was almost overhead when he heard hoof beats approaching. Not knowing if the rider was friend or foe, he slipped into the shadow made by the shacks roof overhang and waited with his trusty 44 in his hand. To his astonishment, the rider turned out to be none other than Rosa.

"Rosa! What in the heck are you doing up here at this hour? You, of all people, should know it's not safe, especially for a woman riding on the open range, much less that dangerous mountain trail at night! What if you had been intercepted by rustlers, thrown from your horse and went over the cliff to land on those boulders? You and the horse might not have been found for days, if ever!"

Rosa did not answer right away. She was intent on tossing the reigns of her horse over the hitching rail before she stomped over to where Emilio was still standing in the shadows next to the shack. She stood with her hands on her ample hips, a frown on her face before she uttered a word. "You need put gun away 'n get self over by fire where Rosa see you more clear! We need talk!"

Emilio walked closer to the fire after stowing the gun in its holster on his right hip. "Is there something wrong at the ranch?"

"You bet something wrong, and it your fault!" she declared.

"You need to come closer to the fire, have a seat on that bale of straw and have a cup of coffee," said the bewildered man. "Then we can talk."

"That good place to start," she replied.

He walked over to dig around in his saddlebag and produce another speckled blue and white granite coffee cup. "I hope you like black coffee. I do not have any sugar, milk or cream the way you like it." He handed her the cup and she took it, blew on the hot liquid, took a small sip and shuddered at the bitter taste. "Now why don't you tell me what has sent you riding up here alone in the dead of night that's my fault. It had better be something serious!"

"Si. It serious, all right! It about JC!" exclaimed Rosa.

Emilio felt his heart start to pound in a rising sense of fear. "Is she sick or hurt?

Rosa took another sip of the strong coffee, made a face to show her displeasure, but managed to swallow instead of spitting it out. "Only if you think broken heart makes for sick or hurt."

"I don't understand. What are you trying to say? You need to spell it out for me, Rosa."

"She cry eyes out every night since day you had words at bunkhouse next day after she come home riding like bat out of hell all dusty, dirty and upset three weeks ago. Rosa hear she call your name when she do manage sleep." Rosa crossed her fingers when she made the statement regarding JC calling out his name, hoping Father Benedictine would forgive her the next time she went to confession, or Emilio didn't think to question the fact that she did not normally spend nights at the ranch house on a regular basis to hear such an utterance.

Emilio didn't know what to say for what seemed like a long time before he spoke. "You're sure she calls out my name?"

"Would Rosa ride up here in dark if that lie?" More finger crossing under the cover of her jacket, knowing it would mean at least six additional Hail Mary's for this lie. "You tell Rosa why you make JC cry!" she demanded.

"Would you believe it was because I told her I loved her? That's when she took off, after she told me we lived in different worlds, and a relationship would never work between us." Rosa could not help but see the sadness in his eyes.

"You loco if believe she not love you no matter what worlds you live! You need woo her like gringos do. If you love her, need keep telling her. Instead, you stay away. That not good!"

Uncomfortable with what Rosa said, Emilio began drawing stick figures in the dirt with the point of the hotdog roasting stick next to the blanket where was seated. "How can I say or do anything to change her mind when she won't talk to me about anything but ranch business, and then only when at least several of the other cowboys are close by?"

"Language of love not always need words," Rosa reminded him. "Send flowers. Ask her go riding or go for dinner. Sing songs outside her window, Take walk together. Use imagination. You smart hombre. You think of something."

Emilio had to chuckle when Rosa suggested he sing. "If she heard me sing, I know I wouldn't stand a chance. I sound like a wounded animal. As for asking her out to dinner, I'm not sure that would go over very well when she makes every effort to avoid me, even for business reasons. Someone sent her roses. She chewed me out thinking they came from me. I tried to tell her I did not send them, but she would not listen. You don't happen to know who sent them, do you?" he questioned. He left out the part where he had slammed the bunkhouse door in her face.

Rosa smiled. "You no have worry who send roses. I check flower shop and learn Bob Wilkins send them. I tell JC 'n she just shake head, laugh and say he waste his money. She not interested."

"Well, at least that's a relief. Rosa, you have to help me find a way to make her understand we can make it work. I don't know if you are aware, but I'm not the uneducated, destitute cowboy most people around here think I am."

"Rosa know you work hard. You save money to own cattle ranch outright next to Scott Ranch. Rosa know about family ranch in Mexico, too. My sister and husband, they work for your father. They tell Rosa how you study books so you smart. You not think for one minute I let any old greaser win heart of my baby, do you?"

Emilio ran his hand through his hair in an effort to hide his discomfort that she knew so much about him. "No, Rosa, I don't think for one second you would let any old greaser win JC's heart."

Rosa squared her shoulders determinedly. "You listen to Rosa, yes? You get invite to JC's birthday party, yes?" Emilio nodded to confirm what she said. "Today Tuesday. That mean you got plenty time buy new suit, white shirt and boots 'n don't forget tie, so you be handsome devil. Then buy flowers for her and go to party."

"But I need to help with cattle drive early on Thursday morning. I'm the foreman and trail boss for heaven's sake! You know we will be lucky to reach Midline by noon on Saturday. I will be covered with dust, sweaty and smell like a steer. How can I be two places at once if we happen to run into a problem and get in late if there should be a thunderstorm or pack of coyotes cause a stampede? Surely you know unforeseen things like that can happen!"

Rosa shrugged her shoulders, but she didn't waste any time before answering. "Party no start 'til seven o'clock, so if you late, you give Rosa call. I make sure JC late, too. Miss Pearl she no like, but she understand when Rosa tell her why. She like you, so be okay. Rent hotel room for Saturday first thing tomorrow for bath 'n quick change before party. Make big entrance at Cattlemen's so JC know you make special effort. Just so you know, she like orchids, not roses, when you order flowers for her."

"But Rosa, the party is at the Cattleman's Country Club. You know they don't allow Mexicans inside, except to clean or make repairs. Some members even complain about lawn care workers being seen too close to the golf course before the first round."

"You no say but to Rosa! Miss Pearl make sure you no have trouble get inside Cattleman's. She make clear to boss man in charge anybody she invite come inside, 'specially when she tell him you more Spanish than Mexican. He no gonna fuss with her. Nobody ever fuss with Miss Pearl! She one tough lady can make for trouble with anyone who not do what she want."

Emilio knew he was beaten. "All right, I will do as you say and come to the party, but we need to compromise. How about I wear a string tie in place of a necktie?"

Rosa smiled. "Okay, you win on string tie. But you need ask JC to dance at party. No take no for answer or you answer to Rosa!"

"What if she slaps my face and tells me to get lost?"

"JC too much lady to do that. Rosa know she love you. She need know, too. How you think Rosa married thirty years to Pablo? I try run away when he ask Rosa marry him, but he no let me go and I no sorry. Pablo good man. Sorry he die. We made good family and that why Rosa come to U.S. to find work for good pay to feed kids."

"How many children do you have, Rosa?"

"Ocho," she blurted out in Spanish before resorting back to broken English. "Eight. They all married. Live in Mexico. Most work for your father, except two Federales. They good boys, no take bribes, no hurt people. They know Momma Rosa skin alive they not be respectful and honest! Rosa has sixteen grandkids, too. Before long it twenty. They come to U.S. visit Rosa here twice in year. You and JC marry. Have beautiful babies I take care of just like Rosa did for JC and Sam." She became quiet and stared into the fire seemingly lost in thought for almost a full minute before she began to speak again. Emilio remained silent content to also stare into the campfire. "Rosa no comprende what happen to Sam; he get same love like JC get. And JC, she love him like only little sister can do, but somehow he different." Rosa had an idea just how different Sam was, but she could not bring herself to say he was gay.

"Rosa, I know you did your best helping to raise Sam, and you would be very good at helping us with any children we may have in our future. But Rosa, I think you are putting the horse in front of the cart. I have to find a way to get her to talk to me privately, let alone marry me and agree to have children. Right now, she doesn't even like me." Although he had heard the rumors, he avoided offering any thoughts on why Sam turned out differently than that expected of Scott men.

"Oh, JC like you okay. In fact, she love you, just don't show yet. You put out campfire fire, lock shack, saddle up and we ride back to ranch tonight. Tomorrow you start woo her." Emilio started to protest, but Rosa would not back down. "We ride back tonight or Rosa ride alone! JC expect Rosa be there to make breakfast."

They both fell silent as the clip clop of their horses' hooves on the rocky trail echoed into the stillness of the night. For some strange reason, the coyotes once again remained silent. Rosa had the feeling she had accomplished what she set out to do in making what could have been a dangerous trip without incident. But she had reservations about really knowing how things would play out in the future for JC and Emilio. Would he end up leaving the Scott Ranch to move on? Would JC end up firing him? Would they marry and live happily ever after? Rosa could not help thinking maybe the coyotes, in their silence, knew something she did not know. She decided only time would give her a definite answer, but not without her best efforts to bring the two of them together.

CHAPTER 20

JC walked down the hallway from her bedroom, passing through the living room on her way toward the ranch house kitchen. The phone in the living room was ringing. "I wonder who is calling this early?" she muttered. "If it's somebody reminding me it's my birthday, I swear I will hang up on them!" To silence the persistent ringing, she picked up the receiver. "Hello. There had better be a good reason for this call!"

"Sounds like somebody got up on the wrong side of the bed. Good morning to you, too, JC!"

"Aunt Pearl, I'm sorry! I didn't mean to be rude. Good morning."

"Well Missy, you were rude, but I'll let it go this time since it's your birthday. I'm callin' to wish you a happy birthday and make sure you are up and ready to go to the spa this fine mornin' and didn't forget about helpin' me at the Cattleman's later tonight."

JC groaned. "That's right. Today is the day for the fundraiser, and here I thought it was tomorrow. I'm not feeling good. I've been up most of the night with an upset stomach. Rosa made fried fish for dinner last night. They were so good I made a pig of myself."

Pearl felt a sense of panic. Everything was all set for the surprise party. Sam arrived on her doorstep last night asking if he could stay there instead of coming to the ranch house. “Don’t you dare tell me you are backin’ out ‘o helpin’ me at the Cattleman’s tonight! You need to take some Pepto Bismol and call me back in an hour. You should be fine by then. In fact, you go take that Pepto right now! Never mind callin’ me back. I’ll be there at nine to pick you up for the ten a.m. spa trip. Goodbye and again, happy birthday.”

JC hung up and continued on toward the kitchen, her tummy feeling more than a little queasy. “Aunt Pearl is probably right. A slug of Pepto, some tea and soda crackers and I’ll be good as new. That’s odd. Rosa isn’t here. She usually arrives before I get up and has the coffee on. Maybe she’s not feeling good, either.” Ten minutes later a very tired, unkept and groggy appearing Rosa entered limping through the back door. “Rosa sorry I get here late. Rosa no sleep much last night.”

“Neither did I. I don’t think last night’s fried fish agreed with me, but that was probably because I ate too many of them. They were really good. I hope we don’t have food poisoning.”

“Rosa no have stomach trouble, so not fish. Rosa just tired. Roberto and Rosa argue last night.” Once again came the crossing of fingers behind her back for telling a lie rather than fessing up to her ride to and from the line shack during the night to meet Emilio that had kept her awake, not an argument with Roberto.

"I just did the Pepto, tea and cracker routine mother always did when I was a little girl those times when I complained of a stomachache when trying to get out of going to school. So far it's helping a little."

"You want Rosa make scrambled eggs, bacon and coffee?"

Just the mere thought of scrambled eggs and especially coffee made JC's stomach threaten to send her scurrying to the bathroom to vomit again. "No, thanks. I think I will stick with tea and crackers and see how it goes. Aunt Pearl is due here in less than an hour. She is insisting on taking me to the Willow Dale Spa this morning, so I'll look a little more presentable when helping her at the fundraiser she's sponsoring at the Cattleman's Country Club tonight. I don't have a choice. I have to feel better, or she will have a conniption fit, and I don't feel up to dealing with that!"

Promptly at nine a.m. Pearl let herself in through the ranch house front door. "JC!" she called. "I'm here. Hope you're feelin' right sassy and rarin' to go on your birthday!" Morning ritual completed, JC snatched up her brown leather purse from a chair in her bedroom and hurried back to the living room to greet her aunt. "I am feeling much better, thank you. Pepto, tea and soda crackers always do the trick. Next time I won't eat so many fried fish. Before we go, I need to let Rosa know it's a grilled cheese sandwich and tomato soup for my dinner tonight."

"Rosa does not need to worry about fixin' dinner. There will be plenty of finger foods served durin' the fundraiser. There's nothin' like free food to bring people in and open their pocketbooks," said Pearl. Her fib regarding finger foods rolled off her tongue like maple syrup on a stack of hot buttered pancakes. *Whew! That was a close one, but I need to give a little more thought about not lying or it could become a habit* was the thought crossing her mind.

"I was hoping to speak with Emilio before we left, but he is nowhere to be found. I swear that man knows when I want to talk to him these days! I need to let him know we need to go over the budget for the coming year. His truck was here yesterday before I went to take a shower and dress for the day. Both he and the truck had disappeared by the time I got dressed and both have been gone ever since."

Rosa spoke up from the kitchen doorway. "You forget he on cattle drive to Midline? He park truck back of horse barn. He back on Saturday after sale."

"Oh, that's right. I must be getting old and forgetful, but I intended to make the drive to town in time to see the check before it gets deposited. That way I will know what's what before the next bank statement arrives, along with discussing a little matter with Mr. Mooney. I've heard on the grapevine about a loan against the ranch and some unpaid bills I received in the mail. But I guess that can wait until I ask Emilio about the check amount tomorrow. I'm sure he will insist on a deposit ticket after what happened this past March."

Aunt Pearl put her index finger to her lips. "Shush. I've taken care of the loan matter. You can ask Emilio about the amount of the check when he gets back. Don't forget we have that spa date this mornin'. I'll tell you all about it on the way there. Come on, we don't have all day! Let's go!" Aunt Pearl remained silent for the first fifteen minutes of the hour-long ride to Willow Dale.

"Okay, when are you going to tell me what the shushing was all about when I mentioned I had spoken with Mr. Mooney?" asked JC.

Pearl took a deep breath. "It's like you suspected, only worse. My sources tell me it's true Mooney not only gave Sam an advance of a twenty-five-thousand-dollar loan against one 'o the best thousand-acre parcel 'o Scott ranchland, they both been skimmin' on the checks from your cattle sales to the tune of three hundred thousand dollars from the ranch trust fund, not includin' interest. I paid off the twenty-five grand, plus interest due for the illegal loan. Mooney agreed he will make restitution for his share 'o the take, plus interest, along with the twenty-five grand, or I threatened to call in the state police and the Feds. He is gonna announce his 'retirement' on Monday mornin'. Sam is not aware I know about the whole shebang, yet. Thought I'd let him stew over the weekend and add to his troubles when he gets a certain bill." Pearl started to sweat. She almost blew the fact the surprise party bill was diverted to Sam for payment, or he was in town to attend the party. "It may take Sam years to pay you back what he took, but by god, he will pay or I'm not Aunt Pearl! Of course, that's unless you want to press charges and have him tossed in the hoosegow. But if you do, he can't begin to pay. Accordin' to my sources, he's past bein' plum dirt broke!" Pearl fell silent again after having her say.

JC slowly let out a deep breath. "How did you manage to learn all of this? I find it hard to believe that Sam and Mr. Mooney would do this to me. From the look on your face, I have the feeling there is something else you are not telling me."

Pearl bit her lower lip and squirmed in her seat while reaching up to adjust the rearview mirror. She did this to give herself time to think of a way to steer the conversation away from even more painful information. "I have my sources when it comes to findin' out things. I told you I could make old Mooney sing like a canary, and he did just that when I told him I had solid proof of him stealin' from not only your trust fund, but mine, along with makin' the fraudulent loan to Sam involvin' some 'o the best grazin' land put up as collateral. Let's just say I named a couple of names that got Mooney's undivided attention. Of course, he didn't know I didn't have jack squat in the way of solid court type evidence until he blabbed. After that, I strongly suggested, on advice of those in the know, the Feds need to do a bank audit. That's when the ornery old cuss fessed up to stealin' from you and the trust fund your Uncle Ira set up to kick in for me after he died, him makin' all that money in the oil business down Houston way. The old fart started blubberin' like a schoolgirl and begged me not to involve the Feds, sayin' he would make restitution, plus interest to both our accounts by this mornin'. That's when I told him I'd keep quiet only if he sold his mansion up on the hill outside 'o town, moved outta Texas within the next six months, sooner if a sale goes through quicker, and he never works at a bank again. I made that six-month provision on the house sale on account of his wife, Penny, in case it takes that long to sell the house, which I doubt, it bein' a prime piece 'o property. I happen to like Penny. She's a woman after my own heart. If she found out what he's been doin' she would tie him to a creosote bush out in the scrub 'n let the scorpions, rattlers 'n coyotes have at him after she beat him to a pulp! I'm dead sure that thought crossed Clarence's mind 'n probably scared the crap outta him more than the Feds comin' in and checkin' out his misdeeds after I mentioned that possibility! Penny's a big girl with an attitude. I wouldn't wanna get on her bad side. Everybody knows she's mighty handy with a bull whip!"

"There's more you are not telling me," insisted JC. "Come on, Aunt Pearl, I know there's more. I'm not that skinny little freckle faced kid anymore. I can handle whatever else you have to say."

Pearl gripped the steering wheel of her Mercedes tighter and wrinkled her face into a grimace. "I was gonna wait 'til Monday to tell you since it's your birthday weekend, but if you must know . . . Sam is gay! He's been spendin' money like flood water flowin' through a busted dam for quite a while now on a feller by the name 'o Ross Vandenberg. He's been livin' with Sam since they was classmates in college. My sources have proof that's where the money been goin' for quite some time. This Ross guy has high expectations; you know, lots 'o spendin' money, drugs, high stakes gamblin', designer clothes, expensive watches, trips, cars, fancy restaurants, 'n so did Sam and Clarence Mooney. That's why that old goat Clarence and Sam cooked up their scheme to steal from us 'n only God knows who else." It dawned on JC why Sam never wanted her to stay overnight at Sam's San Antonio home. She would have questioned him about Ross being there.

"Talk about being hit by a bomb shell! How does Mr. Mooney figure in all of this?" asked JC.

"He's gay, too. My information points to the fact Mooney enticed Sam into havin' a relationship for nigh onto the past four years in order to gain easier access to the ranch trust fund with Sam's co-operation 'n without you, your parents or Rex knowin' about it before they died. Of course, Rex's death made it easier without him around to ask questions and him bein' promoted to loan trust officer. And Sam, always needin' money, thought that was a great way they could both get their hands on it. And by all accounts, it was very profitable for them until now that I've done some serious diggin' around with help from powerful people in the know."

JC leaned forward, put her head in her hands and began to shake her head back and forth. The tears threatened to start. "Oh my God, I find it hard to believe that Sam is gay, but now that you mention it, he has always been a little on the effeminate side. Dad must have known, and that's why they were never close."

"Sam wasn't the only lover Clarence had. There was another guy when he worked in Oklahoma City who has since moved on accordin' to my source. Now don't you go to cryin! Cryin' don't solve nothin' in a situation like this," said Pearl. "You dry those tears in a hurry and hold your head up high. In this case you are NOT your brother's keeper! And as for Mooney, he won't be around much longer if he's got a lick 'o sense! I hate to think what could happen to him when some of those ranchers get wind of what he's been doin', and I strongly hinted that might happen, along with his wife and the Feds findin' out if he don't hold up his end of our bargain. As a little extra insurance, I made him give me his passport, 'n he won't get it back until we get our money back." Pearl was unaware Clarence had made provisions to have an illegal passport made just in case it was needed and was in the process of fleeing right now.

"But Aunt Pearl, how can I hold my head up high when people find out Sam is gay and involved in stealing from the ranch and you? People already feel sorry for me over Rex's death. We both know the rumor mill will have a field day. I will be forced to sell the ranch and move out of the state of Texas!"

"You listen to me, young lady! You will not do any such thing! Anybody who says sometin' outta line will have me to deal with, 'n you know folks 'round here don't wanna deal with me! Now chin up 'n dry them tears! We gotta date to get all gussied up for that fundraiser!" JC could not think of anything more to say, and neither could Aunt Pearl, so they rode in silence the rest of the way to the Spa, each woman deep in their own thoughts.

"Hey there, Miss Pearl. You too, JC! Welcome to Willow Dale Spa. Come on into the changing room, and get those clothes off down to the skivvies and into these robes," ordered a petite, attractive young woman. "They are waiting for you in the massage room. When you get finished there, come back up here, and we'll get right at the facials, hair, makeup and nails. You won't believe the gossip have to tell you!"

"You won't need to wash my hair. I just washed it in the shower before we came," said JC an hour later. "Just cut off the split ends and use whatever goo you need to use to make an updo work."

"Now, you listen to me, JC! Your hair needs a little bit of lovin' in the form of shaping and a good conditioner before we use any of what you call goo! You listen to Bitsy, and we'll get along just fine."

"Bitsy, you haven't changed a bit . . . get it, bit, Bitsy," joked JC in an effort to stuff down the feeling of having been betrayed by Sam and Mr. Mooney.

The petite, freckle faced red head laughed. "You haven't changed, either, JC. Now, step into my parlor, said the spider to the fly . . ." Both ladies took seats in front of the large mirror fastened to the wall atop the counter, allowing Bitsy to begin working her magic following their spa treatment. JC knew Bitsy was not being totally honest about her not changing. She was fully aware of what she looked like when looking in the full-length mirror attached to the closet door of her bedroom, and it wasn't good. She had lost twenty pounds she could not afford to lose. Her cheeks were sunken, her skin still on the dull side, even after the facial. Her once bright sky-blue, sparkling eyes held a look of sadness and pain, even more so since Aunt Pearl divulged that Sam and Mr. Mooney were gay and had been routinely stealing from both of them. But she knew she needed to keep up appearances. She did not want Bitsy falling all over her while expressing sympathy or passing along gossip about her or her family to willing listening ears.

"Okay, out with the gossip. You promised us gossip, Bitsy," demanded JC in an effort to deflect the subject away from anything personal.

Bitsy gave her a fake questioning look reflected in the mirror in front of the salon hair styling station. "Me, promise you two some gossip?" she giggled. "Whatever do you mean? Oh hell, girls! Your ears are gonna be on fire before I'm through! Did you hear about Mary Jane Withers kickin' ole Bob to the curb? Seems he and that whore Lucy Parker got caught, shall we say, in a compromising situation with their pants down in the church basement of all places! Mary Jane got the ranch, the new Jag, three hundred thousand dollars and half interest in the store plus a whole bunch of alimony in the divorce settlement. Bob got the shaft. He's living in one of them nasty second floor one bedroom condos over on the wrong side 'o town over by those smelly dry feed lots next to the railroad loading dock. But you tell me, what did he expect?"

"It sounds like he got what he deserved," commented JC. She didn't mention Bob had sent her roses. In the next hair station beside her, Aunt Pearl agreed. Even though she was aware of Bob's indiscretion resulting in the divorce, she had decided there was no reason to mention it to JC. She knew at some point JC was bound to hear about it on the grapevine, and today was the day.

"Both of you need to be on guard. I hear tell Bob's out looking for a new woman that has money. Not that you aren't nice looking, Miss Pearl, but JC's probably the one he might consider fair game since she owns the Scott Ranch outright." These comments flustered Bitsy, and her face started to glow deep pink as a result of what she just said.

"Don't be embarrassed, Bitsy. I know I'm a dried-up old prune," said Pearl with a wink and a grin.

"That isn't what I've been hearing. The word around town is Sheriff Joe Walker would like nothing more than to hit on you, but he's afraid you might knock out his gold front tooth if he did," said Bitsy.

Pearl thought that was hilarious. "That old geezer wouldn't know what to do with me if he caught me, him bein' a confirmed bachelor." While Pearl laughed it off, she was secretly pleased to know the sheriff was interested in her. Their chatter continued around who was doing who until their hairdos and makeup were done and their finger and toenail polish dry. Then is when Bitsy took the opportunity to voice her thoughts concerning Emilio Vasquez.

"What do you think about that foreman, Emilio Vasquez, you have working out at the ranch JC? He sure is one handsome dreamboat. My friends and I sometimes go to that nasty cantina, The Lonesome Dove, with the hope he will be there. We're always disappointed because he hardly ever shows up. When he does show up, he sits in a corner back booth all alone with his bottle of Dos Equis listening to that crummy little band play for less than an hour before he leaves. I noticed he never responds to the women who literally throw themselves at him beyond giving them a definite, 'no I'm not interested,' so I never got up the nerve to approach him. You have to admit he sure is eye candy. And I do like candy!"

JC felt her stomach lurch at the mention of Emilio's name. "Sorry, Bitsy. We have to leave now. Are you coming to the fundraiser over at the Cattleman's tonight? Aunt Pearl's ladies' group is trying to raise enough money so one of their members can afford to make the trip to Austin for her mom's funeral. I would be willing to bet you will be able to find some good buys if I know Aunt Pearl." This was the only thing she could think of to say in order to steer the conversation away from any more talk about Emilio.

For a moment, Bitsy was at a loss for words before thinking, a fundraiser? So that's what Pearl told JC in order to get her to attend her birthday party. I might have known Pearl would come up with a story like that, so she played along. "Sure am coming to the fundraiser. I plan to be there with bells on if I can pull myself together in time. Goodness sakes! Would you just look at my hair! It's true what they say about beauticians always having the worst looking head of hair. Guess it's because we're too busy taking care of everybody else to take care of ourselves."

"Don't be silly, Bitsy. Your hair always looks good. Well, maybe not always, but you're cute enough to pull it off without having it done," JC responded while she put on her jacket in preparation to leave.

"You don't suppose Emilio will attend the fundraiser, do you? If I thought he would be there I'd have Marlene do my hair and jazz up the eye makeup a little more than usual." Aunt Pearl kept quiet about the fact she knew Emilio would be there after being told he would be there by Rosa. She did not want Bitsy hitting on him.

Without meaning to, JC bristled. "I have no idea what Emilio will or will not do! He usually takes Saturday nights off. He can spend that time however he wants. I am not his babysitter! He doesn't need my permission to do what he wants to do! Come on, Aunt Pearl, we need to get going." JC knew she had to get out of there, and fast, or she would burst into tears. This left Bitsy standing there with a hairbrush in her hand as JC made a dash out the door.

"Wooee! That gal protests too much when it comes to the comings and goings of that buckaroo. It's about time she took notice of the opposite sex and realized life will go on without Rex. I need to keep tabs on where this is going. I have a feeling this could produce a nice little bit of fuel for the gossip mill. Yes siree, I have a feeling JC's mind is off in the clouds when it comes to Emilio Vasquez, and who could blame her? He is one sexy handsome devil!" declared Bitsy.

After lunch where she picked at her food, JC asked Aunt Pearl to drop her off in downtown Midline instead of at the ranch. "I need to do some shopping at the variety store for a new lipstick and some hand lotion."

"How do you plan to get back to the ranch?" asked Pearl.

"Jose always comes into town to pick up supplies about this time on Saturdays," she answered. "He isn't part of the cattle drive this time, since the guys take turns and he went on the spring drive. I will give him a call on my cell phone and have him pick me up at the post office. There is no need for you to wait around while I shop. I think you mentioned earlier that you wanted to take a nap this afternoon before going to the fundraiser."

"If you're sure you don't want me to drive you home, I do need to rest for a little while before I get ready for the fundraiser," Pearl replied.

"Aunt Pearl, I'm sure. I promise I will see you at the Cattleman's promptly at seven tonight, and I'll be wearing the turquoise dress and sparkly earrings."

No sooner than Aunt Pearl had driven away, JC spotted Emilio coming out of the barber shop across the street sporting a fresh haircut and shave. He was wearing clean jeans and a long sleeved light blue shirt. He had what looked like a dark blue suit covered in a clear plastic garment bag draped over one arm along with a boot box in his hand. He appeared to be headed for the flower shop.

"That's odd. I thought he was taking part in the cattle drive." She looked at her watch. It was only three p.m. "Maybe they got in early and he's getting ready for a hot date tonight." A feeling of jealousy caught her by surprise wondering who the lucky lady might be. She slipped behind one of the support pillars of the variety store so as not to be seen. "What in the heck am I hiding for? He won't turn around and see me, and so what if he does? The last time I checked, it's a free country, and I can go anywhere in it I want!" She stepped out and hurried on inside the store. It turned out to be her lucky day. Bob Wilkins had taken the afternoon off from working at the store in order to take a shower, rest and dress for the party, and she had no reason to think Emilio had seen her.

Jose sat patiently waiting in his truck in front of the post office. "You look mighty pretty, Miss JC. Everyone think so when you go help at the fundraiser Miss Pearl have at Cattleman's tonight." He did his best to contain a grin, knowing the fundraiser was just a ruse to get her to come to the birthday party.

"Thank you for the compliment, Jose," she responded. It crossed her mind that everyone might think she looked nice, but the one person she wanted to think so would not be there. He would be spending the evening with a woman other than her. The thought left her feeling depressed, even though she had done nothing more to give Emilio the impression she wanted a relationship with him beyond his duties as the ranch foreman.

CHAPTER 21

JC was still feeling out of sorts when Jose dropped her off at the walkway leading to the ranch house. It didn't help when Rosa met her inside the door grinning from ear to ear as soon as she entered. "Rosa wonder when you come home. Rosa have big news!"

"All right, Rosa, let me hear your news. I hope it is good news," replied JC.

Rosa started to giggle while placing both hands over her mouth but said nothing. Her failure to respond immediately irked JC.

"Okay, out with it. I don't have much time to get ready for the fundraiser."

"Roberto ask Rosa marry him."

That's all I need, thought JC irritably. "Does this mean you are telling me I'm going to lose you?"

"You not lose me. Rosa hoping you let Roberto and me move in apartment upstairs in horse barn since Andy and Maria not need. Roberto's house okay, but very old. I not want live there with three his grown sons, their wives and six grand kids. Too much happen all the time. He real good handyman who fix anything on ranch and I be close by." She paused, giving JC a questioning look. "Rosa think you be happy for us, but no think so. Your eyes, they look sad."

"Forgive me, Rosa. I am incredibly happy for you and Roberto. It's just that this has been a very trying day."

"Rosa understand you not happy you turn thirty today, but you look nice with new hair style and makeup."

"It isn't like I'm unhappy about turning thirty. It is just that I have a lot on my mind right now. Please believe I am incredibly happy you are getting married. You and Roberto are more than welcome to move into the apartment above the horse barn. He appears to be a nice guy and I could use the extra help. I need to know when the wedding will take place so any needed repairs and renovations can be made as quickly as possible."

"Wedding not happen for two months. Need time let families know since they come from many places in Mexico and Texas. Okay they pitch tents in pasture like Andy and Maria's family? You no need bring in portable toilets, water or grill. Roberto, he take care all that and families clean and decorate horse barn for fiesta after wedding ceremony at church if okay."

JC smiled. "Of course it's okay. Roberto will not need to provide toilets, a water tanker or grill. What was done for Andy and Maria's families will be done for your families. I insist. That is only right since you are an important part of my family. Just let me know approximately how many people will be there and the date of the wedding."

"Oh, thank you! I make list of people who come to wedding and give to you. You make Rosa's day good."

"I'm glad somebody is having a good day," JC replied under her breath. "We will talk about your wedding plans next week. Right now, I need get dressed for the fundraiser."

"Rosa take cut in pay for us living in apartment," she called to JC's retreating figure. JC paused and turned. "No, you will not take a cut in pay. I plan to put Roberto to work. In fact, why don't you and Roberto plan on moving into the guest suite down at the far end of the hall here in the ranch house? That will still leave four guest suites available. That way, the vet will still be able to use the barn apartment when he needs to, and I will not need to make any renovations."

If Rosa could do handsprings, she would have. "You not be sorry. We take good care you and ranch. Roberto good mechanic. He make sure tractors, trucks and cars always run good, and he fix what needs fix in house or barns." She hesitated before adding, "Too bad Sam not like you. He should be here helping, not off to play like kid." You have no idea, thought JC. I should have asked Aunt Pearl how I should act toward him if Sam makes an appearance at the Cattleman's fundraiser tonight, but he probably won't make the effort to drive all the way here from San Antonio, since he doesn't even know who the fundraiser is planned to help.

When JC appeared in the living room dressed in the turquoise dress, diamond earrings and silver shoes Rosa gasped. "You look like angel," she declared. "Your momma, daddy and Rex look down from heaven to wonder what you do here on earth!" Rosa's pronouncement brought tears to JC's eyes. "You not cry. You smile, be happy or you make Rosa cry. I no look good when cry. I don't want to look bad when Roberto and I go have dinner with his kids and brothers to tell about wedding. That why I dressed like this ready to go when you leave for fundraiser." She said this knowing it was a fib since she and Roberto were invited to the birthday party.

To no avail, JC kept glancing behind her in the rear-view mirror of her truck hoping to see Emilio's truck following behind her during the drive into town. That was until she remembered the cattle drive and Emilio's clean-shaven appearance, and the clothing bag draped over his arm while heading to the flower shop that had made it look as though he had a hot date.

She wasn't prepared for the crowded street when she pulled into Main Street. There wasn't a parking space to be had within blocks of the Cattleman's Country Club. She was happy Aunt Pearl had insisted she use the valet service. She pulled halfway around the circular drive in front of the clubhouse, where a young man wearing a white shirt and black pants held up his hand for her to stop.

"Good evening, Mrs. Morgan. It's so nice of you to come," he said as he opened the truck door. "You go on inside. Miss Pearl is waiting for you. I will take good care of your truck." She handed him the keys, smiled and thanked him. She paused just long enough to watch him peel off at a high rate of speed.

"I'll just bet you will take good care of my truck! Damn! I'm late, or I would give you a tongue lashing you wouldn't forget for a long time, but Aunt Pearl will already be fuming." Another young man, dressed similarly to the valet, stood there with a silly grin to open the entrance door for her after witnessing the way the other young man sped off with her truck. JC decided not to make an issue of the truck episode. Doing so would not be a good start to a long evening.

"Wow! It looks like Aunt Pearl outdid herself in convincing people to attend the fundraiser," she commented to him. "With all of these people, she is bound to make more than enough money for her friend to travel to Austin in first class style with some money left over."

The young man nodded, gave her a broad smile and agreed. "Yes, ma'am. It looks like just about the whole town and outlying ranch owners are here, but we didn't expect anything less. When Miss Pearl sets her mind to doing something, it's always a winner." JC gave him an affirmative smile.

CHAPTER 22

Bob Wilkins awakened that same Saturday morning feeling slightly better than he had the past few years, having imbibed in only two glasses of wine last night instead of drinking the entire box. He began rummaging around in the messy bedroom closet for his outdated tux, ruffled white shirt and formal black patent leather shoes. Finding the items, he tried them on. Everything was snug, but he figured if he kept his gut pulled in and didn't button the jacket, he would look all right. The tux pants would work if he left the top button unbuttoned and used a safety pin at the waistband underneath the cummerbund. While the tux shirt was a tad on the yellow side, he thought in the dim light that, too, would look just fine after it was washed, starched and ironed. "JC is going to positively go ape over how good I look," he convinced himself.

Whistling a nondescript tune, he set about in search of the rhinestone cufflinks and black bowtie he had worn before Mary Jane divorced him two years ago. The cufflinks were tarnished, but he knew with some toothpaste, an old toothbrush and a little elbow grease they would look presentable in the subdued lighting. So what if he polished a little too much and the pot metal showed through. Into the washing machine went the shirt, along with several other colored items, including a bright red cheap pullover sweater. Bob went to the kitchen for his usual breakfast;

generic cornflakes topped with milk made from a white powder and water while the clothes washed. Finishing his breakfast, he returned to the stackable washer/dryer. He opened the washer lid, and to his horror, the tux shirt was bright pink! "Son-of-a-bitch!" he roared. "I don't have seventy-five extra dollars to buy a new shirt, and I don't have the time to find one at the thrift store two towns over. It would be my luck they wouldn't have one if I did make the drive. I knew I should have bought new evening clothes while I still had the money! Think, Bob! What can you do? Bleach is out of the question. The shirt is so old it would end up in shreds. I know. I'll wear a pink rosebud pinned on the jacket lapel. JC will take one look and think I'm a sensitive guy by wearing a pink rosebud to match the shirt. Problem solved."

A sensitive guy, he managed not only a burned iron print on the back of the shirt but also on the left sleeve. He didn't bother to swear. He determined that, too, would not be seen if he left the jacket on. He didn't want to think about the possibility of sweating profusely when the weather was predicted to turn unseasonably warm on that October day. As soon as he finished ironing the shirt, he placed it on a hanger, hung it on the closet doorknob and left the apartment bound for the flower shop to buy the pink rosebud boutonniere to complete what he thought would be an irresistible look.

"Can I help you, Mr. Wilkins?" asked Billy Joe McClarin, the flower shop's owner.

"I would like one of your best bright pink rosebud boutonnieres."

"Sure thing, Mr. Wilkins, Just give me a minute to check the back cooler and pick out one of our nicest buds." He nodded a greeting in Emilio's direction, who had entered the flower shop a few minutes behind Bob. "Be right with you, sir."

"No big hurry. I'm just here to pick up the white orchid corsage I ordered earlier," replied Emilio.

A few more minutes passed before Billy Joe returned to the front counter. Bob did not bother to turn around to see who entered the shop after him, instead concentrating on the bouquets in the display cooler and swearing under his breath at the prices.

"Sorry, Mr. Wilkins. We are all out of pink buds or pink roses. How about a nice white bud? I can add a pink ribbon and have it sent over to your apartment within the hour."

"I really wanted pink, but if white is all you have, I'll take it and the pink ribbon. How much?"

"That will be eight dollars."

"Eight dollars!" exclaimed Bob. "That's highway robbery! Why, I had dozens of nicer roses growing in my garden than this place has ever seen!"

"Then I suggest you take yourself over to what was your garden and pick one. Of course, Mary Jane might have something to say about it since everybody knows she recently took out a restraining order against you. If you want the white rosebud the price is eight dollars. Take it or leave it!"

"Guess I'll take it," groused Bob. "Seems to me like you could give me a better price after all those roses I ordered, along with those high-priced delivery fees."

"Thank you for reminding me. There will be a two-dollar delivery fee," smirked Billy Joe.

Bob slapped a ten-dollar bill on the counter. "Here, you highway robber!" he declared. "That boutonniere better be nice, or you will definitely hear from me!"

"Thanks for doing business with us," was delivered tongue in cheek by Billy Joe along with a with a distinct note of sarcasm.

Bob was on his way out of the flower shop when he looked up and realized it was Emilio Vasquez waiting to be served. "Aren't you the foreman out at the Scott Ranch? I didn't know JC paid you boys enough to be buying orchids to give to some whore."

"The orchid is for a lady, not some whore, not that it is any of your business who it is for," replied Emilio calmly. He turned his back to Bob and stepped up to the counter. "Is my orchid ready, Billy Joe? Time is starting to run a little short, and I need to get back to the hotel to change clothes."

Bob wasn't about to give up hurling insults. "It must be nice that some greaser like you can afford to buy an orchid all dolled up in a box with a bow on top. And do I detect a suit in that plastic bag draped over your arm? Don't fellas like you usually run around wearing ragged dirty jeans, ten-gallon hats, wrinkled cotton shirts with a grease ring around the neck, along with smelling like cow shit? That orchid wouldn't be for JC Morgan, would it, it being her birthday and all? But that couldn't be since greasers like you aren't welcome at the Cattleman's Country Club. I don't know what made me think you would be going to the party. Riffraff like you don't get invitations to attend parties like that."

Emilio turned around and looked directly in his tormentor's face before stepping back to place his new suit and boots on a nearby chair before he approached Bob. "You placed an order. You ungraciously paid for it. You insulted me. I think it's time for you to do the sensible thing and leave."

"You don't go telling me what to do, you damned greaser! You and your kind need to hightail it back across the Rio Grande! You come over here and take our jobs and defile our women . . ." Bob didn't get a chance to finish the sentence. Emilio grabbed him by the shirt front, forcefully turned him around and ushered him backward out through the front door to land on his back side on the sidewalk. Bob continued to scream obscenities and threats as Emilio closed the door then calmly went back to the counter to collect his belongings and pay for the orchid.

"I'm awful sorry about that, Mr. Vasquez. Bob's gone a little crazy ever since Mary Jane booted him out. If I were you, I'd watch my back. He is known to have a nasty temper," said Billy Joe.

"I sort of figured as much. I hope he doesn't try to sue me, but I just couldn't let him continue to insult me. What do I owe you?"

"Make it thirty-five dollars. Orchid corsages are usually fifty dollars. I'm giving you a discount on account of the way Bob treated you, and you stood up to him." The grin on Billy Joe's face was unmistakable. "And I didn't see a thing, if Bob tries to make a federal case out of what just happened."

"That won't be necessary to discount the orchid, but that is kind of you to offer. Thanks. Are you going to the birthday party for JC at the Cattleman's tonight?" At the same time Emilio handed him a fifty-dollar bill, saying he didn't want any change. Billy Joe didn't argue, tucking the bill under the drawer meant for holding larger bills while offering his thanks.

"I wouldn't miss the party for anything! My girlfriend Stacy 'n me have been looking forward to it ever since Miss Pearl gave us the invite. Miss JC sure is one nice lady, 'n I'm glad to see her getting out again. I was real happy when Miss Pearl gave me the bid to do the floral decorations. I woulda done them for free, but she insisted I be paid the going rate, plus twenty percent since I had to work in a hurry after hours last night to get everything done. She said to send the bill to JC's brother Sam and that money was no object. That was real nice since things have been a little tight with folks not spending as much on flowers since the downturn in the economy. The orchid wouldn't happen to be for JC, would it?"

Emilio just smiled without answering and headed for the door. "See you at the party tonight," he called over his shoulder.

Emilio had seen JC watching him from across the street earlier. Her reflection in the store front plate glass window of the flower shop had stunned him at the sight of her following the spa visit. It took every ounce of restraint he could muster not to walk across the street, approach her and ask if she would join him for coffee so they could talk. "I need to wait until tonight to plead my case," he muttered to himself.

As he walked to his truck after picking up the orchid, a slashed rear tire closest to the curb caught his eye. "Guess I don't need to guess who did this handiwork. Looks like I need to find the time to change it," he mused. "I think I need to ask Miss Pearl if Jose and Juan can attend the party just in case Bob shows up to make a scene."

CHAPTER 23

Absolute terror enveloped Sam Scott! He tried to scream but found he could not make a sound. His throat felt as though he tried to swallow something large and sharp, and it stuck halfway down his windpipe, and he couldn't get his breath. He found it almost unbelievable he had just carried out his plan to murder his lover, Ross Vandenberg. Looking down at what he viewed was a lifeless body in the hot tub, he knew he had to get out of there on the double! Naked and dripping wet, he fled across the wide patio, through the double French doors, across the living room and down the hall into what had been their shared bedroom. He didn't bother to shower, instead drying off and hurriedly putting on his clothes. He gathered up the toiletries and clothing he planned to take to JC's party, haphazardly stuffing them into a suitcase. Then he called Aunt Pearl as soon as he calmed down and regained the ability to speak.

"Hello, Aunt Pearl. It's me, Sam . . . I know it's late. The reason I'm calling is to see if I drove over yet tonight could I stay at your house? . . . I don't want to go to the ranch. JC would start asking questions, and I could blow the cover for the party . . . You don't have to swear, Aunt Pearl . . . and you don't have to wait up. Just leave the front door key in the usual spot. You won't even know I'm there . . . Why do I want to come tonight? I can't sleep. I'm so stressed out and excited about the party. I can't wait to see how you have decorated at the Country Club and hear all about what you said to convince JC to come to the Cattleman's . . . I can stay? Great! Thanks. See you in the morning . . . and no I won't get up too early. Bye." He let out a sigh of relief. "At least I won't have to spend the night here with Ross's body."

If Sam had paused long enough to remember Ross was a champion swimmer and surfer, he should have known he could hold his breath long enough to play dead. Had he done so, it would not have been necessary for him to go into full- blown panic mode.

As soon as Ross realized Sam's intent to drown him, he struggled briefly then allowed his body to go limp. He lay there floating face down, arms hanging limply at his sides. He was able to do this long enough for Sam to think he was dead, allowing him to float until Sam fled in terror.

Driving the interstate across open Texas cattle country on a starlit night gave Sam time to settle down and think. "It was an accident . . . nobody will blame me. Ross won't be found until Monday. I will have been away all weekend, a three-hour drive away. The authorities will think Ross must have had too much do drink and passed out in the warm hot tub water. The cops can't prove I was there, especially when Aunt Pearl tells them I was staying at her house tonight and then I leave for New York City on Monday morning. Thank God I'm rid of that parasite! I'm home free, and to top it off, I won't have any money worries for at least a little while when the life insurance policy I purchased on Ross pays."

Aunt Pearl swore like a sailor after she hung up the phone following Sam's call. Then she burst out laughing. "You think you are stressed now, Sammy Boy. Just wait! You don't have a clue what stress is all about, but you will just as soon as JC, me, the judge and jury gets through with you and you find out what prison life is all about!"

It was one a.m. when Sam arrived to find Pearl still awake watching TV in the den. It was all she could do to remain civil toward her nephew. She did not offer him refreshments, nor did she get up from where she was sitting in a recliner. Her conversation consisted of a minimal, deadpan hello.

"Sorry to barge in on you like this, Aunt Pearl, but I figured you wouldn't mind."

"Second guest room on the right is ready. If I'm not here in the mornin', there will be coffee on the kitchen counter. Bagels and butter in the refrigerator. I'm going to bed." That said, she got up and left the room leaving Sam to take care of settling in for the night.

Pearl figured she would be up and gone early in order to pick up JC for their morning drive to the spa before Sam got his lazy butt out of bed. She got up from her chair, then walked down the hall and slammed her bedroom door behind her. "Sure am glad I won't be here and have to deal with that slimy bastard in the mornin', except for a little while this evenin' just before I leave for the party, and I'll think up an excuse so he can drive there by himself!" she muttered.

Thinking Aunt Pearl was more than a little put out because of him calling at the last minute, Sam dismissed her cool reception. He needed a drink in the worst way but didn't think he should go snooping around to find one at this late hour. Aunt Pearl, being very particular, would notice even an ounce of bourbon missing from one of her lead crystal decanters, so he went to bed.

Along about two a.m., Sam was awakened abruptly from a light sleep. He sat up, looked around and listened. There it was again, that scratching noise on the screen covering the open window next to the bed. The curtains were drawn, and he was too lazy to get out of bed to investigate. A few minutes later the noise, even louder, awakened him again. This time he got up to pull the drapes part way open, looked outside and let out a stifled scream. "That can't be Ross out there! He's dead! It must be a hallucination or a nightmare! Think about all that insurance money instead!" He let the drape drop closed. In his state of panic, he neglected to close and lock the window and went back to bed, where sleep continued to elude him.

Outside the window in the shrubbery, Ross was thoroughly enjoying the look of horror on Sam's face he had seen in the moonlight. "I am going to haunt you until you go stark raving mad," he whispered in a hoarse voice while scraping his fingernails across the screen and said, "boo!" This time Sam did not stifle a blood curdling scream when he got up to close and lock the window, having seen Ross's face pressed against the screen again.

This brought Aunt Pearl on the run. Pounding on the guest room door she called, "Everythin' all right in there, Sam?" Fumbling to get into his robe, he stumbled to the door and opened it.

"My God, you look like you've just seen a ghost!" exclaimed Pearl.

"Just a bad dream, Aunt Pearl. I'm all right. Sorry to disturb you."

Although she wasn't convinced he was all right, she nodded and shuffled back to her bedroom. "Probably havin' nightmares due to guilt since you are nothin' but a thief," she mumbled before leaving to climb back into bed and going to sleep.

Sam lay there wide awake for another hour before he got up, snapped on a bedside table light and sat in a chair he pulled away from the window. To steady his nerves, he tried to read a book he found in the nightstand drawer. All the while, he listened for the scratching noise. He wasn't disappointed. It began again accompanied by loud moaning. He didn't go back to the window to take another look, having closed and locked it after having pulled the heavy curtains closed. He turned off the light and sat in the darkness until five a.m. refusing to believe Ross was out there. Then he went to take a shower and dress. "I'm just imagining I see or hear Ross," he kept telling himself.

"You're up early," said a disgruntled Aunt Pearl, figuring he would sleep late, and she would have gone and not have to interact with him. "Wasn't the bed to your likin'? I thought you would sleep in after that long drive late last night. Don't look like you slept a wink."

"The bed was fine. I guess I didn't sleep late because I'm so excited about the party. I hope you were able to get everything done. If not is there anything I can do to help?"

"Everything has been taken care of for the party," she replied curtly, when she wanted to say, 'you can just stay out of my way, or I might be tempted to kick your ass into the middle of next week!' "With nothin' to do until the party, why don't you go out to the ranch? I'm sure JC would just love to see you." She didn't really want him going out there. She was just looking for a reaction and she got one.

Sam stuttered. "I . . . I don't th . . . think that's a good idea. I might slip up and say something to spoil the surprise."

Pearl persisted. "That's just a bunch of bull! You know she would be delighted if you showed up unexpectedly." *Of course, I don't know if she would tear you limb from limb, but that's not such a bad idea you little prick!* "Oh, I almost forgot, she and I are drivin' over to the spa from her place at nine this mornin'. That means you are on your own for breakfast and lunch. I don't know when I'll be leavin' to go to the Cattleman's, so you will have to drive to the party by yourself. I'm sure you can find somethin' to keep you occupied in the meantime."

"Are you sure there isn't anything I can do for you around the house?" offered Sam in an effort to appease his aunt.

"Well now that you mention it, the shrubbery around back needs a good trimmin'. Know where I mean? It's the ones along the back under the window 'o the room where you just slept. Electric trimmers are in the garage on the shelf next to the water heater. Electrical outlet's back there on the end wall. Help yourself." Sam swallowed hard. Manual labor was hardly his forte, but knew he could not refuse, since he was the one who offered to help. At least trimming the hedges would get him out of going to the ranch and provide activity where he did not have to think about Ross's bloated body or visit JC at the ranch.

During the trimming, he had time to think about coming up with an alibi for Sunday night. Returning to his house in San Antonio was not an option until late Monday morning at the earliest to make sure Ross's body had been found by the cleaning lady and reported to the proper authorities. "I know, I'll hire a prostitute and spend the remainder of the weekend in a hotel with her after the party. That way, she can provide an alibi should one be required since I don't think I will be welcome to stay at Aunt Pearl's on Sunday night after the party." He shuddered at the thought of spending time with a woman in a motel room but decided that was probably the best option since he continued to believe his sexual preference remained unknown in his hometown. “We can spend Sunday afternoon at the zoo or on a picnic at the lake since it’s still warm. I can even invite JC and Aunt Pearl to come along. I’ll just tell the hooker all I want to do is talk when we end up in a motel on Sunday night. Then I’ll send her on her way Monday morning before I drive back to San Antonio to get some money and take off for New York City. I can introduce her to family and friends as a friend’s cousin visiting the area.” After all that thought he decided, as a gay man, he just could not carry out that plan. “I think I will let everyone know I am taking a much needed vacation to New York City and leave the party early Sunday morning, since it will still be going strong until the wee hours. This way I will be home free. By the time the club manager figures out I’m gone, and my credit cards may be maxed out, the Cattleman’s will be left holding the bag. You can’t get money out of a dead guy, and I’m sure as hell I can’t afford to pay them! They can collect from that busybody Aunt Pearl!”

Sam used the automatic garage door opener to open Pearl’s garage doors since Pearl did not invite him to use the door into the garage from the kitchen. He found the hedge trimmers, went around back and plugged them in. Starting at the far end of the house, it didn’t take long before he approached the area under the window where he had slept. The shrubbery was broken, and there were footprints in the dirt the same size as Ross's size twelve shoes. "What the hell, this can't be possible! Ghosts don't leave footprints or break shrubbery! Somebody was out there making that noise during the night, but who was it? It couldn't have been Ross! He's dead!" A feeling of terror overwhelmed him. He dropped the trimmer and ran back toward the garage. "I need to calm down. It was probably the pest control man who broke the shrubs and left the footprints. That's it, he had to break back some of the shrubbery to spray the foundation properly. I need to get back out there or Aunt Pearl will think I'm sandbagging."

Half an hour later, Aunt Pearl stuck her head out the back door into the garage and called out, "Breakfast will be ready in two minutes." She would not have bothered cooking, but she was hungry and could not justify leaving for the ranch at such an early hour.

"Be right there. I'm over here at the utility sink cleaning the trimmer," he called.

"You best not take too long, or I might find some rat poison to flavor your scrambled eggs!" she muttered under her breath after closing the door harder than necessary.

Over breakfast, Pearl found it difficult to carry on a polite conversation with Sam beyond, "How are the shrubs lookin' back there? Pest control man has not been here yet this month. Did you notice any aphids?" was the best she could manage. Sam almost choked on a mouthful of scrambled eggs. There went his theory that broken shrubs and footprints could have been made by the pest control man.

He coughed and took couple of swallows of coffee. "Didn't see any aphids, but some of the shrubs were broken. I did my best to make them blend in with the others," he replied behind his napkin.

"I had fresh soil hauled in back there last month, but since it rained that shoulda been worked in all nice 'n smooth. Broken shrubs would have had more than enough time to recover. I suppose recent breaks coulda been caused by a wanderin' steer. They sometimes get loose over at the feed lots 'n come lookin' for somethin' green to nibble on before they are rounded up. Did you see any hoof prints?" Steers don't leave human footprints, thought Sam. He found himself in a fit of coughing again to cover his fear and agitation.

"Go get yourself some more coffee. A few more swallows will clear the pipes. I have to leave to pick up JC." Pearl wasn't about to serve the coffee to him. "You clear the table and put the dishes in the dishwasher. Sure you don't want me to drop you off at the ranch?" she asked again just to irritate him.

Sam got up and filled his cup, took another big swallow of the scalding hot liquid and burned his lips and tongue. He knew it was going to take more than a few swallows of coffee to wash down the lump of fear caught in his throat.

All he could think was, damn you, bitch! She knows I don't want to go to the ranch and face JC when it is all I can do to just manage to keep my anxiety under control under the current circumstances.

"I'm sure I don't want to go to the ranch," he croaked. Aunt Pearl gave him what could pass for an evil grin. "Suit yourself." She didn't bother to tell him goodbye. She picked up her purse sitting next to her on a chair, got up and walked out of the breakfast room to open the front door and walk through, slamming it behind her. "The more I see of that bastard, the madder I get," she mumbled on the way to her car. "I don't know how my brother-in-law managed to sire such a schmuck!"

CHAPTER 24

JC noticed Bob Wilkins getting out of his car right behind hers at the country club on Saturday evening. She hurried up the walkway in order to avoid engaging in conversation with him. The Club manager stepped forward to greet her when she entered into the glass enclosed foyer. "Good evening, Miss Scott. It is good to see you here with us again."

"Good evening, Bradley. It is nice to be back. Which room are they using to hold the fundraiser Aunt Pearl is sponsoring? I am supposed to give a hand at her booth."

"Empire Room, second door on the left down the east wing," he casually replied. "I will be happy to escort you since it has been quite a while since you were here last, and we've made some changes.".

"Thank you. I remember where it is located, so please don't feel that you need to escort me." But Bradley insisted on using the chance to accompany her. It wasn't every day he was able to spend time with a beautiful single woman, and he wasn't about to miss this opportunity when that woman was JC Scott Morgan.

"Aunt Pearl must be expecting a huge turnout since that is the largest ballroom. If I recall, it has the capacity to seat two hundred and forty people comfortably," she said in an effort to make small talk.

"That it does, and it is packed to the gills tonight." A beeping sound erupted from Bradley's jacket pocket. "You will have to excuse me. The chef is signaling me on my beeper. I need to go see what he wants. Please go ahead into the Empire Room and have a great time."

With Bob Wilkins hot on her heels, JC did not hesitate to enter the Empire Room as quickly as possible, where once inside, she was forced to do a double take. People were milling about on the dance floor talking with drinks in their hands. Waiters were circulating with a variety of appetizers on platters, along with tall, fluted glasses filled with sparkling champagne on silver trays. Twenty tables were covered in starched white linen, with purple orchid centerpieces flanked on each side by silver candles in gleaming crystal holders. Twelve place settings at each table caught her attention, as did the large banner stretched above the stage proclaiming 'Happy 30th Birthday JC!' Hundreds of clear sparkling tiny lights dangling from four-foot-tall live trees set in large colorful pots to surround the dance floor turned the room into a virtual fairyland. A twelve-piece orchestra began to play "Happy Birthday," and guests began to sing soon after she entered the room. "What the heck is going on?" she murmured in astonishment.

"Over here!" shouted Aunt Pearl as the strains of music and the sound of voices drifted away amid applause. Embarrassed, JC managed to make her way through the throng of well-wishers to stand next to Aunt Pearl. "This is certainly some kind of a fundraiser!" she exclaimed. "Aunt Pearl, you had me totally fooled. You should not have gone to so much trouble, but thank you."

"Don't thank me. Your brother is footin' most 'o the bill," she grinned. "I must admit I thought I'd teach the little scumbag a lesson that you don't steal from anyone, 'specially your own family!"

"Aunt Pearl, tell me you didn't have him billed for all of this!" JC whispered.

"You bet your boots I did! Hope he likes a variety of hot and cold appetizers including jumbo shrimp cocktail, charbroiled filet, baked potatoes, mushrooms and baked Alaska along with any kind 'o top shelf booze that suits our guest's preference. I almost forgot, there's that fancy Dom somethin' champagne, too, so step right up 'n have a glass!" Before JC could answer, she felt a firm hand grasp her wrist and heard the words, "May I have this dance?"

It was not a request. It was a demand made while literally being yanked onto the dance floor. She tried to pull away, but Bob Wilkins held on tighter and pulled her closer. "Don't fight it, little lady. I know you must be in need of a little romance, and ole Bob is just the man to provide it. You don't want to be messing around with cowboys. You need a man like me with experience. Let's you and me slip outta here and have ourselves some real fun!" Then without warning, he began to grind his Viagra infused erection into her pelvis as he tried to kiss her. Disgust swept over her, and JC literally wrestled free from the disgusting lecher.

"Mr. Wilkins! How dare you! I have never given you even the slightest impression I wanted a relationship with you, and I assure you I do not! You are totally out of line! Now let go of me and leave or I will scream bloody murder!"

"Is there a problem, JC?" asked a familiar voice.

She turned to find herself looking directly into the face of Emilio Vasquez. "Yes. This gentleman, and I use the term lightly, has just made unwanted advances."

"Would you like for me to have him escorted out of the building?"

She didn't hesitate. "Yes, I would!"

With a nod of his head, two trim, muscled Scott Ranch Mexican ranch hands invited to the party approached. Before Bob had a chance to respond, each one took him by an arm. He became enraged. "You tell these two greasers to take their filthy hands off me!" he growled. "I tried to do this the nice way by sending you roses to express my interest, JC, but you leave me no choice but to tell you I now own the loan Sam made using one thousand prime acres of the ranch as collateral, payable in cash right now for twenty-five thousand dollars, or you will hand over those thousand prime acres to me as specified in this contract!" He was able to wiggle free enough to retrieve the contract and wave it in her face. "You can dance the night away with your damned greaser. Since it's your birthday, I will stop by the ranch for payment first thing in the morning. Maybe by then you will have had time to rethink about having a permanent relationship with me to keep your precious land in the family!"

"You can stop by, but I wouldn't advise it. I can guarantee JC won't waste a minute thinkin' about a relationship with you! You won't get one damned dime or any Scott Ranch land," announced Pearl. "I bought up the loan last night before you could buy it this mornin'. Ole Clarence Mooney scammed you into thinkin' you bought up Sam's loan, so you need to contact him if you expect any money back! Good luck on that happenin' since it's not a legal transaction, and Mooney probably can't be found! Take a good look at the loan papers he gave you. They are copies lackin' the bank's seal! I have the original loan papers." She smiled at Jose and Juan, the two Mexican men who worked at the Scott ranch invited to the party just in case they were needed if Bob got nasty. "Get this poor excuse for a human bein' outta here on the double before I forget I'm a lady!" ordered Pearl. Bob had sense enough to know he didn't stand a chance with those two, so he stopped struggling, but that didn't stop him from yelling threats and obscenities as Jose and Juan literally dragged him across the dance floor between startled couples and through the exit door. People stared and moved out of the way, but assumed he was drunk and continued socializing, eating and drinking as the orchestra continuing to play as if nothing out of the ordinary had taken place.

"Aunt Pearl! You look like you are about ready to faint," said JC after Bob had been unceremoniously escorted out of the club.

"Hell, all I need is a stiff shot of bourbon! Scott women do not faint! I swear if that son-of-a-bitch shows up at the ranch tomorrow mornin' you give me a call. I'll drive out there 'n strangle him with my bare hands!"

"Aunt Pearl! Don't say things like that where people can hear you," cautioned JC. "If something were to happen to Bob, you could end up with a very serious problem."

"That ain't likely. There's enough folks around these parts what want him dead. The sheriff would have a mighty hard time pinpointin' a suspect, 'specially if I drag his sorry ass out into the scrub far enough it won't be found for days, if ever!"

Sheriff Joe Walker, overhearing Pearl's tirade, approached them. "You got that right, Miss Pearl. May I have the next dance, but not until we us find a couple shots of that fine bourbon I've seen being passed around the room. Come this way and I'll show you to my table."

"Sheriff, you're on!" declared Pearl as she took his offered arm, but she gave JC a look that asked if it was all right for her to go with him.

The sheriff, distracted by an acquaintance, did not see JC silently mouth 'I'm all right' before she began to speak out loud. "You go with the sheriff and have a good time. See you at the head table when dinner is about to be served."

Pearl smiled appreciatively. "See you at the head table when they start to serve dinner," she repeated with a grin.

Emilio stood by silently while the women and sheriff continued to talk until he could not remain silent any longer. "JC, didn't you mention the fact you bought out Sam's half of the ranch?"

"Yes, less than fifteen minutes after Mom's will was read stating we were each given half ownership, Sam demanded I buy him out. It was that or he threatened to find someone else who would buy him out. It wasn't easy, but I managed to come up with the cash he demanded after sweet talking Clarence Mooney into releasing funds from the trust. I have a clear title to prove the ranch land listed on that loan was never legally part of the deal."

"If that's the case, Sam had no right to put up any part of the ranch as collateral since he no longer owned any of it. That means he didn't have the legal right, nor did Clarence Mooney have the right to give him the loan. Mr. Mooney had to have known better, being the banks trust manager. They both need to be charged with felony grand theft," Sheriff Walker agreed.

"You are absolutely correct, Emilio and Joe," replied Pearl. "But there is one problem regardin' Clarence. I made a deal with him for restitution of what he pilfered from both JC's and my trust accounts, plus interest, and that he put in notice he is retirin' this comin' Monday mornin', along with sellin' his fancy mansion in order to move out of Texas within the next six months and never work at a bank again. It was that or I'm gonna report him to the Feds and demand a full bank audit along with letting his wife know."

"Pearl, I hope you realize what the two of you agreed to will not be upheld by the court," offered the sheriff.

"I don't give a damn. It seems to have worked so far," replied Pearl.

Neither JC nor Pearl were aware Clarence and his wife had already taken off for his coffee plantation in Brazil without returning any money to Pearl's account stolen over the past eleven years. He felt she had enough money she wouldn't miss it or the interest. He did return the money he had stolen, minus interest, to JC's account, fearful that Emilio or his family members may have contacts in Brazil that could lead to finding him, one of Emilio's brothers having married a girl from a prominent Rio family. It didn't dawn on him that while it might take a while for her to locate him, he wasn't aware Pearl had her contacts in Rio, too, and even God could not help him if she did manage to find him!

Emilio and Sheriff Walker looked shocked. "You sure know how to play hardball, Miss Pearl, but what about the other folks he might have bilked?" asked Emilio.

"They can do some serious investigatin' just like I did. And it's damned sure they will when word gets around concernin' what Clarence has been doin'! Besides, the bank will go into receivership by mid-week after shortages noted will bring in the Feds since JC and I withdrew our money, leaving the coffers a bit bare." The look on her face left no doubt Pearl would make sure the word would get around.

"But Aunt Pearl, will you get the twenty-five thousand back from Sam?" questioned JC. "Even if he pays you back won't it be with your money that was stolen?" "Don't you no never mind, darlin'," she said with a wave of her bejeweled wrist and hand. "When Judge Baumgartner gets through with Sam, I'll get that twenty-five grand back and a whole lot more between him and Clarence Mooney!"

Although she tried, JC could not hold back the tears. Emilio took a handkerchief from his inside coat pocket and gently wiped them away as she mumbled, "I can't believe it . . . my own brother! How could he be a party to all of this?" she whispered softly so as not to bring any more unwanted attention to herself.

"Please excuse us. We are going to find Sam. The sheriff and I need to have a little chat with him," said Emilio. The sheriff nodded his head in agreement.

"Please, don't either one 'o you bother messin' with that scumbag, at least not yet. I want Sam in shape to pay for this party before I lower the boom on his pitiful ass!"

interjected Pearl. "Seem a shame if he should not get to eat the last nice meal he's payin' for."

"Like I said, Aunt Pearl, if he pays -- and that's a big if -- it would be my guess it will be with your stolen money after what you told me concerning his finances when we drove to the spa this morning," insisted JC.

"Didn't you hear what I said not two minutes ago, JC? Sam and Clarence are going to pay me back one way or another, even if part 'o the money comes from the six cents an hour Sam will be earnin' in prison when he makes Texas license plates! Can't you see Sam havin' to pay me back that way will be sweet revenge? Joe, you need to tell me if I'm thinkin' along the right lines."

"I'm not on duty, and I didn't hear any of this," replied Joe as he looked up at the ceiling and rolled his eyes.

Emilio looked at JC with pleading eyes. "Your aunt is right. Let Sam pay back what he stole, even if it takes forever. It could teach him there are consequences to his actions. If you need money to tide you over until Mr. Mooney makes restitution, I will be more than happy to help. No strings attached."

"Thank you, but I keep enough cash on hand for emergencies that I can take care of the payroll you and the other hands are owed for this past month. I understand Mr. Mooney will have made restitution before next month's payroll is due, and the fall sale of cattle will bring in more money, along with increasing the production of the two producing oil wells. With breeding stock sales and trust interest, that should make me solvent for the foreseeable future, even without Sam repaying what he has stolen or Mr. Mooney paying back what he took. By the way, how much money did we make from the sale of the cattle this morning?"

"Seven hundred twelve thousand six hundred and sixty dollars," he replied. "And I demanded a receipt to prove it from the head cashier since Mr. Mooney was not in his office when I arrived." JC let out the breath she had been holding and thanked him for the information, knowing she could at least meet the next payroll for the cowboys and make good on the grocery, vet and feed bills that were in arrears with money left over for unforeseen expenses without dipping into the trust fund.

Emilio smiled, revealing his pearly white teeth and a dimple on each cheek. "Now, why don't you go powder that pretty little nose of yours while I go out to my truck to get something? I'll meet you over by the bandstand in time for the next dance."

"But that means I will be fair game for more whispers and stares, not to mention having to face Sam. I'm not sure if I can do what you ask," she replied.

"I know it won't be easy, but I have no doubt you have what it takes. I've been around here long enough to learn Scott women are tougher than nails when they need to be."

"You got that right, Emilio," said Pearl. "Come on, JC, lets you and me go get ourselves prettied up. I don't know about you, but I don't want to spoil the illusion I've managed to create for the sheriff by havin' lipstick on my teeth or a shiny nose." Pearl gave Joe a wink before starting to walk out into the hall toward the ladies' room, expecting JC to follow. He responded with a grin, saying he would be right here when she returned.

In the privacy of the ladies' lounge area, Aunt Pearl spoke candidly. "You listen to me, young lady! Wipe away those tears along with that sad look on your pretty face! You need to face up to the fact that Sam don't have a pot to piss in, and we know he did us wrong. The law will figure things out. There is one mighty good-lookin' man out there who has eyes only for you, and you'd better wake up before some other cute little chick tries to muscle in, such as Bitsy. There isn't one damned single doubt in my mind she has the hots for Emilio. She's here tonight, dressed to the nines, and without a doubt on the hunt for one hunk of a sexy Scott Ranch foreman!"

"Aunt Pearl! I have never heard you talk that way! What happened to the aunt I know?"

"Honey, you just ain't been watchin' close or listenin'! Now get yourself pulled together and get back out there and dance the night away with Emilio!" JC wiped away her tears and shook her head before trying not to smudge the lipstick she was preparing to apply.

Back in the Empire Room, Sam wiped the sweat from his forehead with one of his white linen monogramed handkerchiefs. He approached a waiter bearing a tray of top shelf drinks. "Who in the hell ordered you to pass around free drinks, top shelf no less!" he demanded.

"I believe it was Miss Pearl, Mr. Scott. Is there a problem?"

Not wanting to appear cheap to guests standing close around him, he told the waiter there was no problem, then turned and started to walk away in search of Aunt Pearl. Not finding her, he decided to go outside to his car and sit long enough to gather his wits before dinner was served. Another waiter intercepted him before he could leave the building.

"Would you like some brandy, sir? You look like you could use a drink," offered the waiter.

"How I look is none of your damned business!" snarled Sam as he continued on his way, muttering under his breath. "Orchid centerpieces, lighted trees, a twelve-piece orchestra, French champagne, top shelf free booze! Aunt Pearl must have lost her friggin' mind! Why, I'll bet they are serving baked Alaska for dessert! I wonder when the clowns and jugglers are going to make their appearance, followed by The William Tell Overture complete with a cannon blast! Dear Jesus! How in the hell does she expect me to pay for all of this?"

When he returned to the Empire Room twenty minutes later, Sam found he was seated for dinner between Aunt Pearl on the left and JC on the right next to Emilio beside her at the head table. He could not help seeing the label on the wine being served with jumbo shrimp cocktails was the very best France had to offer. Sam did not even taste the champagne or shrimp cocktail, feeling he would choke if he tried to swallow. His discomfort grew when the salads were followed by dinner plates bearing charbroiled filet steaks, a huge Idaho baked potato with all the trimmings, flanked by mushrooms simmered in red wine. He took a small bite of steak but found he could not swallow and ended up discreetly depositing it in his napkin. When it approached time for dessert to be served after the sorbet, he asked to be excused. But not before the lights were dimmed and ten waiters, five on each side of the room, appeared with flaming baked Alaska on silver platters held high above their heads, accompanied by the traditional French musical tribute played by the orchestra served to block his exit. The oohs and ahhs of guests were more than he could take. He sat back down and closed his eyes to inhale deeply, allowing the breath to escape from his lungs slowly while the dessert was being served and he could leave.

When he did not partake of dessert, Aunt Pearl leaned over and quietly slurred in his ear. “Whassa matter Sammy Boy? You got your shorts all twisted ‘round your balls? You look like you wanna fart, but you're 'fraid you will shit your pants instead!"

Sam looked at Pearl like she had lost her mind. "I can't believe you just said that! What in the devil has gotten into you Aunt Pearl?"

Pearl settled back in her chair and took several more generous swallows of wine, emptying her fourth glass. "You will fine out sooon 'nough, Sammy Boy. You need to stick round 'n enjoy the food. There will come a daaay yooou wish you had." Her drunken pronouncement ended in a loud burp followed by a giggle.

"What do you mean?" asked Sam.

"Oh, I think you have a pretty damn goood idea. Lass time I checked, they don't serve filet or baaaked Alaska in prison accompanied by a twelve-piece oorchestra. It's cheeeap greasy bologna sanwiches slaaapped between twooo slices 'o stale bread tw - ice aday, seeeven daaays aweek 'n aaany music 'ill be the screamin' or cuss words delivered by oother inmates!"

Sam focused on his Aunt with a continued look of dismay. "Prison?" he questioned. "I don't have any idea what they do or serve in there, and would you please keep your voice down! People are beginning to stare in our direction."

Aunt Pearl ignored his request. "Yooou will know soooon nough 'bout prison life. Yesss sir, you will know sooooon nough, Mr. Playboy. Waiter! More red wine 'n donnn beee chintzy. This genleman is payin'."

"Aunt Pearl you are drunk!" hissed Sam.

"Maybe sooo, but I won' be the one eatin' prison food! It 'ill be yoou, Sammy Boy! Thas wha' happens when yoou steal from anyone, 'specially family! Donn look sooo shocked. I know everythin', yoou slime ball, includin' the deal yoou and Clarence Mooney coooked up involvin' the twenty-five gran' loooan, which I paid off, 'n the three hunerd thousaunn plus inress you owe your siser afer takin' your cut 'o what he stole from her. In plainn Enlish, I'm tellin' you iths your haalf 'o the six-hunred-thousan-gran you and Mooney stole from the ranth truss fun over the pass four years durin' your hooomooo affair. I althso know 'bout Ross Van-den-berr. Hope tha fancy maaanssion, 'n furnishin's, long with the BMW you own brin' in that muss cash when they are soold and the cath is plied to what you will beee judged to owe!"

Stunned, Sam watched as Pearl drained her fifth glass of wine in addition to the unknown number of shots of bourbon she consumed while in the company of Joe Walker before he could respond. "You are drunk and don't know what you are talking about, you old windbag!" he snarled.

Pearl smiled as though she knew an inside joke to which only she knew the punch line. "Oh, buth I dooo know. Your looover Moooney saang likea caanary when I paid him a visit lasss evenin' jus' afore the bank clooosed. How in the hell do you thin' I got the figger of three-hunnerd thousan an his promise to pay baack his half of the stolen six hundred thousan, plus inrest stolen from your sisther? I'll let you in onnn 'nother secret. Mooonnneey plans to 'retire' firss thin' Monday mornin', sell his mansion 'n leave Texthas 'n less thaan sis months or the Fed's 'ill get involved. Donn loook at me that way, you bashard! You had to knooow whath the two of you were doin' wasa crime, let alone immoral! And then therth's tha Ross fell - ow. I donn think I neeed to go into details 'bout what's been happenin' with you 'n him ever thince college." Sam paled and swallowed hard at the mention of Ross's name.

"If we weren't seated here in front of all of these people, I would strangle you, you crazy old bitch!" Pearl only snorted with laughter at what he said and carelessly slapped her hand on the table to emphasize her intoxicated amusement at his reaction.

Sam leaned back in his chair to turn his attention to JC, who was so deep in conversation with Emilio, whom she had asked to join her at the head table. She had not heard much of their conversation. "You need to keep an eye on Aunt Pearl. She is either drunk, she's lost her mind or both! I do not intend to sit here and listen to her alcohol infused accusations! I'm leaving!" announced Sam.

After Sam flounced out of the Empire Room, JC turned to Aunt Pearl. "What in the world did you say to Sam to make him take off out of here like his tail was on fire? He looked like he wanted to kill someone."

Pearl made no attempt to stifle a giggle. "He did wanna kill thom one. He wanna ta kill me."

"Why would he want to kill you? I was aware the two of you were talking, but with all the noise and music, I could not understand more than a word here and there either one of you were saying. I didn't think you were going to confront him about what he's done until later, but you must have, so clue me in."

"Nothin' yoou need ta hear ta night, dear. Waither! Nother glass 'o red wine and maaake it sappy!" she slurred.

When the waiter appeared, JC reached across and placed her hand over Pearl's wine glass. "No more for her tonight."

Pearl waived JC's hand away. "Hell's bells!" she roared. "I'm juss gettin' staarted! Done be sucha spoil sport," she continued to slur, sending the empty wine glass toppling on its side with the sweep of her four-carat diamond ring encrusted right hand. "Aw comon JC. Looten up! Itths a par-ty 'n folks drink a lil ata part-y!" By now Pearl was hanging onto the edge of the table with both hands to keep from falling out of her chair.

JC was too glad to see Sheriff Joe Walker approaching their table. "Joe, would you do me a big favor and take Aunt Pearl home please? I think she has had a little too much to drink."

Sheriff Walker took one look at Pearl, grinned and raised his bushy eyebrows. "I would be mighty pleased to escort Miss Pearl home, JC." He held out his hand toward Pearl. "Come with me, dear lady." Pearl offered no resistance and took his outstretched hand, but it was obvious she needed help to get up and remain standing once she made it onto her feet. Aware she was about to fall, taking Joe down with her, Emilio jumped to his feet, and within seconds, he was supporting both Pearl and Joe as they slowly started to weave their way through the floor filled with dancers on the way toward the exit.

A quarter of the way across the dance floor, Joe stopped to extend his free hand toward Emilio's shoulder to steady himself. "Thank you, Mr. Vasquez. I know your father. I often buy breeding stock from his ranch down Mexico way to add to my stock. Nice place your dad has there. If I were to guess, I'd say it must be at least a couple thousand acres, maybe more." Pearl was giggling and hanging onto both of their arms for dear life in an effort not to fall.

"Nine thousand acres, sir," grimaced Emilio while trying his best to support Pearl's deathlike grasp on his arm.

"Tell you father hello for me next time you see or talk to him," said Joe.

"I will, but I think we need to get Miss Pearl out of here and into your car," replied Emilio.

"Right you are, young man." Joe turned his head to face JC. "A happy birthday to you, young lady. Nice party. Pearl, how about you and me take a little stroll out to my car?" Pearl offered an alcohol-induced giggle. "Itths been a long time thince a good lookin' feller like you assed me to geeet in his caar. Haven't been assed by 'n ugly one lately neither," she giggled. "I'm tellin' you righth up fronn I am not gettin' in the baaack seat, least not yet, 'n I don't kiss ona firss date neither!"

Joe began to blush a deep crimson. "I know you are a lady what don't do those sorts of things, Miss Pearl. Now come on, let's go while Emilio and I can still keep you standing upright!"

All of a sudden, there was a loud commotion at the back of the room near the exit door into the hallway. "Somebody get the Sheriff!" yelled a distraught man at the top of his lungs. "There's a dead guy in a car out in the parking lot!" The orchestra stopped playing. The room became deathly quiet, except for the sound of gasps.

"Emilio, you help Miss Pearl to a seat," instructed Joe. "It's probably just some drunk, but I need to check it out and make sure we aren't dealing with anything more serious. Be back in a couple minutes."

"I would be happy to assist Miss Pearl, Sheriff, but wouldn't you rather I go with you, just in case? Jose and Juan are here, and they can see to Miss Pearl and take her home." He gave another loud whistle and the two men again appeared out of nowhere. "Please take Miss Pearl home. Take JC with you to see that Miss Pearl gets to bed.

I'm going with the sheriff to investigate what appears to be a dead body in the parking lot." The two men's eyes grew large, but they did what he asked without question. At first, JC insisted on accompanying Emilio and Joe to the parking lot, saying she did not want to stay at the party, but a pleading look from Emilio made her change her mind. "Please go with your aunt. You can meet me back here near the stage later."

A few minutes later, Sheriff Walker and Emilio stood beside the BMW where the body had been spotted. "Looks like a feller can't even enjoy an evening out without some jackass getting himself killed," remarked Joe with disgust.

Emilio opened the car door, reached in and felt for a pulse in the man's neck. "He's not dead, Sheriff. I don't smell any alcohol. It looks to me like he has just simply passed out."

Joe could not see the man's face in the poor light from where he stood. "You have any idea who he is?"

"It's Sam Scott, JC's brother. It looks like he might be starting to come around. I'll stay with him if you will go back inside and get Doctor Blake to come out here and check him out."

When Sam fully revived after a couple of whiffs from an ammonia capsule administered under his nose by Doctor Blake, he kept mumbling something garbled that sounded like, "He's is dead. He can't be here!"

Hidden off in the shadows two rows over from where Sam's BMW was parked, Ross Vandenberg and his driver squatted beside the car he had rented. He found it necessary to hold a hand over his mouth and double over in order to keep from laughing out loud at the scene playing out next to Sam's car. "I said the bastard would regret the day we met, and this, along with what I did last night at Pearl's house, is just the beginning," he whispered to his heavily tattooed driver, who was also wearing black.

"Are you ready to head out now, or do you want to stick around and watch the show?" asked the amused driver before adding, "I have to admit that was one heck of a stunt you pulled on that poor bastard outside his aunt's house last night, but you topped that by what you did by scaring the bejesus out of him tonight! There is no way I could ever moan like that!"

Ross gave some thought to sticking around before changing his mind. "No, I don't think I want to stick around. I'm sure someone will call for an ambulance to take him to the hospital psych ward. But then again, I really do want to stick around to see him taken away tied down on a stretcher when he fully wakes up and starts babbling about seeing the ghost of a dead man."

"With the crowd gathering, I'd say we could even get up closer. Nobody will be paying any attention to us," said the driver.

Ross gave the suggestion more thought, but decided against it. "I don't want to take the chance somebody might remember seeing a couple of strangers dressed in black. Especially since everybody around here knows everybody else in this hick town. I think we need to move on and have more fun another day."

"You're the boss since you are the one paying me, and I can't wait to see what you will come up with next," replied the driver. In all the excitement, nobody seemed to notice as they got in their car and pulled out of the parking lot to disappear into the night.

CHAPTER 25

Jumping into his truck, Emilio followed the ambulance taking Sam to the hospital. He called JC on his cell phone to let her know what was happening. She rushed to join him in the ER after finally getting Aunt Pearl into bed, not an easy task. Pearl had kept resisting taking off her clothes and putting on her nightgown while asking where Joe was. "He had to take care of something, so I'm here," she kept telling her.

By the time they got Pearl home and in bed, she had started to sober up, but she continued to slur to her speech after three cups of black coffee. "I'm thorry, JC. I didn't mean tooo embarrass you, but damn it all! I thought I'd haaave a chance to shooow off my pretty underwear to a man, naaaamely Joe Walker. Buy the waaay, where's Joe?"

JC pretended she didn't hear what Pearl just said. She did not want her aunt to go looking for him by mentioning Joe would be staying in one of the guest rooms to check on her at intervals throughout the night. "You get some sleep. You will feel better in the morning." *But probably not that much better before late morning and a couple gallons of black coffee followed by some aspirin* were among the thoughts crossing her niece's mind.

While obviously angry with her brother, JC could not help being concerned that he had been found unconscious in the parking lot. But at the same time, she felt an obligation to make sure Aunt Pearl was delivered safely home. She was grateful when Joe said he would spend the night in the guest room and make sure Pearl was all right by checking in on her.

Two hours would pass before Pearl went to sleep and JC was able to join Emilio in the ER waiting room at midnight. Several other people sat waiting with worried faces to hear information about their loved ones also being treated for a variety of ailments. Two more hours crept by. It was now almost two in the morning. Still Emilio stayed with her, even after she told him to go to the ranch and get some sleep. He refused. He brought her tea from an automat when she said she didn't want coffee. He offered her a handkerchief when tears filled her eyes and began to spill down her cheeks. He held her hand and whispered words of encouragement. "Jose and Juan will make sure things are going all right at the ranch, and Joe Walker is staying with Pearl. They all know what needs to be done. I will stay here with you," he kept telling her.

Finally, a nurse appeared sticking her head through the doorway to the waiting area. "Is there a JC Morgan here?"

JC got to her feet. "I'm JC Morgan. How is my brother, Sam Scott?"

She motioned for JC to come closer for the sake of privacy. "Physically he is doing fine, but the doctor is worried about his mental state. Has he been under a lot of stress lately? He keeps mumbling something about seeing and hearing a dead man's ghost."

JC wanted to tell her, yes, he has been under a lot of stress because he knows he's been systematically stealing from me and not paying ranch bills, and I know it. But she didn't think revealing that information now was prudent. "He is an attorney. I can only presume his work causes a great deal of stress. Can you be more specific why the doctor is concerned about his mental status?"

"I'm sure it's because he keeps babbling about seeing a dead man's ghost."

"I see . . . Perhaps it's because he had too much to drink at my birthday party over at the Cattleman's, but then again, I didn't notice him drinking all that much. In fact, I don't think he drank anything," replied JC.

"Oh, so you are the one having the big birthday bash at the Cattleman's tonight? My boyfriend wanted me to take off work and join him, but as you can see, I had to work. Your aunt invited him and a companion, and that would have been me."

"I am sorry you couldn't make it. I'm sure the party is nice, but I haven't had the opportunity to enjoy much of it with so much going on. Please feel free to go on over and join in when your shift ends. I'm sure the party will continue until the food or booze runs out, and that won't be for hours. Who is your boyfriend?"

"Jose Rodriguez."

JC had to laugh. "Jose works at my ranch. In fact, he's at the party alone. Where did you meet him? What's your name?"

"Nancy Holt. I met Jose at that scuzzy cantina, The Lonesome Dove, about a year ago, and we started dating. Don't say it."

"Don't say what?" inquired JC.

"That I should not be hanging out at a place like that, and I don't normally. But a group of my girlfriends and I were challenged to go there on a dare, and we were stupid enough to go. Otherwise, I would probably have never met Jose, and it turns out he's a great guy."

"Nancy, you do not need to explain yourself to me. I know he's a great guy. I did some pretty stupid things when I was younger, but I don't see what you did as being stupid."

"Thank you for understanding." Nancy nodded in Emilio's direction. "By the way, is that good looking tall gentleman sitting over there with you?"

JC smiled and blushed. "Yes, he is."

"Is he related in some way to Mr. Scott?"

"No. He is my very good friend." Emilio's heart beat faster when he heard those words, very good friend. Those words allowed him to think at least they were a start to a better relationship.

"Let me see if I can find a way to sneak both of you back to see your brother. Be back in a few," and off she dashed.

Nancy had no idea how grateful JC was feeling toward her and Emilio, or that she was feeling her brother could rot in hell for all she cared. Twenty minutes passed before Nancy stood in the doorway to the treatment area again. She motioned for them to follow her down a hall to a green curtained cubicle where Sam lay restrained on a stretcher. He was hooked up to a heart monitor fastened to the wall above his head. The device made strange, squiggly heart tracings on a pale blue lighted screen, along with measuring his blood pressure and a rapid pulse rate. His hands and feet were restrained with white cotton straps to keep him from hurting himself or staff members or getting up and pulling out the IV that fed drop by drop clear solution into the vein of his left arm. He was as white as the sheet covering the lower half of his body.

"What are you doing here, JC? After what Aunt Pearl had to say in her drunken state, you are the last person I expected to see." Sam glared at Emilio. "And what is he doing here?" JC felt the anger she had been holding in check bubble to the surface. "Emilio is here with me in order to help keep me from saying or doing things I might be sorry for later! I'm here out of a sense of obligation since you are my brother, which is a lot more than I can say for you having any consideration for me as your sister or the future of the Scott Ranch!"

"You can consider your obligation fulfilled. Feel free to leave, along with that damned greaser!"

"And just when are you planning to fulfill your obligation to me and the ranch?" she asked accusingly.

Emilio placed a hand on JC's shoulder. She thought about shaking it off, but when she looked into his eyes to see the concern, she decided against taking such an action. "I don't think this is the time or place for this discussion," he told her. "Sam has apparently recovered enough to be rude, so it is time for us to leave and let the medical team and the law take over from here."

Near tears, JC stepped back and turned away from Sam. "I was just getting started, but you are right, Emilio. We need to leave. The law will take care of everything. I no longer have a brother to be concerned about anymore."

"JC, I'm sorry. I didn't mean to be rude. Please don't leave me!" pleaded Sam while struggling against the restraints. His plea fell on deaf ears. "You can tell it to the judge, Sam! You have had plenty of chances. Come on, Emilio. I need some fresh air. This room has the smell of something rotten, and we have a party to get back to and enjoy." Hand in hand, they left the ER, ignoring the pitiful cries coming from Sam pleading for one more chance.

As they walked across the hospital parking lot toward Emilio's truck, he asked, "We aren't really going back to the party, are we?"

"Why shouldn't we? Aunt Pearl mentioned the band and the Empire Room are booked until eight a.m. this morning, longer if the crowd, food and booze hold out.

People will still be dancing, drinking and laughing, even if it's now four in the morning. I don't see any reason why we should not join them. It is my birthday, or at least it was my birthday until midnight, and I can't think of anyone I would rather be with than you. Just don't get any funny ideas just because you are holding me in your arms while we dance, and you gave me the lovely white orchid with the turquoise ribbons and the gold necklace, for which I thank you."

Emilio opened the passenger side door of his truck and helped her inside. Taking a chance, he leaned in to give her a lingering kiss before closing it. To his surprise, she responded to his kiss.

"We still have the rest of the night before you turn into a pumpkin, Cinderella," was all he could think of to say.

When she could catch her breath, she answered, "You are such a lousy romantic. Come on, Emilio! Can't you come up with something more original than calling me Cinderella? By the way, the shoes are silver, not glass. I don't know why I'm sitting in your truck when mine is parked right over there, and I could drive myself back to the party."

"That is entirely up to you to make that call. I have all kinds of things I want to say to you, but only if you are willing to listen." JC realized she was being called out. She didn't know how to react to his obvious flirting or the kiss. "Just start this truck and drive," was all she could say.

Emilio did not miss the smile on her lips. "We can pick up your truck in the morning or even in the afternoon, if we decide to sleep in," he replied suggestively. JC ignored him and continued to stare out the window with a dreamy smile on her face replacing the look of anger directed at her brother.

When they returned to the party, quite a few guests approached JC to inquire about Sam's condition. After dozens of inquiries, she walked up the steps onto stage to make an announcement after the band completed a number and had not yet started another one. The room full of people became quiet. "I just came from the hospital. Sam is in stable condition. The doctor plans to keep him overnight to run some more tests. Thank you for your concern. Please continue dancing, eating and drinking. This is a party!" Everyone clapped, and when they quieted down, she turned to the orchestra leader and asked that they play something slow and romantic. He nodded, turned several pages of sheet music on the stand in front of him, chose one and held up a copy so the musicians could see it. A well-known popular piece, they didn't need copies and began to play.

"I am glad you did that," said Emilio as he drew her closer to him. "Now we can dance in peace. You are going to dance with me, aren't you?"

"I will dance with you, but only if you insist," she coyly replied.

"I insist, Cinderella," he replied with a heart melting grin.

She slid into his arms. "Would you please stop with the Cinderella bit? Didn't I tell you the slippers are silver, not glass, and I promised not to turn into a pumpkin at midnight? That hour has already come and gone."

"But you look like a princess, and I feel like Prince Charming, even if I am only a lowly cowboy," he replied while nuzzling her neck.

CJ snorted softly. "You are a lowly cowboy, my foot! When exactly did you plan to let me know just who you are? It seems everyone knows your father or you, everyone but me!"

"I would be happy to fill you in if you would give me the chance. You haven't exactly been available for any private conversations lately."

CJ's heart began to pound rapidly, and she felt warm all over as she tried to pull away. He responded by pulling her closer to his broad chest while they continued to dance. "I've not been available?" she questioned. "What are you talking about? Every time I try to find you, it seems you are off somewhere, and even the other cowhands don't always seem to know where!" she exclaimed.

Emilio kissed her forehead. "I'm here now, so start talking, dance or be quiet. I strongly suggest you dance and be quiet or I will look like a fool standing out here on the dance floor while it looks like you are giving me what for! We can talk all you want later, preferably up at the line shack when the moon is full, the stars are shining brightly, the campfire is warm and the coyotes are silent." The look of desire he gave her made her legs feel weak. JC could not help thinking about the night of passion they had shared at the line shack only three weeks ago. It sent shivers rippling down the back of her neck, then throughout her entire body. She cuddled closer to Emilio's chest humming the song the orchestra was playing: "I've Got You Under My Skin." It seemed as though her feet were not touching the floor as they swayed to the music. She knew this night would end, but at the same time, she hoped this was the beginning of something wonderful about to unfold between the two of them, even if she was a little unsure how to respond or proceed after what she had said to him up at the line shack.

CHAPTER 26

A few more days passed when nausea, again, swept over JC the minute she awakened from what had been a beautiful dream involving Emilio. She barely made it into the bathroom before vomiting into the toilet. When the dry heaves subsided, she went to the sink, ran some water and rinsed out her mouth. "I don't know what in the hell is the matter with me this past couple of days to make me throw up almost every morning," she muttered. "Too much time has passed for it to be the fried fish."

She washed her face and brushed her teeth before donning a bathrobe over her nightgown. Wandering through the house into the kitchen, she reached for the tea canister and some soda crackers. "This is a routine I can do without," she mumbled. The smell of coffee Rosa had perking threatened to send her scurrying to the hall powder room to vomit again. She took a couple of deep breaths, a bite of soda cracker, and thankfully, the urge to vomit subsided to a tolerable level.

Rosa came into the kitchen a short time later looking more than a little worse for the wear. "You got hangover, too? Nice party last night, but ooh, Rosa's head it pound like somebody hit metal feed barrel with hammer! Good thing Roberto still sleeps. Bet he have hurt in head when wake up, too!"

"Want to join me in some tea and soda crackers?" offered JC.

Rosa gently shook her head no. "I need coffee, lots 'o coffee! You probably need coffee, too. You want Rosa make cup for you?"

"I think I'll pass."

"Why you drink tea and eat crackers? You sick again?"

"I must have some sort of a stomach virus. I threw up as soon as I woke up just like I did when I ate too much fish over a week ago, and I'm tired most of the time. Tea and crackers have helped stop the nausea, at least for now."

Rosa looked at her more closely. "I know you since you born. You never sick much, only cold in nose and chest along with usual kid diseases. You play sick when not want go to school. You feel different anywhere besides stomach?"

"Not really, well maybe a little more tenderness in my breasts than usual, but that is probably due to muscle strain from lifting those large bales of hay to feed the horses when Jose is too busy to do it."

"Rosa not know how to say this, but you been with man lately?"

"Of course not!" she replied indignantly. "You know I have not been dating anyone."

Rosa pursed her lips and frowned. "When you last have woman curse?"

The question caught JC off guard. “I’m not sure. Why would you ask me such a question like that?”

Rosa busied herself at the kitchen counter fussing over preparing her cup of coffee without answering.

“Didn’t you hear my question? I asked why you would ask me such a question.”

Rosa did not turn around to face her. “You know Rosa have eight kids.”

“Of course I do, but what does that have to do with you asking me if I’ve had the curse lately? Stop talking in riddles! I’m in no mood for it!”

“If Rosa not know better she think you pregnant!” she blurted.

Standing beside the kitchen table, JC grasped the edge for support. “Pregnant! Are you out of your mind? I can’t be pregnant!” She ran out of the kitchen, across the living room and down the hall to her bedroom, shut the door and sat on the edge of the bed. “I can’t be pregnant!” she declared. After several minutes passed, she began to think back about that night at the line shack. “Oh my God, we didn’t use protection! What have we done? This can’t be happening! What in the world do I tell Emilio?” She started rocking back and forth to upset to cry while holding onto her bent knees now drawn up to her chest.

Ten minutes later, there was a soft knock on her bedroom door. When she didn’t answer, Rosa walked in to where JC was sitting, sat down beside her and wrapped her arms around the stricken woman. "Oh, Rosa, what in the world am I going to do? I did not get my period this month!"

Rosa stroked her hair. "You tell baby father that what you do. Rosa not ask who father is. She know it be Emilio. She also know it a boy. Emilio, he do right thing by you. He love you and you love him, even you not admit it."

"But Rosa, we have just become good friends since my birthday party. How is he going to react if I walk up to him and tell him he is going to be a father after only one night together?"

"He be fine with news. I see way he look at you every time he see you here on ranch. Last night at party, he look like he want to gobble you up like man starving. He love you very much. You must tell him and soon. He kind of man not want miss one minute of pregnancy."

"Oh Rosa, I wish I had your optimism. I didn't mean for this to happen. I didn't know he would be at the line shack the night I went up there in late September. It was so easy to talk to him, and I was upset about Sam and the overdue bills. The campfire was warm, a full moon and stars were shining, and well, things just sort of happened. You know Rex and I repeatedly tried to have a baby and couldn't, so I never gave a thought to becoming pregnant, nor did Emilio."

"Oh my poor baby!" she exclaimed. "You not blame self. It take two make baby. This happen nice people all the time. You and Emilio nice people make good parents. I pregnant before Pablo and I marry. Having baby only sin if baby not wanted. I know Emilio want this child. I know he want you for wife. You go take shower, dress, come back to kitchen. We talk more then. Right now, Rosa need coffee!" Rosa patted JC's shoulder and kissed her cheek. "Sickness will pass in few weeks. Then you feel real good."

After Rosa had gone, JC stared at herself in the mirror fastened to the back of her bedroom door. She could see a different look in her eyes and a glow on her skin that had not been there before. "I am pregnant," she whispered softly. "I don't need a doctor to confirm it, but I will go see Dr. Blake, just to be sure before I tell Emilio." The only doubt in her mind was how to tell him and how he would react to the news.

Every morning for the next week, Rosa asked if JC had made a doctor's appointment. Every morning after tossing her cookies, JC would tell her tomorrow. On the seventh day, Rosa was adamant. "You make appointment today or Rosa make it for you! You not be fair to Emilio or baby! You sick all the time. You need know baby not grow right if you eat only tea and crackers!" Her outburst frightened JC enough she made the call and reported back. "Dr. Blake will see me tomorrow at two. Are you happy now?"

"Rosa happy now," she beamed. "Not want scrawny baby who have colic. Rosa too old to walk floor at night carry yowling baby boy!" JC smiled. "Why you smile?" she asked. "Colic not joke!"

"I'm not laughing at you or the thought of the baby crying at night with colic. I'm laughing because you called the baby a boy again. How do you know it will be a boy?"

"Rosa just know these things. Rosa know he look just like Emilio." JC shook her head. She knew that was Rosa's stock answer, she knows these things, on almost every question she was ever asked, and she was almost always right. JC hoped she was right this time. "Now you go for walk. No more lifting hay bales. No more cleaning horse stalls. No more racing horse across pasture. No more . . ." JC held up her hand to stop her.

"I will not be coddled! Scott women have always continued living the way they always lived when they were pregnant according to my mother. To hear her talk, it was not unusual for her to pull a calf out in the pasture in the middle of a snowstorm when she was pregnant!"

"She did, but she not tell she lose baby when she pull calf, but Rosa know. You no need do that kinda thing. You got cowboys do work. Your momma didn't back then. When on walk, you think of way to tell Emilio. Now you go!"

"I will tell Emilio right after the doctor's appointment, if he confirms that I am pregnant," promised JC. "Please don't be angry with me for not telling him sooner. Every time I think about telling him, it doesn't seem like the right time."

Rosa stopped peeling the potato she had taken from the bowl sitting on her lap. "Rosa not angry with you, well, maybe just little angry for baby and Emilio. I know it not easy time for you with bad business at bank and Sam, but you need tell Emilio! He not stupid. He figure out soon you tell him or not."

"How do you know what happened with the bank and Sam?" inquired JC.

"Everyone in county knows after what crazy man Bob Wilkins say at party." She hesitated before continuing. "I need tell you I see Sam take money from library safe, too. He tell Rosa keep mouth shut or something bad happen to me and Roberto. He say it his money and I afraid, so I no say anything to nobody."

At this latest revelation regarding her brother, JC felt lightheaded. "Sam threatened to hurt you and Roberto when you saw him steal money from the den safe? That does it! I am getting an attorney and filing a lawsuit against him. What he took was not his money. It was money I earned by helping the children and their parents at the Winchester School. Money I was planning to donate back for the building project. I wasn't going to sue Sam for the other money he owes the trust fund, but that has changed! Rosa, I am so sorry he threatened to hurt you and Roberto."

"You no need say sorry to Rosa. She know long time Sam not good brother or good person!"

The phone in the den began to ring when she passed by. JC continued to let it ring in case it was Sam. She was in no frame of mind to talk to him. Rosa walked over and picked up the receiver, identified herself and listened before handing the receiver to JC.

"It a Mister Bradley at Cattleman's. He needs talk to you."

"Hello, Bradley. I've been meaning to call and tell you it was a fantastic birthday party . . . Sam did what? . . . Oh my god! He left town with no forwarding address and didn't pay the tab? . . . The bill is for two hundred and fifty thousand dollars! . . . Don't be upset. You know Aunt Pearl and I are good for it . . . I will call her just as soon as we hang up and I'll be in town tomorrow at one o'clock to settle with you if that's all right. I have an appointment at two or I will come sooner if you want . . . one will be fine. Thank you. I am sorry Sam left you in the lurch. You are not the only one he stiffed, but I think you and the rest of the county know most of the details after the incident involving Bob Wilkins at the party . . . See you at one, and thank you for your understanding. Goodbye." She felt sick to her stomach, and it wasn't the same feeling associated with pregnancy. As much as she hated to, JC knew she would have to call on Aunt Pearl's generosity, at least until she knew for sure that Clarence Mooney had made good on what he had stolen. She could not even begin to imagine taking Emilio up on his offer of financial assistance. Not with the bombshell she was about to drop on him out of the blue.

"Hello, Aunt Pearl. It's JC. I just got a call from Bradley at the Cattleman's. I would appear Sam has gone on the lam without paying the party bill and left no instructions with his secretary where he could be reached. . . .You know? . . . How? . . . Bradley called you, too? He didn't say anything to me that he talked with you, and we just spoke on the phone . . . That was thoughtful of him not wanting to upset me and that is why he called you, but that doesn't make sense since he ended up calling me . . . Yes, I am planning to meet him tomorrow at one. I can spare two thousand of the two hundred fifty thousand and pay you the rest after Mooney pays what he stole, and the trust fund check clears at the Austin bank . . . You will pay the entire amount including the florist? I can't let you do that! The party was for me, not you . . . I know I didn't arrange it, you did . . . but if you hadn't, I would have never become good friends with a certain ranch foreman we both know . . . Yes, you could say we are on very good speaking terms for now . . . Don't laugh like that! You don't need to tell me he's a good man and what a catch he would be. That's what Rosa keeps saying about him . . . Yes, I'll meet you at the Bluebonnet Café for tea and dessert at three. Sorry I can't do lunch . . . love you, too. Bye." JC sat quietly for a moment following their conversation. She could have met Aunt Pearl for lunch, but she wasn't feeling good enough due to both the morning sickness that left her feeling very tired, along with learning Sam had skipped town. "Aunt Pearl, you may get the news you may become a great aunt before the baby's daddy knows he's going to be a daddy, if Doctor Blake confirms I'm pregnant. Guess it's a good thing you like Emilio since I'm in love with him and more than likely having his baby." JC could only imagine Aunt Pearl's reaction; shock, disgust, joy or a combination or all three? The thought left her feeling more queasy than usual.

CHAPTER 27

Always an early riser, Emilio could not believe it was past seven a.m. when he awakened. The sun had already begun its ascent above the mountains off to the southeast. There were no sounds coming from the main bunkhouse adjoining his separate room. This meant the cowhands had already eaten breakfast and set about the planned activity of continuing to mend fences between the Scott and what had become his ranch. He stretched his arms and yawned, tossing aside the sheet and blanket before sitting up on the side of the bed wearing only his undershorts. He resolved facing a lot of good-natured teasing when he caught up to them. But last night had been worth it when JC invited him to join her for dinner and watch a movie afterward in the den. Three movies later had become two a.m. before either of them noticed the late hour.

"I can hardly believe I was sitting beside her until the wee hours of this morning," he mumbled. He closed his eyes, remembering the smell of her perfume, and how good it had felt when she nestled against his chest as they watched not one, but three movies in the ranch house den after finishing the leisurely dinner Rosa prepared and served before making herself scarce. He also recalled the nasty scenes with Bud Wilkins and Sam Scott. Those are two sons-of-bitches I need to keep a close eye on, he silently vowed.

After a quick shower, hair comb and teeth brushing, Emilio dressed in worn, but clean Levi's and a heavy blue plaid flannel shirt and began pulling on white calf high socks and worn brown leather calf-high boots while he thought about heading to the ranch house kitchen for a cup of coffee and some of Rosa's delicious grub with the hope of seeing JC but decided against it. He didn't want to face Rosa and what he knew would be a barrage of questions, knowing smiles and opinions. The assumption JC would still be asleep helped him make this decision. He went into the bunkhouse kitchen to find only lukewarm coffee in the bottom of the large metal unplugged pot. There was a note from Jose beside it telling him to get his lazy ass out to the fence line near where the river intersected his ranch and the Scott Ranch below the line shack. He quickly wadded up the note and tossed it in the waste basket before pouring a cup of the mud-colored liquid and put it in the microwave. While the coffee heated, he searched the cupboards and found prepackaged hard tack that would serve as breakfast instead of scrambling eggs or crisp fried bacon.

When he finished the makeshift meal, he muttered, "Guess I need to saddle up and go take a look at that fence or I'll never hear the end of it from Jose, the ranch hands or the foreman at my ranch." Almost as an afterthought he decided to strap on the holster and add the Colt 44 to his right hip. "Guess it wouldn't hurt to add the Winchester rifle to my saddle holster, too. Never can tell when they might come in handy. You never know when you might come up on a rattler, mountain lion or two-legged poor excuse for a human bent on causing trouble."

JC was up early in spite of only a few hours of actual sleep, after the late night with Emilio. It was not because she wanted to greet the sunrise or perhaps meet Emilio in the kitchen for coffee before he headed out for the day's work. It was only six a.m. when the wave of nausea swept over her like a wet blanket. She barely made it to the bathroom to stand over the toilet gasping for breath between bouts of dry heaves. When the nausea subsided, she quickly washed her face and rinsed out her mouth, then stood looking out the open window of the bedroom facing toward the bunkhouse. Emilio had stopped walking toward the ranch house and was talking to someone on the two-way radio before he turned and dashed for where Jose had earlier tied his horse. He picked up the reins from the metal rail, jumped into the saddle and took off at a rapid pace.

"I wonder where Emilio is headed for like a bat out of hell?" she couldn't help wondering out loud. Taking a second look she spotted a glimpse of the Winchester in the sheath attached to his saddle. "That means there must be some sort of trouble with one of the herds," she added. She knew coyotes had been attacking the yearlings and there had been signs of rustlers looking for strays below the line shack where the fence had been cut. She thought about riding up to the shack to make sure he didn't face any unsavory characters alone along the way. The thought was interrupted by another round of nausea and a quick trip back to the bathroom. "God, I hope this morning sickness doesn't last much longer!" she gasped. "But that's just wishful thinking since I've heard it usually lasts about three months, and I'm only six weeks along." She patted her stomach and smiled. "Hey, you in there, would you stop with the vomiting already? I don't want us to get off on the wrong foot!" Today was the day she planned to tell Emilio about the pregnancy since that hadn't happened last night. But she had a gut feeling that would probably have to wait until tomorrow.

She slipped into her jeans to find them fitting a little tighter than they were a month ago, but she was still able to fasten the button and zip the fly. The thought of riding up to the line shack persisted, but she felt an obligation to call the hospital to learn the status of Sam first, assuming he had been admitted to the psych ward two weeks ago. She checked for the hospital phone number on her cell phone and dialed. It rang four times before the receptionist answered, identifying the hospital and asking what department was needed. "I need to speak with a doctor or nurse in the Psychiatric Department, please."

"Second floor psych unit, Nancy Holt, R.N. speaking. How may I help you?"

"Hi, Nancy, it's JC. I thought you worked in the ER. I'm checking on my brother Sam . . . Oh, he checked out last week? That doesn't surprise me. I'm not surprised he took off for parts unknown."

"Sam didn't check out. He simply left without bothering to let anyone know he was leaving after conning a new orderly into taking off the restraints. I'm really sorry that happened. We were short staffed on this unit when I was called from the ER to come and give a hand. There was an incident at the other end of the psych ward that demanded immediate attention. In fact, I'm still here pulling another double shift. One of the psych nurses got hurt in the fray."

"You don't have to explain, Nancy. I'm sure Sam didn't want to stick around and have to face the music for what he has done. Please thank everyone who tried to help him . . . No, I don't want to get into a discussion about what he did. I'm sure there will come a time when everyone knows the whole story. Forgive me, but right now I'm not at a place where I can talk about it. I have to run. Goodbye."

"So, the little weasel left," JC muttered. "No wonder he didn't stick around. I hope he has one hell of a headache as a result of guilt! It's Sunday. That means I will have to wait until tomorrow to hire an attorney and possibly a private investigator to find the jerk. One attorney against another attorney . . . that should prove interesting. I hope I have the hometown edge."

Rosa was sitting at the kitchen table cradling a cup of coffee between her hands when JC appeared looking more than a little peaked. "You sick again? You look like hell." JC didn't have the energy to take the bait.

"You don't look so hot yourself, Rosa. Why don't you take it easy today? There isn't anything that needs attention that can't wait until tomorrow."

"Roberto and Rosa have really good time at party with his brothers last night. First time I ever drink like that. I like what called mudslide, so I drink three, but head don't like this morning! Give Rosa few minutes, take aspirin then fix breakfast."

"Don't bother with breakfast. Tea and crackers will do just fine but fix whatever you want."

"You tell Emilio about baby yet?" questioned Rosa.

"No, I didn't want to spoil last night while we had dinner and watched a couple of movies together in the den." She didn't mention it was movies and a little kissy face. "I was planning to let him know this morning when he came by for coffee. But he headed out for what appears to be the upland pasture before I had a chance to talk to him. I will let him know this evening when he comes for dinner, I promise." This time it was JC crossing her fingers behind her back in case that didn't happen, since she was still having trouble finding what she thought was the right time to give him the news he was going to be a father.

"Rosa see how you two look at each other and way you cuddle against his chest night of birthday party and in den. Before I leave last night, I see way you sit close when he come to house to see movie. You fool if don't tell him, and soon, or he be angry you keep him in dark too long!" To change the subject, JC asked her how her wedding plans were progressing.

"We decide put plans off until after baby born."

JC laughed. "Don't tell me you are pregnant, too!"

Rosa did not laugh. "You know Rosa too old for that happen. We wait until after your baby come. Then we have double wedding?"

"Please do not postpone your wedding. As for a double wedding, I'm not sure there will be a wedding for me and Emilio. I would never expect him to marry me just because I'm having his child."

Rosa gave her one of her famous scowls. "You loco if you no think Emilio he not marry you! How many times Rosa tell you he love and want you for wife! You more pigheaded than your father or Mr. Rex! Rosa knows you love him, too!" She shook her head and clucked her tongue. "For smart lady, you sometime very dumb! You sit. I make breakfast. You eat!"

JC knew it was useless to argue. She was able to eat part of the scrambled eggs, toast and bacon, but the coffee was a no go. She excused herself and went to the den. She wanted to check the financials one more time to make sure she wasn't mistaken about the check totals or the empty safe before moving forward with an attorney to file a lawsuit against her brother. The figures and empty safe did not lie. "This is one of the hardest things I will ever have to do . . . well maybe not the hardest . . . I had to bury our parents and my husband, and I still have to let Emilio know he will be a father, but this is not easy. After all is said and done, Sam is still my brother, even if he is a scoundrel."

Sitting in the chair at the desk where her grandfather, father and husband had sat while going over the financial ledgers, JC found herself faced with sudden tears. "When did life make a turn to take away the happiness we all once shared?" she said before taking a deep breath, closing the ledger and getting to her feet. "I can't sit here bawling calf for its mother! I have a doctor's appointment in two hours. Rosa!" she called. "I'm leaving for my doctor's appointment a little early. Do you need anything from town?"

"Don't yell! Rosa has hurt in head! No, Rose not need anything from town."

JC gathered up her purse and started out the door then across the porch headed for her truck. "That's odd," she mused. "What is Emilio's horse Blackjack doing over by the bunkhouse with his saddle still on and there's no sign of him? He would never leave Blackjack standing with the reins dragging on the ground. Guess I need to go take a look and find out why." She hurried across the lawn toward the prancing horse. "Whoa there, Blackjack. Where is your master?" Taking a closer look, she noticed dried blood on the saddle. The Winchester rifle was not in its sheath. Blackjack neighed and began to sidestep, a sure sign of agitation. "Oh, my God!" she exclaimed. "Something terrible has happened to Emilio! Rosa! Jose! Somebody help!"

Rosa came on a dead run from the house just as Jose came running from the horse barn. "What happening?" they shouted in unison.

"I'm not sure. Blackjack's saddle has blood on it and the rifle is gone. I saw Emilio talking on the two-way radio a while ago and he took off toward the mountains in a big hurry. Something has happened, and I intend to find out what that could be!"

The horse seemed to sense JC's urgency. "Take me to Emilio," she told him, springing into the saddle. He headed across the pasture at a full gallop in the direction he would usually take to the line shack. She held on to the saddle horn and reins for dear life. He barely slowed to a trot when approaching the arroyo, river or the steep unstable path up the mountain side. She pretended she did not hear Rosa shout she should not be riding like that.

She was not prepared for the terrible sight that met her eyes when she and Blackjack reached the line shack.

CHAPTER 28

Dr. Blake had been waiting in his office when JC arrived. "Thank you for coming in on Saturday to see me. I didn't want your office staff here to overhear the reason why I'm here."

"I'm sure you have a good reason for that," he replied. "Even though there are privacy laws the word seems to manage to get out." Having been her doctor since before she was born, he also had a sneaking suspicion he knew why she was here on a Saturday when the office was closed after seeing her at the birthday party. "Okay, little lady, out with it. Why are you here?" he asked kindly.

JC's face turned red, and she could not look directly at him. "I think I might be pregnant."

"Tell me why you think you could be pregnant."

"For the past couple of weeks, I've been having bouts of nausea and vomiting, especially in the morning when I smell coffee. My jeans are fitting a little more snuggly than usual, my breasts are tender, and I seem to become tired and cry more easily."

"Have you missed any periods?"

"Yes, this past month."

"Without getting personal, when do you think you could have become pregnant?"

"I know for certain it was six weeks ago. I didn't mean for it to happen."

"There is no need for you to explain. These things happen. I'm here to make sure you and the baby are healthy, not to pass judgment. Your symptoms do lead me to believe you could be pregnant, but to make sure I will need a blood and urine test along with an internal exam." He reached into a cabinet and handed her a pregnancy test kit. "You need to take this into the bathroom and pee on the strip you will find inside the package. You need to be aware sometimes these urine tests are not always accurate and don't show anything or a false positive. Bring it back out here, and we'll take a look."

With shaking hands, JC completed the test. After washing her hands, she could not resist taking a peek at the test strip she had placed on the counter next to the sink. It was a definite positive. Rosa had known what she was talking about.

"Well, it looks like you are pregnant," Doctor Blake said after taking a look at the test strip and performing a pelvic exam. "I'd say you are six weeks along, just as you suspected. That means you will be due around the middle of May. Just keep in mind babies are on their own time schedule. It could be a week either way, but I'm going to say May 15th based on what you have told me. I'm writing a prescription for prenatal vitamins." JC cringed, knowing she would have to obtain the vitamins in a location other than the Midline Pharmacy to delay rumors. Dr. Blake continued giving prenatal care instructions. "No strenuous activities. You don't need to eat for two. That's an old wives tale. We like to keep the weight gain around twenty-five pounds. Just eat healthy, take the prenatal vitamins and add an extra cup of milk a day. Sex is all right, but be careful not to get too excited. See you in a week and again every month for the next six months and then every week for the last month. Call me if you have any questions or experience any pain, vaginal bleeding, headaches or swelling of your hands or feet. You are healthy and should not have any complications. The morning sickness you are experiencing will pass in a few more weeks, but before you go, I need that blood sample." JC winced when he stuck the needle in her arm, finding it necessary to turn away at the sight of blood filling the glass tubes, but it was over quickly.

"Congratulations," said Dr. Blake. "May I give you a hug? You certainly look like you could use one."

"Yes, I could use a hug. I could also use some advice on how to inform the father."

"Just come right out and tell him. I can't imagine you having sex with someone who doesn't care a great deal about you and you caring about him. Whoever he is, he is an incredibly lucky man." Telling him is easier said than done, thought JC.

"Thank you, Dr. Blake. I appreciate you seeing me without your office staff here. They will know soon enough, and the rumors will start flying, not that there aren't already enough rumors after what took place at my birthday party regarding what Bob Wilkins had to say. Just so you know the truth before you hear any current rumors, my brother Sam and the bank trust manager have been stealing from the ranch trust fund and those of Aunt Pearl. The baby's father is Emilio Vasquez," this bit of information regarding Emilio was not what she intended to blurt out.

Doctor Blake smiled. "I know Emilio. He is a good man. As for rumors, how do you think the town gossips would survive without them? I am sorry to hear your brother and Clayton Mooney have been stealing from you. Never did fully trust Mooney, so that doesn't surprise me. Your brother, now that's an entirely different matter. Let the law handle things, and don't let it upset you. I know it won't be easy, but think about the baby and what undue stress can do. If I hear any rumors, you can bet I will do whatever it takes to squelch them. I definitely want to see you in a week for a follow up. Let's continue to make appointments on Saturday for the time being. Now, about that hug." JC left the doctor's office feeling a little better. That was until she thought about getting up the nerve to tell Aunt Pearl when they met for dessert at the café. She knew, without a doubt, it would not be easy. She was wrong.

"How in the heck do you think more than half 'o the family got here?" scoffed Aunt Pearl. "It sure wasn't due to any sort of immaculate conception! What makes you think you are so special? If your Dad's brother hadn't been shootin' blanks, I would have been pregnant long before we got married. And as for Emilio bein' the daddy, you could have done a whole lot worse. Doc Blake was right. Just come right out and tell him. I read people well enough to know he will do right by you. And if he doesn't, well I think you have a good idea what will happen next! Now, how about we order a piece of that delicious lookin' apple pie and a tall, cold glass of moo juice?"

"Thank you for understanding, Aunt Pearl," was all JC could manage to say.

Aunt Pearl smiled and patted her hand. "Just don't go thinkin' I'll be knittin' little booties and tiny sweaters. Never did get the hang of it, and I'm too old to start tryin' to learn now."

CHAPTER 29

Sam had been waiting for a chance to leave the hospital ever since he had been admitted to the psych ward a week ago. He had been able to turn on the charm and talk the new orderly into removing the restraints on his wrists and ankles. The chance to walk out came when there was a loud commotion down at the end of the long hallway that sent the staff running in that direction. He didn't waste any time exchanging the hospital gown for his clothes, except for socks and shoes. Putting those on would take too much time, time he felt he didn't have before being discovered missing. With shoes and socks in hand, he headed straight for the exit sign posted just above the emergency stairway. Fortunately, or unfortunately, the door didn't lock properly when extra personnel responded to the emergency. Less than a minute later, Sam was sitting on a bench off to the side of the parking lot putting on his socks and shoes. He checked his pants pockets and found the two hundred dollars he had placed in his wallet inside his back pocket was still intact along with his cell phone. "I still have one bar. Well, at least I can call a cab to take me back to the Cattleman's and pick up my car. I really don't want to return to my house, but I don't have a choice if I am going to get any more money for the trip to New York City. I just won't go out on the patio to take a look at the hot tub, and I'll be all right." It took an hour, but a cab finally arrived.

"Cattleman's County Club and hurry!" he ordered the driver.

"Look fella, it's after midnight and way past my bedtime. I'm only here because I was next in line to take the call. I'll get you there as quick and safely as I can, and if that isn't good enough, feel free to walk or you can wait another hour before the next sucker takes a call!" His response was surly enough it caused Sam to apologize and remain quiet throughout the remainder of the ride. He even tipped the guy ten bucks, for which the driver did not thank him. He just muttered something unintelligible under his breath and drove away, tires screeching on the club's parking lot pavement.

The keys were still under the mat in the unlocked BMW where he had left them. Music and laughter could be heard coming from the Club. Sam slid into the driver's seat after retrieving the key when he looked into the rearview mirror to see Ross sitting in the back seat. Ross had been keeping informed as to Sam's progress or lack thereof, claiming to be a close relative. He was aware Sam had walked out of the hospital due to the fact he watched him put on his socks and shoes in the hospital parking lot. Ross and his driver knew Sam would call a taxi and head for his car.

Sam screamed and let his head drop against the steering wheel. "No! It is not you! You are dead!" he moaned. Afraid and too distraught to take another look, he didn't hear the rear car door open or see Ross slip out to disappear between other parked cars.

A full five minutes passed before Sam was able to raise his head to take another look. Satisfied he had only been hallucinating, he turned the ignition key. The engine came to life, and he didn't waste any time getting out of town. Three hours later, he arrived at his San Antonio home and retrieved the house key from under the planter on the side porch. Cautiously, he unlocked the side door, refusing to look in the direction of the patio and hot tub.

"Thank God I kept some cash hidden from Ross! Had he known, he would have spent it and not have agreed to lend me the ten grand," declared Sam. He quickly went into the library to find the fake book where the cash had been stashed. The three thousand dollars was still there along with Ross's credit card Sam had put there just in case he needed it. He scooped out the money and card, tossing the fake book on the floor. Grabbing a larger suitcase from the bedroom closet, he filled it with enough clothing to last a week before carefully locking the side door after making his exit. He couldn't walk fast enough toward the BMW where he had left it parked in the driveway. He was certain he had left it unlocked with the key in the ignition, but when he tried the door, it was locked. That was when the sound of loud moaning began. Terrified, Sam raced to the side door, and with trembling fingers unlocked it and grabbed the spare set of car keys kept hanging on a rack next to the door. When he returned to the car, it was unlocked. "What the hell?" he exclaimed. But he didn't wait for an answer, jumped inside, started the motor and tore backward out of the driveway into the street, leaving a trail of black rubber on the pavement after changing gears to move forward.

Ross had hidden in the shrubbery cursing softly. "I sure wish to hell you would land somewhere! It is costing me a bundle to keep hiring this car and driver! But I guess I should not complain. It's coming out of the ten grand I didn't get around to depositing into your account, you bastard!"

In his haste to leave, Sam did not see the black Honda with dark tinted windows parked near the curb two houses away. Nor in his agitated state did he see it pull out behind him without headlights in the predawn light to follow him until they both entered the northbound freeway headed toward New York City before the driver turned on the car's headlights. Sam was so tired he didn't see the same car pull into the rest stop behind him several hours later to park with a car between them, or Ross get out of his car to follow him into the men's room just long enough to be seen before he fled. Sam's screams startled the old man taking a pee in the urinal next to him. The man gave him a funny look, shook the last few drops from his penis, zipped his fly halfway and left in a hurry without washing his hands. The old man and his car were gone by the time Sam pulled himself together enough to return to his car. Looking around, he did not see anyone seated in the black Honda Civic, Ross and his driver having huddled down far enough they could not be seen through the dark tinted windows. They waited until Sam backed out and reached the exit with a rolling stop only briefly before they slowly backed out of their parking space to follow him onto the freeway two car lengths behind.

It was rush hour when Sam pulled up in front of the Waldorf Hotel early the next morning. In an effort to save money, he waived away the parking attendant and bellman, went inside and headed straight to the check-in desk. "I would like a room for five nights," he told the sleepy clerk who had only been on duty for a few minutes.

"Yes, sir. Give me a minute to log onto my computer. I hope you realize by checking in before four p.m. you will be charged an extra day."

"I don't give a damn! Just check me in. I'm tired, and I need some sleep! I've been driving all night!"

"Would you like a single, double, two queens, one queen, king or our deluxe king suite with a hot tub on the balcony?"

It took Sam several seconds to get beyond the mention of a hot tub. "Whatever is the best deal without a hot tub. I have stayed here many times, so I know all the rooms are nice."

"Will that be smoking or non-smoking?"

"I don't care! Just check me in and give me the damned key!" Sam tossed Ross's credit card on the counter, stood back and crossed his arms.

The clerk ran the credit card. "I'm sorry, sir. The card has been declined. Would you like to use another card?" Sam extracted his credit card from his wallet and slapped it on the counter.

The clerk ran that card. "I'm sorry, sir. But this card has also been declined. Would you like to pay with cash? The charges will be three hundred ninety dollars a night, plus ten percent tax for a single room, thirty-five dollars a night for parking, and we require a three hundred fifty-dollar security deposit against any room charges when paying cash."

Sam knew he only had three thousand one hundred dollars and no way to get more cash, and he had to eat and tip the valet each time he wanted to use the car. A quick calculation, and he realized most of his available cash would be taken if he paid cash, leaving barely enough to pay for gas and snack food en route back to San Antonio with very little to spare after he checked out. "Guess it looks like I won't be checking in." he muttered. The clerk looked at him with the typical sneer of a born and bred New Yorker before Sam turned to head back across the lobby toward the door. It was then he got a glimpse of a man that looked exactly like Ross. He did his best to stifle a scream as the man gave him a dirty look, shook his fist with the middle finger of his right hand extended and melted into the crowd. The black Honda and its driver were parked behind Sam's car, but he was in no state of mind to notice when Ross got into the back seat. Sam tossed his suitcase into the trunk, got in his car and stepped on the gas stiffing the attendant. The tires squealed as he pulled into traffic at a fast clip. The Honda followed closely after Ross slid into the back seat and closed the door. With luck and speeds in excess of ninety miles an hour at times, they were back in San Antonio in less than twenty hours with only three pit stops to use the restroom, gas up and buy a bag of chips and a cup of coffee. It had taken Sam an hour longer to get home than Ross due to an accident forcing the Honda to go around him when a police officer forced a lane change. This action left Sam in the lane that had to wait before they could change lanes and move his car forward.

This delay allowed Ross to arrive at their San Antonio home before Sam. This gave him plenty of time to devise another form of terror by forming large puddles of water strewn across the patio, living room and into their bedroom. "Let's see what you make of that, you son-of-a-bitch! I can hardly wait to see your face when I hide behind the closet door where I can see you in the reflection of the wardrobe mirror and give a moan or two. I would be willing to bet you will scream like a girl and piss your pants!" And that's exactly what happened.

Sam did not hang around to find out how or why the puddles of water got there throughout the house. He only knew that he had to get out of there as fast as possible and head back to the only place he would feel safe – the Scott Ranch. “JC won’t be able to turn me away no matter what I’ve done! I’m her brother!”

CHAPTER 30

JC was almost to her car, preparing to make her second doctor's visit. "Rosa," she called. "I'm headed into Midline for my doctor's appointment. Can I get you anything while I'm in town?" Rosa stuck her head out the door to say no. "All right, if you're sure, I will see you later this afternoon."

Sitting there in her truck, she paused to remember the terrible time when she had looked in the direction of the horse barn to see Emilio's horse, Blackjack, nervously prancing and nickering outside the corral as she prepared to leave for the first doctor's appointment. Emilio had been nowhere in sight. Blackjack had not been hobbled and the reins had been dragging on the ground. Even more troubling had been the lack of the Winchester rifle in its customary sheath. That's odd, she could remember thinking. In less than a minute, she had approached the agitated animal. "Whoa there, Blackjack. What's the matter boy? Where is your master?" Then she remembered seeing the dried blood on the saddle! "Somebody help!" she remembered screaming. It had not taken Jose long to emerge from the barn where he had been mucking out stalls to respond, along with Rosa frantically running from the kitchen.

"What happen?" they had both shouted while on a dead run.

“Blackjack is here without Emilio. There’s blood on the saddle and the Winchester is missing.”

“That not good. I saddle up and find other cowboys. We look for Emilio,” declared Jose.

“He was talking on the two-way radio just before he rode out of here in a hurry earlier,” she remembered saying.

“That probably Raul he talk to,” Jose had said. “He and nine other cowboys work on cut fence below line shack. I go there now.”

“I will head up to the line shack in case he ended up there,” JC had insisted. Without waiting for any further comment from Jose along with warnings from Rosa not to ride, she had mounted Blackjack and headed out across the pasture as fast as the horse could run. She thanked God she her reckless behavior had not harmed the baby.

“JC, you no ride horse like that! You know doctor say you not ride fast!” Rosa had yelled. JC now regretted she had ignored her. She continued to sit there clearly remembering Rosa stamping her foot and swearing before heading back into the house muttering loudly. “Damn it! That girl be death of Rosa! She no listen!” JC remembered she had felt bad when she had seen Rosa cross herself and said what she believed to have been a prayer to the Virgin Mary asking for help. But her first course of action had been to determine if Emilio was in serious trouble and needed help.

In record time, JC and Blackjack had arrived at the line shack. She dismounted beside the shack on the south side. A few feet from there stood an old dark blue pickup truck with the driver's side door partially open. Below the door on the ground lay the motionless body of Bob Wilkins in a pool of clotted dark red blood, most of which had already sunk into the ground close to his middle. Without thinking, JC rushed over to find a pulse in his neck. There was none. She had looked around and saw Emilio lying face up, his upper body covered in blood. Her blood ran cold, and she had rushed to his side and began to feel faint. "Now is not the time to panic," she muttered when she approached and knelt down beside him to check for a pulse. When she touched his neck, he moaned. "At least he is still alive, but barely," she would later remember whispering softly. "Emilio, can you hear me? It's JC. Hang on. I'm going to get something to stop the flow of blood from your chest." He tried to say something that sounded like gunshot. "Don't talk, just lie still. I'll be back in a minute." She returned moments later with a blanket, two bed pillows, some towels and a plastic trash bag. She brought the plastic bag because she heard a hissing sound coming from Emilio's chest area when he had tried to move and speak. Red Cross disaster training had taught her that sound could be a sign a lung had been punctured and possibly collapsed. The area needed to be closed off to prevent further damage from diminished oxygen. She raised his head with one pillow and placed the other under his feet to form the shock position. "This is going to hurt, but I have to move you in order to wrap this towel and plastic bag around your chest," she told him. This was when she learned she was capable of far more strength than she ever imagined. Not only was she able to place the towel and plastic bag around his chest, she was literally able to drag him to a sitting position against the shack, allowing him to breathe easier when it became apparent lying flat was not helping him breathe that well. It had been a tough decision whether to treat him for shock or allow him to breathe easier. During the process she kept whispering words of encouragement. "Keep breathing. Don't you dare die on me! It's going to be all right. You need to stay strong for our child." She then reached for the Colt 44 that lay beside him, picked it up and fired three shots into the air to give a prearranged signal to the cowboys gathered below that help was needed in a hurry. This method of signaling had been done for years. There was no cell phone coverage in many areas in the mountains and this location happened to be one of them.

In less than a minute, she recalled hearing the unmistakable sound of three return shots coupled with distant hoof beats. "Help is on the way, sweetheart. Just hang in there!" Five more minutes passed feeling like a lifetime when Jose, Raul, Pedro and Zeke arrived on the scene in a cloud of dust, dismounted and headed straight for where JC was kneeling beside Emilio. They took one look at him and knew there was a serious problem. He was blue around the mouth. His head lulled to one side. He was gasping for air and barely conscious.

"What happen?" asked a wide-eyed Jose.

"I'm not sure, but I think Bob Wilkins shot him and he returned fire before he passed out. Bob appears to be dead over there by his truck, but one of you needs to go check and make sure. I checked and found no pulse in his neck, but I could have been wrong."

Raul had checked Bob's body to proclaim, "He dead all right. Gut shot get him, and he bleed out." He slowly got to his feet to join the others while shaking his head. "Emilio no can ride horse. We use truck take him to hospital? We leave Bob for coyotes!"

"We can't leave Bob for the coyotes, as much as I would like to," JC said. "We need to get Emilio into the middle passenger seat of the truck. He needs to sit there while I keep him upright so he can breathe easier. Zeke and Poncho, you put Bob in the truck bed. Jose, you drive. I'll keep Emilio sitting upright. Poncho, you take Emilio's mount back to the barn."

"It rough ride down mountain. Only deer trail. Truck old," remarked Jose, shaking his head.

"We don't have a choice. We can't drive down the mountain trail. It's too narrow, nor can we wait for a helicopter even if we could call for one. And that's only if the chopper isn't out on another call and the volunteer paramedics are available once we reach the valley floor. We don't have that kind of time! If Bob could make it up here on that deer trail, we can make it down. Let's get moving!" insisted a determined JC.

When they reached a level where there was cell phone reception, JC called Dr. Blake to alert him they would arrive at the hospital in approximately an hour, maybe less, and would he please have a chest surgeon on standby. "Emilio Vasquez has been shot in the chest," she said in response to his inquiry. "I have the bleeding under control and a plastic wrap around his chest, but his breathing isn't good. He is barely alert . . . Yes, I have him in a sitting position with a plastic trash bag wrapped around his chest . . . I had to make a choice of treating him for shock or keep him breathing. I figured breathing was more important." Dr. Blake had let her know she had made the right choice.

A surgical team specializing in chest trauma was ready and waiting when they arrived at the hospital. Emilio was quickly placed on a gurney by a nurse, two residents and an orderly before being wheeled into the ER with JC at his side. Her new nurse acquaintance, Nancy Holt, was on duty. When the hospital supervisor tried to tell JC she could not go into the treatment area, Nancy, as the ER supervisor, interceded in such a determined manner the house nursing supervisor relented, but not in a pleasant manner.

"I will deal with you later, Miss Holt!" she barked before walking away.

"Thanks for what you did, Nancy, although that woman could not have stopped me!" JC assured her. "Let me know if she gives you any trouble. I have connections with board members who wouldn't like it if they did not receive their annual support in the form of a check from the Scott Ranch."

"I never had any doubt you would be stopped, but it gave me the opportunity to put that bitch in her place. She thinks she owns this hospital! However, you are going to have to stay out of the way while we get Emilio undressed, into a gown, hooked up the monitors, get a portable chest x-ray, start an IV, administer oxygen and get blood work, including a type and crossmatch for three units of blood. What type are you in case we need blood faster than the blood bank can provide it? That doesn't mean you can't whisper sweet nothings in his ear while I check his blood pressure. I promise I won't listen to what you say, but then stay out of my way. There is a lot that needs to be done in a big hurry!"

JC remembered a feeling of more overwhelming panic when Nancy asked for her blood type. She knew she could not give blood due to her pregnancy. "Nancy, I am going to tell you something I do not want you to repeat."

"You know I am professionally bound to keep my mouth shut, so be quick about it! I wasn't kidding when I told you there is a lot that needs to be done in a big hurry!" as she continued doing what needed to be done.

"I'm six -- make that seven -- weeks pregnant."

Without missing a beat Nancy replied, "Congratulations. You can tell me all about it later, but only if you want to. In the meantime, I need to get Emilio ready for the operating room. If anyone asks, I'll tell them I asked and you don't have a compatible blood type. If need be, we can use plasma extender until blood arrives from the blood bank. It's done all the time."

Less than thirty minutes passed before JC found herself walking beside Emilio, holding his hand as he drowsily sat upright on the cart transporting him to the OR. A portable oxygen tank lay at his side fastened to the tube running into the oxygen mask covering his nose and mouth. Just before they arrived at the surgery suite doors, she saw a sign attached to one advising only hospital personnel were allowed beyond that point. She leaned over, pulled the mask aside and kissed him on the lips before quickly replacing it. "I love you," she whispered. This brought a slight drowsy smile from Emilio. "I will be here when you wake up." She gave his hand a tighter squeeze, reluctantly let go, and stood watching the cart pushed by an orderly disappear behind closed doors. Only then could she turn and walk toward the waiting room with tears in her eyes. *He has to be all right,* she told herself more than once.

It wasn't long before Rosa, flanked by six cowhands, had arrived to join what would become a seven-hour vigil. "Others be here, too, but somebody need look after ranch," said a tight-lipped Jose. "Thought you should know Sam show up at ranch. He crazy in head! Say he got no place to go and say he see and hear ghost." Jose made a circular motion around the side of his head with the index finger of his right hand to demonstrate Sam was loco. "I send him away. Hope that okay."

"You did the right thing," JC assured him. "Sam can go straight to hell! He is not welcome at the ranch. When you go back there, you can tell him to leave if he comes back again. He owns a house in San Antonio. He can go there. As for seeing and hearing a ghost, that is probably guilt playing games with his mind. I'm sure you all know by now he has been stealing from the ranch trust account since before my father and mother died and even more so after Rex died. If he refuses to leave, call Sheriff Watkins and have Sam escorted off ranch property or charged with breaking and entering if he comes inside the house, the bunkhouse or barns. I don't owe him anything! Sam owes me and the ranch trust fund a lot of money!"

"You no get upset. I take care of Sam. You need take care of Emilio and self," Jose replied.

It was with a profound sense of relief on the way to the doctor's appointment to know she was only mentally reliving that terrible day. But JC knew she had to face facts;

Emilio had been shot and was in the hospital fighting for his life, and she was pregnant with his child.

It was also with an even more profound sense of relief when the surgeon came into the waiting room later to let her know Emilio survived the surgery. "He is in the recovery room where he will be kept closely monitored until fully awake. Then he will be transferred to the surgical intensive care unit. I don't want to get your hopes up too high. He is still in critical condition and has a long way to go before we get him back on his feet. But by the grace of God, we will get him back on his feet! I'm sorry. I didn't introduce myself. I'm Dr. Brandon Barklay. Everybody calls me Dr. Bark." He then smiled. "I can assure you my bark is worse than my bite. I will be working closely with Dr. Gentry and several other doctors who will be assisting in Emilio's care when they arrive from the hospital in Houston. I might add, I've seen firsthand there is a really impressive nursing staff here, even though this hospital is sort of an outpost. In fact, you have more modern equipment here than a lot of larger hospitals where I have practiced." This news passed on an air of much needed confidence to JC.

"Thank you, Dr. Bark. I will hold you to your bark being worse than your bite. This man means a lot to me. I know you will do your best to ensure Emilio's recovery," replied JC.

Five hours later, Emilio was transferred from the recovery room into the ICU unit, and everyone, except JC, left for the ranch to get some rest. She could not be persuaded to leave. "I want to be here when he wakes up. I promised. I can shove two chairs together to make a bed here in the ICU waiting area," she assured them. "I will call Rosa if there is any change in his condition, and she can pass the word." She could not shake the feeling she had been experiencing a bad dream as she curled up between the two chairs in an attempt to sleep.

This is where Dr. Bark found her at five in the morning; half awake and in a cold sweat from, once again, reliving the nightmare. She sat up as he approached, almost afraid to ask, "How is he?"

"He is holding his own after three units of blood and some pain medication. I'm sorry, but we had to remove one lobe of the right lung. The chest tube is helping the remaining part of the damaged lung to slowly re-inflate. I understand you and he do not have a compatible blood type. Forgive me, but I can't help noticing you are in the family way. I have six kids, so I know that look. It isn't hard to tell by the way you glow when his name is mentioned, Emilio is the father isn't he?"

JC started to cry when she whispered, "Yes, he is the father, but he doesn't know yet. I haven't been able to get up the nerve to tell him. We're not married."

"I wouldn't be so sure that he doesn't know about the baby. I heard him mumble something about a baby when he was coming out of the anesthetic. Could you have said something to that effect while you were encouraging him to live? You don't have to answer or be embarrassed. Our first born arrived seven months after we were married, and he wasn't premature."

"Dr. Blake, my GP, told me babies arrive on their own time schedule," said JC. The tears had almost stopped and she began to give him a slight smile. "Thank you for having this conversation. You have no idea how much it helps."

"My pleasure, but I do need to go check on our patient one more time. Then if he's alert enough, I just might have enough pull around here to sneak you into see him for a couple of minutes, even though it isn't visiting time yet."

JC was anxiously waiting outside the automatic ICU double metal doors when he opened them and motioned for her to come inside. "Now don't be frightened by all the equipment with their beeps and squiggly lines, or if you see blood running down a clear plastic tube into a glass container from his chest and another tube carrying away his urine into a plastic bag. This is normal. I'll step over to the nurse's station so you can have some privacy. Maybe I should ask . . . you aren't the fainting kind, are you?"

"As my Aunt Pearl Scott has been known to say, Scott women do not faint! And just so you know, my maiden name was Scott. Morgan was added when Rex Morgan was my husband before he died three years ago."

"I'm sorry. I didn't realize you are a widow. He could not have been that old. What happened?" commented the doctor.

"He was trying to break a wild stallion." Her voice caught, but she continued. "The stallion won. Rex's neck was broken, and his windpipe crushed by the stallion's hooves."

"I'm really sorry that happened. I don't mean to pry. It's just that I seem to have a connection with you and that young man lying there in that bed. Let me get out of the way so you can spend a little time with Emilio. Just call out if you need anything."

JC was grateful Dr. Bark had given her a heads up about what she would encounter. Emilio, while barely awake, was able to give her a slight smile when she leaned over to kiss him on the cheek. He managed to point to his lips in a motion meant to convey that is where the next kiss should be given. She obliged after raising his oxygen mask. He surprised her when he uttered the word "baby" through his oxygen mask after she replaced it. She nodded. "Yes, we are going to have a baby. I hope you are not upset." He mouthed the word no, closed his eyes and went back to a narcotic induced sleep. This was not the way she wanted tell him he was going to be a father. At the same time, she was relieved he now knew.

"I think we had better let him rest now," said Dr. Bark. "I will arrange for you to be allowed to see him as a member of the family from now on until he is sent to a room where you can visit whenever you want."

"Thank you," replied JC. "Oh, my goodness! I need to contact Emilio's family in Mexico. Thank you for reminding me about family. I'm sure Jose or my housekeeper, Rosa, have a phone number. I know Rosa will have it. Several of her family members work for Emilio's father."

"Did I hear you say you live on a ranch?" inquired Dr. Bark.

"Yes. I own the Scott Ranch. Emilio is the foreman."

"I knew your Uncle Ira. I knew we were somehow connected. He and I had an interest in some wild cat oil strikes in the Houston area back a few years ago. He was very good at knowing when a location would end up with a productive strike. That's what paid my way through med school and helped me set up my practice, and that's how he managed to buy more land for the ranch Jeb, his brother, owned. I just knew there had to be a reason I felt that connection. Ira was a good man and that wife of his was a real joy to be around. I recall her name was Pearl. You never knew what she would say or do next. I'm sorry we lost contact over the years."

"You will undoubtedly get your chance to become reacquainted with Pearl shortly. I'm sorry, but Uncle Ira passed away ten years ago. Don't be surprised if Pearl hasn't changed all that much when it comes to saying or doing what's on her mind. I'm sure she will come waltzing in here like a Texas whirlwind giving the nurses what for if they don't do what she thinks should be done! Same goes for you and any other doctor or staff member."

"I look forward to seeing her again. That should be a real hoot!" He could not help chuckling.

"Don't say you haven't been warned," said JC.

"I will take that under consideration, but young woman, I think you need to go home, get something nourishing to eat and rest for a couple of hours. Emilio will get good care and he isn't going anywhere. You both have a long road ahead of you, and you need to think about the baby."

JC returned to her truck to sit in the hospital parking lot after a quick visit to Emilio's bedside once more to find him sleeping. She had kissed his forehead then whispered she would be back soon. After unlocking the door and getting inside, her hands gripped the steering wheel without starting the engine. "How could so much have happened in just a short time?" she lamented. "I know it should be a time for me to move on with my life and be happy; but how can I? There are so many things hanging in the balance, things over which I have little or no control."

A tap on the car's window brought her back to reality. She didn't realize she had been sitting there without the engine running for almost fifteen minutes. It turned out to be Jose asking if she was all right.

"I'm okay, just taking a walk down memory lane before I take care of some business at the ranch and come back to the hospital," she replied after rolling down the window once she realized who was standing there.

"Jose stay here in waiting room. Call you with any news."

"Do you have a phone number where Emilio's father can be reached? I need to let him know what happened."

"Si. I have number. You want me make call?"

"Thank you for offering, but this is something I should do." Before she could locate the cell phone in her purse, Jose pulled up the number and handed her his cell phone. Mr. Vasquez, while upset, was gracious in letting her know he would be coming to Texas as soon as he could arrange for his private pilot to file a flight plan and obtain permission to fly into U.S. air space and land. JC informed him they could use the runway at the ranch for landing. "Just look for the large white S painted on the side of the mountain forty miles south of Midline, Texas. I'm sure your pilot can get the co-ordinates from air traffic control in Austin once you enter U.S. air space. The Scott Ranch is well known to them. The landing strip is visible in the daytime. Just give Jose a call on this number if you will be landing at night, and he will make sure it is lit. My housekeeper's name is Rosa. I will let her know to expect you and your pilot. You are both welcome to stay at the ranch. There will be transportation provided to the Midline hospital by one of the ranch hands." Mr. Vasquez thanked her and said he was anxious to see his son.

"I look forward to meeting you. I am just sorry it has to be under these circumstances," she replied.

"Thank you again for letting me know," answered Mr. Vasquez, but he did not say he was looking forward to meeting her, something that did not go unnoticed by JC. She decided not to dwell on that fact, thinking it was due to his concern about Emilio.

CHAPTER 31

After being turned away at the Scott Ranch for the second time by the determined Rosa, Roberto, and Jose, Sam found driving back to San Antonio more difficult than he had imagined. He could not shake the feeling of Ross's hands on his shoulders while he was seated in the back seat of the BMW. At first, Sam was able to convince himself it was just his imagination, but that was before the strong smell of Ross's aftershave filled his nostrils. Then he heard the sound of Ross's voice as clear as day.

"Surprised to see me, Sam? Don't you miss the smell of my aftershave? You should. It was your favorite before you murdered me!"

"You are not in the back seat of my car! I do not smell your aftershave! You are dead, and I'm not crazy!" Sam shouted in a fit of rage and terror.

"Just keep saying that," said Ross with a cruel laugh. "Sorry, but I will have to leave you for now when you pull off at the next pullout, but you can bet every penny of that two hundred fifty thousand dollars you planned to collect I will return! In fact, I will keep returning until you go completely insane! That's the price you have to pay for murdering me!" Sam was afraid to take another look in the backseat, so he kept his eyes glued to the road, sweat pouring from his forehead making his vision blurry. "I'm not crazy! I'm not crazy! Ross is dead! Ross is dead!" he kept repeating before pulling to the side of the highway to clear the sweat from his eyes with the back of his hand and catch his breath before continuing on. In his current state, Sam had no idea the car pulling off the road behind him was the car and driver Ross hired to whisk him away when he made his exit from Sam's car.

When Sam arrived at the San Antonio house, he entered via the side door. Curiosity made him take a quick glance through the double glass French doors leading out onto the patio where the hot tub was located. He thought it was strange there was no yellow tape surrounding the perimeter authorities usually place around an area at the scene of an accident or a death, but he was confused and much too exhausted to dwell on it. He walked into the kitchen hoping to find something to eat. Finding little beyond a cold slice of stale pizza left in a box sitting on the counter he did not remember leaving there, along with empty bottles of exotic beers and two half full bottles of white wine in the refrigerator, there was nothing else to eat. He ate the slice of stale pizza and ended up chugging two bottles of beer, one after the other, in the hope they would help him sleep.

He could not bring himself to sleep in the bed he had shared with Ross. Instead, he ended up going to one of the guest rooms on the second floor. He threw back the covers, kicked off his shoes and crawled in still wearing his clothes. He had been asleep for less than an hour before there came a scratching sound at the door of the guestroom that grew louder and louder. “Let me in,” pleaded the familiar voice. “It’s cold out here.”

“Go away!” screamed Sam. He got out of bed to check and make sure the bedroom door was locked, along with adding a chair back propped under the doorknob for added security before returning to bed.

“I’m soooo cold,” moaned the voice. “The cleaning woman turned off the heater to the hot tub and the metal drawer at the morgue is soooo cold. Do you know they drained all my blood and put my guts in jars of formaldehyde? It was humiliating being hacked up that way. You have to let me in!”

Sam covered his head with a pillow and put his hands over his ears, but that did not stop the sound of the voice continuing on until daylight, leaving Sam in such a state he could only lay there violently shivering with his eyes closed, pretending he did not hear anything.

CHAPTER 32

When JC returned from the ranch a short time later, seventy-two hours had passed since Emilio was taken from surgery, five of those hours having been spent in the recovery room. JC spent much of this time in the hospital chapel praying between quick visits to the waiting room to meet with members of the ranch staff every fifteen minutes or so to be given updates by the nurses regarding Emilio's condition.

It was on this particular visit she found Aunt Pearl stretched out between two chairs that had been shoved together to form a makeshift bed. It was three in the morning. Someone had given her a pillow and a sheet. "I wonder how she found out so fast," she mumbled. "I hope she doesn't try to take control and end up alienating the doctors and nurses," she said to Jose. The sound of her voice awakened Aunt Pearl who sat up slowly, tossing the pillow on the floor. If the look on her face was any indication of her frame of mind, JC knew she was in for a tongue lashing.

"Why in the hell didn't you call me? I had to hear about this from Rosa? She's all upset that you rode off like some wild Indian on Emilio's stallion! I could barely understand her when she told me what happened! If I hadn't understood the word hospital I would still be in the dark! You need to explain yourself this minute, young lady!"

“I didn’t think you needed to know until I knew for sure what was happening,” replied JC. “Please don’t be angry with me. It has been a very long night, and I don’t want to listen to you blaming me for not calling you. In case you didn’t know, I’m the one who found Emilio severely wounded and Bob Wilkins dead at the line shack! I haven’t had much sleep in the past seventy-two hours, and I don’t want to end up saying anything I might later regret, and I hope you don’t either!” JC could hardly believe she had just stood up to Aunt Pearl.

“I should not have yelled at you,” agreed Pearl. “I’m sorry. It’s just that I am so worried about Emilio.”

“We are all worried, but that doesn’t give you the right to jump all over me or anyone else, including Dr. Bark when he makes his patient rounds.”

Pearl’s face lit up. “You can’t mean Bark Barklay? It has to be the one I knew way back when. Why, I knew that old devil back in the day when he and Ira were wildcatting oil wells together down Houston way before he went off to med school.” She had her back to the waiting room door and did not see the good doctor enter the room.

“The only and only,” said Dr. Bark with a grin. “Hello, Pearl. It’s been a long time. Looks like the years have treated you kindly. I’m sorry to hear about Ira’s passing. Why don’t you come and join me in the doctor’s dining room for some breakfast and a cup of coffee so we can get reacquainted?” The two embraced and he was able to give

JC a wink over his shoulder indicating he would take over with managing Pearl.

"Why, that's a great idea, Bark," she replied. "That's unless JC needs me here."

"No, by all means go have breakfast with Dr. Bark," JC assured her.

"You can join us, JC, or if you would like, I can bring back a tray for you," offered Dr. Bark, knowing what her answer would be.

"I'll take the tray. No coffee, please. Tea would be great. You two have a lot of catching up to do, and I want to be close by here in case there is any news about how Emilio is doing." While Pearl was getting her bearings and gathering up her mammoth black leather purse, Dr. Bark winked at JC again to let her know he would get and keep Pearl under control. "Thank you," she mouthed silently.

"Just so you know, my partner from Houston is with Emilio as we speak," he said. "He is every bit as good as me when it comes to post-op care."

"That sounds like something you would say," said Pearl, grinning when she said it. "Bark never did have the least bit of humility, but that's why we got along since I can't say as I do either. Come on, you old dog, let's get us some vittles. Seein' as how you are a doctor makin' big bucks, you can pay for our breakfasts while we catch up!"

"You are on," laughed Bark while offering his arm to escort her out of the waiting room. JC breathed a sigh of relief as the two of them disappeared beyond her line of sight.

"I sorry I forget tell Rosa she not call Miss Pearl," said Jose who had remained silent in the background, now in obvious distress.

"It's all right, Jose. She would have found out sooner or later. I can only hope Dr. Bark is able to keep her under control. I love my Aunt, but you know how outspoken and controlling she can be. She means well, but sometimes she goes a little too far."

"She good lady," remarked Jose. "She help lot of people and no say anything. I one of them. She pay for my mother's care when she sick and I no have money to pay doctors. She pay for me make trip to Mexico to see Momma, too, and no let me pay back."

"I thought we paid you well enough to be able to live comfortably and take care of such matters," said JC.

"You do pay good, but seven young ones to feed back home and Poppa, he die three years ago same time Mr. Rex die. I send most of pay to Momma so she can take care for family."

"I wish you had told me. I would have helped."

"Jose know ranch in trouble after Mr. Rex die and Sam take money and supplies cut. I no ask Miss Pearl for help. She somehow know I have need and come to me. Just like Rosa, she know things."

"That doesn't surprise me that Aunt Pearl would know more about what is going on at the ranch than I do," responded JC. "Please, Jose, if any of you have a problem with anything, let me know. Don't wait for me to ask. I am so ashamed I have allowed my grief to cloud the needs of others."

"You no think like that! You good lady. You have hands full with ranch. Sam not help and now you have worry about Emilio."

"It may take a while, but things will get better," she assured him. "I want to thank you and the rest of the cowboys for sticking by me and keeping the ranch running. You will all get raises just as soon as the money from the ranch trust fund is settled in the Austin bank."

"None of us plan move on," he strongly replied. "We like family, an family take care 'o family, unless they like Sam. Jose like take him out back of barn and teach lesson with fists and horsewhip!"

"Thank you, but that will not be necessary. The law will take care of Sam," she sadly replied. "Please don't you or any of the other cowhands do anything stupid. I would hate to see any one of you in trouble with the law. Sam is not worth it!"

CHAPTER 33

Dr. Bark's partner stuck his head out of the ICU door asking for JC Morgan. Her heart felt as though it was in her throat when he called her name. She could barely speak to identify herself. "I'm JC Morgan."

"Hello. I'm Dr. Arthur Jackman, Dr. Barkley's partner. Please step inside." He opened one of the double doors wider allowing her to pass. "I just checked on Mr. Vasquez. He is running a fever, but that is to be expected. The antibiotics should take care of it in about thirty-six hours. The chest tube is draining well, and the remaining right lung seems to be expanding, but I will order another chest x-ray to check on its progress. He may need another unit of blood, but I won't order that until the lab work comes back and I can check his hemoglobin level. Are any of you type AB Negative? This type is hard to find since only fifteen percent of the population have that blood type. It would make it a lot easier if one of you have that type." At that comment, JC paled. Three of the cowhands let Dr. Jackman know they would volunteer to be tested to see if they qualified for the blood transfusion should it be needed. Then she remembered Dr. Blake had done a blood test on her first visit to his office that would include this information, and if the AB Negative factor was present, she felt sure he would have mentioned this to her. But she would ask in case he forgot to mention it.

Dr. Jackman nodded toward the three volunteers. "We should know the results of whether one of you is a match in about two hours. Come with me, and we will go to the lab right now and take care of this matter. Ms. Morgan, I suggest you go home, get some rest and a decent meal. Emilio will be taken care of by a very competent group of nurses. I'm sure he will be sleeping during the time you will be gone. He just got a shot of pain killer." This left JC to assume he knew she was pregnant when he did not include her in the blood testing.

"Please call me JC. That's what everyone calls me," she offered.

"All right, then JC it is." But he did not offer to be called by his first name.

Sitting in her truck in the hospital parking lot, once again, JC gripped the steering wheel, until her knuckles turned white. Once again, she did not start the engine. She knew her odds of having type AB blood were slim to none with only a fifteen percent chance of that happening. She wanted to lean her head forward on the steering wheel and cry but recalling Aunt Pearl's earlier words after being told Sam was gay, 'tears don't solve nothin', kept echoing in her head stopped her. Instead of crying she uttered a prayer. "Dear God, please let me be the same blood type as Emilio. I don't think I can go on if something were to happen to him or this child. You have taken my parents and my husband. Please don't take Emilio or our child. Please be merciful in the face of what we did without the benefit of marriage. I know this baby will be loved, cared for and brought up knowing the values I allowed to lapse in moments of weakness." A tap on the window ended her prayer.

"Miss, are you all right?" asked the stranger.

She rolled down the window several inches. "I'm all right, just tired."

"I'm sure you are exhausted. I was also in the ICU waiting room while you were. I couldn't help overhearing the news about your husband or glancing his way when I walked past his cubicle to see my wife. I will say a prayer for his recovery." JC did not correct him about the fact Emilio was not her husband.

"I will do the same for your wife," she responded.

"She didn't make it," he replied. "Please say a prayer for her anyway, and me too." There were tears in his eyes as he walked away. He didn't hear her say she would pray for them or see that she started to cry. Brushing away her tears, she started the truck's engine, backed out of the parking space and headed for the ranch. The unusually warm fall day accented the few remaining colorful leaves still hanging on the tree lined streets in town. Out on the open ranchland covered in creosote bushes and cactus here and there, the distant snowcapped mountains glistening in the sun at any other time would have allowed their beauty to captivate her. Today none of it registered.

Her mind was focused on what she could do to help Emilio recover and the child growing inside her body. The angry sound of a blaring horn brought her back to the task at hand. She had drifted into the oncoming lane without realizing it. She over corrected. This sent the truck skidding off the pavement into a shallow ditch lined with a few struggling bluebonnets as sand and gravel flew. She was wearing her seatbelt, but the accident left her stunned. The driver of the pickup truck skidded to a stop, backed up close to her truck and rolled down his window.

"You stupid bitch!" he screamed. "You could have killed us both! Why don't cha learn how ta drive or stay off the highway!" He didn't ask if she was hurt or offer to help, rolled up his window and sped away leaving JC to figure out how to get the truck back onto the highway. There were no other vehicles in sight. It took several minutes, but she was able to rock the truck back and forth by shifting gears backward and forward until she was, once again, headed down the road toward the ranch a little un-nerved, but otherwise apparently unhurt. The tall pine posts at either side of the ranch entrance emblazoned with the circle S bar brand burned into the sign hanging from the crosspiece never looked to good.

Rosa appeared beside the truck before JC could open her door. "Why you cry? Is Emilio okay?" were the first words out of her mouth. JC slid out and into her familiar arms willing herself not to continue crying. It was good to feel the comfort of a familiar body.

"Emilio is doing as well as can be expected. One of his doctors sent me home for a meal and some rest." She didn't mention the accident due to the embarrassment of having caused it.

"You come inside. Rosa just cook big pot chili and make chalupas. I feed you good. You get shower, then bed."

"You won't get any argument from me. Just don't let me sleep too long. I want to get back to the hospital before Emilio wakes up and realizes I'm gone. The morphine they gave him puts him out for about six hours after each dose. He was given one just before I left. That means I've got about four hours before he wakes up, and one of those remaining hours will be spent driving back to Midline in addition to the one it took me to get here."

Rosa frowned. "You need more sleep time. Not good for baby you no sleep."

"I can sleep at the hospital. My nurse friend, Nancy Holt, is making arrangements for me to use a bed in the nurse's lounge. I need to be there every time Emilio wakes up and asks for me."

"He need learn you no be there beside bed every time he wake up. Rosa know he concerned about you and baby, but he need know you need time for self."

"Right now, he doesn't need to be concerned about either one of us. His energy needs to be focused on getting well! I will be the one concerned about the baby's welfare. Please stop coddling me!"

"You come eat," was all Rosa could say.

Just to be on the safe side and not rely on Rosa, JC set the alarm on her clock radio for two hours after eating. Climbing into bed, she was asleep before her head hit the pillow.

CHAPTER 34

Emilio was semi-awake when JC returned to the hospital. He attempted a weak smile when she entered his cubicle of the ICU unit. "I missed you," he said, his voice slow and somewhat slurred. "I wanted to tell you about the most beautiful dream I had before you left. There was a lady who looked like an angel bending over me. She kept telling me I had to live because I was going to be the father of a son. Can you imagine that – me the father of a son?"

JC felt as though her heart would jump out of her chest. *He doesn't know. He thinks what I said was just a dream, and here I thought he knew.* "I think you would be a good father," she told him. "I am sure it was just a dream due to the pain medications you are receiving." She knew she should have told him the truth, but she could not bring herself to tell him under the current conditions.

"But it seemed so real," insisted Emilio. "When I get well, we could get married and make that dream come true."

JC swallowed hard before answering. "Are you sure you want us to get married and have children?"

"I have never been more certain of anything in my life!" was his weak but fervent reply.

"But what would your parents, the rest of your family and friends think if you married a widow who happens to be a gringo to boot? Just so you know, I made phone contact with your father. He will be flying to the ranch as soon as possible."

"Thank you for calling my father. If he and my mother knew that gringo was you, they would be delighted. They know all about you from my letters and phone calls." He failed to mention he had not used her name, only that she was the woman of his dreams. His parents had questioned him, but he steadfastly refused to give them a name. "I will tell you when the time is right," he kept telling them.

JC made a quick, on the spot decision. "I think it is time to let you know I was the person who told you that you were going to be a father," said JC. "I'm pregnant with your child. Rosa tells me it is a boy, but I would never expect you to marry me just because I'm pregnant."

A dark look passed across Emilio's face. "What do you mean saying such a thing? Of course we will be married! I love you, and I want this baby to have my name. I want to be a father and a husband, but I won't force you into a marriage you do not want." His heart monitor began to beep displaying a crazy irregular beat, and he started violently coughing. Warning bells started to ring. This brought his nurse rushing into the cubicle.

"Please step out into the waiting room," she instructed JC. "I need to find out what's happening. I will let you know when you can come back again."

Several minutes passed when there came a call over the PA system. "Code blue in ICU! Code blue in ICU!" This was followed by the rush of several people dressed in blue scrubs JC recognized as responders to a patient in dire respiratory distress. “Please don’t let it be Emilio,” she kept praying. “I didn’t get the chance to tell him I love him and want to marry him.” She sat unable to move in the waiting room chair. Ten minutes passed. Twenty minutes passed. Thirty-seven minutes passed when the code blue team walked silently out of the ICU unit, every one of them with a look of defeat on their faces. “Oh, no! Please, someone tell me Emilio did not die!” she whispered as tears began to stream down her face. “Rosa was right. I should have told him sooner about the baby and how I felt.” She was so distraught she failed see Emilio’s nurse approach her chair.

“You can come back in now, JC. Emilio has stabilized and is asking for you.”

“But I thought . . .”

“The code blue was for another patient, not Emilio, but he was upset about something and had to be given medication to calm him down. Otherwise, he is stable, but he will be sleeping for a couple of hours. I suggest you take that time to get some rest. Your friend, Nancy Holt, let me know there is a bed ready for you in the nurse’s lounge. She has been checking regularly on Emilio and will let you know if there is any change.”

“Thank you, God, for sparing him,” JC whispered. “And thank you, Miss Conners. Would it be all right if I stepped inside his cubicle for just a minute before I go?” The nurse gave her approval, and JC tiptoed past the cubicle curtain to stand looking down at the sleeping man. “Sleep well. I love you. When you wake up, please don’t be angry with me,” she whispered before reluctantly leaving the bedside of the man she had grown to love and was able to admit without the feeling she was betraying Rex.

CHAPTER 35

The ringing of her cell phone awakened JC. Awakening in the nurse's lounge made her disoriented, so the phone call went to voice mail before she could answer. Her watch told her it was ten a.m. She was annoyed that she had overslept. She struggled to sit up, pressing the appropriate phone button to bring up the message. It was from Rosa.

"Dr. Daniel Preston call you from New York City. Rosa tell him you not here. He say it very important you call him back pronto. He leave phone number." JC rummaged through her purse for a pen and some paper to jot down the number and name before she forgot them. "I wonder who he could be?" she questioned. "I don't know any doctors in New York. Maybe it's someone Dr. Bark is consulting with, so guess I need to return his call. But first I need some of that brew they call coffee, then again maybe not." She got up, slipped into her shoes and walked to the kitchenette to open several drawers before finding some badly wrinkled tea bags and coffee-stained individual packages of sugar. Adding tap water to a heavy-duty paper cup along with the tea bag, she placed it in the less than clean microwave and set the timer for two minutes. When the microwave dinged, she removed the cup, automatically added sugar and stirred it with a wooden stir stick. She had to settle for dried off white colored powder masquerading as cream. Taking a cautious sip of the hot liquid, she walked back and sat down on the edge of the bed, picked up her cell phone from where she left it lying on the pillow, and dialed the number Rosa left on the voice mail message.

"Thank you for calling Mt. Sinai Medical Center. How may I direct your call?" asked a pleasant female voice.

"I'm not sure. I received a phone message that a Dr. Daniel Preston was asking that I return his call as soon as possible."

"That's Dr. Dan, Chief of the psychiatric division. Who should I say is calling?" JC gave her name. "Please hold while I connect you to his office."

The wait listening to elevator music left her with time to wonder who and why a doctor would call her from Mt. Sinai psych unit? She didn't know a soul in the entire state of New York. The two minutes of music did little to answers those questions. It did raise her level of anxiety.

"This is Dr. Preston. May I ask who is calling?" said a pleasant deep male voice.

"Joyce Morgan. I'm returning your call. It was taken by my housekeeper, Rosa."

"Ah, Mrs. Morgan, you are a hard one to track down. Glad we finally made a connection. We found your name, phone number and address in Sam Scott's wallet after he was admitted here, but the phone number was obliterated by something spilled on the paper."

"Why are you calling me? My brother and I do not have a relationship for a very good reason."

"I'm very sorry to hear that, but you are his next of kin, right?"

"You could say we have a biological connection since he is my biological brother. But I'm sure you are aware you cannot choose your family and you can choose your friends. I choose friends over him being a part of my family."

"Would you care to elaborate why?"

"Not really. It's a long, sad story, and I don't have the time or inclination to go into the details. I am right now sitting in the Midline, Texas hospital ICU waiting room praying someone near and dear to me does not die." While not exactly the truth, she didn't want to go into her sleeping arrangements in the nurse's lounge.

"I understand, but . . ."

"No, you do not understand. You have no idea why I no longer have a brother who will undoubtedly end up in prison when or if he returns to Texas."

"Prison? Does that mean he is a fugitive?"

"I don't know if fugitive is the correct word. Law enforcement have not yet been able to serve him with a warrant for his arrest since he takes off whenever he feels them getting close. I believe he keeps ending up in psych wards in an effort to evade taking responsibility for what he has done."

"Does that mean he has been hospitalized for mental problems before?"

"Yes. He walked away from the psych ward here at the Midline, Texas Hospital over a week ago leaving a lot of debt and unanswered questions behind. Debt our aunt and I feel we are responsible for to make good. In case you are wondering, he has led the life of a gay playboy, squandering his inheritance while stealing a large amount of money from me and our aunt. I think I've said enough. You are now his doctor, so it is up to you to determine if he is legally sane and able to stand trial. Let me know as soon as you make that determination so my attorney, along with the judge and jury, can take appropriate action to force him into taking responsibility for what he has done."

JC heard a loud sigh through the connection. "I guess that means you will not be making a trip here to help him return to his right mind?"

"There is no guessing. I will not be coming to New York! I have bent over backward to help him in the past, and for that he lied and stole from me. Unless you have anything further to discuss, such as regarding the weather in New York, I am ending this conversation. Just be sure to let me know about his mental state with regard to him standing trial."

"Please don't hang up! Is there another close family member I could contact who would be willing to make the trip here?" asked Dr. Dan.

"Only our aunt by marriage, Pearl Scott." she replied cautiously.

"May I have her phone number?"

"I will have to check with her first. If she is interested in helping, she will call you. Goodbye."

Nancy Holt stuck her head around the screen put in place for privacy in the nurse's lounge to find JC sitting on the bed staring at the floor in deep thought, a full cup of lukewarm tea in her hand. "Should I stay, or would you rather I didn't?" she asked.

"Pull up a chair and join the pity party. I just got off the phone with a doctor at Mt. Sinai Medical Center psych ward in New York. Seems as though he had high hopes I would come there to help with the recovery of my brother, Sam."

"You aren't going, are you?"

"What do you think?"

"While I am not aware of the whole story, if it were me, I think it would be a definite no based on what I do know," offered Nancy.

"Glad we're on the same page," replied JC. "Is there anything new with Emilio before I get dressed and go back to his bedside? I need to be forewarned. I don't think I can stand much more bad news right now."

"I checked with his nurse about half an hour ago. The good news is they are planning to pull the chest tube today. What remains of the injured lung appears to have re-inflated according to the latest x-ray."

"And the bad news is?"

"He is still running a high fever, so they are changing his antibiotic. He is a little loopy with the fever, pain and narcotics. He keeps telling his nurses he saw an angel who told him he is going to be a father. Am I right in thinking you could be that angel?" When JC didn't answer she added, "You don't have to answer unless you want to, but I do think you need to go back to Emilio's bedside, and when his temperature goes down and he doesn't need another pain shot, you need to clue him in about the pregnancy. That poor man doesn't need to lie there thinking he might be crazy, and his nurses don't need to be dealing with that thought as well."

"Oh Nancy, I've made such a mess of things! I have kept putting off letting him know about the pregnancy. The time just never seemed right to tell him. Then I thought he knew after I said something when I shouldn't have. Now I know I was wrong, but it has taken me almost losing him to realize just how much I love him. I keep begging God to spare him, but it's been over a week since he was shot, and things don't seem to be looking up all that much. Are we being punished because I got pregnant before marriage?"

"God does not work that way, and you know it! So, stop with that line of thinking right now! Emilio was shot by a crazy drunk who thought by blackmailing you into marrying him he could gain control of your ranch, and when that didn't work, he went gunning for Emilio since he saw him as competition. Thank God the bastard got himself killed in the process! That will save the taxpayers of this county a lot of money by not having to go through a trial for the likes of that loser!" The anger in Nancy's voice was unmistakable when she was referring to Bob Wilkins.

"Speaking about a trial, have you heard anything about the Grand Jury investigation? Sheriff Walker hasn't been able to question Emilio about what took place. The only information he has is what I was able to gather from coming on the scene and telling him."

"If I were you, I wouldn't worry about it. Everyone knows Bob Wilkins was a loser with a bad temper. Why else would he have sneaked up to the line shack in a pickup truck on a deer trail except to kill Emilio? He sure as hell didn't go up there with a loaded gun intending to play a game of cards while shooting the breeze and drinking a few beers with him!"

"You are probably right, Nancy. But I won't feel relieved until they meet to make a decision it was justifiable homicide, and they can't do that until Joe Walker interviews him for his side of the story, and only God knows when that will happen."

"Emilio is a strong person. He was healthy and in good shape before being shot. If I were a betting woman, I'd bet he will make it through this with flying colors. That's not to say it won't take time. He lost a lot of blood and will have to deal with diminished lung capacity from the wound and surgery, but that should be minimal in the long run. The body is amazing in its regenerative power."

"What kind of time are we talking about before he's back to normal? A month? A year? Several years? I have a ranch to run. He is -- make that was -- the foreman. That means I will have to replace him, at least temporarily, to keep the ranch running smoothly." Saying she would have to replace Emilio opened the flood gates. Nancy sat down beside her on the bed and put an arm around her shoulder and let her cry for several minutes before speaking.

"I know it isn't easy, but it's a fact of life you need to face. Emilio will understand. He knows what it takes to manage a large cattle ranch. Did he ever mention the name of one of the cowhands being management material should he ever become sick or incapacitated?"

"Jose," was the only person JC could name. "He is the one Emilio usually gives orders to and he then relays them to the other cowhands when Emilio is tied up. You know he speaks and understands relatively good English since you and he have been dating. I would say he is very smart but has never had much in the way of a formal education. His only drawback is a temper when he thinks someone is making fun of him when he speaks broken English."

"Aren't you some sort of a teacher as well as a ranch owner? So, what's to keep you from providing Jose with more education if he is willing to learn?"

"I guess nothing, but he has to understand him being foreman is only temporary until Emilio recovers enough to resume being in charge, and he can't let his temper get the better of him."

"Make that clear from the get-go and see how he reacts before borrowing any trouble. I will be happy to reinforce him controlling his temper every time we see each other should he have plans to continue our relationship, and I don't have any reason to think otherwise," said Nancy, her cheeks flushing a bright pink remembering the last night they had spent together. JC offered her thanks for her offer to help, but it did not take away her anxiety completely.

"Then there's the possibility other ranch hands may think they are more qualified to be the foreman than Jose, especially the gringos. There is one in particular who may raise a fuss and walk away," she said. "I know this man and Jose have had words in the past."

"So, he walks away. It isn't like you won't be able to find someone to take his place. The Scott Ranch is known for how good it treats and pays its cowboys. I'd bet his boots would be filled within a day or two at the most."

"Thanks, Nancy. You have a way of putting things in perspective. I'm sorry I'm being such a pain."

"If it were me in your shoes, I'd be under the bed crying instead of sitting on it. My God, woman! You are pregnant, your brother and the bank manager have been stealing from you, and the man you love, the father of your child, has been shot! That's enough to make a grown man cry!" Nancy took the cup of tea, now cold, JC continued to hold in her hand. "Let me warm up that tea while you wash up and get dressed. Bathroom is just beyond that door. You can't let Emilio see you without your hair combed and some lipstick. You don't want him to have second thoughts about seeing an angel when you walk into his cubicle."

"Nancy, you are the best new friend I could ever want," declared JC.

Nancy wrinkled her nose and gave a snort. "You haven't seen me in action when I'm angry, sleep deprived, hungry or some jerk tries to put unwelcome moves on me in a bar. I turn into a total hellion with a mouth worse than a longshoreman and horns bigger than some of your longhorn steers."

"I somehow doubt that," replied JC.

"Don't doubt a sure thing. Just get your butt in gear and get yourself ready to greet your man. I'll leave your warmed up tea on the counter. I need go get back to raising hell in the ER. There's a new rotation of interns, and I need to keep them running scared. See you at the end of my shift if you are still here and haven't gone to the ranch for some rest and decent food. Sorry to say our chef cooks like he's been out on the trail a little too long." She was out the door before JC could respond.

Leaning back against the pillow, JC could not even cry. "Why me, Lord? Why Emilio? Was what we did so terrible we must be punished?" Five minutes passed before she sat up and picked up her phone. "I hate to do this, Aunt Pearl, but it looks like my only option is to call you."

"Pearl Scott," said the familiar voice.

"It's me, JC. I just spoke with a psychiatrist, a doctor by the name of Daniel Preston, at Mt. Sinai Hospital in New York. It seems Sam is now a patient there. How he got there I don't know. Rosa took the call and sent me a voice mail with his phone number. I called to find out he wanted me to come to New York to help with Sam's recovery. He seems to think seeing a familiar face might bring him out of whatever is going on inside his head. I turned him down for obvious reasons. He then asked if there was another close relative who might lend a hand. I mentioned your name. He wanted your phone number, but I said I would give you his number, and if you wanted to get involved, you would call him. I hope that's okay with you."

"Of course it is, honey. You leave Sam to me," said Aunt Pearl. After they ended their conversation an evil smile played across Pearl's face. "I was wondering how I was going to get even with you, Sammy Boy, you good for nothing spoiled brat!" She picked up the phone again and dialed the number JC had given her. "I need to speak with a Dr. Daniel Preston in the psychiatric division as soon as possible." The elevator music played only a short time before a friendly male voice responded.

"This is Dr. Preston. How can I help you?"

"Daniel Preston, this is Pearl Baxter Scott. You and I shared several college classes back a few years ago, along with a couple of dirty jokes and more than a few beers at the local watering hole just off campus."

"Pearl Baxter! I remember you. Gosh, it's been a long time! You know you broke my heart when you married Ira Scott, don't you? How are you both doing these days?"

"I'm doin' fine, thank you, but Ira passed away nigh onto ten years ago. I'm livin' in a hick town by the name 'o Midline, Texas -- by choice, I might add. I understand you just spoke with my niece, Joyce Morgan, concernin' her brother, my nephew by marriage, Sam Scott. The question is what can I do for you?"

"That's true. I did ask Mrs. Morgan to come to New York to help with her brother's recovery. She declined, with what it sounds like a good reason. I thought it would be a good idea for her to come here and help us get to the bottom of his mental state, but now I'm not so sure that was such a good idea. I had no idea you were related to Sam."

"Well, sadly I am related to him by marriage, but I don't have any intention of traipsin' all the way up to New York to help that poor excuse for a human bein'!" She paused briefly, "I want you to ship his sorry ass back down here to Midline, and I will take on the responsibility for gettin' him the help he needs at a good sanitarium."

"But Pearl, that would cost a fortune, even if the powers that be here will agree to it."

"I don't give a rat's behind how much it would cost! Just make it happen. I can afford it. We have some pretty damn good head doctors down here, too, and I know just the place to send him for help. I'll have an ambulance and nurse waiting to transport him there the minute he lands at the Austin Airport. And if it takes a sizable donation to help put up another wing on your hospital to make that happen, I can handle that, too."

"Let me do some checking and get back to you. Just don't count on bribery to make your case." Ha, thought Pearl. "Dan, you must be livin' in an ivory tower when it comes to 'donations' gettin' things done faster than a lightning bolt hittin' a lone pine tree in a pasture in the midst of a thunderstorm!"

Instead of adding anything more regarding the donation, she said, "You do that checkin', but don't take too long. I've been spendin' a lot of time at our local hospital sittin' with JC, that's what we call her, while the love 'o her life is fightin' for his life. Some crazy yahoo up and shot him."

"I'm really sorry to hear that, Pearl. If you are sure sending Sam to Texas is what you want, I will see what I can do. You know I'll have to arrange for a nurse to accompany him on the flight to Austin, if I get the go ahead, and that's going to cost you too."

"You can send a unit 'o the National Guard along with him if that's what it takes to make you and those stuffed shirts in administration and their legal eagles feel more comfortable!" she declared.

"All right, but like I said before, I'll see what I can do, but don't hold your breath!" replied Dan.

"Dan, you always was the timid one. By this time hasn't life taught you to show people you've grown a pair? One 'o these days I'm comin' up there to New York City 'n give you some lessons in ball bustin'!"

"Pearl, you haven't changed. You are still the outspoken, somewhat outrageous woman I remember. My wife and I will look forward to you visiting. Just give me some lead time to prepare before you plan to arrive."

"I'll be sure to do that," responded Pearl before she hung up. "Damn! He's married. And here I thought we might take up where we left off forty years ago before Ira swept me off my feet," muttered Pearl. "I swear, some days you just can't win!"

Two hours later, Dan called Pearl back. "The powers that be have agreed to your proposal. A sizable donation will be gratefully appreciated according to the Board President. Expect Sam tomorrow on private jet flight #12526 out of JFK to the Austin, Texas airport. He will arrive at three p.m. I hope you realize you are taking full responsibility for Sam, and it's also your dime to send the plane and nurse back to JFK from Austin."

"I assumed as much when it comes to my responsibility for Sam, the plane and nurse. My question is why the private jet flight?"

"We can't risk Sam being aboard a commercial flight, even with an escort. He can get very agitated, even combative when he thinks he sees or hears a ghost, and that would upset the other passengers."

"All right, if that's what you think is best," replied Pearl. "Thanks for your help, and give my best to the missus. It's been real nice talkin' to you." And thanks for not asking the name of the 'sanitarium' I plan to use, she thought with a smile.

Pearl clapped her hands with glee after hanging up. "Sanitarium hell!" she exclaimed. "He's goin' straight to the State Hospital looney bin. We'll just see how long he keeps actin' crazy after bein' locked up with those kinda nut cases!"

True to her word, Pearl wasted little time making the necessary arrangements through a personal friend, who happened to be the State Hospital administrator, to have Sam committed after he spoke briefly with Dr. Preston. It didn't take a rocket scientist to figure out Sam was still acting strange and muttering when he arrived in Austin. If he knew who his aunt was, he gave no indication.

Pearl said nothing to JC about what she had done, nor did she plan to tell her anytime soon. "She's got enough to think about besides that selfish bastard. If I have anything to say about it, there will be plenty of time for her to visit him before he gets released, and that's only if he should get released anytime in the next thirty years! And that isn't going to happen if I have anythin' to say about it, and believe you me, I will have plenty to say should that ever be considered!"

CHAPTER 36

Emilio was just waking up when JC returned to his intensive care cubicle. He smiled weakly and raised his hand a few inches off the bed in a greeting. "I see you are still here. I thought you left and would not come back after our last conversation."

"I have no intention of leaving you. I'm sorry if you had that impression. I slept in the nurse's lounge last night with updates from your nurses and my friend, Nancy Holt, the ER charge nurse who has been checking in on you. She tells me you are running a fever and the doctor has changed your antibiotic. He expects it to kick in soon."

"The fever broke about half an hour ago when sweat soaked me and the bed."

"I'm told they plan to remove the chest tube sometime tomorrow since your lung has expanded, but only if your temperature stays down. They were going to remove it today, but that got cancelled due to the fever."

He nodded slightly and grimaced. "That's what I've been told, but how much longer are we going to beat around the bush before we talk about you being pregnant and us getting married? I meant what I said about loving you and wanting you for my wife, even if I was a little out of my head at the time. I also remember you saying I didn't need to feel I had to marry you just because you are pregnant with my child." He began to cough violently. The nurse wasted little time coming into the cubicle.

"You need to step outside to the waiting room," she said brusquely.

"Please don't make me leave," begged JC. "I will stay out of the way over there in the corner. I need to let Emilio know I love him and want to be his wife."

"That will have to wait until we get his coughing under control. Please, step outside now! The pulmonary team will be rushing in here any minute and we don't need to have you in the way!"

Moments later came a call over the loudspeaker three times: "Dr. Barkley and Respiratory Therapy report to ICU unit STAT!" This time, JC had no doubt the call was for Emilio. She sat down and doubled over to grip her knees. "Please, God. Don't take him away from me. I know what we did at the line shack was wrong, and I am terribly sorry. Our little boy will need a father, and I need a husband who loves me." She was still doubled over rocking back and forth when Father Benedictine's approach sent her into a torrent of sobs. There could be only one reason he had been called since Emilio was a devout Catholic. "Nooo," she wailed.

"Easy there, my child, Emilio is still with us. I serve as the hospital chaplain who responds when there could be a need, and that is why I'm here."

"Thank God! I was afraid he . . ." She couldn't finish the sentence. The priest sat down in the chair beside her.

"I know it has been a while since you've been to confession or church, JC, but that doesn't matter. We are all God's children; he knows what's in our hearts."

"There was a time I hoped and believed, but that got lost when my parents died, and my husband was killed. And now Emilio is in there fighting for his life," she replied with a shrug of defeat.

"I know it is sometimes hard to keep believing when such things happen, but that doesn't mean God does not care. Perhaps there will come a day soon when we can talk about you finding your faith again. In the meantime, how about I go back inside the ICU unit and see what I can learn about what's happening with Emilio? That's one good thing about being a priest at times like this. They don't kick me out. I will return to let you know as soon as I'm given an update." JC merely nodded.

She felt relief when she saw the look on Father Benedictine's face when he returned to the waiting room. "He's doing a lot better. In fact, he was giving them what for because they tried to put a breathing tube down his throat so they could put him on a ventilator. He kept insisting he didn't need the blankety blank thing along with a few more choice four letter words, some even in Spanish!"

“He actually swore? I never heard him utter a swear word but once, even when it involved something I would not have hesitated cutting loose with a whole string of choice words,” she replied.

“Trust me. He can swear with the best of them, even when I knew he could see me standing there.”

“I’m going to take that as a sign he is on the road to recovery. Thank you for stopping by, Father. I will make an effort to find time to meet with you about helping me find my faith again for more than one reason, one being just as important as the other.” She wanted to tell him about the baby but found she couldn’t bring herself to do so right now.

“Just so you know, I can be found here at the hospital when not attending to church matters such as baptisms, conducting mass, confessions or being at a parishioner’s bedside. I always respond to code blue calls when I’m here. It doesn’t matter if patients are of a different religious persuasion. The patient or family members can always tell me to get lost.”

“I can’t imagine anyone telling you to get lost at such a critical time.”

“You would be surprised. It does happen, but not often, thank God. I will be here for another hour or so checking in with members of my flock if you need me. Should I leave just have one of the staff page me and I will find you.”

JC gave him a look of surprise. "Page you? I didn't think anyone used a pager anymore with the advent of cell phones."

Father Benedictine smiled benevolently. "I'm sort of throwback to an earlier time. I do carry a cell phone, but I still prefer a pager." Just then, his pager went off, letting him know he was needed on the fifth floor. "Sorry, I need to be on my way, but I will always find time for you and Emilio."

CHAPTER 37

JC was sitting, with a look of anticipation, in her chair when Emilio's nurse, Evelyn Conners, came into the waiting room after Father Benedictine had gone. "We have sedated Emilio to help bring his blood pressure down and will continue to sedate him for the next eight to ten hours. Dr. Barklay has decided not to pull the chest tube for at least another thirty-six hours until we get another chest x-ray after he wakes up and his temperature stays down. The last x-ray shows some fluid buildup around the lung. This can happen after extensive trauma and surgery like that of a gunshot. His fever is beginning to show a downturn with the current new antibiotic. If you want to leave, I will say you could go back to the ranch for a few hours and get some rest. We will call you if there is any appreciable change. Let me be honest, the way that man reacted earlier leads me to believe he is well on the way to recovery."

"So, I heard from Father Benedictine." JC replied.

The nurse laughed. "I take it you have spoken with Father Ben. He's one heck of a priest. He seems to appear like magic whenever we have the need for him, sometimes before we know we have the need for him. It's like he has a direct line to God. If he weren't a man of the cloth, I'd think he was a witch with supernatural powers."

JC didn't offer further comment other than to say she was heading to the ranch. She knew she could not delay making a decision any longer. It was time to speak with Jose about becoming the temporary ranch foreman.

It was lunch time at the ranch. Everyone who wasn't needed elsewhere had gathered around the massive table in the bunkhouse kitchen. Out of habit and to avoid embarrassment, JC knocked before opening the door. She was greeted with cheers and questions about Emilio's condition. "I'm told he is improving, but there has been a delay in removing his chest drainage tube due to fluid buildup around his lung. He gave the doctors and his nurse hell when they tried to put him on a breathing machine and that's a good sign. Please don't let me interrupt your lunch. Jose, when you are finished eating, I need to speak with you privately in the ranch house den. You don't need to bother knocking. Just come on in."

He jumped to his feet. "I come right now."

"That won't be necessary. Please finish your lunch. I need some time to get something to eat and fill Rosa in on the latest."

"Si. I know Rosa be waiting to hear news, and she make plenty tacos and refried beans." He smacked his lips and returned to his seat and plate full of tacos, refried beans and Spanish rice, but not without wondering why JC wanted to see him in private. Half an hour later found him knocking at the back kitchen door instead of going directly to the den as JC had instructed. Rosa called for him to come inside and have another toco in order to evade his question why JC wanted to see him.

"She wait for you in den. You eat taco. You go find out," was all she would say.

"You know what she want?" he asked again.

"Didn't say, but face look worried. You go see now and find out. Then come back tell Rosa."

Jose's knock on the den door was tentative at best. "Come in and please have a seat." That response scared him. He thought only bad news required a person to be seated. His first thought was Emilio was not doing as well as she had let on to everyone in the bunkhouse. The second thought was that she was going to fire him even though he did not know exactly why – well, maybe it could be because he and Tex had come to blows out on the back forty last week when Tex didn't like being told to dig a couple of new post holes.

"Do it yourself, you damn greaser," Tex had replied. "You ain't no better than the rest of us! Tellin' me what to do don't make it so just because you're JC and Emilio's pet 'n act like you're some sorta lord and master who can order me around!" Tex ended up losing the ensuing fight and took off on his horse swearing a blue streak, leaving them shorthanded. A week passed, and he had not returned to collect his belongings or his truck. Jose had not found the nerve to tell JC what had taken place. He figured he was instructed to come to the main house to be fired because of violating the no fighting rule among the hired hands.

"You don't need look like a jack rabbit being cornered by a coyote," said JC with a smile. "I asked you to come here to see if you would like to take over as temporary ranch foreman until Emilio is back in the saddle again. I don't know how the other cowhands will take this news, especially Tex. I know the two of you don't see eye to eye."

Jose swallowed hard. "You no worry how Tex take news. Tex no work here no more. He leave after . . ." JC stopped him from explaining why Tex no longer worked on the ranch.

"I won't even ask why. I'm sure there is a good reason," said a relieved JC. "I guess that means we need to hire another hand. How do you think the rest of the cowboys will take it if you become the temporary ranch foreman, and do you think you can keep your temper under control when disagreements come up?"

"I get along with all cowboys, except Tex. He no like Mexicans. He think we stupid and lazy, but he lazy one who no like take orders. Jose know good cowboy we hire take his place."

"Is that person a relative of yours?" she inquired.

"No relative. That not good. They not like take orders." JC agreed and told him to go ahead and hire that person and reminded him the terms of employment so he could pass them on to the new cowhand.

"Would you be willing to learn the things you will need to know to make sure the ranch is kept up as it should be?" she questioned.

"Where I learn these things I not already know? Jose not have much school, but I not stupid. Work on Scott Ranch seven years and know what and when things need happen. That why Emilio ask me to let other cowhands know what they do if he busy, just like Andy did before him."

"I will teach you about figuring out how much feed, medicines, supplies, and hay to order, including stocking the bunkhouse, along with posting a monthly list of who does what and when. Above all, you must understand I will not stand for any further angry outbursts involving fighting. I can be a tough taskmaster when it comes to firing you should that be necessary. You must also understand the job is only temporary until Emilio is well again."

"Jose understand and work hard learn, so when Emilio old man I take over."

"Does that mean you will take the job?" Jose broke into a grin and nodded affirmatively. "Your pay will increase by two hundred dollars a month to start. You can take Sundays off unless you are needed for the cattle roundup, branding, drives to market or unforeseen emergencies. Then you will receive another day off or an extra day of pay, your choice. You will get another week of paid vacation above the two weeks you have already earned. Sorry, but sick time will remain the same, two days a month."

Jose sat quietly for a few minutes in thought. “I not take extra pay or vacation. I do it for you and Emilio. What I learn will pay for work.”

“That is kind of you, but I insist on the extra pay and vacation. You will earn it. Lessons begin today. Go tell the others, then report back here to the den. I’ve got two hours to spare before heading back to the hospital. And just so you know, Emilio’s father will be flying in here tomorrow to land on our airstrip. He and his pilot will be my guests. He will call you if it’s a night landing so you have a heads up to make sure the area is lighted and can assign someone to meet and bring them to the ranch house. Rosa will take over from there.”

“Mr. Vasquez, he already call. They land daytime tomorrow in afternoon. I be there to say welcome and bring them to Rosa.”

“Thank you for letting me know when he will arrive, along with agreeing to take the temporary job,” said JC.

Rosa was taken by surprise when Jose yelled, “yahoo” and gave her a hug on his way out the back door. “I got job as temporary foreman,” he shouted.

While he was gone to let the others know, JC gathered up the teaching materials she used at the Winchester School, along with the supply order sheets. It didn’t take long before she was able to recognize Jose was a lot smarter than anyone had given him credit for, including her.

CHAPTER 38

On top of their disagreement over post holes, Tex had taken on the dark thought Jose would be named temporary foreman instead of him. It didn't help his mood when he ended up at the Lonesome Dove Cantina to find Elida cozying up to a man in one of the back booths. "What the hell do you think you are doin'?" he shouted at her. She quickly scrambled out of the booth to face him.

"I am not doing anything bad, mon cheri," she replied. "He is my cousin visiting from France."

"Sure he is, just like I'm the King of France!" Then he struck her across the face with the flat of his hand. "You're nothin' but a whore! I shoulda known with you dancin' and showin' your ass to anybody willin' to take a look." Elida burst into tears and ran out the back door. "Good luck with that cunt," he said to the man who had been sitting with her who gasped as though he had been struck. Then Tex stalked out, got on his horse and took off up a side street to where he knew he could obtain a large amount of dynamite, no questions asked. "I think it's high time I did a little somethin Jose won't be able to order me to fix," he mumbled.

That night, there was a huge explosion that rocked the surrounding buildings within a forty-mile radius of the Scott Ranch. The force was so great it broke windows and caused stampedes. The sound waves could be heard and felt clear over in Midline, along with the glow of the resulting fire that could be seen for miles across the open ranch land. All the ranch hands at the Scott Ranch jumped up from their beds. "What in hell was that?" questioned Jose before he and everyone else ran barefoot out the bunkhouse door in their underwear to take a look and try to figure out what happened. Moments later, Rosa and Roberto ran from the ranch house, her in a white flannel nightgown and Roberto in his black silk underwear covered with red hot peppers.

"Holy Mother of God! It look like line shack on fire!" shouted one of the men.

"Everybody get dressed, saddle up and we ride to mountain," ordered Jose. "Rosa, you and Roberto go in ranch house lock doors. Not open to anyone, especially Tex." Rosa started to ask why Tex was not welcome inside the ranch house. Jose interrupted her. "I tell when come back! You not argue! Just do what Jose say!" They didn't have a choice but to do as they were told unless they wanted to eat the dust made by twenty riders heading toward the mountain at a fast clip.

JC was sleeping in the hospital nurses' lounge when a distant, muted noise followed by a shock wave awakened her. She sat up and rubbed her eyes. "What was that?" she wondered aloud. One of the nurses stuck her head in the lounge to ask if she was all right. "I'm all right, but what made that jolt and sound off in the distance? You can bet whatever it was had to be some sort of an explosion. I hope it wasn't one of the refineries, an oil well or an oil tanker being hauled by the railroad that exploded."

"We aren't sure yet, but one of the orderlies said he thinks it was an explosion somewhere up on the mountain southwest of town. He said you can see the fire from up on the top floor and the hospital roof. I'll fill you in when we know something more. In the meantime, you go back to sleep. Emilio is resting comfortably with his last pain shot keeping him in la-la land in spite of the noise and shock wave." With the news Emilio was resting comfortably and whatever had happened did not involve the hospital, JC lay back down to pull the covers up around her neck and was soon sound asleep. When she awakened at six a.m., she asked Nancy if there was any news regarding the explosion when she stopped by the nurse's lounge during her break for a quick cup of what passed for coffee.

"Nothing official," she replied. "We will have to wait until the sheriff or one of his deputies ends up coming to the ER for their morning coffee to learn the latest. Maybe it was one of the new oil wells that blew up when they burned off the methane. How about joining me for some breakfast in the cafeteria?" She took a sip of the coffee and made a face. "This coffee tastes terrible! I pulled another all-nighter, and I'm hungry. It's hard to ruin scrambled eggs and toast, but then again, have you ever eaten crunchy scrambled eggs with a side of charred toast and black bacon? And I'm not talking about a few flakes of eggshell, bread or bacon more than a little on the dark side."

"I guess it will be all right," replied JC. "I was planning to get dressed and go back to Emilio's cubicle before I had breakfast, but it's early, and his nurse will be giving him his bath and getting him ready for the day. Sure, I'll join you as long as it doesn't take too long, and the food isn't a burnt offering. Give me five minutes."

"No guarantees on the food, but what can the cook do to a tea bag or a bowl of oatmeal? Wait, don't answer that. Maybe you might want cornflakes. I don't recommend the coffee unless you like drinking brown water with an unusual chemical taste. But then I keep forgetting you don't drink coffee these days."

The cafeteria was where Jose found them sitting at a corner table of the hospital cafeteria looking out on the courtyard. The moment JC saw the look on his face she knew something was terribly wrong. He was shaking and looked like he was exhausted and about ready to cry. "You look like you need to sit down," she said patting the empty chair next to her.

"There nothing we could do," he blurted out as he sank into the chair.

JC felt the blood in her veins grow cold. "What do you mean there was nothing you could do?"

"Line shack, it gone. Sheriff say he think somebody probably use dynamite, but no can say until fire marshal come to take look. He tell us stay away."

JC's hands flew to the sides of her face. A look of incredibility followed. "The line shack is gone? How? I don't have any enemies who would do anything like setting it on fire or blowing it up! Maybe the propane tank exploded?"

"Propane tank empty for winter. We wait see what fire marshal say." In his heart, Jose had a good idea what happened and who had done it, but felt he should not point fingers before doing some checking with contacts in town.

Emilio was alert and awake when Nancy came into his cubicle following the conversation with Jose. Upset by the news, JC asked Nancy to let him know she needed to take care of some business at the ranch and would see him later that afternoon. When Nancy arrived, she did her best to smile and act as though nothing out of the ordinary had happened. But she didn't fool him.

The first words out of Emilio's mouth were, "Where's JC?"

"What do you mean? Can't I just drop by for a friendly visit?"

"You know what I mean. I can see it in your eyes. Something is bothering you. Is the baby all right? Is JC all right?" His face had grown more serious when she didn't answer right away. "Please don't lie to me."

"JC asked me to stop by and let you know she had to take care of some business at the ranch this morning, and she will be back later this afternoon. She didn't want you to worry."

"Well, I am worried, so you need to tell me what is going on," he insisted.

Nancy swallowed hard before answering, figuring he would hear sooner or later, and it would be best if he heard it from her. "The line shack at the ranch was blown up last night."

"What?"

"The line shack was blown up during the night," she repeated.

"That's not possible. There wasn't any propane in the tanks. I made sure of that before I closed the place down for the winter."

"Rumor has it the explosion wasn't caused by propane."

"Then what was it caused by?"

"When I talked to Sheriff Walker, he thinks it was dynamite, but that's not official. He is waiting for a ruling by the fire marshal before making a public statement."

"Who in the heck would dynamite that place? We don't have any enemies who would do such a thing. Well, maybe it could be one of the rustlers I've run off. But those guys take being run off in stride as the chance they take. I've never had any of them take offense bad enough to cause that kind of damage in all the years I've been working on cattle ranches."

"I guess we will just have to wait and see what happens. I'm sure JC has insurance, but it breaks my heart to see that place go with all the memories she and now you must have attached to it."

"Me, too, but that's all the more reason she and I should get married and start building new memories with our family. Come spring, it won't take that long to build a new line shack. Maybe this one can be built on the mountain range we share if we join ranks in making both ranches one big ranch."

Nancy smiled and reached for his hand and gave it a squeeze. "That sounds like a real possibility. But first, there's someone she needs to have a serious talk with before you proceed with those plans."

"And who might that be?"

"JC will tell you after they have had that talk and she can more on with a new life with you," replied Nancy.

"That sounds serious."

"Trust me. It is very serious."

"I have trusted you with my life and I will continue to trust you. If you had not been there in the ER to help me after I was brought down off that mountain, we would not be having this conversation." He looked up at her and smiled. "Not to change the subject, but I take it JC told you Rosa thinks we will have a boy? Guess that means we need to start thinking about names." Nancy didn't know what to say, so she smiled and patted his hand. "I think I need to get back to work. See you later."

"Didn't you notice anything different?" he asked before pulling aside the left side of his sheet. "No chest tube. The latest x-ray shows the lung is healing." Nancy leaned over and took a discrete peek before continuing to head toward the door. "Like I said, it's time for me to get back to work. I think you need to keep show and tell between you and JC," a blush flashing across her face, not from looking at him, but for what she was thinking. JC is crazy if she doesn't marry this guy! Even with all those bandages I can see he's ripped!

Emilio was obviously upset when JC arrived later that afternoon. "Why did you send Nancy to tell me about the line shack? I gave serious thought to signing myself out of here and coming out to the ranch and see the damage firsthand!"

"Don't you dare say a thing like that or you will need more than a doctor to save you!" was her heartfelt reply. "By the way, your father will be flying here tomorrow." Emilio's anger quickly subsided when JC told him his father was flying in. "Thank you for calling him. I'm sorry I unloaded on you concerning the line shack, but I wish it had been you to tell me." He didn't miss the look of concern on her face. "I said I was sorry, so why do you look so down?"

“Apology accepted, but I am concerned about meeting your father,” she replied.

“You will like him. I know he will like you.”

“I hope so when he finds out we are having a baby and you plan on marrying a gringo.”

CHAPTER 39

Jose started his quest for information by asking questions around the back streets and alleys of Midline. At first, people were hesitant in providing answers until he ran into a grizzled old prospector who had come into town to buy dynamite for his gold claim and decided to stick around a while. The two of them met at The Lonesome Dove. They ended up sharing a table when the place was crowded.

Jose bought the old man a couple of beers to loosen his tongue. "Wonder what happened to that pretty little French woman what used to dance here," the old man offered. "Think her name was Elidee or some such thing." He nodded in the direction of men lined up at the bar. "One of them buckaroos standin' over yonder at the bar mentioned her boyfriend done smacked her upside the head and called her a whore. She didn't strike me as the type ta be goin' in one 'o them back rooms with men."

"You hear name of boyfriend?" asked Jose. The old man scratched the side of his bearded face and appeared to be in deep thought.

"Seems like it weren't anything unusual . . ." He scrunched up his face. "Think it was Tex." He pointed a finger in the direction of a man standing at the bar. "That one over there said this Tex feller was madder 'n a wet hen 'n seemed sorta crazy like afore he took outta here like a bat outta hell once he hit the woman."

"Do you know how long ago you heard this after Tex hit her?" Deep, head-scratching thought ensued on the part of the miner.

"Not more 'n a day ago. I jest got inta town yesterday right afore that blast over on the mountain over yonder. Sorry I cain't be 'o more help."

Jose' placed a twenty-dollar bill on the table to pay the five-dollar tab. "You are more help than you know. I go now. You keep change after waitress get dollar tip. Good luck in mine."

The old man snatched the change and shoved it in the pocket of his bib overalls as soon as the waitress left it on the table after taking her share. "Thank ye kindly. Ya don't have to hurry off partner," he called to the retreating figure. "We was jest getting started talkin'. Don't get much company out ta the mine."

"Sorry, gotta see man about horse. Maybe we talk next time you come to Dove," replied Jose.

It did not take Jose long to put two and two together. Tex was angry with his girlfriend, angry with hearing Jose had been named foreman, and the purchase of black-market dynamite did not add up to a good combination. His next stop was the rundown building where dynamite could be purchased without any questions being asked.

At first, the owner refused to answer any questions until Jose returned several hours later. This time, he was accompanied by six burly cowboys, six guns in holsters on their hips, hands twitching near their holsters. "You tell who buy dynamite or else," ordered Jose.

"Don't deal in names, but the feller had a Texas accent 'n stood about six feet tall with big beefy hands," answered the man with a wary eye on the cowboys. None of them missed the fact he broke out in a sweat as he spoke. "I don't want no trouble."

"You not get trouble if you answer questions. Man wear a red and black plaid shirt?" questioned Jose.

"Yes, as a matter of fact he did, 'n seemed like he was spittin' mad about somethin', 'n that's about all I kin recollect."

"Thank you, senior," said Jose. "You big help. Man bad hombre. He blow up line shack at Scott Ranch."

"Aw, shit! If I hadda knowed what he was gonna do, I would never have sold him that dine-e-mite. I feel real bad for that poor Morgan woman. She ain't never done nothin' mean ta nobody. If I lay eyes on this feller again, ya kin bet your boots he's a dead man!"

"Only if I don't get him first," declared Jose. "Come on, boys, we got business to do." He glared at the store owner. "Next time you more careful who you sell to, okay?"

"I sure will," replied the frightened man. "I sure will!"

Although Jose and the Scott Ranch cowhands searched high and low, they were unable to find Tex. They finally had to admit defeat a few weeks later. "He probably hightail to Mexico 'n hideout there in mountains. I put out word to family 'n friends there. We get him, but we need get back to ranch in case he come there try hurt Rosa or Roberto," Jose told them. It was a sad and angry group of cowboys who returned to the ranch – so angry they flattened the tires on the pickup Tex had not returned to claim.

It would be deer season the following year when hunters found the badly decomposed bodies of Tex and his horse lying wedged between boulders five hundred feet below what had been the trail up to the line shack. The explosion had caused the narrow path to slide away. They could only speculate this happened in response to his rush to leave the shack before the dynamite blew, the horse apparently lost its footing to send them plunging down onto the rugged and isolated boulders below. A tear in his shirt holding the limb in place between his ribs indicated Tex had been impaled by a dead tree limb. He would never know Elida was faithful to him and was pregnant with what would have been his son had he not lost his temper over not being named foreman at the Scott Ranch. The man he had seen her with was her cousin, plus JC was planning to name him second in command until Emilio recovered. Had he been able to control his temper, he could have made a life for himself and built a house on an acre of land JC would have given him as a wedding present when he married Elida.

CHAPTER 40

JC approached Nancy as she was leaving the ER for her afternoon coffee break the same day Emilio's chest tube was removed. "Would you page Father Ben for me? Tell him I'll meet him in the chapel. We need to talk."

"That sounds ominous," replied Nancy. "When somebody says we need to talk, that's usually a sign it involves something very serious. Anything I can do to help?" From their woman to woman talks, she had already figured out JC needed to speak with Father Ben.

"Thank you for asking if you could help, Nancy, but this is something I need to talk over with Father Ben in private before I am able to move on with my life."

"That sounds heavy duty, so I won't ask questions." She reached into her scrubs pocket and pulled out her cell phone. "We don't use pagers anymore in my department, so I will give him a call. We finally talked him into carrying a cell phone. Let's just hope he answers it," she advised. "It won't be long before the rest of the hospital catches up with the times. Some of the old guard, him being one, are still holdouts." She dialed Father Benedictine's number. It rang nine times before he answered. She identified herself and the nature of her call.

He profusely apologized for the delay in answering. "I don't have the hang of these confounded new electronic devices. I guess that makes me old fashioned, but I'll take a pager any day," he offered apologetically. "Tell JC I will meet her in the chapel in twenty minutes."

"Father Ben says he will meet you in the chapel in twenty minutes. That means you have time to join me for coffee -- woops, make that tea -- in the cafeteria. Sorry, I keep forgetting you can't stand the smell of coffee," announced Nancy. She did most of the talking while they sat at a corner table. JC nodded and smiled in the appropriate places, but her mind was elsewhere trying to figure out how she was going to approach getting back her faith when there had been so many reasons to have lost it.

"I hope you and Father Ben are able to solve whatever problems are plaguing you," said Nancy when it was a few minutes before time for her to return to work. "You know I'm always available if you need someone to talk to. I have broad shoulders, am a good listener and I have a closed mouth when it comes to gossip." She made a zipper like motion across her mouth, along with crossing her eyes and wiggling her nose in an effort to make JC laugh. It worked.

"Leave it to you to make me laugh," said JC. "You should be more careful in offering to listen. One of these days, I just might take you up on your offer and bend your ear more than I've already done."

"All joking aside, I don't extend such offers unless I mean it. Now you need to get going to the chapel before Father Ben decides he needs to be someplace else. I swear that man must have been a track star before he became a priest! Now you see him, now you don't because he's off and running to handle the next crisis or problem."

"Are you sure you two aren't related when it comes to the appearing and disappearing acts?" Nancy just smiled and disappeared inside the elevator without waiting for JC to enter before the door slid shut.

Father Ben was already waiting when JC arrived in the chapel. Although a busy man, he never gave the impression he didn't have time to spend with whomever he was meeting. "JC, it is good to see you, my child. I take it you've had time to do some serious soul searching?"

"Yes, Father, but I really don't know where to start."

"Pick a place, and we'll take it from there."

"As you know, I have not been to church or confession since the funerals of my parents and Rex. I don't know why I should be, but I think I am still angry with God. He took away the three most important people in my life! Now that I have come to terms with possibly finding a new love with Emilio, he was shot and almost killed, and he's still not totally out of the woods when it comes to his recovery." She paused and lowered her head struggling to find the right words to continue the conversation.

She was obviously struggling, so Father Ben added, "You know there isn't anything you can't tell me. Everything we talk about is in strict confidence, even though we are not in a church confessional."

"It might be easier if we were," said JC. "Then I wouldn't have to look you in the face and tell you I'm almost two months pregnant and not married to the father of this baby."

"Do you love this man, and does he love you?" he inquired.

"Yes, I think so," she answered.

"Love is not something you have to think about. You either love him or you don't. He either loves you or he doesn't," countered Father Ben.

"He tells me he loves me with all his heart, and he wants to marry me."

"Do you believe this to be the truth? And if so, how do you feel about him?"

"I love and want to marry him, but at the same time I feel like I am betraying the memory of Rex."

"Do you remember your wedding vows?"

"Yes, of course I do."

"Then surely you recall the promise to be faithful to each other until death you do part. In the eyes of the church and God, you are free to marry again without any feelings of guilt. Rex has gone to his reward, and that does not include you. Of course, you will always have a place in your heart for him, but that does not mean there isn't room for Emilio and the child in your life."

"I don't remember telling you the name of the baby's father is Emilio. How did you know?"

Father Ben smiled his usual benevolent smile. "It is obvious by the way you look at each other, the way he is always asking for you, the way you are never far away. I think I would hang up my robe and collar if I weren't aware of the love you have for each other, along with the love both of you have for this child. As for losing your faith, people often struggle with the loss of loved ones or tragic events over which they have little or no control. It is human nature, and God understands and does not fault you for these feelings. But at the same time, I believe He feels a sense of sadness one of His flock has lost their way. JC, it isn't too late to ask for forgiveness. He will lead you back into the fold, but only if you allow Him to."

"I have already asked for forgiveness for becoming pregnant before marriage."

Father Ben beamed. "That, my child, is a crucial step for you to reclaim your faith. The next step is to accept the loss of your parents and Rex, followed by marrying Emilio and giving your child the gift of his father's name."

"That's where I'm on shaky ground, Father. I don't want Emilio to feel he must marry me just because I'm pregnant with his child."

"Didn't you just tell me he asked you to become his wife? Hasn't he told you he wants this child?"

"Yes, to both questions."

"Then what is the problem?"

"He has to get well and be released from the hospital first, and that could give him enough time to change his mind, especially if his family objects."

"That need not be a problem. You could get married here in the hospital chapel, unless you want a big fancy wedding. As for his family, you aren't marrying them, and I know your Aunt Pearl will approve."

"I hadn't thought of using the chapel as an option," replied JC. "But that is a very good idea, but only if Emilio and Dr. Bark think it's a good idea, too, and no, I do not want a fancy wedding."

"Let's you and I go ask Dr. Barklay what he thinks. I think I have a good idea what Emilio will think."

JC's eyes opened wide. "Do you mean right now?"

"Why not right now?" Father Ben questioned. "There is no better time than the present. I don't know who said those immortal words, but whoever it was, they were right, especially in this case." JC could not help but see he was politely glancing in the direction of her slightly expanding belly coupled with a blush.

"You are right. I'll really be beginning to show in a couple more weeks. Just enough time will have passed before the birth and wedding to have the town gossips counting on their fingers when the baby arrives. Will you perform the ceremony if Emilio agrees and Dr. Bark approves?"

"Of course, I will. Who else did you think would do it since I'm the only priest for miles around?" They left the chapel smiling, arm in arm on the way to find Dr. Barklay. He was just leaving ICU when they spotted him. His smile grew by leaps and bounds into outright laughter as he listened to JC's request to have the wedding in the hospital chapel on the coming Saturday morning.

"I could not have ordered a more potent medicine," he told her. "Congratulations, almost Mrs. Emilio Vasquez," he said as he gave her a fatherly hug. "Please tell me I can walk you down the aisle and give you away, but let's not get ahead of ourselves. We need to give Emilio a few more days in ICU before he gets caught up in all the excitement of becoming a husband, and you have time to come up with a wedding dress, maid of honor and put together a reception in the doctors' dining room for a few friends and staff. That is something I can help with since my father paid big bucks to have that room built. Of course, you realize the honeymoon will have to wait, but I don't see any reason why an extra bed can't be moved into Emilio's room when he's transferred out of ICU onto the stepdown unit by this coming Tuesday. Hopefully if that goes well, he should be able to be moved to a private room on the surgical floor by Friday, followed by being one of the major participants in a wedding on Saturday morning."

"Will it be all right if I let him know right now?" asked JC.

"Like I said, knowing one of his dreams is about to come true by making you his wife is the best possible medicine. That man is absolutely head over heels in love with you, along with the knowledge he will be a father. In fact, I would like to be a fly on the wall when you let him know you will marry him. Of course, I'm speaking metaphorically about being a fly. We don't allow flies in ICU, but I'll be standing by at a discreet distance." JC felt her face turn a delicate shade of pink but agreed it would be okay if Dr. Bark stood by outside Emilio's cubicle when she accepted Emilio's proposal and suggested a hospital chapel wedding on Saturday morning.

"What about me?" asked Father Ben with a fake pout.

"Maybe it would be a good idea if both of you stood by, just in case he goes into heart failure," replied JC before she stepped inside his cubicle to inform Emilio she would marry him.

"Bite your tongue!" said Dr. Bark with a grin. "Along with no flies, we don't allow heart failure when a woman tells the man she loves yes to his proposal." He looked down at the green scrub suit he was wearing. "It seems like I should be dressed a little more formally for the occasion, but why stand on ceremony? Let me re-phrase that – I will be dressed more formally when I give the bride away at the wedding ceremony." They did their best to control their laughter as the three of them entered Emilio's cubicle.

The look on Emilio's face was one of confusion. "Why are all three of you here? Does that mean you have bad news?"

"Only if you object to learning JC is accepting your proposal of marriage. Oops. Maybe I should not have said that. I hope you will forgive me, JC," said Father Ben.

"It's all right, Father," she replied.

Emilio's eyes grew wide followed a wide grin, followed by tears of sheer joy. "You aren't just saying that to make me feel better are you, Father?"

"No, he isn't," answered JC. "I love and want to marry you, the sooner the better. I don't want to waste any more time being unsure like I have been in the past. I love you. I want to be your wife. I want to have your babies. I want us to grow old together."

"Father Ben, I think this is where you and I need to exit stage left," said Dr. Bark. "I'll let the nurses know they don't need to panic when his heart and blood pressure monitors go bonkers for the next few minutes."

"If I thought I would not fall flat on the floor, I would get out of this bed and do somersaults after I kiss you," said Emilio. "But I'll settle for a kiss until we can . . ." Her lips on his prevented him from completing the sentence. Just as Dr. Bark predicted, the monitors went completely haywire, but the rosy color in his cheeks didn't show any evidence of respiratory distress when they came up for air.

"Now you need to tell me what changed your mind?" questioned Emilio.

"That is between Father Ben and me," she replied. "Let's just say he helped me put things back in proper perspective when true love comes calling and leave it at that," she responded.

CHAPTER 41

It was easy to see where Emilio got his good looks. He was the image of his handsome father, whom JC immediately recognized as he approached the ICU waiting room. "You must be JC," he said, offering his hand. She stood to shake the offered hand.

"Mr. Vasquez, it is nice to meet you. Emilio speaks highly of you."

"He has spoken of you," he replied. His voice or face did not give any indication of his response being a positive or negative reaction.

"I am sure you don't want to waste any time before seeing your son. Family visiting hours are for ten minutes for up to two people every three hours." She looked at her watch. "That means we will have to wait another half hour. Please have a seat. May I get you some coffee?"

"No, thank you. My pilot and I had lunch at a place called Willow Dale Resort after we checked in there and arranged for a rental car," replied Mr. Vasquez.

"I thought you would be staying at my ranch. There would have been transportation available here to the hospital, and Rosa would have made you comfortable."

"I thought it best we not impose."

"You would not be imposing. In fact, Rosa Gonzales, my housekeeper, was looking forward to seeing you again, and we have plenty of guest suites."

"Rosa works for you? We have known each other since childhood. She will be disappointed. I do not wish to disappoint my friend, so I will call my pilot and have him let the resort know there has been a change in plans. But I think we will keep the rental car. If you provide directions to your ranch, I will pick him up after the visit with my son since I drove it here." JC provided numbers and names identifying county roads. He thanked her, and they fell into an awkward silence for several minutes until he asked her to tell him, again, what had transpired at the line shack the day Emilio was shot. "The connection during our phone call was not good," he explained. JC told him again what she believed to have taken place.

"So, the authorities have not yet ruled it was justifiable homicide?" he questioned.

"No, they haven't, but I'm sure that will happen after Sheriff Walker hears what Emilio has to say, and that should take place later today or tomorrow at the latest. The man who shot him was known to have a bad temper."

"I see . . . and what caused him to lash out and attempt to kill my son?"

The question made JC very uncomfortable. "I'm not sure, but I think he saw Emilio as competition."

"Competition? I do not understand this competition."

"Emilio and I are good friends. The shooter didn't like it."

"And why was that?"

JC cleared her throat nervously. “The shooter thought he could force me into marrying him, and I turned him down.”

“Was this the same man who did what I overheard at Willow Dale was damage to the line shack? From the air when we flew over the area, it looked like a bomb had been dropped.”

“No. It is highly suspected it was done by a disgruntled cowhand.”

Mr. Vasquez frowned. “I see. Why . . .?” JC was saved from answering another question when the ICU charge nurse opened the unit door to announce it was visiting time. She looked inquisitively in the direction of the new person. JC graciously introduced him and told Mr. Vasquez to go in alone since she was sure he and Emilio would need some private time. “Are you sure you don’t want to join us?” he asked.

“I’m sure. I have been able to see him throughout his ordeal.” Mr. Vasquez raised his eyebrows at this response but didn’t say anything as he followed the nurse into the unit.

“Emilio, wake up.” said the nurse. He slowly opened his eyes. “Look who’s here.”

“Dad! When did you get here? JC said she called you, but she wasn’t sure when you would arrive.” He smiled sheepishly before adding, “Isn’t she lovely?”

"She is very beautiful." This was all he said with a straight face unaccompanied by a smile.

"I sense you have reservations."

"She is your employer. I sense there is more to your relationship, but we will talk about it later. How are you feeling?"

"I am doing much better, but we need to talk about my relationship with JC now. Time is critical."

Mr. Vasquez frowned. "What do you mean time is critical? Is there something you are not telling me about your recovery?"

"No, Dad. I need to let you know I'm in love with JC, and she is in love with me. We plan to be married on Saturday morning here in the hospital chapel, and I want your blessing."

"I do not understand why it is critical you are married here in the hospital. Your mother and I, along with other family members, have been waiting for you to return home, choose a local senorita, marry and take over the responsibility for our ranch."

"I know that was the plan, but that has changed."

"And when did this change happen?" questioned his father.

"The day I first saw JC more than five years ago," replied Emilio.

"Ah, she is the mystery woman of whom you have spoken and written? Why has it taken you five years to make this woman known to me? Is it because she is a gringo?"

"No. She was married at the time."

The look of shock on his father's face was unmistakable. "She is a divorced woman? You know that is not acceptable in the eyes of the church! I will not stand by to see you excommunicated for marrying a divorced woman! No! You will not have my blessing on this unholy union!"

"Dad, please hear me out. JC is a widow. Her husband was killed three years ago. I apologize for not telling you her name when I mentioned in my letters and phone calls I had found the woman of my dreams. I did not know for sure if she returned my love until recently. I did not want to get you or mother's hopes up."

"And pray tell, what brought about this recent revelation on the part of this mystery woman?"

Emilio looked uncomfortable. "That is personal, something that needs to remain private for now."

"Is she carrying your child?" he asked bluntly.

"Yes, Dad, she is, and no, we did not plan on that happening, but I take full responsibility. I love her and want this child, along with her as my wife."

His father lowered his head and appeared to be studying the pattern on the floor tiles. "And she bears no responsibility? I find this hard to believe. She could have said no when you made your move to have sex with her. Some women use this weakness in men to spread their seed knowing they can get what they want if a child is the result. How do you know this baby is yours? She has been a widow for three years. There could have been other men besides you."

"She is not that kind of woman, Dad! There have been no other men, or I would know. She seldom leaves the ranch unless she accompanied by her aunt, except to help at The Winchester School three afternoons a week, and there have been no men associated with the school hanging around the ranch."

"This Winchester School . . . It is the place where I send money to help migrant workers and their children?"

"Yes."

"Then I will ask men there if they know her in the biblical sense."

"I am telling you she has not been with other men!"

"Son, we have a proud heritage to uphold. It is bad enough she is a gringo. Your mother will be disappointed, along with her sisters, your sister and brother."

"When they get to know her, I can assure you they will not be disappointed. JC is a very caring, honest person who has gone out of her way to make sure everyone working on the ranch is treated like one of the family. I assume she made the offer for you and your pilot to stay there. That will give you the chance to ask her housekeeper Rosa what she thinks. I have no doubt she will tell you what I've just told you. Rosa has known JC since the day she was brought home from the hospital, and if anyone can vouch for her, it will be Rosa. Dad, you have to give JC a chance before you question her character and morals!"

"I can see you are very strong in your feelings and assessment of this woman. Yes, she did invite me and my pilot to stay at her ranch. I must admit I accepted only after I learned Rosa would be disappointed if we did not accept. Not only will I have a talk with Rosa, but I will speak with the ranch hands man to man!"

"You do what you feel you must. I just hope you are prepared to ask for her forgiveness when you make a fool of yourself by questioning her character. You need to be aware I will marry her even if we do not have your blessing. It will be on your shoulders if we no longer have a father and son relationship!"

"Those are strong words, son. I will see what the ranch hands and Rosa have to say before I make my final decision. I know Rosa to be honest."

"As well you should when it comes to the hands and especially Rosa. I have always known you to be fair and hope I can continue to have that feeling in the future."

"I have no wish to upset you, but it is obvious that I have, so I think it is time for me to go. Just know I have your best interest at heart. I will return tomorrow when we have both had time to reflect on our opinions." He patted his son's hand, got up and left the cubicle, feeling he had every right to question the character and morals of the woman who would become the mother of his grandchild. JC was puzzled when Mr. Vasquez come back into the waiting room before the allotted time was up. "Did something happen to end your visit?" she asked anxiously.

"Emilio was tired, and I didn't want to cause him harm," was all he said. "If you will excuse me, I need to go get my pilot and run a small errand. I should be able to be at your ranch by six p.m., if the invitation to stay there is still open for me and my pilot."

"Of course it is. Rosa will be delighted. I called her, and she informed me she will be making traditional dishes for dinner she knows you will enjoy, and I look forward to getting to know you better. Since there is five minutes left for visiting hours, I will slip back inside to let Emilio know we will return tomorrow morning. I usually spend the night sleeping in the nurse's lounge, but it will be late by the time we finish dinner, and he will be asleep by then. And I'm sure it has been a long tiring and emotional day for both of you."

"Have you spent every night here in the hospital since he was shot? That seems a little unusual for an employer to be doing," questioned Mr. Vasquez.

JC blushed. "Am I to assume he did not tell you?"

"Tell me what?"

"That we have developed feelings for each other." She did not know what Emilio had told him, so she did not elaborate about the baby.

"He mentioned the fact he cares for you."

"Oh," was all JC could manage to say.

"I think I need to be on my way, or I will be late for this dinner Rosa has planned." He walked away leaving JC feeling like he would not accept her as Emilio's wife, let alone be a grandfather to their baby. The feeling did not leave her when she returned to ICU to tell Emilio good night. Emilio was evasive about what he and his father had discussed, claiming he was tired, and they would talk about it tomorrow. It was with a heavy heart she made the forty-mile drive back to the ranch.

Mr. Vasquez wasted little time driving to The Winchester School as soon as he got directions from one of the hospital security guards. If he expected to learn JC was a woman of questionable character and morals, he was disappointed. Every man he spoke to sang her praises, as did their wives and children. Of course, they would say things like she is an angel and a wonderful person, and she never came on to or accepted offers from men. She is the one who helps them prepare to become citizens, he kept telling himself on the drive to pick up his pilot. As a proud man who felt he was looking out for his son's best interest and the heritage of his family, Mr. Vasquez still did not allow it to register as positive what everyone he had spoken to had said about JC was the truth.

CHAPTER 42

Rosa was not happy when Mr. Vasquez and his pilot arrived at the ranch half an hour late. "Miguel Emilio Vasquez! It about time you get here!" she announced when answering his knock before she wrapped her arms around his chest in a heartfelt hug and kissed him on both cheeks. "You late and make Rosa's salad and enchiladas soggy! JC forgive you, but Rosa not sure she forgive you! I remember when we children, you always late when you come to momma and poppa's house. Who is man with you?"

"This is my pilot, Manuel." Manuel extended his hand. She shook it while appraising him. "You fly airplane?"

"Yes, ma'am. I fly old goat wherever he want go." This statement brought a belly laugh from Rosa.

"Rosa like you call him old goat and speak like Mexican, and he no get upset. He always push Emilio and self to speak like gringo. Yes, Rosa like you, Manuel, so you come inside with old goat. I tell JC you here."

JC did her best to appear calm as she welcomed her guests, but her stomach was in knots. "Good evening, Mr. Vasquez. I presume this is your pilot. Welcome to the Scott Ranch. Please allow me to show you to your rooms where you can freshen up before dinner." Mr. Vasquez did not offer his hand, nor did he offer to be addressed by his first name when he introduced his pilot. This did nothing to lessen her nerves, but she continued to smile as she led them to their quarters following the brief introduction to Manuel. I wonder if he is always this cold, she silently wondered. "Please come to the dining room as soon as you can. Rosa is beside herself that her enchiladas are not fresh out of the oven." She immediately regretted saying that for fear Mr. Vasquez would take it as a rebuke for being late. He surprised her when he smiled and said he had no wish to distress Rosa any more than he already had done and hoped JC would forgive him. She smiled and told him it was not a problem on her part.

"You are not familiar with the roads around here, so it is understandable you arrived a little late," she replied as she led them down the hall to their suites. "I will leave you gentlemen to settle in and look forward to you joining us in the dining room. Just let me know if there is anything you need. I hope it does not distress you that Rosa and her new husband, Roberto, will be dining with us if you are not used to having the hired help join you for meals. Rosa and Roberto are more than just hired help. Rosa has been a part of this family longer than me," she went on to explain. "I know you will find Roberto a delightful and interesting individual. Manuel is also welcome to join us."

"That will not be a problem if they join us. Rosa and I are old friends and if she has chosen Roberto for her husband that makes him a friend of mine."

"I am happy that you agree," said JC as she turned to walk away.

"She nice lady and much beautiful, too," offered Manuel when she was out of ear shot.

"Beauty is as beauty does," replied Mr. Vasquez in what Manuel thought was a cold tone of voice. "We shall learn just how beautiful she is during the next two or three hours." This statement left Manuel wondering if his boss had lost his mind when he barked, "Go get cleaned up and meet me in the hallway outside my room in fifteen minutes! I don't want to keep Rosa waiting."

"Yes, boss," Manuel meekly replied.

Dinner was tense. Mr. Vasquez answered question asked by JC with as few terse words as possible, while being charming with Rosa and Roberto. "When we have finished with dinner, Rosa, would you be so kind as to take me on a tour of the grounds and outbuildings? The moon is full, so we will have no trouble being able to see." Then he turned to Manuel. "Would you be so kind as to help clear the table and wash the dishes? It only seems fair that you help." Manuel felt he had no choice but to do as his boss asked. Rosa thought Mr. Vasquez had a lot of nerve, but she said nothing and began gathering up the dishes, as did JC.

On their way across the path toward the bunkhouse Rosa asked her childhood friend why he was being such an ass. "You rude to JC! She does not do dishes when company come here! That Rosa's job!" she declared. "You need tell Rosa why you rude."

"I needed to speak with you alone, Rosa."

"You can say anything in front of everyone at dinner, most of all JC! She offer place for you and Manuel stay. You put feet under her table! You eat her food! Why you act this way? It not like you!"

"Emilio and I had a talk when we visited this afternoon. He let me know he plans to marry this woman on Saturday in the hospital chapel. He also tells me she is pregnant with his child. While I am deeply disturbed she is a gringo, my main concern is if the child belongs to Emilio. I will not give my blessing until I am satisfied she is of good character and morals! That is why I want to talk with you and the other ranch hands to make sure."

Rosa stopped walking, turned and slapped his face. "You are worse than old goat! How dare you question character and morals of JC! She have more character in little finger than you have in whole body! Rosa ashamed of you! JC good woman. She no carry on with men! She not even date man since husband killed three years ago. What happen with Emilio is what happen when two people love each other! You fool if you not believe Rosa, and I no want you for friend!"

Mr. Vasquez was still rubbing his face when he answered. "I'm sorry, Rosa. I should not have told you what happened between Emilio and I."

"Yes, you should tell Rosa, so you know truth! They love each other. They want child. You have no reason think it not Emilio's child! Rosa know this true! I here every day an see how hard JC work to keep ranch going. She no have time sleep around! You need be proud to have her for daughter! You big fool you not accept baby for grandson! I go back to house now. I no want to walk or talk with you until you think more straight!" As she was leaving, she turned back. "And if you try talk to cowhands, I shoot you! They all know JC good woman!"

Mr. Vasquez knew Rosa well enough that her treat to shoot him was real, so he called out to her. "I believe you Rosa. Please do not shoot me. They shall have my blessing, along with that of my wife and family. I will contact my wife yet tonight to let her know she will have another daughter and be a grandmother. In the morning, Manuel will fly back to Mexico and bring her, her sisters, our daughter and son here to the ranch. I hope this will be all right with JC that I continue to say here at the ranch, and she can forgive me for thinking bad thoughts."

"You no say more! You come back to ranch house and you tell JC plan for wife and family to come so she can make plan. You act better toward her, and Rosa will act like we never have this conversation in yard, but you not ask cowhands any question. They not know about baby or wedding yet. JC plan to tell them in morning so some come to wedding on Saturday. Chapel at hospital too small for all come. The all come but some must stay behind take care of ranch. They all come when we have fiesta when Emilio is well. Then you see how much they love and respect her!"

CHAPTER 43

The next morning, Emilio was surprised to see JC arrive at his bedside alone. “Where is my father?” he questioned. “Has he gone back to his ranch in Mexico?”

“No, he is still at the ranch. He said he had business he needed to take care of. He will be here later this afternoon. What makes you think he would leave?”

“I wasn’t going to say anything, but we had a disagreement when he was here yesterday.”

“It was about me, wasn’t it? I had the feeling he would never accept me, then his attitude suddenly changed for some strange reason after he and Rosa went for a walk after dinner. He was like a different person then, and he is still acting that way this morning. I wonder what they talked about?”

Emilio was at a loss for words. He did not want to reveal the conversation between him and his father and hurt JC’s feelings. “Maybe he was tired, or it was Rosa’s good home cooking that put him in a better mood.” JC chose to accept his response rather than pressing for a further explanation.

“You are probably right,” she responded. In her heart, she felt Rosa’s cooking wasn’t the answer to his father’s almost hostile behavior prior to the walk with her. The change in his attitude had been dramatic, but she knew sometimes it is better not to question the motives of people unless you want to be hit between the eyes with an answer. “I understand from Dr. Bark you will be getting out of bed to go for a little walk yet this morning, and if all goes well, you will be moved into the stepdown unit for a day or two before being moved to a regular post-surgical room by Friday morning.”

Emilio grinned. “That’s what I’ve been told will happen so I can get back enough strength to make you my legal wife on Saturday afternoon. I’m letting you know those will be the longest few days of my life!”

“At least you can lie there and have your meals served and pretty nurses to take care of you while I buy a wedding dress and plan a small reception for a few of our friends and staff members. Dr. Bark has offered the use of the doctor’s dining room, and he wants to walk me down the aisle and give me away.” She did not mention the arrival of Mrs. Vasquez and his family to keep it a surprise.

“Why do you need to buy a wedding dress? The turquoise dress you wore at your birthday party would make a lovely wedding dress. Just the thought of seeing you in it again gives me chills.”

“I had not thought of that,” she confessed. “That is a wonderful idea. That means I do not have to darken the doors at the She Shoppe.”

Emilio grinned. “Sometimes a husband-to-be has a purpose besides showing up at the altar.”

“Just wait until you become a full-time husband! I can assure you that you will have many purposes!”

Emilio's walk went well that afternoon, along with his transfer to the stepdown unit. He was incredibly happy to have the surprise visit from his mother, aunts, brother and sister along with his parents' blessing. Things got a little shaky on Friday afternoon on the regular surgical ward when he attempted to get out of bed and take a walk without alerting his nurse. When making rounds, she found him sitting on the floor leaning against the wall.

"Mr. Vasquez, what in the world are you doing?" she demanded. "You know you are supposed to ring for assistance before getting out of bed!"

"I'm sorry. I thought I could make it to the bathroom without calling you. I simply slid down the wall and sat down for a rest. Nothing is broken. If you will give me a hand, I'm sure I can get up."

"I will do nothing of the kind until we have Dr. Bark check you out! Stay put, and I will give him a call." That said, she left the room.

Dr. Bark was beside himself when he learned Emilio got out of bed without calling for assistance. "What in the heck do you think you are doing?" he yelled. "A lot of people have worked hard to help you get well, and you show your appreciation by trying to be the bigshot and end up falling on your ass when all you had to do was push a button for help! In case you forgot, you are getting married tomorrow, and you will become a father in about seven months unless you keep doing stuff like this and end up killing yourself!"

"I'm sorry. It won't happen again," said a sheepish Emilio.

"It damn well better not happen again or you will find yourself looking for another doctor! Now give me a hand, and I will help the orderly get you up on your feet and back to bed." After checking him and not finding any further injury, Dr. Bark apologized for yelling at him. "I should not have yelled at you, but dang it all, you have become more than a patient, and JC is more like a daughter. I have never allowed myself to become attached to patients ... until you two."

"I deserved to be yelled at," conceded Emilio. "It was selfish on my part. I hope you can forgive my stupid move. Please do not mention this to JC. It will only upset her."

"You are forgiven, but I think you need to be forthcoming with JC. There should not be secrets between a husband and wife," replied the obviously shaken man. "You behave yourself, and I will see you tomorrow before I walk your bride down the chapel aisle, and before you ask, no, you will not walk to the chapel. You will ride in a wheelchair, and that is final!" Emilio did not argue, nor did he promise to discuss the episode with JC.

CHAPTER 44

JC felt tense. The plane carrying Mrs. Vasquez, her daughter, son and sisters was due to arrive in less than half an hour, just in time for lunch. She had spent the morning helping Rosa polish her mother's silver and removing water spots from the crystal. A white linen tablecloth graced the dining room table instead of the usual placemats. A crystal vase filled with pink carnations and fern adorned the middle of the table.

Rosa nixed the idea of adding candles. "It too much for lunchtime," she insisted. "Mrs. Vasquez and sisters all nice ladies. You like them, and they like you. Brother he okay. Problem be with daughter. She spoiled 'n think all should bow down to wishes and sun rise and set over her."

That wasn't something JC wanted to hear in light of everything else happening in her life. "I will think positive when it comes to Emilio's sister. What is her name so I can greet her properly by name?"

"Inez," replied Rosa before leaving for the kitchen to finish preparing lunch.

The ranch house was squeaky clean, Roberto having washed all the windows, vacuumed and dusted in every room. This was in addition to sweeping the porch and making sure all the flower beds were in perfect order, along with luring the dogs into the barn with food and water. The dishes Rosa prepared filled the house with a delicious aroma.

"I think we have all the bases covered," said JC with a sigh. "If it is not good enough, that's too bad. Excuse me while I go change into some clean clothes, dab on some lipstick and put my hair in a ponytail."

Rosa was right. Mrs. Vasquez and her sisters all gave JC a hug and said the house was beautiful. The daughter hung back, not even offering her hand. She looked around the living room with the look of someone smelling a bad odor. Instead of ignoring her, JC went up to her and gave her a hug. "It is so nice to meet you, Inez. You must be tired after the flight here from Mexico. Welcome to my humble home." Taken aback by the friendly gesture, Inez found herself smiling. "Please come with me, and I will show all of you to your rooms. There you can freshen up, then join Rosa and me for lunch. After lunch, I will give you a fifty-cent tour of the house along with a little history of how it came to be when my great grandfather settled here. We can tour the ranch tomorrow since I know you are anxious to visit Emilio this afternoon."

Lunch fared better than JC expected. Everyone was polite and tried to keep up their end of the conversation. The only tense moment occurred when Inez leaned over to her mother and whispered loud enough for Rosa to hear, "Why does JC allow the hired help to dine with us?" Obviously embarrassed, Mrs. Vasquez quietly told her to mind her manners, that things were different in the United States and they would discuss it in private.

Rosa spoke up. "You discuss it now! You need understand Rosa raise JC since baby. She more like daughter than work for her. Make for more chance to love her when we eat together." JC nodded in agreement. Inez lowered her gaze to concentrate on the flan served for dessert, thinking she would be labeled a snob. To her surprise, JC spoke up and offered to take her riding in the morning. Rosa smiled and said that was a good idea. That's one hurdle taken care of, thought JC.

"Be ready to ride by sunup which happens around six a.m. It will be cold, so wear appropriate clothing. We will have coffee before we leave, but breakfast won't happen until eight a.m. Isn't that right, Rosa?" Rosa thought about making it nine a.m. just to make Inez wait but agreed to the earlier time for the sake of JC, who was used to eating at eight a.m. or even earlier.

When the two of them reached the barn the following morning, Inez laughed with delight when she saw JoJo. "I want to ride that one," she insisted. Being a beauty at age twenty-one, she was used to everyone meeting her demands.

"I am sorry, but JoJo is my horse. I have another one for you in mind. She is every bit as lovely and spirited as JoJo. I would love nothing more than to have a good relationship with you, Inez, but do not expect me to give in to your every demand, nor should you expect my employees to meet your every need. That is not how things are done here on the Scott Ranch. We work together as a family. I know things are different for you in Mexico, but you must keep in mind you are now a guest in the United States. Now let's saddle up and get started or we will miss breakfast." The words were not delivered in anger, just firmly.

"I do not know what my brother sees in you! You act more masculine than feminine. You dress like hired hand," retorted Inez. "I do not see us becoming friends, nor will I ride the nag you suggest!"

"That is your call. I have lived my life without you in it for thirty years, and I expect to live at least twice that many more years as the wife of your brother."

"We shall see about that!" snarled Inez. "My brother and I are very close. He will do as I ask, and you can be sure I will ask that he not marry you! There are many lovely senoritas where we live, any one of which would be more than willing to be his wife."

"I have no wish to carry on this conversation. Perhaps it would be best if we postpone the ride for another day when you come to the realization I will become your sister-in-law whether you like it or not." That said, JC turned and walked away back to the ranch house, leaving Inez standing there in a state near hysteria.

"Do not walk away from me!" she screamed. JC kept on walking.

Breakfast was tense, even though Inez did not grace them with her presence. JC explained to Mrs. Vasquez what had transpired between them in the barn earlier. "You will have to forgive my daughter's bad manners. It is the fault of me and her father for allowing her to become high spirited." High spirited in pig's eye, thought Rosa as she helped herself to more fried bacon. Inez is plain spoiled brat!

"Perhaps it would be best if Inez not accompany us to the hospital," offered Mrs. Vasquez. "She will only upset Emilio."

"Emilio is a grown man who is able to make is own mind known," replied JC. "I think it would be good for both of them for her to see him and express her opinion. I know she loves her brother. She is young and has not learned that true love can handle such outbursts. I want you to know I truly love your son and will do everything in my power to be a good wife in sickness and in health. I have every reason to believe he feels the same way about me."

"You are truly an amazing woman! I can see why Emilio and your employees love you. I am sure, in time, Inez will see it, too," replied Mrs. Vasquez.

"Don't be ridiculous," were the first words out of Emilio's mouth when confronted by Inez in his hospital room. "I love you dearly, but you are being unfair and very foolish when you speak ill of JC. You just met her, and I'm sure you didn't like it when she stood up to you. I will NOT have you making a spectacle of yourself at our wedding this afternoon! One word out of your mouth and it will be an awfully long time before we see each other again!" Inez started to cry. "Save your tears. They will not work this time, and I expect you to be civil to JC." She left the room in a huff to storm past her mother and JC patiently waiting in the hall outside Emilio's room.

CHAPTER 45

Emilio's wheelchair had been decorated with dozens of ribbons and a sign JUST MARRIED placed on the back of the seat signed by the staff, including everyone taking part in his care. He was not aware there would be a cluster of tin cans tied to the rear of the chair just before he and JC exited the chapel as husband and wife. The doctor's dining room was unrecognizable with all the flowers, potted plants and tables laden with food for the reception. Guests had cried when he and JC exchanged their personally written vows in addition to the protocol delivered by Father Benedictine in the chapel. More flowers, bows, gifts and rose petals adorned the hospital room where the two would spend their first night as a married couple.

A week later, Emilio was released to go home to the ranch with private nurses. JC declined the offer of having private nurses. "I will take good care of him. After all, I have nursed horses and cattle a whole lot bigger than him," she quipped. Dr. Bark laughed at that remark but agreed with the understanding Emilio would need physical therapy and occasional visits from him until Emilio was able to resume normal activities.

Being the determined man he was, it didn't take long before Emilio was back in the saddle for an hour or two to start, but that gradually increased as the days went on. Jose continued to act as foreman during this time. Seven months later, Emilio found himself pacing the hallway of the maternity ward for nine hours waiting to be handed his eight-pound bouncing baby boy. Once again, Rosa was right in her predictions.

Both Emilio and JC were relieved to learn the Grand Jury ruled justifiable homicide in the death of Bob Wilkins.

Nancy Holt and Jose Rodriguez were married six months later and now live on the acre of land given to them as a wedding present to build a home on the Scott-Vasquez Ranch, now comprised of thirty-two thousand acres.

Not surprising to anyone, Aunt Pearl and Sheriff Joe Walker have moved in together at her home but have yet to name a wedding day. She does sport a lovely diamond engagement ring.

Pearl did locate Clarence Mooney in Rio. He did pay more than what he owed, plus interest. His wife, Penny, divorced him (after the use of a horsewhip on Clarence's backside) and took up with a bullfighter who moved in with her at the coffee plantation given to her by Pearl after it had been awarded to her as part of the settlement. Clarence ended a broken man after being extradited back to the United States to stand trial for embezzlement and found guilty. He still resides as a guest of the state of Texas and will remain so for the next thirty years.

And yes, the little old ladies of the Wednesday night prayer group did count on their fingers and came up a little short on JC's first pregnancy gestation period. But after seeing the beautiful baby boy with dark hair and dimples they kept gossip to a bare minimum.

Sam Scott remains a resident at the Texas State Hospital. He continues to claim he sees and hears a ghost in conjunction with the monthly visits from someone who signs the visitor's roster as Ross Smith, a distant cousin, a claim backed up by his Aunt Pearl.

And oh, there was a new line shack built near the location of the one that was dynamited. This was after the new road was built up the mountain side to gain access to both ranches. Emilio and JC spend a lot of time up there when the weather co-operates, the moon is full, the stars shine brightly, the campfire is warm, and the coyotes remain silent.

Rosa and Roberto did get married and have become surrogate Grandma and Grandpa to Jeb Emilio Vasquez, who is the spitting image of his father, just as Rosa predicted before he was born.

Unfortunately, Inez and Emilio have yet to reunite. The elder Vasquez couple have become regular visitors to the renamed Circle SV ranch to spend time with their grandson. They refer to JC as their daughter.

JC Scott Morgan Vasquez is incredibly happy, she decided. The time had come to move on. Their second child, according to Rosa, is a girl due in eight months.

QUESTIONS FOR BOOK CLUB READERS DISCUSSION

1. Is it healthy for JC to refuse to participate in celebrations following her husband's death? If not, why not?
2. Should three years after his death be time enough passed before she starts thinking about reassessing her life and moving on?
3. Has JC been wearing blinders when she overlooks the signs her brother is taking advantage of her? Should she have trusted Sam when he asked for the chance to be a better brother?
4. Was Andy Mendoza wrong not to voice his reasons for disliking JC's brother?
5. Does Aunt Pearl have the right to enter into an agreement on behalf of Sam to pay for JC's birthday party? Should she have minded her own business?
6. Is Ross Vandenberg justified in terrorizing Sam for his attempt to kill him?
7. Is Aunt Pearl justified in revenge for Sam's theft of her and JC's money by making sure he remains in the state mental hospital?
8. Was JC wrong in waiting to tell Emilio he was going to be the father of their baby?

9. Should Tex have been made ranch foreman or should he have been fired before he destroyed the line shack?
10. Did JC have the right to confront Emilio's sister when she voiced the opinion she and her brother should not be married?
11. Should CJ make the first move at reconciliation with Emilio's sister Inez?
12. Was it time for JC to move on with Emilio?

ABOUT THE AUTHOR

Linda Ellen (Petty) Lynch was born on a small farm in Franklin County, Ohio. She is a retired R.N. and business owner. She now resides in Southern California.

Other books by Linda Ellen Lynch

Secrets on Sand Beach
Blood
Emerald Valley
What the Heart Wants

Made in the USA
Columbia, SC
02 December 2021

50096462R00215